D0176012

HOLD
BACK THE
NIGHT

Also by
SEAN LYNCH

COTTONMOUTH

HOLD BACK THE NIGHT

SEAN LYNCH

PINNACLE BOOKS
Kensington Publishing Corp.
www.kensingtonbooks.com

PINNACLE BOOKS are published by

Kensington Publishing Corp.
119 West 40th Street
New York, NY 10018

All Kensington titles, imprints, and distributed lines are available at special quantity discounts for bulk purchases for sales promotions, premiums, fund-raising, educational, or institutional use. Special book excerpts or customized printings can also be created to fit specific needs. For details, write or phone the office of the Kensington sales manager: Kensington Publishing Corp., 119 West 40th Street, New York, NY 10018, attn: Sales Department; phone 1-800-221-2647.

PINNACLE BOOKS and the Pinnacle logo are Reg. U.S. Pat. & TM Off.

ISBN-13: 978-0-7860-4779-6
ISBN-10: 0-7860-4779-8

First Pinnacle paperback printing: May 2021

10 9 8 7 6 5 4 3 2 1

Printed in the United States of America

Electronic edition:

ISBN-13: 978-0-7860-4780-2 (e-book)
ISBN-10: 0-7860-4780-1 (e-book)

*This book is dedicated to
my daughter, Brynne,
a young woman of exceptional courage.*

PART ONE
FUEL

CHAPTER ONE

Deputy Leanne Strayer wriggled herself into the least uncomfortable position she could manage without encroaching on the deputies at either side of her. This was no small feat since she was one of ten people crammed into a standard-sized delivery van. It didn't help her predicament that the van's other occupants were all male, larger than she was, and everyone including her was clad in urban-pattern fatigues and burdened with at least twenty-five pounds of weapons, armor, and gear.

Adding to her discomfort was the fact that Northern California's Indian summer was in full swing. The mercury on this late October afternoon had risen well into the nineties. The elevated temperature inside the cramped van, as it jostled over the pothole-strewn country road, was close to intolerable. Beads of sweat formed on Strayer's face under her ballistic glasses, and her perspiration-soaked uniform stuck to her skin beneath her uniform and body armor.

"We're in the park," Sergeant Bennerman announced from the front seat. "One minute to location."

The eight deputies in the back of the vehicle had no way to verify their sergeant's claim. The delivery van had no rear or side windows, and a partition separated the front and rear compartments. They checked their weapons a final time, donned their helmets, and prepared to disembark.

Bennerman keyed his transceiver as the van came to a halt. "Tac is ten-twenty-three," he broadcast.

"Tactical team on scene," the dispatcher's aloof voice acknowledged. "Medical and air support standing by."

"Go!" Bennerman commanded. The rear and side doors opened, and Strayer and her fellow deputies scrambled from the vehicle. Like her teammates, she was instantly relieved to escape the confines of the hot, cramped, van.

Though she'd never been to this particular trailer park before, the landscape that greeted her wasn't unfamiliar. Strayer grew up in a rural trailer park not unlike the one where she and her Special Weapons and Tactics team now found themselves.

Strayer raced toward the single-wide, recognizing it from photographs shown at the operational briefing earlier that morning. She flicked the selector lever on her Heckler & Koch UMP-40 submachine gun down from Safe to Sustained Fire.

Strayer wasn't on the entry team today, instead assigned to perimeter duty. It was her job, along with three other deputies, to assume containment positions on the four corners of the trailer while a five-deputy team, led by Sergeant Bennerman, forced entry through the front door.

The S.W.A.T. team was serving a "no-knock" arrest warrant on an armed and extremely dangerous homicide suspect. The likelihood the suspect might resist arrest with a firearm resulted in the deputy district attorney issuing a warrant that didn't require the arresting deputies to knock on the trailer's door and announce their presence before entering.

Two days previously, a twenty-nine-year-old fugitive parolee and verified Mexican Mafia gang member named Ernesto Machado walked nonchalantly into a downtown Farnham restaurant. The eatery was affiliated with Nuestra Familia, the Mexican Mafia's sworn rivals. Once inside, he produced a fully automatic AK-47 from under his jacket and cut loose.

When the brass settled, two people were dead. This included the restaurant's owner, who was the gunman's intended target. Seven patrons were also injured, two critically. Security camera footage from inside the restaurant clearly identified Machado, well known to the county's Gang Task Force, as the shooter. Machado fled the scene in a stolen Toyota sedan and disappeared.

The following day, an informant tipped off a dope detective in the county's Narcotics Unit that Machado was hiding out in a trailer park in rural Farnham County, smoking meth, and awaiting Mexican Mafia–sanctioned passage south to Mexico. The densely populated park was inhabited by a large number of probationers, parolees, and others hostile to law enforcement and housed many known Hispanic gang members. Any attempts by detectives to confirm Machado's whereabouts by traditional surveillance methods would certainly have been spotted and resulted in the suspect's flight.

It was only through the use of an aerial drone with night-vision capability, which captured Machado's image as he accepted delivery of a pizza, that the informant's tip was verified. A warrant was subsequently obtained and Bennerman's squad of S.W.A.T. deputies tasked with serving it.

The experienced S.W.A.T. sergeant elected to have his team surreptitiously enter the Pleasant Pines Trailer Park and approach the suspect's unit concealed in a commandeered online retailer's delivery van. Strayer, the only female deputy currently assigned to the Farnham County S.W.A.T. Unit, was a member of Bennerman's team.

Like all fifteen full-time Special Weapons and Tactics deputies at the Farnham County Sheriff's Department, Strayer worked a triad rotation schedule. Each of the three five-operator squads were either on duty, in training, or on their days off. This ensured at least ten S.W.A.T.-trained deputies were available for deployment at all times. Bennerman's crew happened to be one of the two squads on hand when the order to serve the high-risk warrant came down.

Strayer took her assigned position at the corner of the trailer and lost sight of the entry team as it moved from her field of view. The deputies in front of and behind her, assigned to the other corners, took up their positions to her left and right.

The trailer had once been white with a lateral green stripe, but years of neglect and disrepair left its battered aluminum exterior a dingy gray. The miniature yard was devoid of grass and littered with beer and soda cans, cigarette butts, and discarded fast-food wrappers. The trailer's four windows, one on each side, were covered with black plastic sheets.

The trailers surrounding Machado's, like all mobile homes in the park, were situated close to one another with little more than the width of a single-vehicle driveway between lots. The double-wide mobile home directly behind Strayer had a tricycle on its sparse lawn, and the cracked driveway was decorated with multicolored chalk drawings typical of grade-school-aged children.

Strayer heard the sound of metal rending and glass breaking and surmised the entry team had torn off the front door with their breaching tool. Seconds later a pair of earsplitting explosions erupted.

She felt and heard dual concussions as a pair of distraction devices, commonly known as a flashbangs or stun grenades, were detonated inside. She knew the entry team would be rushing into the trailer directly behind the blasts.

She next heard men's muffled, shouting, voices. Then came a noise she'd hoped she wouldn't hear; the unmistakable signature of a fully automatic AK-47. Strayer knew the unwelcome sound all too well from her two tours in Afghanistan.

Strayer instinctively took a knee and brought her weapon up from low-ready to her shoulder. The AK-47 was firing steadily, in one long burst, and she knew the trailer's flimsy construction would be no match for the full-metal-jacket rounds it digested. As if to confirm this, holes began sporadically materializing in the trailer's exterior walls. Bullets ripped through the thin sheet-metal panels leaving puffs of insulation in their wake.

Strayer dropped to a prone position as bullets exited

the suspect's trailer and sailed overhead. She could hear them impacting the trailer behind her. She scanned to her left and right. To her dismay, she noticed her fellow perimeter deputies hadn't dropped to the ground. Both were crouching with their weapons shouldered, but still standing.

Seconds after the fully automatic AK-47 opened up, the contrasting reports of multiple AR-15s, the standard-issue weapon of the Farnham County S.W.A.T. team, erupted. The telltale bark of semiautomatic gunfire, in contrast to the fully automatic fire, told Strayer her team was in a firefight. Among the cacophony of dueling weapons, she also detected the report of the .40 caliber submachine gun, like hers, carried by Sergeant Bennerman.

Strayer wasn't comforted by the knowledge that her fellow deputies were all wearing ceramic body armor rated to withstand the 7.62x39 military cartridge and wielding ballistic shields. There were still plenty of exposed areas on a S.W.A.T. team member's body not covered by bullet-resistant armor, such as the face and extremities. More than once while deployed, she'd witnessed the serious injury or death of another soldier when an unlucky bullet found its way under, around, or even through the hapless troop's body armor. In the fierce, close-quarters battle currently unfolding inside the single-wide trailer, the likelihood a bullet might find its way to a deputy's vulnerable spot was high.

The number of bullets piercing the trailer walls from inside the unit and entering the park outside increased dramatically, keeping pace with the volume of gunfire raging within. Strayer heard someone announce, "Shots fired!" over the radio through her earpiece but didn't immediately recognize the excited voice, and therefore didn't know if the transmission emanated from a deputy inside or outside the trailer.

The perimeter deputy to Strayer's left, posted at the opposite rear corner of the trailer, suddenly cried out, fell onto his back, and grabbed his neck with both hands. He'd been struck by one of the bullets that tore through the trailer's walls.

Strayer instantly rose to a kneeling position. She hesitated, torn between her duty to remain at her post and maintain the perimeter and her instinct to rush to the wounded deputy and render first aid.

Before she could choose, Strayer's course of action was decided for her. The trailer's rear window shattered outward and a human body came crashing through. The body belonged to a shirtless, barefoot, man who was howling maniacally and covered in blood.

She instantly recognized Machado, from his long hair and what she could see of the tattoos beneath the smeared blood on his chest and arms. His face and build, despite his macabre appearance, matched the booking photographs shown to the team during the briefing. He was still carrying his AK-47 rifle.

Machado had leapt through the window to escape the deputies inside. He landed headfirst amid a cascade of wood splinters, plastic sheeting, and shattered glass, and rolled to a standing position only a couple of yards from the downed deputy to Strayer's left. Had he rolled the opposite direction upon landing, he would have faced her. Instead, he loomed over the wounded man lying at his feet.

The injured deputy kept one hand to his neck to stanch

the flow of blood and with the other fumbled for the .45 caliber pistol holstered at his thigh.

Machado lowered his rifle, at point-blank range, to the deputy's head. The bloodied gunman's maniacal grin widened, and his finger closed on the trigger.

Strayer brought up her sub-gun's front sight to Machado's center of mass, paused her breathing, and squeezed the trigger. A three-round burst of .40 caliber slugs tore into his back.

Machado, anesthetized on methamphetamine and adrenaline and in the throes of the drug-induced state known to law enforcement and emergency medical personnel as excited delirium, merely fell to one knee. He swung his body toward Strayer, his face a mask of berserker fury. At the same time, he attempted to bring his Kalashnikov around to bear on her.

She reacted this time by triggering a six-round burst from her sub-gun, tipping the barrel up ever so slightly at the end of the firing sequence. Like the previous burst, all of her rounds struck Machado. The last two impacted his chin and forehead.

Machado fell forward onto his face and didn't move. Strayer, per her training, continued to cover him with her Heckler & Koch. Seconds later, Bennerman and the entry team came running out of the trailer. A pair of entry-team deputies immediately began to attend to their wounded comrade, while another handcuffed Machado and began checking his vitals.

Strayer slowly stood up, lowered her weapon, and flicked the selector lever back up to Safe.

"You okay?" Bennerman asked her.

"Yeah," Strayer said, exhaling.

One of the deputies checking Machado gave Bennerman a thumbs-down. "Injuries inconsistent with life," he said. "Non-revivable."

Bennerman looked from Machado's body to Strayer and shook his head. "Why did it have to be you again?" he said with a grunt.

Strayer met her sergeant's disdainful expression with an indifferent one. The indifference took effort. Inside, she was seething.

Sirens could be heard in the distance, along with the hum of a helicopter. People slowly began to exit their trailers and take in the scene before them. Most merely stared, but more than a few glared at the heavily armed S.W.A.T. deputies and cursed in Spanish.

"Sarge," one of the men attending to the wounded deputy called out, "we gotta get Steve to the trauma center."

"Ambulance is en route," Bennerman said. "Tell him to hang on."

A woman's scream rang out. It was stark and piercing and easily overpowered the sounds of milling bystanders, approaching sirens, and the helicopter above. The scream carried within it a mother's anguish, and came from the trailer directly behind Machado's.

The trailer's door flew open, and a young Hispanic woman emerged. She was wailing and cradling the inert body of a little girl, perhaps six or seven years old. The woman's hands, and the child's body, were covered in blood.

CHAPTER TWO

Granite Bay, California

Marjorie Guthrie extinguished the first cigarette she'd smoked in over thirteen years on the porch steps of her upscale residence. Her husband Theodore, whom she'd always known as Tad, was due to arrive any minute. He'd texted his wife from the Sacramento airport, as he typically did when returning from a business trip, to let her know his plane had landed and he was on the way home.

She lit a second cigarette, extracted from the first pack of Marlboro Lights she'd purchased in more than thirteen years, with a butane lighter held in trembling hands. It wasn't fear that added the tremor, but a combination of multiple emotions. A cocktail of feelings seasoned over time and ripened by a final straw.

Anger.

Betrayal.

Loathing.

Resolve.

Marjorie took the smoke into her lungs, mildly surprised it tasted so good after having been a nonsmoker for so long. That many years after quitting, she expected the cigarette to taste unpleasant. She realized, with some irony, that it wasn't her only expectation during the last thirteen years that turned out wrong.

Her nine-year-old son, Joel, and his five-year-old sister, Jennifer, had been deposited at a friend's house after school. Marjorie explained to her friend she was experiencing a family emergency, which wasn't untrue, and would pick them up later that evening. She had a lot to do.

After visiting the pharmacy, she made a trip to the bank. Then she stopped at a gas station to top off the Range Rover's fuel tank. There, on impulse, she'd purchased the cigarettes.

On the way home, she telephoned her parents, who resided in a modest restored farmhouse in rural Farnham County on the other side of Folsom Lake. They weren't pleased with what she had to tell them, but understood.

Once back home, she began to pack. Marjorie emptied a plastic bin containing Christmas ornaments and filled it with documents. She took her personal, financial, and medical records, those belonging to the children, the backup hard drive to the family's desktop computer, and her laptop. Then she packed as many clothes, for both herself and the kids, as she could, along with toiletries and other personal items, into several large suitcases. She'd learned what to pack after the last incident.

The first incident, which had occurred three years prior, was sparked when Tad inadvertently left his work laptop on in his study after returning home from a business trip to Phoenix. Unable to resist the temptation, Marjorie perused the contents while he was in the shower. It didn't take long for her to discover irrefutable, and graphic, photographic evidence of his affair with a buxom young coworker at the wireless company that employed them both.

The confrontation was explosive. Tad, whom Marjorie had known since they were both undergraduates at UC Davis, couldn't deny the infidelity. Instead, he chose to blame her.

He berated his wife for being what he called a "nosy, suspicious, bitch," and rationalized his unfaithful behavior on his sexual needs while away from her on business. She responded to his insulting attempt to hold her accountable for his infidelity by calling him a "disgusting, selfish, pig."

That's when he slapped her.

Instantly remorseful, Tad begged for forgiveness and pleaded with Marjorie not to call the police. He tearfully insisted he loved her, and their two young children, and promised to end the affair. He further swore he would never, ever, hit her again. He also pointed out, once again putting accountability for his actions on her, that his arrest would result in their family's breakup and financial ruin.

Desiring to keep her family together, and at the same time still in love with her husband, Marjorie relented. She chose to believe him because she wanted to. She agreed to forgive and elicited a promise from Tad to resign from his current job, never communicate with his former coworker again, and to attend family counseling with her. He eagerly consented.

She told her friends at the gym, when they inquired about her bruised cheek, that her son had accidentally struck her while playing with one of his toys.

As she sat smoking on her porch and waiting for her husband to arrive home, Marjorie berated herself as weak and gullible to have believed anything that had come out of Tad Guthrie's mouth.

When Marjorie first met Tad, he was Hollywood handsome, exuded confidence and charm, was fit and tan from being on the water polo team, and hailed from an uber-rich family. Half the girls on campus had been in his bed or were trying to be.

The darkly beautiful Marjorie Hernandez was not impressed by his strategically orchestrated and well-practiced advances, and wasn't afraid to show it. Which, as it turned out, only piqued his interest and fueled his desire for her.

After weeks of fending him off, she eventually relented and agreed to go out with him. To her surprise, Marjorie found Tad Guthrie seemingly not nearly as shallow as his frat-boy demeanor led others to believe. Or so she thought at the time. Reluctantly, she began to succumb to his charms. So did her younger sister Mary and her parents.

When Tad met Hector Hernandez, a retired construction supervisor, and his wife Margaret, a homemaker, he was polite and respectful, despite the fact that the Hernandez family was clearly of a social station far below his own. Marjorie's younger sister Mary, a sophomore in high school at the time, didn't attempt to conceal her envy over what she called her older sister's "totally awesome catch."

Their romance blossomed. It took Tad, not the most committed of students, an additional two years to obtain his undergraduate degree, the result of too much partying and switching majors multiple times over the course of his college experience. Marjorie decided to stay on campus to be with him after her own graduation. They moved in together, to the dismay of her parents, while Tad finished an undergraduate degree in marketing and she pursued a master's degree in business administration. He proposed to her on the day they both graduated; him for the first time, her for the second.

Tad's wedding present to his wife was to quit smoking weed. Hers was to quit smoking cigarettes.

Unlike most newlyweds, money wasn't a problem for Tad and Marjorie Guthrie. Tad was able to provide his bride a lavish lifestyle through the bounty of his wealthy parents, who'd purchased a deluxe Granite Bay home for the couple as a wedding gift. Tad's father, a highly successful Sacramento plastic surgeon and commercial landlord, had always ensured his only child had the best of everything.

Today, as she sat in contemplation over cigarettes on her porch steps, Marjorie finally embraced her denial regarding her husband's true character and accepted the realization his hyper-privileged upbringing had much more to do with his narcissism, lack of ambition, poor discipline, and weak impulse control than she'd originally thought. She considered herself a blind fool for refusing to see Tad Guthrie for who he was long ago. She blamed herself, not him, and the choices she'd made, for her predicament.

Things had been okay up until a few years after the kids came. Tad's father paid their bills, provided new cars for his son and wife to drive every other year, and funded elaborate family vacations each summer. Marjorie quit her job as a marketing consultant when she became pregnant with Joel and never went back to work, electing to stay home and raise their son. When Jennifer arrived four years later, it only affirmed her decision to relinquish her career for full-time motherhood.

Tad stumbled along, bouncing from firm to firm, spending much of his workweek away on sales junkets and most weekends ignoring his children and playing golf. Joel was six years old, and Jennifer only two, when Marjorie discovered the extramarital affair, forgave him, and moved on.

A little more than two years after that incident came another. Tad, who'd been a heavy drinker in college but tapered off after graduation, began drinking heavily again not long after Marjorie caught him cheating.

Tad's drinking habit started up again gradually, beginning with single-martini business luncheons, a glass or two of wine with dinner each night, and the occasional overindulgence during weekend golf with his buddies. But it soon escalated into Irish coffee each morning at breakfast, four-martini luncheons, whether he was conducting business or not, at least a bottle of wine every night, and all-day beer benders on weekends.

As Tad's drinking habit worsened, his moods darkened, he withdrew from his family, his waistline increased, and he became irritable and more argumentative. When Marjorie, who'd always maintained a positive outlook and a very athletic figure, tried to confront her husband about his spiraling alcohol consumption and change in behavior, or nudge him to accompany her to the gym, she was angrily rebuked.

Their arguments became increasingly abusive, with Tad often implying that he never wanted children, and without him she wouldn't be living in a four-thousand-square-foot home in Granite Bay or enjoying the luxury of being a stay-at-home mom, as if full-time motherhood wasn't a vocation itself.

Marjorie never reminded Tad, during those heated exchanges, that she held a master's degree and he only a bachelor's. Or that without his parents' generosity he wouldn't be living in a Granite Bay McMansion, either. He was usually too intoxicated by that point in the argument to listen, anyway.

One afternoon while Marjorie and preschool-aged Jennifer were at a car dealership having her sport utility vehicle serviced, she received a call on her cell phone from an officer with the Granite Bay Police Department. It seemed her husband, tasked with leaving work early to pick up Joel at his elementary school since she was indisposed, had been involved in a traffic collision.

Tad inadvertently ran a red light in his Porsche and broadsided a Subaru driven by another parent who was also picking up a child after school. Fortunately, despite the fact that both cars sustained significant damage, no one was hurt.

Unfortunately, the Subaru's driver, while exchanging insurance information with Tad, noticed his red, watery, bloodshot eyes, slurred speech, and the heavy odor of an alcoholic beverage on his pungent breath. The police officers she called to the scene noticed, too.

An indignant Tad failed his field sobriety tests. Despite his pleas, and subsequent threats, he was arrested on suspicion of drunk driving. He was also charged with child endangerment since his son was in the car. The police officer phoned Marjorie at the car dealership to come to the station and retrieve Joel. Tad would have to remain in custody for at least six hours until he sobered up.

When Tad phoned home six hours later, a furious

Marjorie refused to come and get him. He showed up twenty minutes after the call, by way of an Uber, since his badly damaged Porsche had been towed from the crash scene.

He first tried to minimize the significance of the crash and arrest, then explain, rationalize, and finally, to half-heartedly apologize. According to Tad, the real blame for the incident rested with the other driver, "a total bitch," and Granite Bay's, "stupid, nit-picking, hall monitor, cops."

All Marjorie said to her husband in reply was that she was sleeping in the guest room, but it was enough to send Tad into a rage. He forcefully grabbed her by the arm as she walked away. When she tried to pull her arm from his grasp, he backhanded her.

Marjorie took the kids and drove to her parents' home an hour away in Farnham County. Tad called multiple times each day and pleaded with her to return. She ignored his calls and consulted with a friend's husband who was a divorce attorney.

Five days after his arrest, Tad ignored her demand not to show up at her parents' home. Her mother let him in.

Tad implored his wife to hear him out. He insisted the slap was an "accident," which was at least partially her fault, since it had occurred in the heat of an argument. As a result, he argued, he hadn't really broken his earlier promise never to strike her again. He swore he'd quit drinking and was attending Alcoholics Anonymous meetings, and assured her that his father's high-powered attorney was handling the criminal charges against him.

He tearfully begged Marjorie for another chance. Her resolve was further whittled away by her mother, eavesdropping from another room. She interjected herself, and insisted to her daughter that a husband saying he was sorry could make up for putting his hands on his wife in anger and shouldn't necessarily be cause for breaking up a marriage. Marjorie demanded Tad leave, but told him she'd think about what he'd said. She also agreed to take his calls.

By the end of the week Tad's barrage of telephone pleas, her mother's entreaties, and Marjorie's own doubt and guilt wore down her resistance. Against her better judgment, she and the kids returned home.

Tad made good on his promise to remain sober and continued to attend AA meetings. Their marriage counseling also continued. Her father-in-law's attorney got the drunk driving charge against Tad reduced to reckless driving, a civil settlement was reached with the Subaru's driver, and the child-endangerment charge was dropped. Over the course of the following year, things gradually returned to some semblance of what had once been normal in the Guthrie household.

Tad switched companies again, and without alcohol seemed less discontented with his career. He spent more time at home on weekends, and at least made a pretense of parenting. Marjorie convinced herself that her spouse had made real changes, was hopeful about his progress and the progress of their marriage, and consoled herself with the notion that the unfaithful and violent behaviors he'd previously exhibited were a product of the booze and not inherent in his character. She hadn't forgotten what Tad had done, but she'd come to a sort of peace with it. She loved her children, enjoyed her lifestyle, and accepted her husband for who she convinced herself he was. It seemed to be enough.

Until a week ago.

It was the day before Tad was to fly to Salt Lake City for

a sales conference, and Marjorie began to fall ill. The illness began with a fever, and then severe cramps. Tad offered to stay home and help care for the kids while she recovered from what they both assumed was a bout of the flu, but she insisted he go on the business trip. She didn't want him to jeopardize his new job. The flu bug had been making the rounds at the elementary school Jennifer and Joel attended, both had already been through it during the previous month, and Marjorie believed she would likely be over the ailment before her husband returned at week's end.

Instead, Marjorie's symptoms worsened. Her fever intensified, and in addition to cramps she developed joint aches, a burning sensation while urinating, and discovered she was emitting a milky, odorous, vaginal discharge. She made an appointment to see the doctor the following day and provided blood and urine samples to facilitate a battery of tests. Three days later, on the morning of the day Tad was scheduled to return home from his business trip, her doctor's office phoned with the results.

The taste of Marjorie's second cigarette soured. She looked at her hands and noticed they were no longer trembling.

Tad's car pulled into the driveway, the engine switched off, and he got out. Instead of greeting him with a hug, his wife ground out her smoke, stood, gave him a disgusted look, turned her back to him, and walked through the open front door into the house.

"What's wrong?" Tad said, with no attempt to hide his exasperation. "Where are the kids?" His wife ignored his questions as he followed her.

"What're you so pissed off about?" he said, once they were both inside. Marjorie stopped a dozen feet inside the hallway and turned to face him with her arms folded across her chest.

"What gives?" Tad demanded. "Why the cold shoulder?"

Marjorie remained silent, staring at her husband.

Tad's face started to redden. Her refusal to speak was beginning to anger him. His next sentence was another question, but came out as an accusation. "When did you start smoking again?"

"When you gave me chlamydia," she said evenly.

The flush that had only seconds before colored his features drained from his face. His jaw slackened, and he took too many seconds to respond.

"What are you talking about?" he finally stammered.

"I'm talking about a sexually transmitted infection," Marjorie said. "An infection I was diagnosed with while you were away. I'm on antibiotics now. Evidently you should be, too. The doctor said it's possible you don't even know you're infected. Frankly, I don't give a damn. As far as I'm concerned, your little pecker can rot off."

"There's an explanation . . ."

She cut him off. "Of course, there is. Since I haven't had sex with anyone but you since we met, and certainly didn't catch chlamydia from a public toilet seat, we both know what that explanation is, don't we?"

"Marjorie, listen to me . . ."

"No," she interrupted him again. "I've listened to your lies and excuses and bullshit for the last time. I only stuck around today to tell you in person."

"I don't understand?" he said. "Tell me what?"

"That I'm gone. I took half the money from the accounts. That's only fair. I'm also taking my car, and I'm taking the children. Not that you'd care about them. Don't bother coming after me."

"Marjorie, wait a minute . . ."

"No," she cut him off a third time. "We're done. Don't try to stop me, don't call me, and don't come over to my folks' house. If you do, I'll get a restraining order. You'll be hearing from a lawyer soon. We can work out the child custody and money issues through the courts. I never want to see you, or speak to you, again."

Tad looked at the ceiling and ran his hands through his hair. "This isn't happening," he said.

"Sure, it is," Marjorie said. "People get divorced every day. My turn was a long time ago. I was just too naïve and stupid to know it."

Marjorie started to walk past Tad to the door. He blocked her path.

"Please step aside," Marjorie said.

"You're not leaving," Tad said. "Not until we talk this out."

"We're done talking. Get out of my way."

"If you think I'm going to let you walk out of our marriage," he said, tension building in his voice, "you're out of your mind."

"I don't have time for this," Marjorie said. She tried once more to step around him to the door. Instead of merely blocking her path again, Tad grabbed both of her arms. "Listen to me," he said. It wasn't a request.

"Get your hands off me," she insisted. "I've got nothing more to say. This marriage is over."

She tried to pull away, but Tad's grip tightened. His face turned crimson again, this time behind a snarl. She tried to wriggle free. He slammed her against the wall.

The impact stunned Marjorie, tore the breath from her lungs, and dislodged a large picture frame hanging in the hallway which fell and shattered at her feet. Tad's grip on her biceps tightened.

"You're . . . hurting . . . me," she gasped. "Let . . . me . . . go."

"You aren't going anywhere," Tad hissed, pinning her against the wall. "It'll be a cold day in hell before I let you walk out on me again."

Marjorie's next words, rehearsed over and over in her mind in the hours before her husband's arrival, elicited exactly the reaction she anticipated.

"Fuck you," she said.

Theodore "Tad" Guthrie cocked his right fist. He punched Marjorie, his wife of thirteen years and the mother of his children, squarely in the face. She collapsed to the floor amid the broken glass, dazed and barely conscious. Blood poured from her shattered nose as she looked up at her enraged husband. He stood over her with both fists clenched and his chest heaving.

Marjorie shook her head to dispel the lights dancing before her eyes, fought the urge to vomit, slipped her hand into her jacket, and pushed the panic button on the remote in her pocket. The expensive residential alarm system they'd installed featured a function that summoned the police at the touch of a key on a pocket-sized remote.

The system also featured high-resolution interior video cameras. One of those cameras was mounted above the entryway.

It didn't occur to Tad, until he was being placed in handcuffs, that his wife Marjorie had deliberately chosen the location in the hallway for their confrontation.

CHAPTER THREE

Farnham National Forest
Sierra Nevadas, western range

Donald Paris guided his new Dodge truck over the abandoned logging road while his brother-in-law, Tim Cummings, directed his lever-action .30/.30 rifle through the open passenger window. Both men had deer tags for this zone, but neither had any luck sighting a buck during almost an entire day spent navigating the forest in search of game.

The pair had been as far up as seventy-five-hundred feet, and were now below four-thousand. They were about to abandon the hunt and return to the small town of Rockwell, a few miles outside the Farnham National Forest, where they both resided with their families.

The U.S. Forest Service had declared another Red Flag Fire Hazard Day in the Farnham National Forest, situated between the Tahoe and El Dorado National Forests, due to the extreme fire danger. Though it was almost November, there'd been no rain since April, typical for the Sierra Nevadas

All of Northern California had been experiencing

several years of drought, with commensurately lower winter snowpack totals. Consequently, the Sierra Nevadas' densely wooded forests, which were abundantly populated with white, red, and Douglas fir, ponderosa, Jeffrey, and sugar pine, and plentiful incense cedar, were tinderbox dry.

This year brought a later-than-usual Indian summer, with unseasonably warm temperatures extending well into the autumn. Both Paris and Cummings guessed the day had peaked somewhere in the nineties, which was high for that month and elevation.

But by late afternoon the temperature had dropped dramatically. The drastic, sudden shift in temperature, not uncommon for that time of year in the Sierra Nevadas, created the perfect incubator for the Mono Winds.

Named after Mono Lake, the Mono Winds differed from the Diablo Winds, which plagued Northern California, and Southern California's infamous Santa Ana Winds, because they were fueled by cold, instead of warm, air. The Mono Winds, however, could be just as destructive as the Diablos and Santa Anas, especially during California's notoriously virulent fire season.

Beginning in October and usually abating in April, the Sierra Nevada Mono Winds arose when a high-pressure system formed above the Great Basin. They could produce winds ranging from fifty to as high as one hundred miles per hour.

Colder air created by the high-pressure system was forced over the Sierras. It would pick up speed as it rushed down the western slopes, exponentially increasing in velocity as it dried out. The topography would further funnel the swiftly rushing air, increasing its speed even more and intensifying its effects.

Mono Winds could be highly damaging to the landscape, felling trees by the hundreds and launching high-speed dust and debris at anything, or anyone, unfortunate enough to be in their path. The real danger of the Mono Winds, however, was their contribution to the fire risk.

A forest fire driven by the Mono Winds might easily become a firestorm that could spread extremely rapidly. Fed by an abundant supply of fuel in the form of countless dead and drought-stricken trees, copious amounts of dry brush, and endless grasslands, such a wildfire was capable of consuming huge swaths of territory.

Tragically, such wind-powered fires weren't uncommon in the Sierra Nevadas, nor elsewhere in California. They were especially prevalent during late summer and early autumn, before the arrival of annual rains, when the air and land were driest. Catastrophic fires like the Oakland Hills Fire, energized by the Diablos, and the most destructive fire in California's history, the Camp Fire, were Indian-summer fires stoked by such high winds.

Due to the coming darkness, blowing wind, and swirling dust, Cummings reluctantly pulled in his rifle and rolled up the window.

"We surely ain't gonna bag a deer now," Cummings said. "Not with all this dust blowing. I can't see more'n twenty feet."

"Let's call it a day," Paris said. "It's getting dark, anyways."

Paris and Cummings, neither experienced outdoorsmen, noticed the steeply decreasing temperature and sharply increasing winds but weren't knowledgeable enough to be overly concerned. What worried them most, which wasn't greatly due to their ignorance, was the rapidly diminishing visibility. Though it was still technically an hour from sunset, the sun had begun to dip below the tree line. The resulting loss of light, along with the escalating dust caused by the sudden emergence of high winds, should have prompted them to decrease the truck's speed on the narrow, switchback dirt road. Instead, anxious to get home, Paris drove faster.

Both men, though disappointed they hadn't scored a deer, were looking forward to trading the mountain's bumpy dirt roads for the asphalt highway home to dinner and a beer.

Suddenly a large buck appeared directly in front of them. Paris swerved the truck and slammed on the brakes. The truck skidded sideways off the dirt road, narrowly missing the big animal as it bounded off and disappeared into the wood line.

"Jesus," Paris exclaimed, as the Dodge came to rest in the ditch along the road. "That was close."

"Closest we came to a deer all day," Cummings remarked.

Both men laughed, releasing the tension from their near miss, and stepped out of the truck. The Dodge was pointed nose down in the dead brown grass of the steep ditch.

"Can we back it out?" Cummings asked, surveying the vehicle's awkward position.

"Only one way to find out," Paris said.

"We'd better not be stuck," Cummings said. "I sure don't want to spend the night up here. It's windy as hell. It's gonna get cold, too, and we didn't bring any overnight gear."

"That's 'cause we didn't plan on being stuck in a ditch," Paris said. "Stand back, while I try to back 'er out."

Paris got behind the wheel, put the truck in four-wheel drive, nodded to Cummings, who'd gotten clear, and shifted into reverse. He slowly began pressing the accelerator until it was floored.

The engine roared, the tires spun, geysers of dirt flew from beneath the wheels, but the truck barely budged.

"Shit!" Cummings shouted. "She's really stuck!"

"Have a little faith," Paris retorted. He switched the gears back and forth from forward to reverse several times, punching the gas pedal sharply each time. He hoped the rocking motion would allow the tires to gain traction and dislodge the truck. The wheels cycled rapidly, first forward and then in reverse, as the roaring noise continued to emanate from the furiously laboring engine. The truck slowly began to move.

"You'd better ease up," Cummings hollered over the screaming engine and howling wind. "You're gonna blow the motor."

"You wanna walk down the mountain?" Paris yelled back.

He gave it one more try. To his relief, the Dodge lurched backward and out of the ditch.

"I wouldn't want to repeat that experience," Paris said, as his relieved partner climbed back into the vehicle's cabin. "At least we didn't hit the damn deer and bang up my new truck."

"Just get us the hell outta here," Cummings said. "This wind is kickin' up somethin' fierce. And slow down, huh? Try to keep it on the road this time?"

"Tell that to the next buck we run into," Paris said. He

put the truck back on the narrow dirt road and they resumed their trek.

As the Dodge once again continued to wind its way down the mountain, neither man noticed a tiny flicker of flame smoldering in the ditch behind them. Even if they'd been inclined to look back, the darkness, blowing wind, and the dust the truck's tires kicked up on the dirt road combined to obscure their view.

It didn't occur to either of the hunters that the over-heated exhaust pipe of their truck, which had been toiling to free itself from the ditch, might have sparked the bone-dry grass and ignited it.

CHAPTER FOUR

Duane Mims sat in the cage with his eyes closed and tried to ignore the annoying chatter of the inmate seated across from him. This required more concentration than he cared to expend. He couldn't plug his ears because both of his hands were chained to a thick leather belt at his waist.

The only other occupant of the rear compartment of the California Department of Corrections and Rehabilitation's prisoner transportation van, the convict currently talking his ears off, was freakishly skinny, tattoo-covered, and looked to be in his mid-twenties. He sported a shaved head and corroded teeth, and seemed delighted to be sharing a ride in a moving cage with Mims.

". . . things were pretty cool for a while, after I got discharged," the skinny con continued babbling. "Never liked the army much, anyways. But civilian life wasn't no better. I went to work pounding nails for a roofing outfit in West Sacramento owned by my old lady's dad. That's when I first got into meth. That shit will get your engine goin', lemme tell ya. You ever do crank?"

Mims kept his eyes closed and didn't answer, hoping his fellow passenger would get the hint. He did not.

"I got into caffeine in the 'Stan while I was deployed," the convict went on. "Poundin' Red Bulls and Rip Its down like they was Kool-Aid. Six, maybe seven, cans a night. F-Bomb was my favorite flavor, but I dug Red Zone, too. That stuff'll keep your ass awake, that's a fact. I guess all them Rip Its and Red Bulls was what started me on my taste for speed."

Mims and the overly talkative convict were being transported from the California Medical Facility in Solano County, thirty miles west of Sacramento, to Folsom Prison. For Mims, it was a return trip.

Duane Audie Mims was almost nine years into a life-without-possibility-of-parole sentence being served at Folsom State Prison. Two weeks previously, as part of compliance requirements mandated by a federal consent decree and a research project funded by the State of California's Department of Corrections and Rehabilitation, he'd been sent to the California Medical Facility in Vacaville for what was to have been a weeklong psychiatric evaluation.

During the physical examination he received on arrival, it was discovered Mims was in the advanced stages of appendicitis. The corrective surgery, and complications that arose due to an infection, turned his one-week hospital stay into two.

After he was medically cleared for return to Folsom, Mims was secured in transportation chains that bound him at wrist and ankle. Then he was loaded into the caged van, along with the similarly restrained inmate who was incessantly blabbing. Since both were deemed violent, high-risk, offenders, they were required to be restrained when out of their cells for any reason.

It was nearing sunset, and the van had been on the road for over two hours. It occurred to Mims, largely because of the tedious nature of the one-sided conversation he was enduring, that they should have arrived at the prison long ago.

Mims also noticed two other things.

The van had stopped, and a strong scent of woodsmoke permeated the cabin. Since there were no windows in the caged vehicle, he couldn't look outside and ascertain the cause of his dual observations.

". . . tried coke and oxy and smoked a lot of weed," the inmate droned on, "but crank was my all-time favorite. Me and crank got to be real good buddies. At first, my girlfriend didn't mind me doin' meth 'cause when I was cranked up I could go all night, if ya know what I mean. But she eventually changed her tune, like bitches always do. Started naggin' the shit outta me about usin' meth. It got to be a real drag. Next thing I know her dad fired me, she dumped my ass, and she was about to kick me out of her crib."

The skinny convict leaned forward in his seat. "Have you ever been dumped?" he asked.

"Do you ever shut up?" Mims countered.

"Hey, man," the skinny convict protested. "There ain't no need for you to . . ."

"Shut up," Mims cut him off. The order was issued in a baritone accustomed to having commands obeyed. The younger inmate, far smaller than the tall, burly, older man seated across from him, momentarily forgot they were both restrained and shut up.

"Officer," Mims called through the small screen separating the driver's cabin and the cage behind it. "Why are we stopped? And what's burning?"

The partition slid open. "Take it easy, Mims," the correctional officer in the passenger seat said. He was an obese man in his forties wearing sergeant's stripes on the sleeves of his uniform. "You in a hurry to get back to your cell?"

"I smell smoke," Mims said. "A lot of smoke."

"We're stuck in a massive traffic jam," the driver, an equally obese corrections officer, said. "Both sides of the highway are a frickin' parking lot. Nothing to worry yourself over. You used to be a deputy sheriff, didn't you? You should know how California traffic gets during the evening commute."

"That doesn't explain the smoke," Mims argued.

"A wildfire started somewhere up in the Farnham National Forest last night," the sergeant said. "Supposed to be a pretty big one. You're smelling smoke from a fire that's a long way off, that's all."

"Don't smell a long way off to me," the skinny inmate spoke up.

"Didn't you boys notice the winds last night?" the driver asked the inmates. "Of course not," he chuckled, answering his own question. "You two chumps were locked down. For your information, it must have been blowing forty miles an hour overnight. Always does at this time of year. That's probably the reason you're smelling the smoke from so far away. It's just the wind."

"Weather lady on the news said the wind was closer to

fifty down here in the flatlands," the sergeant added. "She said up in the mountains it gusted up to seventy-five. Even a hundred, in some places."

"Every year it's the same thing with these frickin' wildfires," the driver lamented. "Breathing California air during the fire season is like smoking a pack a day."

"Is the wind blowing our direction?" Mims asked.

"Listen to Mister Public Safety behind me," the sergeant remarked, "asking for a weather report from the back of a prisoner van? Chillax, Mims. I have no idea which way the wind is blowing, and as you can see, I don't care."

"Maybe you should?" Mims said.

"When I need advice from a con, I'll let you know," he said. "Last I checked, we're the ones wearing the badges and you're the ones wearing the chains."

"You may as well smoke 'em if you got 'em," the driver said, chuckling at his pun. "Like I already told you boys, the road's a frickin' parking lot in both directions. We can't go anywhere even if we wanted to. Traffic'll clear up when it clears up. Besides, it ain't like you fellas are late for a date, are you?" His partner laughed at the taunt and closed the partition.

A faint rumbling noise, like a train off in the distance, could now be heard. Vehicle horns began to honk. First a few, then dozens more car horns blared all around the prisoner van.

Suddenly a gust of wind, powerful enough to rock the van from side to side, struck the vehicle. All four of the occupants were jostled. The rumbling noise continued to increase steadily until it became a roar that rivaled the many automobile horns blaring.

"What the hell is that?" the skinny inmate asked, raising

his voice to be heard above the din outside. Mims ignored him, listening.

People outside were shouting and screaming, many with the unmistakable tinge of panic in their voices. Vehicle doors could be heard opening. Many of them.

Another barrage of wind buffeted the van, and the odor of smoke became stifling. "It sounds like a riot's goin' on out there," the younger inmate said. "What do you suppose is happening?"

"Why don't you ask our keepers?" Mims said.

"Hey!" the skinny inmate yelled at the closed partition. "What's goin' on!"

The partition reopened. Both inmates leaned forward and glimpsed through the small barred window. They could see an orange glow permeating the driver's cabin. The two corrections officers were no longer cracking jokes. The driver was trying to operate the vehicle's dash-mounted Motorola transceiver, and the sergeant was attempting to make a call on his phone.

"You two shut up back there," the sergeant said.

"Radio's not working," the driver announced. "Not even CLEMARS." He was referring to the California Law Enforcement Mutual Aid Radio System.

"We're too far from a repeater," the sergeant said. "My phone's not working, either. The towers in the vicinity must be out."

"We have to get out of here," Mims said calmly. "Now."

"You ain't going anywhere," the sergeant snapped. The tension in his voice belied his mounting fear. "I don't need a goddamned con telling me how to do my job."

"It isn't about cons or guards anymore," Mims said. "It's about all four of us not getting cooked alive. This van's stuck. We're trapped, and the fire's going to be on us any minute."

"What fire?" the younger inmate said, his voice rising. "Where?"

Mims ignored the other inmate and continued addressing the corrections officers.

"Can't you feel that wind?" he asked them. "This isn't a wildfire, it's a firestorm, and it's coming our way. That's why people are abandoning their cars and running for their lives. If we don't do the same, and get out of here immediately, we're going to be incinerated."

"He's right," the driver said to his partner, unable to contain the fear in his own voice. "Look at those flames." He pointed through the windshield. "It's a frickin' wall of fire and heading right for us. I've never seen anything like it."

"Okay, okay," the sergeant said. He didn't need any more convincing. "We'll leave on foot." He turned to the inmates in back of the van. "If either of you two try anything . . ."

"Just get us out of this van," Mims cut him off, "before it becomes an oven. We're not going to try to escape, I swear. We don't want to get roasted any more than you do."

A moment later the van's rear doors opened. A blast of extremely hot air instantly struck the inmates, accompanied by eye-stinging smoke. Ashes, sparks, embers, and burning debris could be seen floating in the air. Everything around them was tinged with an orange glow.

Both inmates quickly shuffled toward the rear of the vehicle. They could only take baby steps due to their ankle chains.

"Sit down," the sergeant ordered. The inmates hopped

from the van, sat on the rear bumper, and extended their legs. The sergeant went to one knee and began unlocking Mims's leg restraints.

Mims took in the landscape. It was as bad as he'd surmised.

A solid wall of flame, at least one hundred feet in height and stretching as far as he could see, bore down on them from the east. The fire was less than fifty yards away and moving rapidly. The flames and accompanying smoke completely obscured the view of the Sierra Nevadas.

The tattoo-covered inmate coughed and squinted through the smoke, wind, and heat. "If we don't get movin'," he said, "we're gonna be burned to a crisp!"

"You figure that out all by yourself?" Mims said.

As the driver earlier noted, the van was trapped on all sides by other immobilized vehicles. Some of them, farther down the highway near the wall of fire, were already igniting and becoming engulfed. But what really got Mims's attention was the vehicle resting beside the prisoner van.

In the lane directly adjacent to the van, to Mims's consternation, was a semi-tractor truck linked to a tanker adorned with the logo of a major petroleum company. The tank wore diamond-shaped Department of Transportation placards identifying its contents as explosively flammable. Motorists could be seen abandoning their vehicles and running west, away from the highway, the tanker truck, and the massive inferno bearing down on them.

"I'm leaving their waist chains on," the sergeant said to his partner. He was beginning to cough and choke.

"Whatever you do," the driver answered between coughs, "do it quick."

The roar of the approaching blaze sounded like an oncoming freight train. The heat, too, was becoming noticeable. Gale force winds buffeted, pelting the four men with dust, sparks, flaming debris, and burning embers.

"Hurry up," the driver pleaded. "You see that frickin' gas tanker? We've got to get away from here before it blows." He was barely able to keep the tide of panic from overtaking him.

"Of course, I see the damned tanker," the sergeant angrily shot back. He squinted through the smoke and wind as his shaking hands fumbled with the keys. "You think this is where I want to be right now?"

"Leave them!" the driver yelled to his partner. "The fire's almost at the front of the tanker! Let's go!"

"We can't just leave them, you idiot," the sergeant argued. His shaking hands fumbled, and he dropped the keys.

"They're a couple of frickin' murderers," the driver shouted back. "One of them's a baby-killer, for Chrissakes! Nobody'll care! C'mon, let's go!"

Mims looked over at the fuel truck. Just as the corrections officer said, the fire had consumed most of the cars ahead, and flames were now licking at the front of the tanker. Other motorists in the vicinity had all fled, including the fuel truck's driver.

Mims wondered how many of the vehicle's occupants farther ahead didn't get out in time and were being immolated inside their automobiles. He looked over at the driver, who appeared terrified. He seemed to be on the verge of bolting, leaving his partner, and the two chained inmates, behind.

"I ain't staying any longer," the driver shrieked, his

voice cracking. "Stick around if you want to, but I'm not going to die over a couple of killers!"

"Hold on," the sergeant said, recovering the keys and resuming his task. "I'm almost done."

A few seconds later, Mims's legs were free. The sergeant turned to unlock the leg restraints on the other inmate.

Mims waited until the sergeant was focused on unlocking his fellow inmate's leg irons before he pounced. The other corrections officer's attention was still riveted on the fuel truck and the approaching wall of fire growing closer by the second. He didn't see Mims moving toward him until it was too late.

Mims kicked the driver in the groin with everything he had. The corrections officer convulsed and fell to his knees, in so much pain he couldn't even scream. Mims kicked him again, this time in the head. The officer dropped to the ground on his face, unconscious.

The sergeant had removed one of the other inmate's leg restraints when he sensed motion behind him and looked up. He had just enough time to raise a forearm to block Mims's kick to his cranium. He stopped the kick to his head, but the force of the strike shattered his ulna and sent him sprawling backward.

The sergeant fell onto his back, desperately reaching for the .40 caliber Glock at his hip. Mims, his hands still chained to the belt at his waist, threw himself on top of the frantic corrections officer.

Mims was taller than his adversary, and quite a large man himself, but the sergeant had fifty pounds on him. Mims headbutted him, and thrashed as hard as he could, but the big corrections officer had the advantage in the use of at least one of his hands.

He shoved Mims off and scooted backward. The big convict struggled to a crouch, preparing to launch his body at the officer again. The sergeant drew his pistol. He aimed it at his attacker, one-handed, with his broken left forearm draped across his chest.

Mims stared into the unblinking eye of the pistol's barrel. The impassive face he'd worn a moment before his attack had transformed into an expression of primal malevolence. The sergeant's finger closed on the trigger.

The tattoo-covered convict kicked the sergeant in the head, from behind, instantly knocking him out.

The vehicle in front of the fuel truck, a sedan that was already on fire, exploded as its gas tank ruptured. Both inmates flinched. The raging inferno was consuming car after car.

"Come here," Mims shouted over the din. He squatted down and retrieved the correction's officer's dropped keys. The other inmate hesitated.

"Do you want to live," Mims asked him, "or die? We don't have much time."

The inmate overcame his doubt and stepped over to help Mims. Even with his hands restrained, Mims was able to expertly unlock the handcuffs securing the younger man's hands. Then he handed the keys over.

"Unlock me," Mims ordered.

The younger convict hesitated again. "What about them two guards?" he said.

"They were going to leave us to burn," Mims answered.

"Only one of 'em."

"Forget them," Mims said. "They're already cremated, they just don't know it. Do you want to join them?"

The younger man, free of his own chains, looked up at

the older, larger convict. Mims could see he was on the verge of fleeing.

"What's done is done," argued Mims, the roar of the fire nearly drowning out his voice. The skin on their faces and exposed forearms was beginning to blister. "Without me, you'll never make it out of here alive. Even if you do survive, you'll be caught. I'm your only chance."

The younger man bit his lip and hesitated another few seconds. Then he unlocked Mims's handcuffs.

Both men removed their heavy leather transportation belts. Mims also stripped off his light blue tunic, decorated with the stenciled initials CDCR, leaving him clad in only dungarees, canvas shoes, and a white T-shirt. The younger convict followed suit. Mims then recovered the pistol from the unconscious sergeant. He removed the gun from the security holster of his equally unconscious partner, familiar with its safety features supposedly designed to prevent anyone but the wearer from accessing the firearm. He stuck both guns in the waistband of his trousers under his shirt.

"Follow me," Mims said. He ran west, away from the fire, with the young, tattoo-covered convict on his heels.

They crossed the opposite lanes of the highway and descended a steep embankment. The smoke was so thick visibility was reduced to mere feet. At the bottom of the slope, to their relief, was a creek. Mims waded into the chest-deep water, followed by the other convict.

They found dozens of other motorists taking refuge in the water. Many were sobbing and holding each other. Some were praying.

A tremendous explosion erupted from up on the road, creating a mushroom cloud of fire that billowed into the red sea of flame surrounding it. It was loud enough to temporarily eclipse the overwhelming roar of the wind-fueled firestorm, and the concussion it released could be felt as well as heard.

"That's gotta be the tanker blowin'," the younger inmate remarked, keeping his voice low. "We got out just in time. Them two guards are crispy critters fer sure."

"I agree on both counts," Mims said.

"What're our chances?"

"Better than when we were chained in the back of a prison van," Mims answered, "parked next to a fuel truck, in the middle of a firestorm."

"What'll we do now?"

"Stay here in the water and breathe shallow," Mims said, submerging himself to his chin. "The air above us is superheated; it can burn your lungs even if the flames don't reach us. That gasoline truck up on the road will keep the fire fed for a while, but this windstorm is moving fast. Once all the cars are burned out, and their fuel's exhausted, the firestorm will blow over us and move on."

"What then?"

"Then we'll get the hell out of here," Mims said, "and disappear."

"Won't the cops be lookin' for us?"

"This fire isn't going out anytime soon," Mims said, "and it'll get a lot bigger. Believe me, the authorities are going to have their hands full. I doubt they'll be looking for us at all."

"What are you sayin'?"

"I'm saying," Mims said with a slight grin, "we both just got pardoned, courtesy of this firestorm."

"I don't get it," the younger inmate said.

"I've seen firestorms this hot before," Mims said. "They disintegrate pretty much everything in their path. That fuel truck going off next to us didn't hurt, either. That prison van will soon be nothing more than a burned-out shell. Everything around it will be vaporized."

"Even them two guards?"

"There won't even be ashes left of those two fools."

"You think," the inmate said, "the cops'll figure we got burned up, too?"

"If we're lucky," Mims said.

"We're lucky, all right," the younger man said. "One minute we were in chains on the way to Folsom and about to get burned alive, and the next minute we're free as birds. It don't get any luckier than that."

"Don't start your end zone dance," Mims cautioned, gesturing toward the dozens of terrified people taking refuge in the water and the wall of flame barreling toward the creek. "We aren't out of the frying pan yet."

"My name's Randy Purdue," the tattooed convict said. "My friends call me 'Skink.'" He raised his right hand from the muddy water. "Thanks for savin' my bacon back there. And for gettin' me my freedom."

"Seems you did the same for me," Mims said. He shook the offered hand. "Pleased to make your acquaintance, Skink. You can call me Duane."

Chapter Five

Strayer entered the office of her S.W.A.T. commander, Lieutenant Russell. He wasn't alone. Undersheriff Torres was sitting in one of the only two chairs in the room with his arms folded across his sizeable belly and a rolled-up newspaper in one fist. Russell motioned for her to sit down.

It had been four days since the firefight in the Pleasant Pines Trailer Park. Deputy Strayer, along with everyone else in her squad except Deputy Steven Calley, who was still in the hospital recovering from a gunshot wound to his neck, had been placed on administrative leave. This was standard protocol for deputies involved in a shooting.

In the hours after the firefight Strayer, along with the other S.W.A.T. deputies at the scene, including Calley at the hospital, were all separately interviewed by detectives from both her department and inspectors from the Farnham County District Attorney's Office. Her H & K submachine gun and duty pistol, a .45 caliber Sig Sauer 1911, were taken as evidence by technicians from the Crime Scene Unit. They also confiscated the weapons from each of her squad mates.

Strayer was accompanied by an attorney paid for by the Deputy Sheriff's Association's Legal Defense Fund during the interview, which was standard practice for any deputy involved in a lethal force investigation where criminal charges might potentially result.

Technically, Strayer was a homicide suspect. The officer-involved shooting investigation would eventually determine whether the lethal force she used when she shot and killed Ernesto Machado was legally justified and within departmental policy or not. If not, she would be criminally charged like anyone else.

Strayer was read her Miranda rights, waived them, and voluntarily answered every question posed by the investigators. She calmly related what transpired, from her perspective, during the attempted arrest and subsequent death of an armed and dangerous homicide suspect by members of her S.W.A.T. team.

When she walked out over an hour later, Strayer's attorney assured her she had nothing legally to worry about. The lawyer told her she did her duty, followed the law, complied with departmental rules, regulations, policies, and procedures, and saved a fellow deputy's life.

Strayer wasn't especially comforted. Her attorney said nothing reassuring about her political jeopardy.

"You wanted to see me?" she asked the lieutenant as she sat down. The Special Weapons and Tactics commander had previously summoned every other member of Sergeant Bennington's team for a one-on-one meeting. Strayer was the last deputy to be interviewed by the investigators since she'd been the last deputy to fire her weapon.

"I've got some news you may not like," Lieutenant Russell said. He was a no-nonsense former Marine who, despite being in his early fifties, was extremely fit. Not a man to waste words, he got right to the point. "You're being reassigned, pending your clearance to full duty by the departmental psychologist."

"What am I being reassigned for?" she asked, trying to keep the disappointment from her voice. "I didn't do anything wrong."

"It's not a punitive transfer," Russell said, "and it isn't just you. Everybody on Sergeant Bennington's team is getting reassigned once they're cleared for duty."

"With all due respect, Lieutenant," Strayer said, looking sideways at the undersheriff, "that's bullshit."

"Maybe so," Russell said, "but that's how it is."

"I busted my ass to get assigned to S.W.A.T.," she protested. "I put my time in Custody and Patrol. I aced the selection trials, too. I earned that assignment."

"I know," Russell said. "Nobody said anything about putting you back into the Custody or Patrol Divisions. You're getting another special assignment."

"Where am I going?"

"The Investigations Division," Lieutenant Russell said. "Juvenile Unit."

"You've got to be kidding?"

"Think of it as career development," Russell said. "A lot of deputies would give their right arm for a slot in the Investigations Division."

"Lazy ones," Strayer said scornfully, "who want day-shift hours, weekends off, and to get their butts off the street. I don't want to fly a desk, Lieutenant. I'm a first responder, not a rear-echelon puke."

"You mean like me?" Torres said disdainfully.

Strayer winced. That hadn't come out the way she intended.

"Detectives spend plenty of time in the field," Russell said, getting the conversation back on track. He didn't like that Torres insisted on being present when he gave Strayer the news, particularly since he'd issued the reassignment orders to the other S.W.A.T. deputies alone. Russell understood the necessity of having a witness when interacting one-on-one with a female deputy, a reality of the modern law enforcement environment in the #MeToo age. But he disliked the optics of appearing to double-team her while issuing what was clearly being interpreted as a negative order.

"I don't care how much time they spend in the field," Strayer countered. "I don't like paperwork, I don't want to be a detective, and I damn sure don't want to be a kiddie cop."

"Nobody's asking what you like or want, Deputy," Undersheriff Torres interjected. "For your information, the sheriff has the authority to transfer his personnel wherever he wants, whenever he wants, as long as it isn't a demotion in rank or punitive in nature. Your pay grade will remain the same, and the lieutenant already explained that your reassignment is a lateral transfer from one special assignment to another. So there's nothing to beef through the union."

"Did anybody else on my team get reassigned to Investigations?" Strayer asked.

"No," Russell admitted. "The rest of your team is being assigned to the Custody or Patrol Divisions, depending on their preference. I'm only telling you because you'll find out eventually."

Strayer could guess why her fellow S.W.A.T. deputies

chose to return to Custody or Patrol. The Custody and Patrol Divisions, like S.W.A.T., operated on a 3-12 schedule. This meant they worked three twelve-hour days, with four days off.

Four days off each week translated into more leisure and family time, and offered greater opportunity for lucrative overtime pay if called in while on a regularly scheduled day off.

Investigations Division personnel worked a 4-10 schedule, with weekends off. While detectives certainly enjoyed plenty of overtime opportunity, and weekends off allowed a semblance of normality typically not afforded to law enforcement officers, an assignment to Investigations meant a deputy would have to give up one of their days off.

"Why can't I go to the Patrol Division?" Strayer said. "If I have to leave S.W.A.T., I'd rather be a road deputy than a detective."

"Not going to happen," Torres said. "The sheriff believes you'd best serve the department's needs in the Investigations Division."

"Explain to me again," Strayer asked, her jaw tightening, "why the only female on S.W.A.T., who also happens to be half-Asian, is getting shuffled to Investigations and everybody else is going to Custody or Patrol?"

"Don't try to play that card," Torres said. "Your gender or race has nothing to do with it. I already told you, the transfer isn't punitive. By the way, the command staff of this department doesn't owe individual deputies explanations for their staffing decisions."

"Then maybe the command staff would like to explain the transfer to my attorney?" she retorted. "Or the department's Equal Employment Opportunity Commission representative over in Human Resources?"

Undersheriff Torres exhaled, rolled his eyes, and slapped his thigh with his rolled-up newspaper. He started to speak again, then recrossed his arms, leaned back in his chair, and nodded for the lieutenant to continue.

"The sheriff feels," Russell began, uncomfortable with having to explain an order he neither issued nor agreed with, "it would be best right now for both your career, and the department's image, if you were to assume a less high-profile position. He believes at this time it's in everyone's interest that you take on a follow-up role in Investigations, as opposed to a frontline function as a first responder in the Patrol Division."

"It's because of my other shootings," Strayer said, "isn't it?"

"Personally," Russell said, "I can't confirm or deny whether your previous officer-involved shootings played a role in your reassignment." It was his turn to look sideways at Undersheriff Torres. "That decision is above my pay grade."

"What did you expect?" Torres said, his exasperation overcoming his silence. "The Machado incident was your third fatal shooting in less than three years. You're a hot potato right now, Deputy Strayer."

"Each of my shootings was justified, lawful, and within departmental policy," Strayer said defensively.

"Nobody said you did anything wrong," Torres acknowledged. "But the department has to deal with the political and legal fallout the same as if you did. Were you aware those cop-hating reporters over at the *Farnham Times-Journal* have christened you with a nickname?"

He tossed the newspaper on the desk in front of her.

"They've dubbed you 'Deadeye.' Not exactly the kind of press the department needs right now."

Strayer examined the newspaper. The headline of the *Farnham Times-Journal* read, "Deadeye Deputy Strikes Again."

"I couldn't care less what a hack reporter writes," Strayer said. She dropped the newspaper into the recycling bin beside the lieutenant's desk.

"Maybe you don't care," Strayer said, "but the sheriff does. He's got an election to win in a few days. This kind of media coverage doesn't exactly improve his reelection chances."

"That's what this is all about," Strayer said, "isn't it? I committed the cardinal sin of causing the Farnham County Sheriff's Department bad press."

"You said it," Torres said with a shrug, "not me."

"Shame on me for my lousy political instincts," Strayer said bitterly. "Maybe next time I'll let a murder suspect with an assault rifle execute one of my fellow deputies, and spare the department any potential embarrassment."

"You're out of line, Deputy," Lieutenant Russell said.

"I wonder if Deputy Calley would prefer I hadn't inconvenienced the sheriff's reelection campaign?"

"That's enough," Russell said sharply. "There's more on the table than your career, and you know it."

Strayer knew what her former commander was referring to. In addition to a dead suspect, and a seriously wounded deputy, a seven-year-old girl named Amalia Gallantes was in the Intensive Care Unit as a result of the botched raid.

One of the many rounds fired from inside the mobile home during the brief but intense firefight between the desperate murder suspect and the deputies attempting to arrest him penetrated its flimsy walls. The bullet entered the adjacent trailer and struck the sleeping Amalia in her bed. Though expected to survive, Amalia was in critical condition. The child's mother, and many others in the community, were understandably outraged.

While it was too early in the investigation to determine which weapon, the suspect's or a S.W.A.T. deputy's, fired the offending bullet, to the community at large it didn't matter. Their collective rage fueled three days of angry protests in front of departmental headquarters in the Town of Farnham, which was also the county seat.

The blisteringly negative media coverage that accompanied the protests made it abundantly clear many felt blame for the child's injury rested squarely on the shoulders of the law enforcement agency conducting the high-risk arrest, and not on the murder suspect they were attempting to capture.

The timing of the shoot-out couldn't have been worse. The incident occurred a little more than a week before Election Day, with the sheriff in the final throes of a re-election fight in which he held only a razor-thin lead in the polls. Strayer didn't have to be a political pundit to recognize the political firestorm the gun battle in the trailer park ignited in the community or within the department. Nor was she naïve enough to believe her transfer wasn't connected to both.

There was no doubt that her reassignment, and the reassignment of her entire S.W.A.T. team, was nothing more than damage control. The sheriff wanted to get ahead of the political and legal fallout. And Strayer knew there was nothing, short of turning in her star, that she could do about it.

"I didn't shoot the little girl," Strayer said.

"Never said you did," Russell answered. "The round that hit her came from inside the trailer. As far as the community is concerned, everyone on Bennerman's team is responsible."

"Not everyone on Bennerman's team is going to Investigations," Strayer pointed out.

"Not everyone on Bennerman's team has your record," Torres said.

"Don't have a choice," Strayer said, with no effort to conceal her disgust, "do I?"

"No," Russell said, "you don't. You're a vet, and you've been a deputy sheriff for almost five years. Surely this isn't the first time you've received an order you didn't like?"

"That's true, Lieutenant," she said. "I've received my share of lousy orders in the army, and more than a few here at the department. But this is the first time a superior officer ever pissed on my head and told me it was raining."

"Take some advice," Russell said, not unkindly, "from somebody with more military and law enforcement time in the saddle than you. Try to make lemonade out of lemons, will you? Nobody said this would be a permanent transfer, or that at some future date reassignment back to the Patrol Division, or even S.W.A.T., isn't an option. But for now, it's not. That's just how it is. Who knows? You might like being a Juvenile Detective?"

"Don't hold your breath," she said, standing up. "Will that be all?"

"No," the lieutenant said. "There's one more thing." He handed her a slip of paper. "Your appointment tomorrow with the department's psychologist for your mandatory counseling session. Don't miss it. You know the drill;

you're still on administrative leave until officially declared fit to return to full-duty status. You won't even be going to the Investigations Division if the psychologist doesn't approve."

"I know the drill, Lieutenant," Strayer said. "I've been through the post-shooting psych evaluation twice before, remember?"

"Roll with this punch and drive on," Russell said.

"I can't make any promises," she said.

"Is there going to be a problem, Deputy?" Torres said.

"No problem," she answered, staring straight ahead.

"Then you're dismissed."

CHAPTER SIX

Strayer walked out of the lieutenant's office, resisting the urge to slam the door. She passed the elevator and took the stairs down to the basement, taking chi breaths while clenching and unclenching her fists to release her anger and frustration. Once underground and in a state again resembling calm, she walked past the gym, the indoor firing range, and locker rooms to the S.W.A.T. armory.

To her surprise, the armory was filled with S.W.A.T. deputies. Some had been on Bennerman's team, but the rest were from the other two squads. The deputies from Strayer's squad, like her, were there to strip personal effects from their lockers and vacate them in light of their new assignments. None looked any happier about the task than she was.

There was only one reason the other two S.W.A.T. squads—the off-duty squad and the squad on training rotation—would have been called in; something was up.

Several deputies from her former squad nodded silently to Strayer as she unlocked her locker and began to remove her personal gear. The others ignored her. As the only woman previously assigned to an otherwise all-male tactical unit, she was accustomed to it.

"What gives?" she asked one of the deputies on her former team. "Riot duty, for the protestors outside?"

"Nope," he said. He was a short, stocky, Caucasian deputy named Colby she didn't know especially well but who had always been professional and cordial, something she couldn't say for all the deputies assigned to S.W.A.T. He'd been on the entry team and inside the trailer during the shoot-out.

"Full callout," Colby said, "department-wide. They've opened up the Emergency Operating Center, too. Everybody still on S.W.A.T., which ain't you and me anymore, is getting called in. They're even calling in the reserve deputies."

"What's the big emergency?"

"Didn't you hear?" another deputy said, butting into the conversation. His name was Meyers. He was tall and heavily built, with a face scarred by steroid-induced acne, and wasn't assigned to Strayer's former squad. She often caught him leering at her during joint tactical training, along with more than a few of the other S.W.A.T. deputies. She'd learned to ignore being checked out by men in uniform long ago while in the army.

"I've been in I.A. all afternoon," Strayer said, "getting grilled. What didn't I hear?"

"That wildfire that broke out last night up in the national forest?" Colby said. "It's turned into a full-blown firestorm. Sheriff's declared a countywide state of emergency. The governor's expected to do the same later today. County's going to be crawling with firefighters from all over the state."

"I heard something about it on the news driving into the station," Strayer said. "I could smell the smoke, too."

"This one's supposed to be big," Colby said, "and totally out of control."

"I'm not surprised." Strayer shrugged. "The high-country timber is always dry as a bone this time of year."

"I guess the Monos have been doing their thing again. Winds are blowing like crazy up there. They're saying this blaze could be as big as the Camp Fire."

"That ain't good," Strayer said, not really listening. She was stewing over the fact that everyone else but she and her former squad were getting dressed to be deployed.

"The fire's burned almost to Tuckerville and Drayton," Colby continued. "Cal Fire isn't making a dent. It's eating up farms and ranches all over eastern Farnham County."

"Any fatalities?"

"Nothing official, but that's only because it's early yet. Tons of missing people are being reported. A bunch of motorists got trapped on the highway south of Folsom. People had to abandon their cars and run for their lives. From what I heard, quite a few didn't make it."

"Poor bastards," Strayer said, filling her nylon gear bag.

"Fire's so hot," Colby said, "firefighters can't even get close. Coroner's office has no idea how many are missing or dead."

"Can you imagine going out that way?" Meyers blurted. "Cooked alive in your own car like a frozen burrito in a microwave oven? That must righteously suck. Just thinking about all those burned-up folks gives me the creeps. I'll bet most of the ones who got charbroiled were the oldsters and kids, since they can't run as fast."

"You're truly an asshole," Colby said, "do you know that?"

"Maybe so," Meyers quipped, "but at least I'm still on S.W.A.T."

"Ignore him," Strayer said to Colby. "He's a moron."

"I heard that," Meyers said to her.

"You were meant to," Strayer said, giving Meyers a sarcastic thumbs-up. "Mission accomplished." Several other deputies in the locker room laughed.

"C'mon," she said to Colby. "Let's get packed up and get out of here." They resumed clearing out their lockers.

"What else have you heard?" Strayer asked him, changing the conversation back to the fire to get his mind off Meyers's remark. She could tell by his reddened face the comment about being reassigned stung. It stung her, too.

"I heard that all the firefighters and first responders can do right now is evacuate residents," Colby said to Strayer. "That's what we'd be doing if we were still on the team. Helping to evacuate and conducting looter-suppression sweeps."

"There ain't gonna be any looters breaking into homes in that inferno," Meyers said, still eavesdropping on their conversation. "There's gotta be homes left for looters to break into. Yessiree, there's gonna be a lot of homeless folks in Farnham County tonight. I'll probably be hangin' out at the staging area or one of the shelters, sipping Red Cross coffee and making bank in overtime pay." He laughed. "How about you two? What are your plans tonight?"

"Are you always such an asshole," Colby asked, "or is today special?"

Meyers grinned and gave him the finger. "Good luck writing traffic tickets back in the Patrol Division," he said.

"Forget him," Strayer said. "He's just trying to rile you."

Colby took her advice. He closed his locker and headed for the door.

Strayer felt her own anger and frustration rise again, but she didn't show it. She didn't want to give Meyers, or anyone else, any satisfaction. She knew Colby and the rest of her squad, like her, were upset because they weren't getting geared up for deployment to the fire zone. Instead, they were unpacking their lockers and moving out.

Strayer finished collecting her gear, zipped up her canvas bag, and closed her empty locker. She followed Colby toward the armory door.

"I heard you were getting transferred over to Dicks," Meyers called after her, using the traditional law enforcement slang term for detectives. He laughed again and said, "Good luck with that, Strayer. I'll bet you've got plenty of experience working with dicks."

"Shut up, Meyers," she heard a S.W.A.T. deputy behind her say.

"Yeah," echoed another, "shut the fuck up. I don't want to get interviewed by I.A. as a witness to a sexual harassment beef on account of your stupid mouth."

Strayer walked out, biting back a desire to drop her gear bag, conduct an about-face, and roundhouse kick Deputy Meyers squarely in the center of his stupid mouth.

CHAPTER SEVEN

Tad Guthrie sat at the large mahogany table and drummed his fingers on the polished surface. His father was seated on one side of him and his father's lawyer, Vincent Holloway, on the other. They were in a conference room in the Sacramento law offices of Holloway, Carruthers, and Stern, discussing how to proceed with Tad's "predicament," as his father called it.

"You're telling me," Tad whined at the attorney, "that I can't even visit my own kids?"

"Not yet," Holloway said. "Your wife's attorney has filed for, and been granted, a temporary emergency restraining order against you. The order governs the children, as well. It will remain in effect until the permanent restraining order she's filed is reviewed by a judge. Based on what I know about your case, I believe it is highly likely that permanent order will be granted."

"What does all that mean?"

"It means," Holloway continued, "you will have to stay at least one hundred yards away from your wife at all times, not attempt to contact her in person, by phone, or other electronic means, such as email or text, or try to contact her through a third party. If you do, you will be arrested, charged with violating a court order, which judges take personally, by the way, and remanded back into custody."

"I can't contact my kids, either?"

"For the time being. Eventually, some sort of supervised visitation schedule will be arranged, but that's a ways down the road. For now, there must be no contact with your children or your spouse. You'll get to visit your children, in a supervised setting, once you're out on probation and after you show proof you've attended counseling and anger-management classes. But as I said, that's a ways off. You're putting the cart ahead of the horse, Tad. Our focus right now is to minimize the amount of actual jail time you'll have to serve."

"Jail time!" Tad exclaimed. "What are you talking about? I already spent three days in jail! Isn't that enough?"

"Take it easy, Teddy," Tad's father, Dr. Maury Guthrie, said. He called his son Teddy, which was short for Theodore. Tad despised the nickname, which was why he began calling himself Tad in high school. "It took longer than we thought to arrange your release. The judge wouldn't let you out."

"Why not?"

"California law gives judges the leeway to deny bail and keep a defendant in a domestic-violence case incarcerated for a reasonable enough time to allow the victim to make other living arrangements," Holloway explained. "Keep in mind, you're only out on bail pending your next court date, which will be your arraignment. Some incarceration time, even if I'm able to arrange a plea bargain, is inevitable."

"You've got to be kidding?" Tad moaned. "I'm going back to jail? Seriously? For one little slap in the face?"

He turned to his father. "What are you paying this guy for, Dad? I know he's your friend, and he's represented you for a long time, but can't you find a lawyer who can keep me out of jail?"

"Calm down, Teddy," Guthrie said to his son. "I have every confidence in Vincent."

"You can afford to have confidence in him," Tad smirked. "You aren't the one who's going to jail if he screws up."

"It's not my screwup that's going to send you to jail," Holloway said, "it's yours. This time, Tad, you really stepped in it."

"I got into a little argument with my wife," Tad scoffed. "A lot of married couples argue now and then. What's the big deal?"

"The big deal," Holloway began, as if explaining something to a small child, "is corporal injury to a spouse, which is how the California Penal Code defines what you did. During your 'little argument,' as you called it, you slammed your wife into a wall, punched her in the face with a closed fist, and knocked her to the ground. These acts resulted in your wife suffering a fractured nose, lacerations to her knee requiring stitches, and a concussion. That's called a felony, not a 'little argument,' and is punishable by no less than one year in the county jail and up to four years in the state penitentiary."

"She set me up!" Tad said hotly. "Marjorie deliberately provoked me into losing my temper, and she did it where she knew our security camera would record it! I didn't even know the interior cameras were switched on!"

"As your attorney," Holloway said calmly, "I'm compelled

to advise you that claiming your wife is responsible for you beating her up is a very poor legal strategy. Especially when the entire incident was, as you pointed out, recorded on high-resolution video."

"Can't you work out some kind of a plea bargain?" Tad pleaded with Holloway. "Get me off with probation, like you did with that drunk driving thing? Isn't that how this legal stuff is supposed to work?"

"It's not that easy," Holloway continued. "In most of these types of cases, it's the victim's word against the defendant's. Even with medically documented injuries, and your wife has plenty of those, an argument can sometimes be made that the victim did something to provoke the defendant, like attacked first, or at least participated vigorously in the physical altercation which led to their injury."

Holloway paused to look at Dr. Guthrie, who stared meekly at his hands. "But in your case, Tad," he went on, "you chose to commit an utterly unprovoked assault on your petite wife in full view of an operational video camera. I've seen the footage, and so has the deputy district attorney. You can bet when a judge and jury see it, sympathy and mercy aren't going to be on their minds."

"So what you're saying—"

"What I'm saying," Holloway cut in, "is you've given me very little to plea bargain with. If this case goes all the way to trial, you'll get slam-dunk convicted, and the D.A. knows it. And if we put the county through the expense and inconvenience of such a trial and lose, which we will, the judge will issue the maximum sentence. That's presumably the incentive for pretrial plea bargains in the first place. As you said, that's 'how this legal stuff is supposed to work.' In your case, that maximum sentence will be four years in state prison. Which gives the deputy district attorney very little motivation to cut a deal involving no custody time."

"What can we realistically expect?" Guthrie asked.

"At this point," Holloway said, "I would be very lucky to get your son off with a year in the county jail, followed by three years of formal probation."

"A year in jail?" Tad exploded, rising to his feet. "Are you nuts?"

"You might not have to do the entire year," Holloway said. "You could be out in eight or nine months if you behaved yourself while inside."

"Eight or nine months?"

"I don't make the laws, Tad."

Tad slunk back into his chair and put his face in his hands.

"You don't think there's any chance a jury would let him off?" Dr. Guthrie asked.

"Not a snowball's chance in hell," Holloway said flatly. "The trial will essentially be over the minute the jury finds out that Tad and his wife were arguing about him infecting her with a venereal disease, which is documented in her medical records. After they're shown the photographs of her injuries, and get a gander at that video, I doubt she'll even have to testify."

"Wait a minute," Tad said, looking up and snapping his fingers. "That gives me an idea. What if Marjorie dropped the charges?"

"It wouldn't matter," the attorney said. "The victim is the State of California, not your wife. Even if she recanted, the D.A. would probably still charge you."

"You said 'probably,'" Tad argued. "That means there's

a chance the district attorney might dismiss the charges, right?"

"I suppose anything is possible," Holloway said. "In any case the point is moot, since you're prohibited from contacting your wife."

"I'll take those odds," Tad said. "It beats nine months in jail. Especially since I'm sure I could get Marjorie to drop the charges against me. Then all you'd have to do, Mister Holloway, is convince the D.A. to cut me some slack." He rubbed his chin as his mind raced. "I just need to get her alone for a few minutes."

"As your attorney," Holloway said, "I would strongly advise you not to attempt to contact your wife. Remember, you're under a restraining order which was served while you were in custody at the Placer County Jail. If you try to contact Marjorie, even if you're unsuccessful, you'd be committing another felony. You'd be arrested, locked up, denied bail, and I can practically guarantee a state prison sentence."

"I'll take your advice under consideration," Tad said, grinning. He stood up again. "C'mon, Dad. Let's get out of here."

CHAPTER EIGHT

Mims and Skink walked together through the smoke and darkness. Up ahead, they could see the tail reflectors of two parked vehicles at the side of the road with their engines turned off. They immediately left the road and slunk into the ditch, creeping toward the parked vehicles as quietly as they could.

Less than five minutes after they took refuge in the creek, the fire reached them. Fortunately for the duo, and the dozens of other motorists who'd fled their trapped automobiles as the firestorm approached, the steep incline acted as somewhat of a windbreak. This permitted the fiercest of the wind-driven flames to pass largely overhead.

The fire nonetheless progressed down toward the creek rapidly through the dry grass. Soon both banks were aflame.

The two convicts lay on their backs under the water with only their noses above the surface. The air they took in, through shallow breaths, was acrid and hot. What they could see of the sky through the muddy stream was aglow.

After what seemed like hours, but was probably no more than thirty minutes, the air cooled noticeably and the glowing sky faded to darkness. Mims patted Skink's elbow, and they both slowly rose from the water.

All around them were sporadic flames, but it wasn't the inferno they'd fled from the highway. The landscape was blackened, and the smoke was so dense neither could see more than a dozen feet in any direction.

They could hear people moaning and crying off in the dark. A woman started yelling for help but they couldn't see her nor anyone else.

"We've got to get out of here," Mims said between coughs. He stripped off his soaking shirt and wrapped it around the lower portion of his face as an improvised filter. Skink followed suit, revealing a torso covered in crude tattoos.

"Which way should we go?" Skink asked.

"Upstream," Mims said.

"Won't that put us back towards the fire?"

"We've got no choice," Mims answered. "We can't outrun the firestorm. It's moving too fast. Even if we could, we'd run smack-dab into an army of firefighters and cops coming to meet it. Our best bet is to make our way through the areas that're already burned out. There're bound to be places that have been evacuated where we might find an abandoned home or farmhouse to hole up in."

"I wouldn't mind finding a car," Skink said.

"I was thinking the same thing. Let's go."

The shirtless convicts began making their way upstream, wading and swimming, through the chest-deep water. They passed a number of dazed, filthy, and terrified people huddled in the creek.

"Are you going for help?" an elderly woman, her face black with soot, asked Mims as he went by.

"That's exactly what we're doing," came the muffled reply through his T-shirt. "You folks hang on. We'll be back with help soon."

"God bless you," the woman said, patting his arm.

After a few minutes, they encountered no more people in the water. They continued on for another half hour, before darkness completely enveloped them. The smoke was so thick they didn't even see the sun go down.

Every so often they'd dip under the surface and resoak the towels over their faces. They fumbled along through the dark for the next couple of hours, feeling their way up the creek, until gradually the smoke cleared somewhat and a few stars became visible through the haze overhead.

Both men crawled, shivering and exhausted, to the bank. Their bodies were numb from the strenuous trek through the creek and from being immersed for so long. They gulped in fresh air, though it was still tinged heavily with the scent of smoke.

"Looks like we're out of the fire zone," Skink said, through chattering teeth. "At least for now."

"Let's have a look around," Mims said.

Mims and Skink clawed their way up the embankment and found they were next to a dirt road. There was no traffic on it.

"I wonder where we are?" Skink said.

"I think I know," Mims answered. "It's a county road, somewhere south of Folsom."

"Folsom?" Skink spat. "I don't want to go anywhere near that place."

"I didn't say we were going to Folsom Prison," Mims said. "I told you where we are, that's all. But I agree with you, I don't want to go near Folsom, either. Too great a chance somebody might recognize us."

"Recognize you, maybe," Skink corrected him. "I ain't never been to the town of Folsom. I don't know a soul there."

They reached the road and began walking west.

"I heard that guard in the van say you was a deputy once," Skink said, unable to keep silent any longer. "Is that true? You sure worked that handcuff key like a pro."

"Maybe," Mims said, "in another life."

"So tell me," Skink said, "what did a deputy sheriff do to get locked up in Folsom?"

"You've never been to prison before," Mims answered with a question of his own, "have you?"

"Nope," Skink admitted, "just county jail."

"If you'd been to prison," Mims said, "you'd know better than to ask somebody what they're inside for."

"Why not?" Skink said.

"Because they might show you," Mims said.

They walked in silence for another hour, chilled, fatigued, and hungry, until they saw the trucks parked along the side of the road.

"Follow me," Mims said, returning to the ditch. The pair crept slowly forward until they got within a few yards of the vehicles.

One of the trucks was a semi-tractor hooked to a flatbed, and the other a pickup truck. The flatbed had a bulldozer chained on it.

The trucks were stopped at a fork in the dirt road. Two men in baseball caps were standing near them smoking cigarettes. One was speaking on a portable transceiver.

Mims and Skink quietly maneuvered close enough to hear their conversation.

". . . don't give a damn what's happening at your end," the man speaking into the walkie-talkie said. Frustration was evident in his voice. "I know things are burning all over. I just need to know where you want the damned dozer? I don't care whether it's the firebreak at Coloma or the break at Farnham. That's your call, not mine. But you've got to tell me now. We're at the fork, and I can't move on until I know where you want it."

"Gimme one of those guns," Skink whispered. "We'll jack 'em and take their pickup truck."

"Don't be an idiot," Mims whispered back. "If we do that, we'll have to kill them."

"You didn't have no trouble killin' them prison guards," Skink pointed out.

"We didn't kill them," Mims said. "The fire did."

"If you say so," Skink said.

"Use your head," Mims said. "Did you forget we're supposed to be dead? If we kill those two guys out here away from the fire, people will know they didn't die accidentally, unlike those corrections officers. We'll be hunted for sure."

"I didn't think of that."

"Don't do any more thinking," Mims said. "Just do what I tell you, okay?"

"Okay," a humbled Skink said. "What's the plan?"

"Wait until they get back into their trucks," Mims said. "Once they start up the engines again, they won't hear us move. We'll hop on that flatbed and stow away."

"Wouldn't it be safer to walk?" Skink said.

"I don't know about you," Mims said, "but I'm cold,

hungry, and exhausted. How far do you think we'd get on foot before we ran into somebody else? Maybe a law enforcement officer this time or a crew of firefighters? We have to leave this area and find a place to hide while we figure out our next move. This is as good an opportunity as we're going to get."

"Sure, Duane," Skink said. "Whatever you say."

"Ten-four," the man said into his transceiver. "It's about time somebody made a goddamn decision."

He pocketed the transceiver and turned to his fellow trucker. "Farnham it is," he said. "Let's get movin'."

Both truckers returned to their vehicles and fired up the engines. Mims and Skink scurried from the ditch to the back of the flatbed trailer and clambered aboard. They crawled beneath the bulldozer's tracks and huddled together, shivering, as the big rig got under way toward Farnham County.

CHAPTER NINE

"Mom," Joel yelled from somewhere within the house. "The TV doesn't work."

"That's because the power's out," Marjorie said. "The phones are out, too." She sniffed the air. "Did you close the window in your room like I told you?"

"Uh . . . I forgot."

"Go upstairs this minute and close that window," she ordered her son. "Can't you smell the smoke?"

"Okay, okay," Joel's voice replied.

"Bring your sister with you when you come back down," she called after him. "It'll be dark soon. I want us all to stay together."

"There's no need to yell at him," Margaret Hernandez said, emerging from the basement. She was carrying a box full of candles. "He's just a little boy."

"He's in the fourth grade, Mom," Marjorie said. "He's not a baby anymore."

"Still," her mother clucked, "you don't have to be so hard on him."

"Telling him to do something twice isn't being hard on him. It's called parenting."

"I seem to remember having to remind you and your sister to do your chores more than once," Margaret said with a laugh.

Three days before, Marjorie, along with her nine-year-old son Joel and five-year-old daughter Jennifer, had showed up at her parents' door. When her sixty-four-year-old father, Hector, and his sixty-one-year-old wife, Margaret, saw their daughter's face, he grimaced and she wept.

The bridge of Marjorie's nose was adorned with a plaster cast and both of her eyes were badly swollen and encircled with angry-colored bruises, lending her a raccoon-like appearance. She also had several stitches in her right knee, an abrasion-covered bump on the back of her head, and hand-shaped contusions on both of her upper arms.

The couple nonetheless eagerly welcomed their eldest daughter and only two grandchildren into their home.

Hector and Margaret Hernandez resided in a modest two-story restored farmhouse in rural Farnham County, almost a dozen miles outside the Farnham town limits. Marjorie moved back into her old bedroom, and Jennifer and Joel were boarded in Marjorie's younger sister Mary's old room.

"Shouldn't Dad be back by now?" Marjorie asked. "It's getting late.

"I wouldn't worry," Margaret said. "He'll probably be home any minute."

Hector had driven into Farnham to fuel his truck and obtain emergency supplies at the grocery and hardware stores. Normally Margaret would have accompanied him, and they'd have spent the day together shopping, eating lunch at one of their favorite diners, and leisurely enjoying their regular weekly outing. But today's shopping was anything but leisurely.

Two nights before, a forest fire broke out in the Farnham National Forest. By the following morning it was out of control. The Mono Winds had appeared and turned the wildfire into a firestorm that rapidly consumed thousands of acres of woodlands and was showing no signs of abating. The wind, rugged terrain, and extremely hot and dry conditions made it virtually impossible for the California Department of Forestry and Fire Protection to contain the spreading blaze, much less extinguish it.

By the second morning the wildfire, officially dubbed the Farnham Fire by the governor's office, had rampaged south into the El Dorado National Forest, down into the Farnham Valley, and west toward Folsom.

Marjorie and her family watched in dismay at news reports of a group of motorists who'd been stranded by the fire on a stretch of Highway 50. People had to abandon their vehicles and flee for their lives as the wind-fueled firestorm descended upon them. According to the solemn newscaster, as many as three dozen people didn't make it off the highway and were immolated in their cars.

Marjorie and her parents noticed the increasing smoke and watched as the sky turned brown and darkened. They diligently listened to the news, paying careful attention to the progress of the fire. While the residents of Farnham and the surrounding area hadn't yet been ordered to evacuate, the sheriff's department advised all residents in the region to prepare to leave at a moment's notice.

The tiny town of Tuckerville, only sixteen miles away, had been completely destroyed. There were several confirmed deaths, most of the townsfolk were now homeless, and dozens of residents were missing and unaccounted for.

Earlier that afternoon, shortly after Hector departed to obtain supplies, the electric power at the house went out. Fortunately, Margaret and her husband still owned an old battery-powered AM/FM radio. She and her daughter kept it on all day as they packed up the Range Rover.

"Here's your father now," Margaret said, glancing out the window.

Hector parked his old Ford truck and began carrying boxes up the porch steps.

"Joel!" Marjorie called out. "Go outside and help your grandpa with the groceries!"

Joel ran downstairs with his sister on his heels to comply with his mother's order.

"It's getting dark upstairs, Grandma," Jennifer said.

"Don't worry," Margaret said to her granddaughter, giving her a reassuring hug. She gave Joel and his sister hugs every chance she could. "Grampa has a lantern, and we have candles. Soon we'll have plenty of light. Why don't you help me light some of them?"

"Okay!" Jennifer exclaimed.

Marjorie knew the refrigerator, stove, and washer and dryer were older-style appliances that operated on propane from the tank outside. But all of the other electrically powered conveniences in the home, such as the lights, television, desktop computer, and microwave, were without power.

Joel and Hector brought in a half-dozen cardboard boxes and set them on the kitchen table. Marjorie and her mother began to unpack the contents. Most contained groceries, but one was filled with batteries, spare flashlights, a pair of battery-operated camping lanterns, medical supplies, and a box of twelve-gauge, 00 buck shotgun shells.

"Looks like the power's out here, too," Hector remarked, glancing around.

"Has been," his wife said, "since just after you left."

"It ain't just us," he said. "Most of Farnham is down, too." He began putting batteries into flashlights and handed one to Marjorie and Joel. "Save the lights for when you need them," he cautioned.

"Can I have a flashlight, too?" Jennifer asked.

"Of course, you can," Hector said to his granddaughter, handing her a light. He leaned down and kissed her on the forehead.

"What are those for?" Marjorie said, pointing to the box of shotgun ammunition.

"Varmints," Hector said.

"You know I don't like guns," she said. "Especially when the kids are around."

"Better to have a gun and not need it," he said. "You know the rest." He walked over to the closet by the front door and withdrew an old, but well-cared-for, Remington 870 Wingmaster. Joel's eyes widened at the sight of his grandfather's shotgun.

"Dad," Marjorie said, "what do you think you're doing?"

"Taking precautions," he said. He checked the weapon to ensure it was unloaded, then opened the box of shells and put four into the tubular magazine. He left the chamber empty.

"You're not loading that thing, are you?" Marjorie said.

"There's nothing in all the world," her father said, "more useless than an unloaded gun."

"Will you teach me to shoot it, Grandpa?" Joel asked.

"No," Marjorie answered her son, "he will not."

"Why not?" Hector said. "I taught you and Mary how to handle this gun when you were about Joel's age. You were a pretty good shot, if I remember?"

"And I haven't touched one since."

"At least you know how. It was my duty to teach you, just like I taught you to swim. To keep you safe."

"That's nonsense."

"No," Hector said, "it isn't. You've been a city girl too long, Marjorie. You've forgotten what it's like to live out here in the country. We can't call nine-one-one and have a policeman on our doorstep in a couple of minutes. Hell, right now we can't call nine-one-one at all. This fire could bring all manner of dangerous critters scampering our direction. It's the two-legged ones that're usually the most dangerous."

"Guns don't make people safer," Marjorie said.

"Then why do police carry them?"

Marjorie shook her head, choosing to end the debate with her silence. Hector put the shotgun back in the closet.

"You are not to go near that closet door," she admonished Joel. "Do you understand?"

"Yes, Mom," Joel said. "I'm not a total dummy."

"Did you get everything on our list?" Margaret asked her husband.

"Most of it," he answered. "Stores were crowded as hell. Important thing is, I gassed up the Ford and picked up ten extra gallons of fuel. I was lucky to get it before the power at the pumps went out. I left the can in the truck in case we have to get out of here quick."

"That's a good idea," she said. "We have water, food, and propane to fire up the oven and keep the fridge and washer and dryer working." She patted Jennifer's head. "We'll be snug as bugs in a rug, even if it is a little dark."

"Hopefully they'll have the fire out before it reaches Farnham," Marjorie said. "If not . . ."

"If not," Hector interrupted, "we'll load ourselves up and drive out of here in a hurry." He turned to his wife. "Did you get all of the important stuff packed?"

"Yes," she said. "Marjorie and I spent all morning packing up photographs and documents. They're already outside in her car. I surely do hope we don't have to evacuate. I'd hate to leave the house."

"Me too," Hector said, putting his arm around his wife.

There was an unspoken fear between Hector and Margaret. They knew, if they had to evacuate the home as a result of the fire, it likely wouldn't be there when they returned.

A series of knocks sounded at the door. The insistent pounding startled everyone.

"Who could that be?" Margaret said.

"Let's find out," Hector said. He retrieved the shotgun from the closet and headed for the front door.

"Dad," Marjorie said. "What do you think you're doing? Put that thing away!"

"Be quiet," he silenced his daughter. The pounding on the door continued.

"Who is it?" Hector asked.

"It's me," a familiar voice said. "Open up, I have to pee!"

"It's Mary," Hector said, unlocking and opening the door.

Mary Hernandez, five years younger than her sister Marjorie, rushed inside, dropped a large shoulder bag in the doorway, and dashed wordlessly past everyone to the downstairs bathroom.

"That's our Mary," Hector said, returning the shotgun once again to the closet.

Mary emerged moments later to the sound of a toilet flushing behind her. "You feel a lot gladder when your bladder is flatter," she declared. Joel giggled.

"Aunt Mary!" Jennifer exclaimed, running into her arms. Mary hugged her niece and gave Joel, who accepted it awkwardly, a hug as well.

"Was the shotgun for me, Dad," she asked her father, "or do you always answer the door armed to the teeth?"

"Hello, Mary," Hector said, returning the weapon to the closet. "Been a while. A long while."

Margaret stepped forward and gave Mary a hug. "How are you, dear?"

"Can't complain," she said. She noticed Marjorie's face.

"Holy shit," Mary whistled. "Tad really did a number on you this time, didn't he?"

"None of that kind of talk," Margaret scolded. "Especially in front of Joel and Jennie."

"It ain't like they can't see the damage for themselves," Mary said. She extracted a Marlboro and stuck it between her lips.

"Not in here," Hector said sternly. "You know we don't allow smoking in this house."

"Sor-ry," Mary said snarkily, transferring the cigarette from her lips to behind an ear.

Mary Hernandez stood as tall as her sister but was twenty pounds lighter, which lent her a somewhat emaciated appearance. She wore her coal-black hair short and spiky with blue streaks in it, and both ears were adorned with multiple piercings. Her left arm, from shoulder to wrist, was covered in an ornate sleeve tattoo, and her onyx nail polish matched her lipstick. She was clad in jeans, Converse high-tops, and a T-shirt bearing the logo of the Sacramento nightclub where she once worked as a bartender.

"So," Marjorie said, "what brings you here?"

"Is there a law against visiting my own parents?" Mary said

"We're supposed to believe you got homesick?"

"Believe what you like," Mary said. "You always did believe in fairy tales. How'd that work out for you?"

"You're both always welcome," Margaret spoke up, before Marjorie could fire off a retort to her younger sister. She hoped to head off an argument and knew her daughters well enough to realize one was almost always imminent when they were together.

"We weren't expecting you," Hector said to Mary, "that's all. As you can see, we have a full house. It would have been considerate of you to call before coming over."

"I tried," Mary said. "I couldn't get through."

"The phones are out," Hector admitted.

"That's why I came," Mary said. "The Farnham Fire is all over the news. I couldn't get in touch, so I got worried."

"Since when did you acquire this concern for your family?" Hector asked. "We haven't heard a word from you in over a year."

Mary glared at her father. "I'm going outside for a smoke," she said. Marjorie followed her through the front door.

Outside, the air smelled heavily of smoke, and there were no stars visible through the haze. Marjorie noticed a late-model Lincoln sedan parked in the gravel driveway behind her father's truck. The last time she'd seen Mary, her sister had been driving a beat-up ten-year-old Hyundai.

"Like the wheels?" Mary said, noticing her sister eyeing the car. She removed the cigarette from behind her ear.

"Moving up in the world?" Marjorie said.

"Don't draw any conclusions," Mary said, lighting her cigarette. "It's only a rental. I'm barely in the door and everybody's busting my chops. Home sweet home."

"What did you expect?" Marjorie said. "We never hear from you. We don't even know where you live. Then you show up out of nowhere, unannounced. We're your family, Mary. We worry about you."

"What's to worry about?" Mary said. "I'm doing all right. Just because I didn't marry a cubicle dweller, settle in the burbs, and pop out a couple of crumb snatchers doesn't mean I'm incapable of taking care of myself."

"Quit being so defensive," Marjorie said. "Mom and Dad only want what's best for you. So do I."

"Like what you have?" Mary said, exhaling a stream of smoke. "An expensive house, a fancy car, and a husband who uses you for an Everlast bag?"

"I don't want to fight with you," Marjorie said wearily. "I've had a rough enough week already." She turned and started back up the porch steps.

"Don't get your panties in a bunch," Mary chided. "Apparently you can dish it out but can't take it."

"Everything you said is true," Marjorie began. "I'm not throwing stones. I screwed up my life, and my face is the proof. I have to live with that, and do my best to make sure my lousy choices don't screw up Joel and Jennifer's lives. That's my cross to bear, and I've got nobody but myself to blame. Choices and consequences, right? What's your excuse?"

"Wow," Mary said. "First Mom and Dad, and now you. Am I going to get the 'responsibility' lecture again? I haven't been home ten minutes and you're all giving me shit. That's a new record, even for you."

"Who's giving who shit?" Marjorie said. "I have to be here, and so do my kids. We don't have any place else to go. But you don't. You can peddle your Suicide Girl routine anywhere you want. Go back to slinging drinks and dealing coke and banging bikers and carnies, or whatever else it is you do to feed your habit."

"There's the big sister I remember," Mary said. "I knew the inner bitch would eventually come out. She just needed a little coaxing."

"I don't know why you're trying so hard to pick a fight with me," Marjorie said. "You didn't even know I was going to be here. Which makes me wonder, why did you really come home tonight? Because if you think I buy that bullshit about claiming to be worried about Mom and Dad because of the fire, you're even more baked than you look. You need money again, don't you?"

"I've got plenty of money," Mary said angrily. She threw away her cigarette and withdrew a thick roll of cash from her hip pocket. "Over two thousand dollars." She waved the wad in Marjorie's face. "And I can get more anytime I want."

"You're dealing again, aren't you?"

"No, I'm not."

"Then where did you get that kind of money?"

Mary put the cash back into her pocket and lit another cigarette. "If you only knew," she said with a furtive smile.

"I don't care where you got it," Marjorie said. "If you won the lottery, you'd be broke the next day. You pissed your college money away fast enough."

"I pay my own way," Mary said.

"Oh yeah?" Marjorie countered. "Then why did Mom and Dad have to take out a second mortgage on the house to pay for your first stint in rehab? I paid for your second, by the way. Paid off your car, too, after you totaled it, but you probably don't remember that because you were so wasted at the time."

"You mean Tad's parents paid it off, don't you?"

"You're an ungrateful little bitch," Marjorie said.

"Forgive me for not being fucking perfect," Mary said, "like you are, with a master's degree, a rich husband, two darling kids, and a *Real Housewives* lifestyle. Always have to rub it in, don't you?"

"You think I live my life to show you up?" Marjorie asked incredulously. "Jesus, Mary, all those drugs really have fried your brain. Newsflash, little sister; not everything revolves around you."

"Kiss my ass," Mary said.

"I don't want to do this," Marjorie said. "Your drama I didn't expect and don't need. How about for as long as we're both here we agree to a truce and leave each other alone?"

"I'm sorry," Mary said, casting her eyes down. "Really, I apologize. I didn't mean to go off on you. I get nasty sometimes, and my mouth gets ahead of my brain. I tend to take things out on the people around me."

"You don't say?" Marjorie said. "Normally I'd ignore it, but I don't have the energy to spar with you, and I won't allow you to start fights with me or our folks in front of the kids. Joel and Jennifer have been through enough of that lately."

"No more fights," Mary said. "I swear. I'll be cool."

"See that you are," Marjorie said, returning to the house.

CHAPTER TEN

"My name is Dr. Wozniak. Please come in. You can call me Carol, if you like?"

"I'm Deputy Strayer," Strayer said, entering the room. "You can call me Deputy Strayer."

"What do your friends call you?"

"We're not friends," Strayer said.

"Can I offer you something?" Wozniak asked, nonplussed. "Water, coffee, or tea? A soft drink perhaps?"

"No, thank you," Strayer said. "If it's all right with you, I'd like to get this over with as quickly as possible."

"Then let's get started," Wozniak said cheerfully. "Sit where you like."

Strayer surveyed the room. Dr. Wozniak's office was spacious but cluttered, with a cozy, relaxed, lived-in appearance that Strayer's trained observer's mind thought matched its resident. One entire wall was bookshelves, and the desk at the far end of the room was littered with files and papers. A pair of large plush couches were situated in the center with a small coffee table between them. A jumbo-sized box of tissues sat expectantly on its glass top. She saw no pictures of family, nor any degrees or certificates, adorning the office walls.

Wozniak appeared to be in her late forties. She was a nondescript-looking woman with a pleasant face and dirty-blond hair. She wore glasses, a loose-fitting blouse, a skirt, and flat shoes.

Strayer had chosen more formal attire, the suit she wore to court when testifying, even though she'd been informed she could wear casual clothes to her psychological evaluation. Her hair was in a ponytail and her shoes gleamed with polish. She took a seat on one of the couches.

Wozniak sat on the opposite couch, bringing along a can of Diet Coke with a straw inserted and a thick file. She placed the soda can on the table and opened the file on her lap.

"I gather," Wozniak began, looking down at the file, "that you don't particularly want to be here?"

"My feelings are entirely inconsequential," Strayer said evenly. "It's a job requirement, so here I am."

Wozniak nodded. "It's important for you to know, Deputy Strayer, that everything spoken between us will be kept under the strictest confidence. Nothing you say will leave this room."

"If you say so," Strayer said.

"You don't believe me?" Wozniak said, looking up.

"The department is paying you, right?"

"Yes, my fees are being paid by your sheriff's department."

"This is a post-shooting fitness-for-duty evaluation," Strayer said. "If the department is paying for it, they're going to want a report on whatever your findings are. I've been through this drill before."

"All your department gets from me is a thumbs-up or

thumbs-down," Wozniak said. "Nothing more. You're either fit for duty or you're not. Nothing else leaves this room."

"Like I said," Strayer stated, "I've been through this drill before."

"Then you should be familiar with the process."

"This isn't the process I've been through before," Strayer said.

"How's this time different?"

"You aren't the departmental psychologist I saw after both of my previous shooting incidents."

"And you're naturally suspicious as to why you've been sent here, to me, instead of seeing the regular departmental psychologist?"

"Wouldn't you be?"

"Do you think it's because of your previous shootings?"

"Maybe," Strayer said, glaring at Wozniak. "Or maybe it's because I'm female."

"You believe discrimination is possibly at play?"

"I figure the department is trying to kill two birds with one stone. Having me evaluated by another woman makes the department look sensitive, and at the same time heads off a potential sexual discrimination beef."

"So," Wozniak said, "if I'm hearing you correctly, you believe that sexism may have played a role in my being tasked with your post-shooting evaluation?"

"Does Pinocchio have wooden balls?" Strayer said with a grunt. "There are guys on my team who've been in shootings before. I'll bet they're all seeing the regular departmental psychologist instead of an out-of-town psychiatrist?"

Wozniak set the file aside and took off her glasses. "It might be best," she began, still smiling, "if I told you a little about my practice. I don't know if this will assuage your concerns, but in the interest of trying to reassure you I hope you'll show me the courtesy of hearing me out. If you don't like what I have to say, and still feel being assigned to see me is discriminatory after I've said my piece, you have my word, Deputy Strayer, that I'll recuse myself from your evaluation and recommend, without prejudice, that someone else conduct your post-shooting fitness-for-duty evaluation. Fair enough?"

Strayer exhaled and willed herself to relax. She realized she'd come into Wozniak's office front-loaded with hostility, especially after she discovered the department wasn't sending her to their own in-house psychologist, but instead to a *psychiatrist* all the way in Folsom.

"I just want to get back to work, Doctor," Strayer said, softening her tone. "I don't want to be treated differently."

"After reading your personnel file, which includes your background investigation packet, I can understand your reservations. I'm not going to insult you by trying to convince you to trust me. Trust is a very hard-earned commodity, as I'm sure you know."

"Tough to replace, too," Strayer said.

"As you already pointed out," Wozniak explained, "I'm a psychiatrist, not a psychologist. That doesn't mean I don't do psychological examinations. All being a psychiatrist means, as opposed to psychologist, is that I have advanced medical training. Much of what I do is very similar to what your departmental psychologist provides. In fact, I do contract work for a number of federal, state, and local agencies, as well as all branches of the military. Most of my practice involves work with police officers, firefighters, and military personnel. I specialize in critical incident review and patients suffering from post-traumatic stress disorder."

"I don't have PTSD," Strayer said.

"I never said you did." Wozniak said. "Would you like to continue, Deputy Strayer, or should I end this session and have your department refer you to someone else?"

"I guess I'm okay with seeing you," Strayer found herself saying.

Dr. Wozniak seemed easy enough to talk to and didn't appear insulted when Strayer initially displayed such overt enmity. Strayer was aware the psychiatrist was undoubtedly trained to put her at ease but found the woman likeable despite her reservations. That Wozniak claimed to have experience working with veterans was also a mark in her favor. Also, if she declined the evaluation with Dr. Wozniak, the department would simply reassign her to someone else who might potentially be worse.

"I'm glad," Dr. Wozniak said. She put her glasses back on and picked up the file. "Let's talk about you."

Wozniak scanned the documents. "Leanne Eu-Ji Strayer," she began. "Twenty-seven years old. Born and raised in Farnham County, I see. Both parents deceased. Looks like you have one sibling, a brother."

"Half brother," Strayer corrected.

"If I may ask," Wozniak said, "what is your heritage?"

"My mother was Korean, and my father was an American of Danish ancestry," Strayer said. "They met when my dad was in the Air Force, stationed at Osan Air Base."

"That would explain the blue eyes and freckles," Wozniak said.

"Among other things," Strayer said.

"You enlisted in the army at age seventeen," Wozniak

continued. "Your mother signed you in. You served five years on active duty in military occupational specialty thirty-one bravo; Military Police. It says here you were deployed twice to Afghanistan, and once to the Horn of Africa." She looked up. "Somalia?"

"Djibouti," Strayer said.

Wozniak nodded and returned her gaze to the papers. "You left the service at the rank of E-4 with an honorable discharge, a Combat Action Badge, a Bronze Star with a valor device, and a Purple Heart. I see you also obtained your associate degree in Criminal Justice while serving in the military."

"Online courses," Strayer shrugged. "It beat the monotony."

"Why didn't you stay in?" Wozniak asked, looking up again. "Seems to me you had a solid career going. You could have continued to pursue your education. Maybe even gone to Officer Candidate School and obtained a commission."

"Green isn't my color," Strayer said.

Wozniak changed documents "You entered the sheriff's academy almost immediately upon leaving the army. Your academy records indicate you graduated second in your class academically, fourth in physical fitness, and first in marksmanship. Impressive."

"Not really," Strayer said. "My military experience helped."

"Evidently," Wozniak said. She read on. "You did a tour in the Custody Division, like all newly minted deputies, and were then assigned to Patrol. That's where you were involved in your first shooting incident, wasn't it?"

"Yes," Strayer said, glad the interview was finally steering away from her personal history and to what she believed it was supposed to be focused on; her recent officer-involved shooting. "It happened while I was a rookie in the Field Training Program."

"Tell me about it?" Wozniak put the file aside again, removed her glasses, and picked up her Diet Coke.

"Not much to tell," Strayer said, aware that Dr. Wozniak had access to the officer-involved shooting report and had probably already read it. "I was with my first field-training officer. We pulled over what we thought was a drunk driver on a rural road near Tuckerville. The driver was a woman, who was drunk and high, and the passenger was a parolee with an eight ball of meth and a nine-millimeter Glock in his pocket. He opened up on my training officer. He was hit several times and went down. I returned fire and neutralized the threat."

"By 'neutralized the threat' you mean you shot him?"

"Yeah."

"Did you kill him?"

"Yeah."

"This wasn't the first person you've killed, was it?"

"No."

"Military action?"

"Yeah."

"Did your training officer survive?"

"He did," Strayer said. "All of the suspect's rounds hit his ballistic vest. He wasn't even badly hurt, but he resigned a few days afterwards."

"It's not uncommon," Wozniak said, "for a person to leave the profession after a life-threatening critical incident. It's one of the reasons less than eight percent of law enforcement officers reach a full-service retirement."

"I didn't hold it against him," Strayer said indifferently.

"I never said you did. Your second shooting occurred a couple of years later, didn't it? Tell me about that one?"

"I was working the dogwatch shift in the Town of Farnham."

"Your hometown, right?"

"Not really. I went to school there, but I grew up outside of town."

"In a mobile home park, with your mother and brother?"

"Half brother," Strayer corrected Wozniak again, "and whatever boyfriend-of-the-week my mom had living with us at the time."

"I apologize for interrupting," Wozniak said. "You were telling me about your second shooting?"

"Got a call of a man with a gun at a homeless shelter. When I arrived, I found a guy with a government-model forty-five holding a bunch of residents hostage. He'd been evicted the day before for violating the shelter's conduct policy."

"What did he do?"

"I didn't know it at the time, but I learned later that he stole some prescription drugs from one resident and beat up another."

"What prompted the shooting?"

"He was yelling, making threats, and waving his gun around. When I entered the shelter, he aimed it at me."

"And you shot him?"

"I take it kinda personal when people point guns at me, Doc."

"Did he die?"

"Not at the scene, like the first guy. He died in the ambulance on the way to the ER."

"There was some controversy associated with that shooting, wasn't there?"

"Not from my end," Strayer said.

"It wasn't a real gun, was it?"

"No," Strayer said. "It was one of those replica firearms, they call them. Shoots little plastic balls. Looks exactly like a real gun, though. Same size, same weight, and even had the Colt logo stamped on it."

"So he was essentially unarmed?"

"According to some," Strayer said. "That's what the newspapers wrote, anyway."

"Do you think it was a suicide by cop?"

"I don't presume to understand the motives of a violent, homeless junkie," Strayer said. "All I know is that he pointed a gun at me, ignored a command to drop it, and suffered the consequences."

"There was another deputy with you, wasn't there?"

"There was."

"Did that deputy fire his weapon?"

"No."

"Do you know why not?" Wozniak asked.

"I know the reason he gave the investigators," Strayer said. "He claimed he 'sensed' the suspect wasn't going to shoot, even though he was aiming a gun at me. That's why he didn't fire. He implied the shooting resulted from my inexperience. He threw me under the bus."

"You believe that deputy froze, don't you?"

"I didn't say that," Strayer said.

"You took heat from some of your fellow deputies, didn't you?"

"I did."

"Some of them thought you were too quick on the trigger, isn't that right?"

"Maybe," Strayer said. "Maybe I'm just decisive. Or maybe the deputy with me that night was a popular 'good ole boy' who needed to come up with an excuse for why he stood there with a slack jaw and piss running down his leg and didn't even draw his weapon."

"What happened to him?"

"He took a stress retirement a few months after the shooting. Now he can do his drinking out in the open instead of hiding a bottle in his squad car."

Wozniak sipped soda. "And you went on to be assigned to S.W.A.T.?"

"It isn't like they gave me the assignment," Strayer said, "like a birthday present. I had to compete for that slot against more than fifty other deputies, every one of them senior to me. The department conducts competitive trials for selection to S.W.A.T. It's one of the few special assignments where popularity and politics don't entirely determine the outcome."

"What were the trials like?"

"At least as challenging as the hiring process," Strayer said. "A physical fitness and agility test, a firearms competency test, an oral board, and a psychological evaluation."

"Any other female deputies try out for the team?"

"No."

"How'd you place?"

"I came out number one."

"Do you think some of the other deputies, senior to you and all male, foster resentment towards you for your selection to S.W.A.T. over them?"

"Are we going to discuss Pinocchio's balls again?" Strayer said.

Wozniak smiled once more. "How well, would you say, do you get along with your coworkers?"

"It's a bell curve," Strayer said. "Some I respect, and some I wouldn't piss on if they were on fire. Most I ignore. They're just folks I work with."

"You seem very guarded, Deputy Strayer. Do you think this behavior comes from your military experience or from somewhere else?"

"You've never served, have you Dr. Wozniak?"

"As a matter of fact," Wozniak said, pausing to take another sip through her straw, "I have. I still do, in fact. I'm a colonel in the National Guard. Medical Corps."

Strayer didn't see that coming, and it took her aback. Nothing about Dr. Wozniak's appearance or demeanor implied military bearing.

"I may not look like G.I. Joe," Wozniak said, reading Strayer's astonishment, "but I certainly know what it's like to be a woman in a hypermasculine, male-dominated, ultracompetitive environment. Half the guys are trying to get into your pants, and the other half are threatened by you. If you screw up it's not because you're human, and everybody makes mistakes, it's because you're a woman. And if you excel at something, it's not because of your hard work or competence, it's only because you were given preferential treatment because of your gender. Am I right?"

"I'm sorry," Strayer said. "I didn't realize . . ."

"Don't be so hard on yourself," Wozniak cut her off. "There aren't any pictures on my walls for a reason. As I said, I work with a lot of cops. Cops are nosy by nature and training. Many of them are veterans, like you. I don't want my patients to have preconceived notions about me. It can create barriers."

"Were you assigned to do my post-shooting psych evaluation because of your military background?" Strayer asked.

"It's possible," Wozniak admitted. "I don't know for sure. I only know we're both here now. Why don't we agree to make the best of it? Isn't that what soldiers do?"

"Yeah," Strayer said. "We solve the problem and drive on."

"Getting back to your coworkers," Wozniak resumed, "do you have any close friends on the department? You've been there over five years."

"I keep to myself," Strayer said, not directly answering the question. "That way, none of the other deputies can figure out which one of the Three O's I am."

"The Three O's?" Wozniak said. "I'm not familiar with that term. What are the 'Three O's'?"

"I'm surprised you've never heard of the Three O's," Strayer said, "especially since you said you work extensively with law enforcement agencies."

"Would you enlighten me?"

"Male cops and deputies typically assume all female law enforcement officers are one or more of the Three O's," Strayer said. "A lesbo, a nympho, or a psycho."

"I've never heard it put quite like that before," Wozniak said. "But it certainly encapsulates the prejudice many male law enforcement officers harbor towards their female counterparts."

"You get used to it," Strayer said.

The hollow slurp emanating from Wozniak's soda can indicated her beverage was finished. "Do you have any questions for me?" she asked. The abrupt shift in the conversation took Strayer by surprise.

"Uh . . . no. Are we done?"

"We are," Wozniak said. "For today, anyway. I'm releasing you to full duty, effective immediately. But I want to ask you a favor."

"A favor?" Strayer was still absorbing Wozniak's unexpected declaration that she was being cleared to return to duty.

"I very much enjoyed speaking with you. I would like to invite you to come back and speak with me again."

"I'm confused," Strayer said. "If you're releasing me to full duty I don't have to come back and see you, do I?"

"You do not," Wozniak said. "I'm simply extending an invitation. It's not mandatory. You can decline, if you want."

Strayer was baffled. Dr. Wozniak didn't even ask her about the recent shooting, or how she was dealing with its aftermath. In her previous post-shooting evaluations, that's all the psychologists wanted to discuss.

"What would we talk about?"

"Anything we want," Wozniak said. "You're not afraid to speak with me again, are you Deputy Strayer?"

"Of course not," Strayer answered, a little too rapidly.

"Then why don't you come back and visit me?"

"I suppose I could make time," Strayer said.

"Let's put something on the calendar," Wozniak said. "Otherwise it'll become one of those 'let's do lunch' things, and it'll never happen. Okay?"

"Okay," Strayer heard herself say. Before she realized it or could protest, Dr. Wozniak had penciled her in for another appointment.

CHAPTER ELEVEN

Mims knelt and observed the farmhouse from the cover of the wood line. Skink lay on the cold ground next to him grimacing in pain, shivering, and nursing his injured arm. The sun had been up for over an hour.

Mims and Skink hid under the tracks of the bulldozer, atop the flatbed semitruck, as it slowly navigated rough logging roads for most of the night. At times the air was relatively clear, and at others it was so smoky they could barely see beyond the rear edge of the truck. But at all times the horizon to the north, east, and south glowed with the angry orange of the expanding wildfire.

Despite the jostling of the truck on the bumpy dirt road, Skink dozed off. Mims remained awake, constantly alert, scanning their surroundings. After several hours of bitterly cold travel, Mims awakened the skinny convict.

"Wake up," Mims said. "We're getting off."

"Huh?" Skink complained, slowly bringing himself to wakefulness. "Where are we?"

"Farnham County," Mims said.

"Where the fuck is that?"

"About forty miles northeast of Folsom," Mims said.

"What's in Farnham County," Skink asked, "and why are we gettin' off here?"

"I know this country," Mims said. "I used to work around here. The fire hasn't reached this area yet."

Mims was right. The winds had swept the wildfire south from the Farnham National Forest into the El Dorado National Forest, and then west towards Folsom along Highway 50. This burn pattern created a horseshoe-shaped region in Farnham County untouched by fire, despite being surrounded by the massive blaze on three sides.

"Can't we ride a while longer?"

"No," Mims said flatly. "We have to get off now. It'll be daylight, soon, and this truck is heading to the fire line. Do you want to be surrounded by firefighters and cops?"

"Hell, no."

"Then follow me."

Mims crawled out from under the bulldozer to the edge of the truck. The semi was only traveling about ten miles an hour over the dirt road, but everything behind it was obscured in a cloud of dust.

"Shouldn't we wait until this thing stops?" Skink said.

"It isn't going to stop," Mims said, "until it gets to its destination. By then it'll be too late."

"You know," Skink said, staring at the ground rushing by below him, "a guy could get hurt jumping off a moving truck."

"Did you receive airborne training in the army?" Mims asked.

"No," Skink replied. "I was a wheeled vehicle mechanic. Ninety-one bravo."

"All you have to do when you hit the ground is roll," Mims said, "and keep rolling. Don't try to break your fall or slow your momentum by sticking out your arms or legs, or they'll snap. Just curl into a ball and roll until you come to a stop. Like this."

Mims jumped and disappeared into the dust cloud created in the truck's wake.

Skink hesitated a few seconds and then jumped, afraid he'd lose Mims if he didn't.

Mims's advice was quickly forgotten. When Skink hit the ground, he didn't roll. He fell forward, sticking out both arms to break his fall.

He struck the dirt road with his head and right shoulder. The impact stunned him, and he nearly lost consciousness. When he finally skidded to a halt, dazed and covered in abrasions, he found his right arm didn't work.

Skink rolled onto his back and looked up. He found Mims standing over him as the dust cloud dissipated and the sound of the truck's engines faded. Mims, though still damp and filthy from their earlier trek through the stream and engulfed landscape, looked no different than he had the instant before he leapt off the truck.

"Didn't you hear me tell you to roll?" Mims said.

"I thought I did," Skink said groggily. When he tried to sit up, a bolt of agony shot through his right shoulder. He cried out.

"Take it easy," Mims said. "Looks like your collarbone is busted."

"Shit," Skink said through the pain.

"Let's get off this road," Mims said, "and I'll set it for you."

Skink let Mims help him to his feet and guide him into the woods. He sat down on a fallen tree while Mims removed his wet T-shirt and examined him.

"Can't be sure it's a clean break," Mims said. "Might be all splintered up inside. All we can do for now is immobilize your arm." He began tearing Skink's shirt to fashion a sling. "It's going to hurt."

"You can say that again," Skink moaned.

Both men were weakened to the brink of exhaustion. Neither had eaten since breakfast the day before, and in the twenty-four hours since had been nearly immolated while chained inside a prison van, overpowered their guards and escaped, survived a rampaging firestorm by taking refuge underwater, hiked miles through a creek and overland through dense woods, stowed away on a truck hauling heavy machinery, and now found themselves hungry, shivering, and on foot in a heavily forested area. If these challenges weren't enough, Skink now found himself suffering a broken collarbone that left him in severe pain and rendered his right arm useless.

Mims suspended Skink's arm in the makeshift sling using the torn T-shirt.

"Did you learn first aid when you were a deputy?" Skink asked.

"Something like that," Mims said. "Can you walk?"

"I think so," Skink said, though he felt woozy and his stomach churned.

"We need to find a place to rest," Mims said, "and get something to eat. Let's go."

With Skink leaning heavily on his larger companion, the duo made their way through the forest. They walked for over an hour, growing more weak and tired, until they reached a clearing that revealed a house. Skink collapsed, spent, while Mims knelt and scrutinized the property.

The house was a well-kept two-story former farmhouse

that looked to have been constructed long before World War II. There was no barn, shed, or other structure on the property, but it featured a well with a pump, a windmill, and an exterior propane tank.

Mims detected no signs of a dog or other livestock. Three vehicles, an American-made luxury sedan, a European sport utility vehicle, and an older, but well-maintained, pickup truck were parked in the gravel driveway.

"There could be a quite a few folks in there," Skink said, "by the number of cars out front. Maybe we should find someplace else?"

"The nearest place might be miles away," Mims said. "Besides, I haven't got enough gas in my tank to go anywhere else. Do you?"

"No," Skink admitted. "I ain't even sure I can stand up again."

"Not to mention," Mims said, "even if we could find another house within miles of here, who's to say there won't be just as many people there?"

"Good point," Skinks said. "What should we do?"

"Wait a little while longer," Mims said, "and watch. Sun's up now. People will be moving around soon. I don't want to make a move until we get a better idea of who's inside."

"I'm with you all the way," Skink said.

"Good morning," Hector greeted Marjorie as she entered the kitchen. He was already dressed and enjoying the day's first cup of coffee. "You're up early."

"I never really went to bed," Marjorie said. "Haven't been sleeping too well lately."

"It's only because you're sleeping in a strange bed," Hector said.

"This is the house I grew up in, Dad," Marjorie said, wrinkling her bandaged nose at him. "I'm sleeping in my old bedroom, in my childhood bed. How could that be strange?"

"You know what I mean," he smiled. "Coffee?"

"Sure," Marjorie said, sitting down at the table.

Hector poured. "How do you feel?"

"Despite my face looking like a catcher's mitt," she said, accepting the mug, "I feel okay."

In the days since she'd been assaulted by Tad, her eyes had faded from black to dark purple and were now transitioning to a bluish green. But the swelling in her nose hadn't diminished much, and the ER doctor told her she might eventually need surgery to realign her septum. The only good news regarding her health was that her chlamydia infection was clearing up, to her relief, as a result of the antibiotics. She expected that by the time her two-week antibiotic regimen was concluded she'd be completely cured.

"How are Joel and Jennifer holding up?"

Marjorie shrugged. "Hard to say. This is fresh for all of us. We haven't discussed it much. I think Joel senses what happened is going to change our lives, but Jennifer still thinks she's going back to Granite Bay to live with Mommy and Daddy in the same house like nothing happened."

"You haven't heard from Tad?"

"No," she said sharply, "and he'd better not try. Like I already told you and Mom, he's been served with a restraining order. If he calls, comes out here, or has somebody else try to contact me for him, I'll have him arrested."

"Take it easy," Hector said, "I was only asking. Your mother's the one who always wanted you two to work things out, not me. As far as I'm concerned, if Tad shows his face around here, he'll become one of the varmints I loaded up my shotgun for."

"I doubt if he'll come all the way out here," Marjorie said. "He's not *that* stupid."

"He came out here before," Hector reminded her. "After the last time he put his hands to you."

"And Mom let him in," she reminded him.

"At least we don't have to worry about him calling," Hector said. "The phones are out, same as the power. I'm sure the lines are down all over the county on account of the fire. Probably be days, if not weeks, before the power and phones are restored."

"He can't call me on my cell phone, either," Marjorie said. She blew across the surface of her mug. "Even if you and Mom had cell service out here, which you don't, I changed my number."

"Do you always get up this early?" Mary said, entering the kitchen.

"Good morning," Hector greeted his youngest daughter. "You don't remember that I get up at first light?"

"I was talking to Marjorie," she said.

Mary was wearing an oversized T-shirt over panties with no bra. She had bedhead, had an unlit cigarette in her mouth, and clutched her cell device. "Any more coffee?" she asked.

"There's plenty of coffee," Hector said. "Do you have any more clothes?"

"Relax," Mary said around her cigarette. "Joel isn't up

yet." She sat at the table and accepted a steaming mug from her father.

"Anybody else having trouble getting cell service?" Mary asked, staring at her phone. She put her cigarette behind her ear.

"We were just talking about that," Hector said. "There's no cell service out here. If you visited us once in a while, you might know that."

"Figures," Mary said with a frown. She set her phone on the table. "I suppose your internet is down, too?"

"Our internet comes in through the satellite dish," Hector said, "along with the television. If the power is out, do you really think we'd have an internet connection?"

"I keep forgetting," Mary said dryly, "that I grew up in the Little House on the Prairie."

"If you need to make a call," Marjorie said, "you'll have to go into town. Cell service picks up about a half-mile outside of Farnham."

"I have to go into town today anyway," Mary said. "I'm almost out of cigarettes."

"What a tragedy," Hector said.

"I'll be leaving this afternoon myself," Marjorie said. "The kids want to go trick-or-treating tonight back in their old neighborhood."

"Do you think that's a good idea?" Hector said. "Granite Bay's almost an hour away on a good traffic day. With this wildfire, and all the road blockages, you could end up stuck on the highway for hours. Besides, wouldn't going back to your old neighborhood put you in violation of your own restraining order?"

"Not if we don't encounter Tad," Marjorie said. "With any luck, he'll never know we were there. I have to, Dad.

The kids are so excited for Halloween, especially Jennifer. I don't have the heart to tell them they can't go."

"Why can't they do their trick-or-treating in Farnham?" Hector suggested. "That's where I always took you girls on Halloween night. Seems to me the candy in Farnham tastes the same as the candy in Granite Bay?"

"Not the same," Marjorie said.

"Marjorie's right, Dad," Mary said. "The kids will want to trick-or-treat in their own neighborhood." She looked across the table at her older sister, and their eyes met. "Especially if it's for the last time."

CHAPTER TWELVE

Strayer took the stairs up from the basement to the Investigations Division on the third floor, eschewing the elevator. She was one of the few deputies with a five-year hashmark on her uniform sleeve who weighed the same as the day she graduated from the academy. Choosing the stairs over the elevator was only one of the reasons.

A deputy typically left the academy in the best shape of their life. A regimen of intense daily exercise, a balanced diet, and the demands of formal, high-stress, law enforcement training ensured a high level of physical fitness for those who could stick it out.

Upon graduating from the academy, everything changed. Instead of a training sergeant supervising daily runs, extensive physical training, and a healthy diet, rookie deputies found themselves immediately assigned to the jail on the dogwatch shift.

Soon the combination of night working, day sleeping, an eighty-hour workweek in the form of mandatory overtime, a fast-food diet, lack of exercise, and the realities of their new and dangerous working environment could quickly transform a fit, fresh-faced, eager young recruit into an overweight, haggard, burned-out, and cynical deputy sheriff.

Strayer's commitment to maintaining her physical fitness with daily workouts was sparked in the military, long before she became a deputy sheriff. Unlike most soldiers, after completing basic and advanced individual training, she worked out beyond her mandatory physical training. She made it a daily habit, and even took up martial arts. During her five years on active duty, in between overseas deployments, she even managed to obtain her 1st Dan in tae kwon do.

After her honorable discharge from military service and completion of the sheriff's academy, Strayer continued to work out, unlike nearly all of her fellow deputies. Her daily physical fitness routine became even easier to maintain once she was selected for assignment to the Special Weapons and Tactics Unit, where she was paid to work out on duty.

S.W.A.T. deputies, requiring a much higher level of physical fitness to perform their duties, were allocated on-duty workout time. In fact, it was primarily the physical fitness requirement of S.W.A.T. duty that discouraged most deputies from trying out for the team.

Strayer arrived at the department a couple of hours before her new assignment to the Investigations Division for two reasons. In addition to getting in her regular workout and a shower, she had to report to the armory. There a departmental rangemaster was slated to issue her a new duty pistol. Her previously issued duty pistol was still in the Property and Evidence Section, along with her submachine gun and the weapons belonging to the other members of her former S.W.A.T. squad.

As a detective, Strayer would normally have been issued a Sig Sauer P229, a more compact version of the full-sized .40 caliber pistol issued to all deputies as the department's standard duty sidearm.

Since she was S.W.A.T. certified, Strayer was authorized, with a rangemaster's permission, to utilize a single-action, .45 caliber, pistol even if assigned to the Patrol or Investigations Divisions. The customized Sig Sauer 1911 Tactical .45 was considered an informal badge of honor among those deputies who'd earned the right to carry them.

The rangemaster was a red-haired former army grunt and S.W.A.T. operator who'd been her firearms instructor at the academy. Strayer respected him, and knew he respected her for being arguably one of the best pistol shots on the S.W.A.T. team, if not the department.

Strayer took pride in her skill with firearms. Shooting ability was gender-neutral, and qualification scores don't lie. Nobody could assert that her tactical abilities and firearms proficiency were a result of preferential treatment. Those things came only from training, practice, and hard work.

The rangemaster confessed to her once, after one of her regular training sessions, that in his experience female recruits learned to shoot proficiently more quickly than their male counterparts. He believed this was because they listened better and weren't as competitive as males about their firearms training. He felt women simply wanted to learn and improve their skill, while men were always trying to compete with, and best, each other.

The rangemaster issued Strayer a new pistol identical to the one she'd lost to the evidence technicians, a plain-clothes holster, and three eight-round magazines. She then fired a standard qualification course, as required with any newly issued weapon. Not surprisingly, she achieved the maximum score. She cleaned and lubricated the weapon and loaded it up with departmentally authorized 230-grain hollow-point ammunition.

"Heard about your transfer to the third floor," was all the rangemaster said as Strayer finished. "Tough break. You ever want to let off some steam, the range is always open."

Strayer shook his hand, thanked him, and headed for the stairs and the third floor.

Like most deputies not previously assigned to the Detective Division, Strayer hadn't spent a lot of time on the third floor. The basement of the departmental headquarters consisted of the Patrol Division, S.W.A.T. Unit, locker rooms, gym, range, armory, and training rooms, including the daily briefing room. The second floor consisted of the Records Section, Traffic Division, and the civilian administrative offices. The third floor was exclusively reserved for the Investigations Division, and on the fourth floor were the offices of the command staff and sheriff.

With few exceptions, Strayer had spent her entire career in either the academy, which was a separate facility across the plaza from the administration building, the Jail Division, which was across the street, or in the Patrol Division or S.W.A.T. Unit, which were both headquartered in the basement of the administration building. As she opened the main door into the Investigations Division, she felt like an outlander about to set foot on a foreign shore.

"Lieutenant McDillon is expecting you," the receptionist said to Strayer when she entered the lobby. "First door on the right."

She entered the Investigations Division's long hallway, nicknamed the "bowling alley" by the detectives who worked there. There were multiple doors on each side, along with a series of interview rooms, restrooms, a break room, and a large briefing room at the far end.

The Investigations Division was commanded by a lieutenant. It was divided into five separate sections, each supervised by a sergeant and assigned between five and twelve detectives.

The Crimes Against Persons Unit encompassed homicide, robbery, assault, rape and other sex crimes, domestic violence, physical elder abuse, kidnapping, and any other major crime committed against an adult victim.

The Property Crimes Unit handled felony thefts, burglary, auto theft, forgery, fraud, embezzlement, computer crimes, identity theft, financial elder abuse, and any major crime involving loss of property.

The Vice & Narcotics and Gang Units, as their names implied, handled vice, drug, and gang-related crime, respectively, within Farnham County. The biggest unit in the Investigative Division, however, was the Juvenile Unit.

The Juvenile Unit was the largest, by virtue of the fact that it was tasked with investigating *all* felonies committed by juveniles, regardless of crime category, and *all* felony crimes where a juvenile was the victim. If a burglary suspect was an adult, for example, the Property Crimes Unit handled it; if the suspect was a juvenile, the Juvenile Unit took the case.

This model meant that detectives assigned to the Juvenile Unit had to be well-versed in many types of investigations, not just specialists in one crime classification like the detectives assigned to the other units. There was a running joke among deputies assigned to the Juvenile Unit that if the suspect or victim of a crime was a juvenile, *or had ever been a juvenile,* the case got dumped on them. In addition, the Juvenile Unit handled all status offenses, such as runaways, truancy, and school-resource issues.

As a result of this heavy caseload, the Juvenile Unit was staffed with the most detectives. The unit was authorized a complement of twelve detectives, but was currently down one position due to a detective being out on long-term medical leave pending retirement. This was the slot Strayer had been assigned to fill.

Strayer knocked on the door marked COMMANDER, INVESTIGATIONS DIVISION. "Come in," a voice from within ordered.

Strayer entered, and found two people seated in the room. Behind the desk sat a jowly blond man in his late forties wearing glasses and an expensive suit that was carefully tailored to minimize the appearance of obesity. She was always struck by how few of her fellow deputies, regardless of age, rank, or tenure, were not overweight.

Across from him was an African American woman who looked to be in her late thirties. She was thin, appeared quite fit, had a very dark complexion, and wore her hair closely cropped and dyed white. Strayer had seen both of them around the department before, but had never spoken to either.

"Deputy Strayer, reporting as directed."

"I'm Lieutenant Rich McDillon," the man said, without standing up. "I'm in charge of the Investigations Division. This is Sergeant Tasha Simpson. She supervises the Juvenile Unit. You'll be working for her."

Strayer nodded to both.

"We've been going over your personnel file," McDillon said. "You have above-standard or outstanding evaluations from all of your previous commanders and supervisors. But you have less than two years of street time as a patrol deputy, despite being on the department for over five years."

"I've been assigned to S.W.A.T. for the past three years," Strayer said.

"So I noticed," McDillon said. "You realize, of course, that S.W.A.T. is more of a paramilitary type assignment. S.W.A.T. deputies operate as members of a strictly supervised team, as opposed to working independently by themselves. Detectives must be free thinkers who are independent and intuitive. Do you think you can manage that?"

"I'm not sure what you're asking me," Strayer said. "I didn't request this assignment, and I suspect you don't want me here. I can't make any promises about how I'll perform in a job I didn't want, haven't been trained for, and have no experience doing. All I can tell you is that I don't shirk and I've always gotten the job done, whatever it was."

McDillon frowned. "I heard you could be difficult."

"Is that in my file?" Strayer asked. "Or did you pick that up in the locker room?"

McDillon's face reddened. Before he could speak again, Simpson stood up.

"I'll show Deputy Strayer around the division," she said with a smile. "Get her settled in and introduce her to some of the other supervisors and detectives."

"You do that," McDillon said through his teeth.

Simpson ushered Strayer out of the lieutenant's office

and down the hall to the door labeled JUVENILE UNIT. Once inside, she led her straight into her own office. It was neat, with several framed pictures on the walls. One showed a younger Simpson in navy dress whites decorated with the rank of petty officer. Another showed her at the finish line of the Bay to Breakers run in San Francisco, in shorts and a numbered placard. A final photo showed the Juvenile Unit sergeant and a very attractive Caucasian woman holding a baby. She closed the door.

"Sit down," Simpson said.

"I'd rather stand," Strayer said.

"I wasn't asking, Deputy." Strayer took a seat. Simpson sat down behind her desk.

"I don't know where you picked up that chip on your shoulder," Simpson began, "and I give zero shits. I gather you don't want to be in my unit. Boo-fucking-hoo."

Strayer said nothing, waiting expectantly for the rest of her new supervisor's "welcome to the unit" speech.

"I've read your file, *Deadeye,* and I've heard the scuttlebutt. And it wasn't in the locker room, either. I don't care whether you want to be here, and I'm sure you don't much care whether I do or not. In any case, I've got too much on my plate to deal with your personal baggage. You're going to unload it, right here and right now. That's an order."

Strayer could easily imagine Simpson as the petty officer in charge of a detachment of shipboard sailors. It wasn't difficult to do. The bluntness of her speech, delivered so casually and professionally, told Strayer she knew how to deal with difficult subordinates. Strayer was impressed, despite herself.

"We have an important mission here in the Juvenile Unit," Simpson went on, "whether you think so or not.

I've got some of the hardest-working and most dedicated motherfuckers in the department under my supervision. I will not have their efforts, or our mission, impeded by the immature, self-absorbed, petulant, tantrums of a tender-foot detective who hasn't earned the right to pout in my presence. Are we clear?"

"As glass," Strayer said. Getting chewed out notwith-standing, she couldn't help but like Simpson and the no-nonsense manner with which she conducted herself.

"Very well," Simpson said. "Now that the air is cleared between us, let's get down to business."

"I'm all ears, Sergeant," Strayer said.

"Because of the short notice I got on your assignment here," Simpson said, "I wasn't able to get Personnel and Training to schedule your Basic P.O.S.T. Investigator's course in Sacramento until a month from now. Until you get the basic course completed, you're technically not a detective yet."

P.O.S.T. was the acronym for Peace Officers Standards in Training, the governing body that certified and quali-fied all peace officers in the State of California. P.O.S.T. ensured all police and sheriff's departments throughout the state met the same exacting criteria for all phases of their sworn employees' law enforcement careers, from the acad-emy, to specific job titles like detective, S.W.A.T. operator, or background investigator, all the way up to supervisor, command officer, police chief, or sheriff.

"I understand," Strayer said.

"After the basic course, we'll get you scheduled for the Interview and Interrogation course, Sexual Assault Inves-tigation course, and the Juvenile Crimes Investigation course. Those are all required, and important for you to have under your belt. But the truth is, you'll learn the real business of being an investigator from the other detectives you interact with in the unit. By getting your feet wet and actually working cases."

"Whatever you say," Strayer said.

"I've assigned you to partner up with one of our senior detectives for a while. His name is Reynaldo Benavides. You could learn a lot from him. I did."

"I look forward to meeting him."

"There's something else I'd better tell you up front," Simpson said, in a pleasant but matter-of-fact tone. "I'm in charge of this unit, not that dipshit McDillon. He's never been a detective; he came up from the jail. All that bullshit he told you about being a 'free thinker,' and 'independent,' and 'intuitive' is a load of garbage. The number one quality a detective needs is tenacity. From what little I know about you, Strayer, you've got it in spades."

"Thank you," Strayer said.

"It wasn't a compliment, only an observation. McDillon's nothing but a good ol' boy REMF who's trying to ass-kiss his way up the ranks. He only got himself assigned to the Investigations Division to polish his résumé, and cares about the Juvenile Unit even less than you do. If he thinks you're going to create a problem for him, he'll squash you like a bug. He'll also think nothing of squashing me and my other detectives if we get in the way of him squashing you."

Simpson leaned back in her chair and folded her hands behind her head. "You were in the army, so you already know shit rolls downhill. I don't like shit. So if you have a problem or a complaint or just want to vent, you come to me. My door is always open, twenty-four/seven, three-sixty-five. Is there a problem with that?"

"I'm familiar with my chain of command," Strayer said.

"I know you are," Simpson said. "I'm aware of your military record."

Simpson appraised Strayer. "I know you believe you've been given a raw deal. In a way, that means I have, too. That gives us something in common. All I ask is that you give me and my unit a chance. We're always behind the eight ball here, and could use the help. If you could handle the 'Stan, working here should be a cakewalk."

"I'll do my best," Strayer said.

"I'm sure you will," Simpson said, as she stood and opened her office door. "One more thing I should warn you about; you may encounter a bit of flak from a few of the other detectives. A couple of them had buddies they were politicking to get assigned up here before you got the job. Besides resenting you for that, you're young, good-looking, and a have a rep as a gunfighter. Some of these good ol' boys and gals won't handle that too well. Don't let it get to you."

"It hasn't yet," Strayer lied.

Chapter Thirteen

"Get up," Mims said to Skink. "It's time to make our move."

Skink sat slowly up. Every movement was agony. His right arm and shoulder launched missiles of sharp pain that coursed throughout his entire body. In addition, his numerous seeping abrasions stung, he had a tremendous headache, and he'd developed a fever. He was also light-headed and extremely weak. If these symptoms weren't enough, he felt ravenous hunger and the urge to vomit at the same time. But his dominant feeling was thirst. Skink's mouth felt so dry he thought he could spit dust.

"I don't feel so good," he croaked.

"You aren't going to feel any better until we get inside that house," Mims said, "and get some food, water, and rest. Let's go."

Mims and Skink waited in the woods all morning, as the sun arced higher in the sky. The heat increased dramatically, even though the sunlight was filtered through a heavy layer of dirty brown smoke.

Skink had dozed fitfully during what was left of the night as Mims kept watch. In the early morning, Mims saw a thin, pretty, short-haired woman about thirty years old come outside to the porch and smoke a couple of cigarettes. She wore only a T-shirt and panties, and her left arm was a full-sleeve tattoo. He stared, fixated, at her long legs, bare feet, and small, sharply outlined, breasts. After smoking, she returned to the house.

Mims had occasionally been exposed to female guards at San Quentin. There were also the rare instances when he had to go to the infirmary and might encounter a female nurse. But in each of those cases he'd been either locked in his cell or chained hand and foot and escorted by a pair of stout corrections officers. Today was the first time, in over nine years, that Duane Audie Mims was in close proximity to a young, attractive, woman with nothing between them but his urges.

At mid-morning, a man who looked to be in his mid-sixties exited the house through the back door. He was of average height and medium build and sported a mustache and a full head of salt-and-pepper hair. He was clad in jeans and a short-sleeved collared shirt, and was carrying a toolbox. He went over to the windmill's pump and began to fiddle with it.

Fifteen minutes later, the short-haired, punk-rock-looking woman reemerged from the house. This time she was wearing skintight jeans, sneakers, and a bra under her T-shirt. She had a large purse over one shoulder, and lit a cigarette as she got into the Lincoln sedan and drove off. The older man paused in his task long enough to wave as she drove away.

Less than an hour later, another woman came out of the house. This one looked older than the previous woman by a few years. She had long, dark, hair pulled into a ponytail, and a fabulous figure, and Mims could tell she was quite beautiful, even with the two black eyes and a bandage decorating her nose, which he presumed was from cosmetic surgery. Two children accompanied her, as well as a much older woman who possessed a clear physical resemblance to both of the other adult females.

The older woman hugged the children, one boy and one girl, and waved as they got into the Range Rover and drove off with the ponytailed woman behind the wheel. The older woman then walked across the yard and joined the man at the pump.

That was when Mims roused Skink. "What's up?" the skinny convict asked.

"An old man and woman came outside," Mims explained. "Two adult females, and two kids, drove off. I haven't seen any signs of any other men. Now's our chance."

Mims hauled Skink to his feet and drew one of the .40 caliber Glock pistols taken from the prison guards.

"Let's go."

With a Glock in one hand, and Skink in the other, Mims steered them from the woods. They circled around the property and approached from the side opposite the windmill, using the house to cover their advance.

Several times Skink stumbled, and would have fallen, if not for Mims. He half-carried and half-dragged his injured companion along.

Mims entered the back door first and pulled Skink, who hobbled on wobbly legs, behind him. The rear door led up a short flight of steps directly into the kitchen. Mims sat Skink on a kitchen chair and continued into the house.

With his pistol raised in a textbook two-handed Weaver stance, Mims hurriedly searched the downstairs. Finding no one on the lower floor, he quickly ascended the stairs.

In less than a minute he'd gone from room to room and satisfied himself there was no one else in the home. He scurried downstairs again and found Skink passed out in his chair. His head was resting on the kitchen table.

Mims surveyed the kitchen. He saw the older-style gas-operated refrigerator and stove, and correctly surmised they were powered by the propane tank outside. He found no electronic appliances operating, such as the clocks above the microwave oven or on the face of the cordless phone. He risked flicking on the wall switch to confirm that the power was indeed out. Then he picked up the telephone receiver and verified the line was dead.

That's when he noticed there was a second door in the kitchen. There was a dead bolt installed at head level, which he suspected had been put there as a child safety measure to keep small children from opening the door.

Mims opened the door and discovered why. He found a steep, narrow, stone stairwell leading down into darkness.

He turned his attention to several grocery boxes on the countertops. A hasty perusal told him they were filled with recently purchased supplies the residents must have obtained as a result of the fire emergency. Several flashlights were among them.

Mims grabbed a light and headed down the narrow stairs with his gun in front of him.

The basement was dark and dank, and had once been the old farmhouse's preserve cellar in the days before electric refrigeration. The stone walls were lined with shelves containing the sorts of items families typically stored in the garages of more modern homes, such as old lawn furniture, unused tools, and recreational items like badminton racquets and croquet mallets. There was a cot set up in one corner, and a card table with folding chairs in the center of the main room.

There was a smaller, secondary room in back of the cellar, which housed the furnace and ducting leading up into the house. There were no windows in the basement, and it appeared to Mims the only way in or out of the musty underground storeroom was to take the stairs leading up into the kitchen.

Mims remounted the steps. Skink was still asleep at the kitchen table. In one of the boxes he found a bottle of extra-strength ibuprofen, and in the refrigerator was an unopened carton of orange juice.

"Wake up," he said to Skink, slapping him lightly in the face until he awoke and sat up. He handed the groggy convict several pills and the orange juice. "Take these."

Skink gagged and coughed as he greedily slurped, but got the pills down.

Mims helped himself to a couple of painkillers and the rest of the orange juice. Though exhausted, he felt immediately better after drinking it. He was wiping his mouth on his forearm when Skink pointed to a key ring with a Ford logo on the kitchen table.

"Look," Skink said, pointing to the keys. "We could take the truck and split."

"We wouldn't get far," Mims said, shaking his head. "Not the way we look. Too many emergency vehicles and police on these county roads on account of the fire. Besides, before we can travel, we both need to eat and rest. You've got to get your strength back, and we have to clean ourselves up and find some new clothes." He patted Skink on his good shoulder and looked around.

"This place is perfect," he said. "We'll stay right here,

Goldilocks, in this cozy, just-right little house. At least for now."

"What about those folks outside?"

"Don't worry," he said. "We'll deal with them when the time comes."

"You mean kill 'em, don't you?" Skink asked. "Like them two guards in the van?"

"I didn't say that."

"I'm confused," Skink said. "You said we didn't kill them guards? You told me it was the fire that done it?"

"That's right." Mims nodded. "That's what I said. Are you saying different?"

"No," Skink said. "What I'm sayin' is with the guards everything happened so fast because of the fire bearin' down on us. I didn't have time to think about it. But now it's . . . I dunno . . . different."

"What about those two truckers?" Mims said. "You were ready to kill them, weren't you? You even asked me for a gun."

"No," Skink corrected him. "I wasn't gonna end 'em, just jack 'em. I only wanted to use the piece to scare 'em off, so they'd give up their truck and run away."

"That wasn't very smart," Mims said. "I had to remind you if they saw us, we'd have to kill them."

"I didn't forget," Skink said. "So what are we gonna do?"

"I don't know about you," Mims said, "but one thing I'm not going to do is go back to prison. I'll do whatever it takes to keep breathing free air."

"Free smoky air, you mean," Skink said. "I don't want to go back any more than you do. But what if them two gals and those kids you told me about come back? What'll we do then?"

"Don't worry," Mims said again.

Actually, Mims had been thinking about the women nonstop since he'd seen them.

"Maybe they aren't going to return," Mims suggested. "My guess is, the old folks sent them away because of the fire. For now, we'll play it cool."

"If you say so," Skink said. "You got us this far, I'll give you that."

"You keep forgetting," Mims said, sensing Skin's hesitation, "we're dead. Nobody searches for dead men. We've got nothing to worry about, as long as we remain dead."

"I guess you're right," Skink said. "We're like ghosts now, and ghosts can do anything they want."

"Exactly," Mims said.

What Mims didn't tell Skink was the other reason, besides their imminent need to rest, refuel, and hide out, that he wanted to stay at the farmhouse instead of stealing the truck and taking off.

The two dark-haired women he'd observed from the wood line. Contrary to what he'd told Skink, Mims sincerely hoped they'd return.

PART TWO
OXYGEN

CHAPTER FOURTEEN

"Reynaldo Benavides," the detective said, extending his hand. "Everybody calls me Benny."

Strayer shook a thick, heavily calloused, hand. It belonged to someone accustomed to hard physical labor over a very long time. She appraised its owner.

Detective Reynaldo Benavides was shorter than her by at least two inches, and looked to be in his late forties. He had a husky build, a full head of thick, gray, closely cropped hair, a bushy mustache, and a sun-darkened complexion. He wore a rumpled suit and a wide, genuine, smile featuring a lot of white teeth.

"How do you do," Strayer said. She found his grip surprisingly strong, and only the slightest hint of an accent in his speech.

"I'll leave you two to your work," Sergeant Simpson said. "Set her up in a desk, will you Benny?"

"I'll try to get around to it," Benavides said, "but I've got a full day ahead, Sarge. Ain't gonna be in the barn much."

"Whatever," Simpson said, already walking away.

"C'mon," Benavides said, tucking a digital audio recorder, clipboard, and laptop under one arm and grabbing a travel mug full of coffee in the other hand. "We gotta get on the road."

"Where're we going?"

"Folsom."

Strayer followed Benavides out of the Investigations Division and down to the first floor via the elevator. She was tempted to tell him she'd meet him below and take the stairs, but decided against it. He'd find out soon enough.

They exited the administration building through the rear door into the secure parking lot. Benavides got behind the wheel of an unmarked gray Dodge Charger.

"I'll drive on the way there," he said. "You can drive on the way back. I'll be writing on my laptop by then. You want to stop and get coffee before we go?"

"No thanks," Strayer said. "What's in Folsom?"

"I need to interview a three-year-old girl at Mercy Hospital," he said. "Get her to make an I.D., and pick up a copy of her medical records."

"Okay," Strayer said. They drove in silence through the streets of Farnham until they reached the highway onramp.

"So, you want to be a detective?" Benavides said, once they were on the highway.

"Not particularly," Strayer said.

"I heard that," he said. "Funny, ain't it? How life take us places we never thought we'd go?"

"Funny isn't the word I'd choose."

"Take me, for example," Benavides went on, undaunted by her sarcastic tone. "I always thought I was going to be a bricklayer. My father was a bricklayer, and his dad a bricklayer before him. I was born in Mexico, but grew up here in Farnham County. If you'd told me when I was a kid

I'd be a law enforcement officer, instead of a bricklayer, I'd have laughed in your face."

Strayer stared out the passenger window, wondering if Benavides was going to talk the whole way. It was over forty miles to Folsom. That was less than an hour's drive, assuming the Farnham Fire didn't have the roads completely screwed up, and could conceivably take much longer. She could tell the gregarious detective was talkative by nature and wasn't looking forward to hearing him prattle on for the entire trip.

"Life sure does take you places," Benavides repeated, "you never imagined you'd go. By the time I was in high school, I was your typical teenaged boy; stupider-than-Jupiter, cocky as hell, and thought I knew everything. I was running with a gang, smoking a lot of weed, and doing all that dumbass shit boys do when they're young, dumb, full of cum, and believe they're invincible."

Strayer said nothing. She wasn't comfortable hearing his history and hoped he didn't expect her to divulge her own as some kind of "get to know your new partner" ritual. If he did, she thought, he was going to be disappointed.

"Then I got arrested for stealing a car. Maybe not as smart as I thought, huh?"

Strayer remained silent.

"My dad kicked my ass all the way up to my eyebrows." Benavides laughed, reminiscing. His laugh faded. "Then he signed me into the Marines. I was seventeen."

Strayer turned her attention away from the landscape rushing by through the passenger window and looked over at him.

"The Corps changed my religion," he said. "Showed me what a piece of shit I was on the way to becoming. Taught me a few things. True things. Four years later, when I got out, I was a different animal. I'd learned a little about the world, and a lot about myself. You know what I mean?"

"Yeah," Strayer finally said. "I know what you mean. I went into the service at seventeen myself."

Benavides nodded, as if confirming something he'd already guessed. "After my hitch, I went back to civilian life as a bricklayer," he said, his smile returning. "This time," he said, laughing, "my dad had to pay me. I was on what I thought was going to be my life path."

His smile once again vanished. "Then my dad got killed. He was on a job site and caught a couple of junkies breaking into his truck to steal his tools. One of them hit him in the head and knocked him unconscious. He never woke up."

"I'm sorry to hear that."

Benavides shrugged. "It wasn't your fault, but I thank you for the sentiment. I was very angry," he continued. "If I could have found those punks, I'm certain I would have killed them."

"I know the feeling," Strayer said.

"I met the detective who handled my dad's homicide case," Benavides said. "A Farnham County deputy named Donaldson. He retired long ago, and has since passed away. I got to know him pretty well over the course of the year following my father's murder. I don't think it was his intention, but he also taught me a lot of things about the world, and myself, just like the Marine Corps. When my mom died of a broken heart, less than a year after my father, he came to the funeral."

"Detective Donaldson inspired you to become a deputy?" Strayer heard herself asking.

"Yep," Benavides said. "My heart wasn't in laying bricks any longer. It wasn't the same without my dad. So I applied to become a Farnham County deputy sheriff, and the rest is history. What about you? How did you end up wearing a Farnham County star?"

"You wouldn't believe me if I told you," Strayer said, returning her gaze to the window.

They drove in silence for another ten minutes before Benavides spoke again. "In my clipboard is the initial crime report and my supplemental investigation," he said. "Why don't you familiarize yourself with them before we get to the hospital?"

Strayer spent the next half hour reading. Traffic on the highway wasn't as bad as she expected, but the air quality and visibility, due to the massive wildfire, made it seem like they were driving through a light fog.

Benavides pulled into the parking lot of Mercy Hospital and parked in a space designated for law enforcement vehicles only.

Strayer put the report back into Benavides's clipboard. "What do you think of the case?" he asked her.

"Horrific," she said, "but open-and-shut. I presume we're here today to shore up the responding deputy's initial report?"

"That's right," Benavides said as they got out of the car. "Exclude any others on the scene at the time of the offense and have the victim formally I.D. the suspect."

"But the suspect is her uncle?" Strayer said. "She knows him."

"True," Benavides said. "The D.A. still needs a formal identification in order to charge."

"You honestly believe we're going to get a positive I.D.

from a three-year-old?" Strayer said, as they walked through the parking lot.

"You'd be surprised," Benavides said through his perennial smile, "what you can get from a three-year-old."

They entered the hospital and were directed to an upper floor. When they walked out of the elevator, they were met by a gray-haired woman who didn't appear old enough to have gray hair wearing a skirt and carrying a clipboard. A young nurse in scrubs adorned with a jack o' lantern pattern was with her.

"Hiya, Paula." Benavides greeted the gray-haired woman and introduced Strayer.

"Hello, Benny," she replied. "Always nice to see you. I just wish it wasn't always under these circumstances."

"I'm Paula Robeson," the older woman said to Strayer, "with Child Protective Services." She gestured to the nurse. "This is Brenda. She's caring for Cassie." They shook hands all around.

"How's she doing?" Benavides asked, as Brenda led them down the hallway.

"Her hand is healing," Brenda said, "but she's definitely going to need skin grafts. Too early to tell if there'll be permanent nerve damage, but the doctors are confident that with therapy she'll make a full recovery. Other than the scarring, of course. I have a copy of the updated medical report at the nurses' station for you."

"We'll pick it up on the way out," Benavides said.

They entered a hospital room. A haggard-looking young woman in her twenties, wearing the uniform of a popular fast-food chain, was sitting in a chair next to the bed. At Robeson's request she wordlessly got up and left the room along with the nurse.

In the bed was a brown-haired little girl with her right hand wrapped entirely in gauze. She was clutching a Barbie in her left. She smiled when she saw Paula.

"Hi, Cassie," Paula said.

"Hi, Paula," Cassie said, her eyes brightening.

"I brought some people to meet you," Robeson said. "This is Benny and his friend Leanne. They want to talk to you. Is that okay?"

Cassie nodded.

"Hello, Cassie," Benavides said, launching his trademark smile.

"Hi, Cassie," Strayer said, unable to keep from smiling at the adorable little girl.

"Hi," Cassie said softly. She pointed her Barbie at Straycr. "You're pretty."

"Thank you," Strayer said. "I think you're pretty, too." Cassie smiled from ear to ear.

Looking at three-year-old Cassie lying in the hospital bed, Strayer's mind was flooded with images corresponding to the police report she'd read on the way over to the hospital.

She'd read about the child's struggling, unmarried, twenty-one-year-old mother, living in Folsom but working at a fast-food restaurant in Farnham, and how she was forced to drop off her daughter each day to be babysat by her brother there because she couldn't afford childcare.

The report listed Cassie's uncle, the suspect, as a twenty-five-year-old unemployed janitor living in a basement apartment in Farnham. He had prior arrests for petty theft, vandalism, and possession of opioids without a prescription. He claimed he was boiling a pan of water on the stove to cook a box of processed macaroni and cheese for his niece's lunch when she somehow, accidentally, put her right hand into the water.

The child's mother found Cassie catatonic when she arrived to pick her up. Her hand, from the wrist down, was covered in second- and third-degree burns. Much of the skin had simply boiled off, like overly done chicken from the bone.

All the brother reputedly had to say to his sister when confronted, according to the mother's statement taken by the patrol deputy at the emergency room, was "It wasn't my fault. It was an accident. Cassie's just a clumsy kid. Don't worry, though; kids are tough."

The doctors told the deputy that Cassie's injury could only have occurred by continuous immersion of her hand in boiling water for an extended period, perhaps minutes. The suspect's claim that Cassie accidentally dunked her hand in the boiling pan did not match the severity of her injury, or explain how she got her hand into water inside a pan on top of a stove that was taller than her.

"I have three questions," Benavides said to Cassie. "Can you answer them for me?"

She nodded. He switched on his digital audio recorder and noted the date, time, and location.

"When your hand got hurt," he began, "was there anybody else in the apartment with you besides your Uncle Jim?"

"No," she said, shaking her head vigorously from side to side.

"Is this your Uncle Jim?" Benavides asked, holding up a California Department of Motor Vehicle photograph of the suspect.

"That's Uncle Jim!" she declared, pointing at the picture with her Barbie.

"Did you put your hand in the water, or did Uncle Jim put your hand in the water?"

"Uncle Jim," she said, her smile vanishing. "I wetted myself. He got mad at me. He said I was a little fitch."

"You mean a 'little bitch'?"

"Yeah!" she said.

Benavides noted the time again, and switched off the recorder. He produced a small bag of Oreo cookies from inside his pocket.

"Paula told me you liked Oreos," Benavides said. "Was she telling me the truth?"

Cassie nodded again, her smile returning as fast as it had disappeared.

"Thank you for talking to me, Cassie," Benavides said, handing her the cookies. "It was very nice to meet you." He motioned for Strayer to follow him and headed for the door.

"Will you come back and play Barbies with me?" Cassie asked her.

"I'd very much like to," Strayer said, "but I can't. I have to go to work now. Maybe I'll come back later?"

She followed Benavides out.

"Do you have children?" Benavides asked Strayer, as they walked to the nurses' station.

"No," Strayer said, mildly surprised he asked.

"Take a piece of advice from someone who's done this job a long time," he said. "Never make a promise to a child you cannot keep."

"You're right," Strayer conceded. "I shouldn't have told her I might return. I didn't want to disappoint her, that's all."

"I know," Benavides said. "But you aren't on S.W.A.T. anymore. In this job, each child will take a piece of you if you allow them. You must remember to keep enough of yourself."

"I won't forget," Strayer said.

They collected a copy of Cassie's medical report, said their good-byes to Robeson, and took the elevator down to their car. Benavides tossed the keys to Strayer.

"You're driving, remember?" he said. "I'm writing."

"Arrest warrant?"

"You got it," he said through his smile. "I have most of it already framed out. I should be finished by the time we get back to Farnham. We'll go to the district attorney's office first, get the warrant signed by a judge, and then pay a visit to Uncle Jim. Unless you're hungry? We can stop for lunch first, if you like?"

"To hell with lunch," Strayer said, starting the ignition. "I want to meet Uncle Jim."

CHAPTER FIFTEEN

"I can't wait to go home," Jennifer declared from the back seat. "I like Grandma's house, but I like my own bed better. I miss Daddy."

"You're not going to sleep in your own bed anymore," Joel snapped at his younger sister from the front seat. "And you're not going to see Dad. He's in jail, so just forget about it."

Startled by the harshness of her brother's rebuke, Jennifer started to cry.

"Joel," Marjorie scolded, "why would you say such a thing to your sister?"

"Because it's true," he retorted. "She might as well figure it out now."

After leaving her parent's home in rural Farnham County, Marjorie was relieved to learn the power was back on in the town of Farnham. She decided to stop at a local restaurant and feed Joel and Jennifer their lunch before going on to Granite Bay, unsure of how long they might be on the road due to traffic delays because of the fire.

During the meal, Jennifer talked incessantly between bites about how much she missed her father, and her room, and her stuffed animals, and how she was looking forward to returning to kindergarten to see her teacher, and her friends, and how exited she was about going trick-or-treating, and a dozen other topics related to her life back in Granite Bay.

While Jennifer chattered, Joel ate in silence. Marjorie had little appetite herself. She sipped a glass of water from behind her sunglasses and ignored the stares from patrons ogling the two children and the woman with the black eyes and bandage on her nose.

Once back on the road, Jennifer continued to express her excitement about returning home. Joel hadn't spoken a word since they'd left his grandparents' until he unleashed the tirade upon his sister.

"Please don't cry," Marjorie implored, as Jennifer's sobs intensified from the back seat.

"I'm never going to see Daddy again," she wailed.

"That was a very cruel thing to say, Joel."

"Telling the truth isn't cruel," he said. "It's just the truth. She's got to learn sometime."

"Who says that's the truth?" Marjorie said. "And even if it is, you don't have to say it so harshly. She's only five, Joel. Apologize to your sister."

"I won't," Joel said. "I don't care how old she is. I'm not going to apologize for telling her the truth. Dad's in jail, and I don't want to live with Grandpa any more than she does. I want to go home. Not just for tonight, to trick-or-treat, but for always, like before. I want to go to my school in Granite Bay, and be with my friends, not go to some stupid school in Farnham. Because of you, that's all gone."

"What did you just say?" Marjorie said.

"You heard me," Joel said, raising his voice and turning in the passenger seat to face his mother. His face was red. "If you hadn't made Dad mad, and had him arrested, everything would be like it's supposed to be. This is all your fault."

Marjorie pulled the Range Rover over to the side of the road. Leaving the engine on to power the air conditioner, she got out. She climbed into the rear seat and held her daughter, soothing her until she stopped crying. Joel remained in the front and fumed.

"Wait here," she told Jennifer, once her daughter had ceased crying and regained most of her composure. "I'll be right back."

Marjorie left the car again and opened the front passenger door. "Come here," she motioned for her son to exit the Range Rover. "We need to talk."

"I don't want to get out of the car," he said, staring sullenly at his feet. "It's hot and smoky outside."

"Get out," she said. She unbuckled Joel's seat belt, took his arm, and escorted him to the rear of the car.

Joel allowed himself to be led, looking down at the ground. "I don't want to talk right now."

"You were all for talking when you made your sister cry," Marjorie said. "But I guess you can't take it yourself?"

"Take what?"

"The truth, young man. You want it so bad, here it is. We don't always get what we want."

"I know that," he said under his breath. His gaze was still fixed on the concrete at his feet.

"Do you?" Marjorie leaned over and took Joel's chin.

She gently, but firmly, tilted his head up. Despite his upraised head, he refused to meet her eyes, choosing to focus on a point somewhere above his mother in the smoke-filled sky.

"Look at my face, Joel," Marjorie said. She removed her sunglasses. "Look at it. Does this look like my fault?"

"You made Dad mad," he said, finally meeting Marjorie's eyes. "He lost his temper. It was an accident."

"It wasn't an accident. He's done it before."

She let go of Joel's chin and stood up. Cars passed by them on the road. The afternoon air was brown, thick, and stiflingly hot.

"What you told Jennifer was the truth," she began, speaking as much to herself as her son. "It hurt her, and made her cry, but you told her anyway. You said you didn't care how old she was. 'She's got to learn sometime,' you said. Well, now it's your turn."

Marjorie put her sunglasses back on. "You were right when you told Jennifer we aren't going back. Your father and I are finished. We're not getting back together and moving back into our house in Granite Bay. It will never be like it was. I don't want to see him again. Ever. That's the truth."

A tear began to seep from the corner of one of Joel's eyes, but he stuck out his jaw and looked up defiantly at her.

"You can blame me if you want," Marjorie went on. "That's your choice. But if your sister is old enough to hear the truth, so are you."

"I can take it."

"Good," she said, "because here it comes. You love your father. I get it. I did once, too. You miss your life back in

Granite Bay. So do I. You resent me for taking it from you, and you lashed out at Jennifer because of the anger you feel towards me. You believe the breakup of our marriage is my fault. That somehow if I'd behaved differently towards your father, he and I would still be together, right?"

Insolent silence was Joel's answer.

"You're forgetting half of the equation: your father's behavior. Don't you think he might have something to do with the way things turned out?"

"I know my dad," he said.

"Do you?" Marjorie challenged. "Take another look at my face. Who do you think beat me up? The tooth fairy?"

Joel clenched his fists and his jaw.

"Let me tell you about the father you don't know," she went on. "He lied to me. He lied a lot. I took it for a long time, because I loved him. He cheated on me. I took that for a long time, too, because I loved him."

Joel's eyes widened.

"I was going to divorce him a few years ago, when you weren't much older than Jennifer. But he begged me not to. He promised he wouldn't lie to me or cheat on me ever again. I wanted to believe him, so I did. And I forgave him. I thought I was doing the right thing by trying to keep our family together."

Joel's face went slack, and he released his fists.

"But then your father lied and cheated on me again," Marjorie said, her voice cracking. "This time, he cheated with a woman who was sick. Because of that, I got sick. It's the kind of sickness that could have infected you and Jennifer."

Joel's mouth opened as if to speak, but no words came out.

Tears began to eke out from under Marjorie's sunglasses. "I told myself I was never going to tell you or Jennifer any of this," she said. "I didn't want my children to hate their father, no matter what he'd done. But I won't take all the blame. I'm not going to let you hate me for what he did. He's not getting off the hook this time. And I'm sure as hell not going to do it to protect him from you finding out what kind of a man he really is."

Marjorie removed her sunglasses again and wiped her eyes angrily on a forearm. It was her turn to refuse to look into her son's eyes.

"When I confronted your father, he didn't man up. He wouldn't admit how he'd wronged me and our family, or even say he was sorry. He tried to lie to me again. When I caught him in that lie, he beat me up."

She pointed to herself. "He broke my face, Joel. I'm going to have to have surgery to fix it. That's why he was arrested. Not because I made him mad. Because of what he did to me, and to our family, with his own choices and his own two hands. It's your father's fault he went to jail, not mine. You said you could take the truth? There it is."

Joel's face paled. Cars continued to drive by, some slowing as their drivers paused to gape at the crying woman with the banged-up face talking animatedly to a young boy on the sidewalk.

"But in a way," Marjorie said, "you're right. This is my fault. Because if I'd had the strength to leave your father when I found out what kind of man he really was, years ago, none of this would be happening now. He never hid what he was. He was a lousy father and a worse husband, but I wouldn't see it. I had to have the truth about your father beaten into me."

Mother and son stared at each other in silence for a long minute.

"I'm sorry for the way things turned out," she finally said, through her tears.

"So am I," he said, almost inaudibly.

"But I'm not so sorry that I'm going back," she said. "I'm not going to pretend that he didn't lie to me, or cheat on me, or beat me. Those days are over. I may be a fool for being stupid enough to believe your father's lies and letting him cheat on me for so long, but I'm not going to be his punching bag. Not anymore."

"I know that, Mom."

"I'm just like you," she said. "There're plenty of things I don't want. I don't want to take you and Jennifer away from your home and your school and your friends. I don't want to live out in the sticks, in Farnham County where I grew up, any more than you and your sister do. But that's where we are now. We don't have a choice. What I want isn't important anymore. The only thing that's important is taking care of you and Jennifer."

Joel's shoulders slumped, and he looked down again.

"I know that's not what you wanted to hear," Marjorie said. "And I honestly don't know what's going to happen to the three of us, going forward. But one thing I know for certain: We're going to be okay. We're still a family— you, me, and Jennifer—and nothing will ever change that. Your dad will always be your father, too, but he is no longer my husband. He's never coming near me again. That's just the way it is."

She put her sunglasses back on. "That's all of it. You can be angry with me and lash out at your sister all you want, but it doesn't change anything. We have to deal with the way things are, not the way we want them to be. That's the real truth, son."

Joel rushed into his mother's arms. He hugged her fiercely and sobbed as he hadn't since he was three years old. Marjorie stood on the sidewalk, held her son to her chest, and stroked his head as she'd done when he was a very small boy.

Automobiles rolled by through the haze and smoke, slowing to allow their occupants to gape as they passed. They went unnoticed by the woman and boy, embracing each other and crying together on the sidewalk.

One of the passing cars, a newer Lincoln sedan, slowed more than the others.

CHAPTER SIXTEEN

Mary Hernandez parked the Lincoln and turned off the engine. She didn't think Marjorie or the kids saw her as she drove by them on the street, but couldn't be sure. She hoped they hadn't, since she was driving in the wrong direction to be going back to their parents' house.

She was surprised to see them stopped at the side of the road in downtown Farnham. Her initial thought was that they'd experienced car trouble, but when she saw Marjorie holding Joel on the sidewalk and crying, she realized they were having a "family moment," as her mother used to call them.

Mary drove quickly past and pulled into a strip mall parking lot a block away. Fifteen minutes later she was relieved to see her sister's Range Rover drive by toward the freeway.

While in the strip mall lot, Mary dug into her purse and retrieved the small glass jar containing a quarter-ounce of methamphetamine she'd purchased in Rio Linda the day before. She'd been thinking about it all morning.

Mary ducked her head below the dash, scooped out a pinky-nail's worth of the tan-colored paste, and snorted it.

The rush took her immediately. She sat up, blinked several times to clear the watering in her eyes, and took a few deep breaths to dilute the stinging in her nostrils, throat, and lungs.

She replaced the jar's cap, careful not to spill any of its contents, and lit a cigarette. Normally she would have rolled down the car's window while smoking, but it wasn't significantly less smoky outside.

Mary checked her device while she sat in the lot and smoked. She'd regained cell service the moment she reached the Farnham town limits. Several text messages had come in.

WHERE R U? the first text message read. It was dated an hour earlier. The message repeated multiple times.

NEARBY, she texted back. BE THERE IN A FEW.

ROOM 115, came the reply.

Mary took a final drag, cracked open the Lincoln's driver's door, and tossed out her cigarette. She could feel her heart pounding inside her chest, and her skin tingled. She sniffed several times, wiped her nose on the back of her hand, fired up the Lincoln again, and got back on the road.

It took Hector longer than he'd anticipated to change out the well's pump filter. In addition to replacing the filter, he inspected and oiled the mechanism, satisfied it was working properly.

The home was on rural water, supplied by the county, but Hector had always supplemented it with the ancient well. Given the power outage, and the potential for local water lines to be disrupted due to the fire, he wanted to ensure the water supply to the house from the well was dependable.

He was mentally kicking himself, and told his wife as much, for not having previously purchased a gas-operated generator. He tried to buy one in town during his shopping trip the day before, but the hardware store was understandably sold out.

Margaret allayed her husband's concerns about their lack of a portable generator by reminding him that in all the years they'd owned the property, the power had only gone out a couple of times annually, and when it did, it was typically restored within an hour or so. The power grid in Farnham County was usually reliable, and until the Farnham Fire they'd never anticipated being without electrical power for an extended period of time.

By the time the well pump was checked and maintained, Hector had worked up a mild sweat. He and Margaret walked back to the house together in the sweltering afternoon heat, made more uncomfortable by the scent of smoke that filled the air.

When they got to the house, Hector set the toolbox on the back steps and held the rear door open for his wife. The first thing he and Margaret noticed as they entered was the strong smell of human body odor. It permeated the kitchen, and overwhelmed even the ever-present scent of smoke.

The second thing they noticed were the two filthy men in their kitchen.

CHAPTER SEVENTEEN

"How do you want to play this?" Strayer asked, as Benavides parked the unmarked Dodge a half-block from the suspect's home. They were in a residential neighborhood in one of Farnham's rougher districts. Most of the single-family homes on the street were unkempt and run down, and many had been broken up into individual apartments. More than a few of these apartments were low-income units and subsidized by government entitlement programs.

"What do you mean?" Benavides said. Before she could respond, he radioed dispatch their location.

"Shouldn't we ask for cover officers from Patrol if we're making an arrest?"

"You're not on S.W.A.T. anymore," Benavides said with a smile. "You're a detective now. We make our own collars in the Investigations Division."

Strayer shrugged and followed Benavides as he locked the car and ambled down the street.

By the time they'd returned to Farnham, Benavides had completed his warrant affidavit. They drove directly to the courthouse and the District Attorney's office, where he printed the paperwork. They avoided the middleman of a court clerk by turning it in to a deputy D.A. whom Benavides had previously briefed about the case. He escorted them to the duty judge. Ten minutes later, armed with a felony arrest warrant, Strayer and Benavides arrived at their destination.

James Andrew Tully, who according to the felony warrant in Benavides's pocket was a Caucasian male twenty-five years old standing five feet nine inches tall and weighing one hundred and sixty-five pounds, lived in the basement unit of one of the seedier houses broken up into multiple low-income, apartments.

"What if he decides to run?" Strayer asked. "Shouldn't we at least have another deputy roving nearby?"

"Don't need another deputy," Benavides answered. "If you remember from the crime scene description in the initial report, the suspect lives in the basement. There's only one way in, or out, of his apartment."

Strayer was mildly embarrassed she'd missed that detail when reading the report. She'd been focused on the elements of the crime, and glossed over the reporting officer's scene description. She made a mental note not to make that mistake again.

"You will find," Benavides said, "as a detective, that sometimes the little details count. Besides," he continued, his ever-present grin widening, "we've got you, don't we? You're young and fast, and from what I hear a certified badass. If he gets out and makes a run for it, you can shag him down, can't you?"

They walked through the yard of a particularly shabby, two-story, house, and around to the back. There was a rickety door at the base of a set of concrete steps. They descended, and each took a position on either side of the doorway. Like all trained deputies and cops, neither Strayer nor Benavides would stand in front of a door if it could be avoided.

They could hear the sounds of a video game being played inside, and slivers of electric light filtered through cracks in the weathered door. In a basement apartment, having lights on during mid-afternoon wasn't out of the ordinary.

Benavides knocked on the door three times. The video game silenced. A moment later, the door opened a few inches.

The face peering out was pale, zit-covered, unshaven, and the eyes within it were glazed and red-rimmed. What the owner thought was a mustache adorned his upper lip, matched by an even scragglier goatee.

"What do you want?" the face demanded. It matched the DMV photo of James Tully that Benavides had shown Cassie.

"I'm Detective Benavides, from the Farnham County Sheriff's Department. May we come in?"

"I already talked to them other deputies," Tully said. "I got nuthin' more to say."

"We didn't come to talk," Benavides said. "We have a warrant for your arrest."

Tully tried to slam the door shut, but Benavides had already wedged his foot in the doorway. He shouldered it open and Tully stumbled backward. Both deputies rushed inside.

Even with the lights on, it was dim within the apartment. The interior smelled strongly enough of marijuana smoke and unwashed body to drown out the scent of the pervading woodsmoke outside. The unit was quite small and was furnished with only a worn couch, a folding table, and of course a flat-screen television with a video game console attached. *Call of Duty* was paused on the screen, with the controller discarded on the couch.

Tully was wearing only a pair of shorts under a filthy bathrobe. He looked and smelled as if he hadn't bathed in days.

"You got no right," Tully said, backing away from the two deputies toward the tiny kitchenette.

"More right than you have," Benavides said, no longer wearing a smile, "to torture a three-year-old girl."

Strayer noticed that without his characteristic smile, the squat former bricklayer's face was as hard as the stone he once worked with. His eyes had darkened, too. Not a glint of mirth remained.

"I didn't do nuthin' to Cassie," Tully protested. "I don't care what my sister says. Her kid's lyin'. It was an accident. Clumsy little brat did it to herself." Tully backed up, while Strayer and Benavides slowly flanked him on either side of the couch.

"I already told you we didn't come to talk," Benavides said. "You're under arrest. Turn around, put your hands behind your back, and don't resist."

"I ain't goin' to jail," Tully stated. "No fuckin' way."

"You have no idea how much I was hoping you'd say that," Benavides said, moving a step closer.

"You and the little lady gonna take me in?" Tully asked. "Is that what you think?"

"I think you can go to jail," Benavides said, "or you can go to the hospital and then go to jail. One way or the other, you're going to jail."

"Fuck you," Tully said, emboldened. "If you think I'm gonna let some old Mexican dude and a badge bitch take me in, you're outta your motherfuckin' mind."

"Make your move, tough guy," Benavides said, stepping even closer.

Tully had a choice to make. Two deputies were blocking his path to the door. One was male, much shorter than him, at least twenty years older, and at least fifty pounds heavier. The other was female, slightly shorter, and at least twenty pounds lighter. He made his decision.

He released a guttural howl and rushed directly toward Strayer. Tully ducked his head and shoulders like a full-back, expecting to bowl the female deputy down, run over her, and make his escape through the open apartment door.

Tully hoped his charge would flatten her, knock the wind out of her, and maybe even knock her out. He knew the rotund old detective would never catch him. All he had to do was hop over a few fences, scurry through some backyards, and he'd lose his pursuers. He presumed the female deputy wouldn't be able to get up very quickly after he stampeded her, if at all.

Tully had several friends in the neighborhood who didn't like deputies or cops any more than he did. This included a neighbor three doors down, whom he bought his dope from, and who would gladly hide him out. After he lost the deputies with his felony parkour routine around the neighborhood, he planned to circle back and hole up with him.

The only problem with Tully's plan, as he gleefully began to implement it, was the unanticipated heel of the female deputy's right shoe.

Instead of absorbing Tully's headlong charge, Strayer sidestepped, pivoted, and executed a perfectly aimed turn-back-kick. She fully extended her hip, locking her leg as her heel came to rest squarely in his mustache zone.

Tully's war cry ceased in mid-screech. Despite his extreme forward momentum, the force of Strayer's kick snapped his head violently rearward while his lower body continued on. His legs flew out from under him and he landed on his back, with his cranium striking the ground before his torso. It looked to Benavides like he'd run full-speed into a clothesline.

Tully's nose and jaw were instantly shattered, and all four of his upper and lower front teeth were knocked out. He lay on his back, semiconscious, spewing blood and tooth fragments. He blinked repeatedly, rolled his head from side to side, and looked up blankly at the two deputies standing over him.

Benavides turned Tully roughly over onto his stomach. He knelt on his back with his full weight, ignoring Tully's agonized scream, and expertly handcuffed him.

"Thith ith polithe brutality," Tully wailed through his busted mouth.

"Shut up," Benavides said, "or I'll let her kick you again."

"I'm gonna thue you both," Tully hollered.

Benavides ignored him and stood up. "Nice move," he complimented Strayer. "Uncle Jim never knew what hit him. I may have to change your nickname from Deadeye to Deadfoot."

"If you ever call me either one of those names again," she said, putting her hands on her hips, "I'll kick you in the mouth."

"Okay, okay," Benavides said, showing his palms.

"You knew he'd go for me," Strayer challenged, "instead of you, because I'm a woman. You deliberately steered him my way."

"Whaddya know?" Benavides replied, as his trademark smile returned. "We might make a detective out of you yet?"

CHAPTER EIGHTEEN

"Who are you?" Hector demanded. He stepped protectively in front of his wife. "What do you want?"

"Take it easy," Mims said, holding up his empty hands. "We didn't know anybody was home. We thought this house was evacuated because of the fire."

When Hector and Margaret Hernandez reentered their house from the barn, they found Mims and Skink in the kitchen. Mims had donned his damp, soiled T-shirt, and concealed both of the Glock pistols beneath it.

"So you decided to come inside and help yourselves?" Hector challenged. "In normal times, that's called trespassing and burglary. With the wildfire burning, it's called looting."

"You've got us all wrong," Mims said. "We aren't looters. We had no choice. We're just looking for a phone."

Hector assessed the two men in his kitchen. The one standing was a tall man in his forties, with a solid build, dark eyes, and a military haircut. The one seated at his table was very thin, of medium height, and in his twenties. He was shirtless, sported a shaved head, and his naked upper torso was covered in tattoos.

Both men looked exhausted, were covered in dirt and soot, and were wearing identical clothing: rubber-sole canvas shoes, ill-fitting denim trousers, and what were once white T-shirts. The big man was wearing his soiled shirt, and the other man's shirt had been fashioned into a sling supporting his right arm. The larger man wore a weary, entreating, smile. The smaller man looked nervously back and forth from his partner to the homeowners.

"Do I know you?" Hector asked Mims. His eyes narrowed. "You look familiar. Seems like I've seen you somewhere before?"

"I don't think so," Mims said.

"What's wrong with your arm?" Margaret asked, pointing to Skink's sling.

"Me and my friend got stuck in a traffic jam when the wildfire hit the highway," Mims answered before Skink could. "The firestorm blew over us like a hurricane. We had to abandon our vehicle and make a run for it."

While what he said was technically true. Mims conveniently neglected to mention why he and Skink were on the road in the first place.

"Marjorie and I heard something about that on the radio," Margaret said to Hector. "The broadcaster said a bunch of people were trapped in their cars by the fire out on Highway 50. Some of them didn't make it out."

"The radio wasn't lying, Ma'am," Mims said. "It was an inferno. There were folks who didn't make it. We saw them burn. We barely got out with our lives."

"Good Lord," Margaret said.

"That's quite a ways from here," Hector remarked.

"After we left our vehicle," Mims continued, ignoring Hector's comment, "we got lost in the woods. It was so smoky and dark we couldn't see our hands in front of our faces. My friend here fell down a ravine and busted his collarbone. I patched him up as best I could, and we've been wandering the forest all night trying to find help. Yours was the first place we came to."

"How come we didn't see you boys walk up?" Hector said. "We were out front, working on the well pump."

"I guess you didn't see us because we came up to your house from out of the woods in back," Mims answered smoothly. "I knocked on your rear door, but nobody answered. It was unlocked, so we came inside. In our shoes, mister, you'd have done the same."

"If they did come onto the property from the back woods," Margaret pointed out to Hector, "we wouldn't have seen them."

"Do you have a cell phone we can use?" Mims asked. "Like you said, your land line is out." He pointed to the phone mounted on the kitchen wall. "We already tried it."

"Don't own a cell phone," Hector said. "Wouldn't do you any good if we did. There's no cell coverage out here. You've got to be near town for that."

"We're sorry to have barged into your home," Mims continued lying. "We wouldn't have done it if we weren't in trouble. We'd sure appreciate any help you could give us."

"This ain't a hotel," Hector said. He eyed the two men warily.

"Hector," Margaret scolded, "can't you see these fellows have been through hell? We can at least give them something to eat and a ride into town. One of them's hurt. It's the Christian thing to do."

"We'd surely be obliged," Mims said earnestly.

"Of course, we'll help," Hector finally said.

"I'm Margaret Hernandez. This is my husband, Hector."

"I'm Duane," Mims said, "and this is Randy." Skink nodded uneasily.

"Why don't you fix them some food," Hector said to Margaret. "I'll go see if I can rustle up some dry clothes. After they've eaten, I'll drive them into town."

"Randy looks about your size," Margaret called after Hector as he headed down the hallway. "I think there're some of Tad's clothes upstairs in Marjorie's old room which might fit Duane. Tad certainly isn't going to be back for them."

"Okay," Hector answered. "I'm pretty sure Tad left most of his clothes in the downstairs closet last time he was here. I'll take a look."

Once down the hall from the kitchen, Hector hastily opened the closet door and sifted through garments hanging within. He suddenly turned around and brought up the Remington shotgun. He pumped the action with a loud *clack-clack,* but froze in place before shouldering the weapon.

Standing rigidly before him in the hallway was Margaret. She wore a terrified expression. Behind her, using the woman as a shield, stood Mims. His face was no longer tired and beseeching. His eyes had become flat and hard. He pressed the muzzle of a black semiautomatic, pistol against her temple.

"Go ahead and shoot," Mims said. "You'll get as much of Margaret as me with that scattergun."

"Don't hurt her," Hector pleaded.

"Drop the gun," Mims said, "or I'll paint the walls with your wife."

Hector released his grip on the Remington and let it fall

to the floor. "Step back," Mims ordered. Hector complied, keeping his hands in the air.

Mims removed the Glock from Margaret's head and pointed it at Hector. He walked over, picked up the shotgun, and returned the pistol to his waistband. Margaret ran into Hector's arms.

"Serves me right," Mims said, as he unloaded the Remington by repeatedly cycling the action. "I should have known there was a gun in the house. Everybody out here in the boondocks has one."

He knelt and recovered the Remington's ejected shells. "Do you have any more firearms, Hector? If you do, tell me now. Because if you're holding out on me, I'll gutshoot your wife and let you watch her bleed out."

"That twelve-gauge pump is the only gun I own," Hector said, wrapping his arms tighter around Margaret. "I swear."

"Where are the rest of the shells?"

"All I've got is one box. Here in the closet." He handed them over.

"You'd best be telling me the truth."

"I am."

"What gave us away?" Mims asked.

"Highway 50 is more than forty miles from here," Hector said. "There's no way you could have covered that distance in one night on foot. Not in this country, with the fire burning."

"You're right," Mims agreed. "It was a dumb thing for me to say. We stowed away on the back of a truck. Anything else tip our hand?"

"Your friend looks like a criminal," Hector said. "Also, you're both wearing the same clothes. Especially the shoes. I've seen shoes like yours on work-furlough crews. You two are escaped prisoners, aren't you?"

"Not bad," Mims said. "You're a pretty smart guy, Hector."

"You're wrong," Hector said. "I'm not a smart man. I'm a man who doesn't want any trouble. Take whatever you want and go. You know we can't call the sheriff. The keys to the truck are in the kitchen. Just don't hurt us."

"What's going on?" Skink called out from back in the kitchen. He appeared in the hallway, walking on unsteady legs. He stopped and leaned against the wall when he saw the couple clinging to one another and Mims standing before them with the shotgun.

"What gives?" Skink said. "I thought you said we was gonna play it cool."

"Change of plans," Mims said.

CHAPTER NINETEEN

Marjorie, Joel, and Jennifer walked silently into the house. Marjorie held Jennifer's hand. Joel came in tentatively behind them.

"Is Daddy here?" Jennifer asked meekly, as they entered through the door leading into the garage.

"No," Marjorie said. "He's at work."

In truth, Marjorie didn't know where Tad was. But she knew he wasn't at work.

When they arrived in Granite Bay, she phoned his workplace and was told that Mr. Guthrie was no longer employed by the company. She guessed as soon as his new boss discovered he'd been arrested, and for what, Tad's current employer had become another one of his many ex-employers. One more line on a résumé littered with former employers.

Marjorie drove past the home twice before stopping several houses down and parking on the street. Tad's Porsche wasn't in the driveway. She got out alone, walked up to the house, and peered into the garage window. There were no vehicles inside.

Just to be safe, Marjorie rang the doorbell several

times. No one answered. She returned to her car, drove to the house, and activated the garage door opener. As she suspected, Tad hadn't changed the electronic code. She backed her Range Rover in and re-closed the garage door behind it.

Marjorie still had her house key, and guessed if Tad hadn't changed the garage door code, he wouldn't have changed the locks. She knew how irresponsible he could be and surmised his habits hadn't improved in the days since she and the kids left. She didn't need the key, however. Not only wasn't the door between the garage and interior locked, but the alarm wasn't activated, either.

"Wow," Jennifer said, once they were inside. "It's messy."

Jennifer was right. Though they'd been gone less than a week, the kitchen was a maelstrom of dirty, piled-up dishes, used glassware, pizza boxes, and fast-food wrappers. But what concerned Marjorie most were the dozens of empty beer cans and the pair of empty jumbo-size vodka bottles discarded on the countertop. Clearly Tad was no longer practicing sobriety.

Marjorie wasted no time. It was only early afternoon, but Tad wasn't at work and she didn't know where he was or when he might return. When she opened a cabinet under the sink to obtain plastic trash bags, she noticed the garbage bin was stuffed to overflowing, mostly with more empty beer cans. She handed a bag each to Joel and Jennifer.

"Go to your rooms," she said to them. "Get your Halloween costumes, and anything else you want." She knelt and caressed Jennifer's hair, looking into her daughter's eyes. "Take what you can," she said softly. "I don't know if we'll be coming back anytime soon."

"C'mon," Joel said, taking his little sister's hand. "I'll help you."

Marjorie stood, smiled, and gave her son's shoulder a squeeze. He smiled weakly back, and led his little sister from the kitchen.

"Hurry up," Marjorie called after them. "We're leaving in fifteen minutes."

Marjorie sat at the kitchen table and dialed her cell phone.

"Law Offices," a female voice answered.

"Is Mark Gould in? This is Marjorie Guthrie."

"One moment."

"Hello Marjorie," a man's voice said. "I've been trying to call you for several days. Are you and the kids okay?"

Mark Gould was an attorney, and the husband of one Marjorie's friends from the health club. He'd provided free legal advice when she'd contemplated leaving Tad several years prior, and was formally handling her divorce now.

"We're okay," she said. "We're out near Farnham with my folks. The phones are down, and cell service is non-existent."

"That's close to where the fire's burning, isn't it?"

"It is," she said, "although it hasn't reached us and hopefully won't. That's why I'm calling. If we have to evacuate, what are my options?"

"I've already told you," he said, "you could be back in your own house right now. You have a restraining order against Tad, remember? All you have to do go to the house, call the Granite Bay PD, and have them come over and conduct a civil standby while he moves out. If he comes back after that, have him arrested."

"That's where I am now," Marjorie admitted.

"Where's Tad? He's not there, is he?"

"No," she said. "I already called his work, and he's not there, either. Evidently he's been let go."

"That could impact the divorce," Gould said. "Why'd you come back?"

"I brought the kids to get a few things and to take them trick-or-treating in their old neighborhood."

"Do you want me to call the police for you?"

"No," Marjorie said. "We'll be out of here in a few minutes."

"It wasn't a good idea to go there without a police escort," Gould admonished. "What if Tad returns? You could be in danger, not to mention in violation of your own restraining order, which could nullify it."

"We'll be all right."

"There's no reason," Gould said, "that you should have to move out of your own house. Tad was the one who was arrested."

"Tad's father bought the house. It belongs to Tad. It doesn't seem right to kick him out, especially since I'm the one who left the marriage and is filing for divorce."

"That's nonsense," Mark said. "The house is paid off, and the deed is in both your and Tad's names. You legally own half of it, no matter who bought it. I told you this before. You're being too honorable, Marjorie. You have to think of yourself and the kids."

"I know," Marjorie said. "If Tad goes to jail, maybe I'll consider moving back in. But for now, I don't want to be here."

"I understand."

"How's the divorce progressing?"

"I've filed your separation papers, which is the first

step in a divorce proceeding. This is going to take a while, Marjorie. Months, at least. We can't really go forward until we find out what Tad is looking at as far as his criminal sentencing is concerned. His legal predicament could have a big impact on the divorce."

"What'll we live on until then?"

"Don't worry about that," Gould said. "Tad's been ordered to provide temporary child support and subsistence payments until the formal amounts are set in stone when the divorce is finalized. It's too soon to know how his being unemployed will play out."

"It's not like Tad's paying the bills. Daddy is. Probably paying for his attorney, too."

"Speaking of attorney's fees," Gould said, "there's something I'm obligated to inform you. While Tad is prohibited by the restraining order from contacting you, or having anyone else try to contact you as his proxy, since I'm your legal representative his lawyer is under no such prohibition from contacting me."

"Let me guess," Marjorie said. "Vincent Holloway reached out to you, didn't he?"

"You know him?"

"I've met him a few times over the years at family functions. He's a close friend of Tad's father. His law firm cleans all of the Guthrie family's dirty laundry. It was Vince Holloway who got Tad out from under his drunk driving arrest."

"As with any divorce proceeding," Gould explained, "mediation is mandated, to potentially work out a settlement which might spare further court involvement."

"What did Holloway want?"

"You know what he wants. He wants you to withdraw

your divorce filing, abandon your petition for full custody of Joel and Jennifer, drop all criminal charges against Tad, and refuse to cooperate further with the prosecution efforts against him by the Placer County D.A.'s office."

"Not a chance," Marjorie said.

"I figured that would be your answer," Gould said, "but as your attorney I'm still obligated to convey the offer. As an incentive, in hopes of convincing you to relent, Holloway offered to draw up a last-chance contract."

"A 'last-chance contract'? What's that?"

"It's a legally binding postmarital, agreement designed to allay your concerns and give Tad one more chance. Through such a contract, if Tad were to misbehave in the future and you chose to end the marriage, he would cede all marital rights. You would get sole custody of Joel and Jennifer, the house would be deeded exclusively in your name, and a significant financial settlement would result. There's also a very generous sum to be paid up front, as additional incentive for you to accept the offer."

"Money," she sneered. "That's the Guthrie family's answer to everything. Tell Holloway to go to hell."

"You do realize," Gould continued, "if Tad goes to jail or prison for any length of time, which is a real possibility, he'd be unable to pay alimony or child support? And his father would be under no legal obligation to pay it for him?"

"I don't care," Marjorie said. "I just want that asshole out of my life and the lives of my children."

"If Tad gets locked up that'll take care of itself. At least temporarily."

"Doubtful," Marjorie said. "The eminent Dr. Maury Guthrie will never allow his only son to go to jail. He and his crony Holloway will find a way to get Tad off the hook, no matter how much it costs."

"I'm not so sure," Gould said. "Tad's in deep water this time, and he knows it. The only way Dr. Guthrie and his attorney have a chance at getting him off is through you."

"Then Tad's in a world of hurt," Marjorie said.

"I'm only required to convey the offer," Gould said. "I wasn't trying to convince you either way. I'm your lawyer, not your father. You get to make the call."

"I know," Marjorie said, "and I appreciate it. I've got to run, Mark. I don't want to be here any longer than I have to."

"If I can't get ahold of you," Gould instructed, "at least try to call me once a week. There're things we'll need to discuss."

"Thanks, Mark. And thanks for letting me store our things in your garage."

"No problem."

Marjorie ended the call, left the kitchen, and went upstairs. She entered Jennifer's room first. She found her daughter lying on the bed, coloring in a book. She looked like she did on any afternoon, as if she wasn't potentially leaving her home forever. Jennifer didn't notice her mother peering in.

She went to Joel's room and found him sitting forlornly on the floor. He had his baseball glove and Little League team cap on and looked up with red eyes as Marjorie entered.

"We have to go now," she said softly.

Joel nodded and stood up. He put his cap and glove in the trash bag and slung it over his shoulder.

"Help your sister pack," she said to him. "I'll meet you both downstairs in a minute."

While Joel went into Jennifer's room, Marjorie went across the upstairs hallway to the master bedroom. The first thing she noticed was that the room was nearly as messy as the kitchen. Clothing and items were scattered on the floor. Like the kitchen below, there were also empty beer cans strewn about.

The second thing she noticed was the scent of stale cigarette smoke. Since Tad didn't smoke cigarettes, she scanned the room and located a ceramic cereal bowl on the nightstand. Closer inspection revealed it had been used as an ashtray. There were a half-dozen Marlboro cigarette butts in the bowl, and the remnants of two hand-rolled joints. Each discarded cigarette butt had very dark lipstick on it.

Marjorie shook her head in disgust. She felt no jealousy, only contempt.

It had been just under a week since Tad had assaulted her and been arrested. She knew from Mark Gould he'd spent at least three of those days in jail. For a separated husband who'd hired a high-priced attorney to convince his estranged wife not to divorce him, he didn't waste much time filling his bed.

Marjorie left the bedroom and went downstairs. She found Joel and Jennifer waiting in the kitchen. Joel was carrying both of their bags.

She gave them each a long hug. "Let's get out of here," she said.

CHAPTER TWENTY

Because they spent the remainder of their shift in the emergency room, it was late afternoon by the time Strayer and Benavides got back to the Investigations Division. In the ER, Tully was examined, given X-rays and an MRI, and treated, at taxpayers' expense, for a concussion, broken jaw, and multiple avulsed teeth.

Benavides took several photographs of Tully's injuries for his report. He and Strayer spent the time it took for the ER physician to certify their prisoner as fit for incarceration completing the arrest report and use-of-force forms.

When read his Miranda rights, before his jaw was wired shut, and asked if he wished to provide a statement further explaining his version of the events surrounding the injury to his niece and his arrest, all Tully said was, "Kith my ath, you cockthucking mothoofuckooth."

"Betcha can't say that three times fast," Benavides retorted. Even Strayer couldn't resist a grin at the quip.

They booked Tully into the Farnham County Jail and walked across the street to the administration building.

Benavides rode the elevator up to the third floor while Strayer took the stairs.

When she arrived in the Juvenile Unit, she found Benavides and Simpson talking together in hushed tones in the bowling alley. They stopped speaking as she approached.

"Benny tells me you did a good job today," Simpson greeted her.

"He's being kind," Strayer said, glancing sideways at Benavides. "I did my job."

"Maybe so," Simpson said. "It was still a nice pinch. Paperwork's done?"

"Here it is," Benavides answered, handing her the forms. "All the I's are dotted and the T's are crossed. It's Miller time."

"Not quite yet," Simpson said. "McDillon wants to see us."

"Oh brother," Benavides muttered.

"Let's get this over with," Simpson said. "I want to get home to my daughter. She's waiting to go trick-or-treating."

Simpson led Benavides and Strayer into McDillon's office.

"You wanted to see us, Lieutenant?" Simpson said.

"That's right," McDillon said, removing his glasses. He withdrew a small spray bottle and cloth from a desk drawer and began to clean the lenses.

"If we could abbreviate this," Simpson said, "I would appreciate it. I've got a five-year-old at home waiting to get into a princess costume and collect candy. You don't get those times back."

McDillon didn't look up at them from behind his desk. He continued to silently, and very slowly, wipe his glasses.

Simpson exhaled loudly. Benavides rolled his eyes. Strayer remained impassive.

"Tell me about your arrest today," McDillon finally said.

"It's detailed in our report," Benavides said.

"I don't care about your report," McDillion said. "I want to hear from Deputy Strayer how her first arrest on her first day in my division ended up in the emergency room?"

"It was a clean use of force," Benavides said. "The suspect attacked her. What he got he had coming."

"I wasn't asking you, Detective Benavides. I want to know how a routine arrest resulted in a suspect suffering significant injuries requiring extensive medical treatment."

"Would you rather it had been the other way around?" Strayer asked.

McDillon looked up. "A formal complaint against you for brutality and unlawful use of force is likely coming. What happened?"

"Like Detective Benavides told you," Strayer said, "it's in our report."

McDillon stood up. "Are you refusing a direct order?"

"No," Strayer said, "I'm simply protecting myself. If there's potential for departmental discipline or criminal charges, as you just implied, I'm entitled under the Peace Officer Bill of Rights to stand exclusively on my written account until formally interviewed by Internal Affairs. If you still want a verbal report, I'll be happy to read my written account to you."

"Don't be flippant," McDillon said. "If I wanted to

know what was in your written report, I'd read it myself. I want to hear from your own lips what went down today."

"Sounds to me like you've already made up your mind," Strayer said.

"What are you implying?"

"Only that I know my rights. I may be new to your division, Lieutenant, but I've been a deputy for five years. I'm familiar with how this game is played."

"What are you talking about? What game?"

"The discrepancy trap," Strayer said. "If a complaint is going to be lodged against me, Internal Affairs will conduct a recorded interview. Asking me to give you another, unrecorded, verbal report puts me at risk for an allegation that I said something different in each interview, which could be used against me in a disciplinary action. No thanks, Lieutenant. Like I said, I'll stand on my report."

"Are you accusing me of trying to entrap you?"

"I don't know." Strayer shrugged. "Maybe by burning me you could score brownie points with the undersheriff."

"That's insubordinate," McDillon said. "I could bring you up on charges." The look on his face showed Strayer had hit a nerve.

"Honestly answering a direct question you asked me isn't insubordination," Strayer said, "just because you don't like the answer."

"She's right," Simpson said. "You asked, Lieutenant."

McDillon's face reddened. "When I need a departmental regulations lesson from a sergeant under my command," he said through tight lips, "I'll let you know. Your deputy, Sergeant Simpson, like all deputies, is required to give an initial verbal report of any significant incident to a superior officer."

"You're right, Lieutenant," Simpson said, "but only one. Deputy Strayer already gave her initial verbal report to me before we came into your office."

McDillon's eyes narrowed. "Are you sure about that, Sergeant?"

"Absolutely," Simpson said. "For the record, Deputy Strayer's verbal report was consistent with her written account. Both adequately covered today's arrest and the level of force used to effect it."

Long seconds passed while McDillon glared at Simpson. She smiled innocently back. Benavides looked at the ceiling. Strayer stared straight ahead.

"Then I guess I'll have to forgo the verbal report," McDillon said, "won't I?" He pointed his extremely clean glasses at her. "I want that arrest report on my desk, ASAP."

"I'll make you a copy as soon as we're done here," Simpson said pleasantly.

McDillon turned his eyes back to Strayer. "I understand the suspect got kicked in the head. Last I checked, that's not one of the defensive tactics techniques they teach at the academy."

"The street isn't the academy, Lieutenant," Benavides said.

"Shut up, Detective," McDillon said. "I wasn't talking to you."

"Was that a question?" Strayer said.

"No, Deputy." McDillon smirked. "I wouldn't want to be accused of trying to make you repeat a verbal report you've already given to your supervisor in violation of your POBAR protections. It was just an observation. I was merely remarking on the mystery of how a suspect ended up with a busted face during a routine arrest."

"I suppose it would be a mystery," Strayer said, moving her eyes to meet McDillon's, "to someone behind a desk. Street deputies know there's no such thing as a routine arrest."

McDillon's eyes flashed, and his cheeks flushed a darker crimson. He glowered at Strayer but said nothing.

"Is there anything else, Lieutenant?" Simpson finally asked. She tapped her wristwatch. "Halloween is waiting."

"Yes," McDillon said, "there is. Information has come into our Gang Unit that indicates there may be attempts at reprisal against our deputies by members of the Mexican Mafia and their affiliates for the death of Ernesto Machado. Specific threats have been made against you, Deputy Strayer. An 'eye for an eye,' is what the informants are telling us."

"The hits just keep on coming," Strayer muttered.

"I've called a meeting for all Investigations Division personnel at zero-eight-hundred, so bring your coffee with you. The Gang Unit supervisor is going to brief us."

"This is just great," Simpson said. "Every gangster wannabe in Farnham County looking to earn a rep will be gunning for us."

"All sworn personnel are being notified to take extra officer-safety precautions," McDillon said. "That goes double for you, Deputy Strayer."

"I'll be sure to look both ways before I cross the street," she said.

"That is all," McDillon said, returning to his seat.

"That went well," Benavides chuckled, once the trio were out of McDillon's office.

"The hell it did," Simpson said. She began feeding Strayer's and Benavides's reports into the industrial-sized photocopier in the bowling alley.

"You didn't have to do that," Strayer said to Simpson.

"Do what?"

"Cover my back."

"Screw you, Strayer," Simpson said, not harshly. "I had a hunch you were going to be a pain in my backside the instant I laid eyes on you."

"Give her a break, Sarge," Benavides said. "It's her first day, for Chrissakes."

"And what a first day it was?" Simpson said. "Do me a favor, will you, Benny? Try to get her through tomorrow without whipping me up a triple-decker shit sandwich?"

"I apologize," Strayer said, "if I caused any trouble for you."

Simpson pressed the start button and turned to face Strayer, as the individual sheets of their reports began to feed through the copier.

"I'm starting to think 'Trouble' is your middle name," Simpson said. "Get out of here, the both of you. I'm outta here myself, as soon as I turn in this paperwork."

Strayer parked her car in her designated spot and got wearily out. She was tired, hungry, and frustrated. Her first day in her new assignment had turned out even worse than she'd anticipated.

Though her apartment complex was only a couple of miles from the administration building, it took her longer than usual to drive home. It was just past the dinner hour, and the streets were filled with throngs of costumed children scurrying excitedly from house to house. She drove slowly and with extra caution. The dwindling daylight combined with the hazy smoke to diminish twilight visibility even more than usual.

It was windy, and it was unseasonably warm for late October. Despite the dangerous air-quality warnings, and the countless children who had asthma, Strayer was comforted knowing the Farnham Fire didn't stop Halloween from launching an army of gleeful kids outdoors in search of treats.

She couldn't help thinking about the thousands of firefighters, most from the California Department of Forestry and Fire Protection, but many others hailing from fire departments all over the state, who were spending their Halloween not with their children, but instead risking their lives fighting the Farnham Fire.

Like all Californians at this time of year, on the eve of the advent of the rainy season, she fervently wished for rain. She knew, like the hard-pressed firefighters, that despite their valiant efforts and the millions of dollars being spent combating the massive wildfire, the flames wouldn't be extinguished until the annual rains arrived sometime in November.

Until then, Strayer knew all the firefighters could hope to do was try to contain the mammoth blaze long enough to evacuate those towns, villages, and occupied rural areas unfortunate enough to be in the path of its voracious appetite for carnage.

The towns of Tuckerville and Drayton, both rural communities within Farnham County, had been entirely wiped out by the fire. Most of their residents had been evacuated to emergency shelters in Farnham. Hundreds of people, however, had been listed as missing and the death toll, as reported by the newscaster on Strayer's car radio, was listed at over fifty and projected to climb.

Strayer caught the shadow of a silhouette from behind the tall hedges that bordered her ground-level apartment. Torn between the opposing extremes of a possible trick-or-treater about to jump out and yell "Boo!" or a Mexican Mafia gangster with a gun and desire to earn his bones, she opted to take no chances.

Strayer continued to walk nonchalantly toward her apartment door but pocketed her keys, discreetly drew her pistol, and bootlegged it along her thigh. She thumbed the safety down, keeping her trigger finger out of the guard along the right side of the Sig Sauer's frame as her training dictated.

When she was ten feet from the hedges, Strayer brought up her pistol and placed the tritium front sight at a spot approximately chest-high to an adult male.

"Deputy sheriff," she called out. "I'm armed. Come out and show me your hands."

"Take it easy," a male voice said. "Don't shoot. I'm coming out."

Strayer recognized the voice an instant before its owner emerged. She flicked up the thumb-safety and holstered her gun.

"What's wrong with you, Robbie?" she said. "Lurking in the bushes outside my apartment is a good way to get yourself shot."

"I didn't figure my own sister would put a bullet in me."

"I'm not your sister," Strayer corrected him. "I'm only your half sister, if that. What do you want?"

Robert "Robbie" Hennisten shared the same mother as Strayer, but a different father. He was sired by one of the many men who came in and out of the single-wide she inhabited with her mother in the Sierra Vista Trailer Park, in rural Farnham County, after her father died.

Hennisten was the only thing resembling a sibling Strayer had. Her mother's descent into alcoholism and despair after her husband's death at the hands of a drunk driver led to a number of doomed relationships, but he was the only child who resulted.

Hennisten was six years younger than Strayer, and they hadn't been close as children. His father, an itinerant logger, would often take him away for lengthy periods of time. Once he was gone with his dad for more than a year.

When Hennisten did return, typically abandoned by his father, he was a sullen, spiteful child, whose age discrepancy with Strayer precluded much of a relationship. Of course, his constantly rebellious behavior and regular heated arguments with their mother in the tiny trailer had more than a little to do with their estrangement.

Hennisten was in middle school, and away again with his father, when Strayer enlisted in the army. When their mother died a year later, while she was on her first tour in Afghanistan, she was granted leave to come home. Hennisten and his father showed up.

After the funeral, Hennisten's father took him back to Spokane to live. She wasn't sorry to see her half brother go and didn't expect to ever see him again. It would be almost six years before she did.

More than a year after she got out of the army, returned to Farnham, and became a deputy sheriff, she was surprised to discover Hennisten had also returned. Strayer was working as a rookie intake deputy in the Custody Division when he was booked into the Farnham County Jail on charges of burglary and narcotics possession. She didn't recognize him before seeing his name on the booking forms because of his long hair, scraggly beard, and emaciated, drugged-out, appearance. He recognized her right away.

Neither Strayer nor Hennisten wanted anyone in the jail to know they were related. Strayer because she was disgusted and ashamed, and Hennisten because it would have resulted in potential trouble with other inmates.

Strayer, however, immediately notified her supervisor as required. Departmental regulations mandated a deputy notify their superior if a relative was in custody.

Hennisten remained in the Farnham County Jail for four months. His charges were eventually reduced from burglary to criminal trespass, and he was released.

Ironically, the circumstances of Hennisten's incarceration led to Strayer being transferred to the Patrol Division early, even though she wasn't slated to be eligible for a transfer out of the Custody Division for another month.

As a rookie patrol deputy Strayer would occasionally see Hennisten's name on the daily arrest log, usually for petty theft or minor narcotics-related offenses. She knew he was still living locally but didn't encounter him herself for many months. It wasn't until she'd been a road deputy for almost a year, well after her first shooting incident, that they interacted again.

She was checking doors at a strip mall early one morning and found Hennisten sleeping in the bushes behind a dumpster. He wasn't under the influence of drugs at the time, had no outstanding warrants, and was guilty of no crime other than trespassing and vagrancy.

Before she let him go, Strayer learned that after their mother's death he'd dropped out of school, ran away from his father, and lived on the streets of Seattle until he turned eighteen. After running afoul of some local drug dealers, he drifted south to his native California and eventually wound up back in Farnham County.

In the more than four years since, Strayer had run into him only a handful of times. Each time she was off duty, shopping or running errands in town, and each time he begged for money, which she never gave him. During that period, her half brother spent a couple of separate stints in the Farnham County Jail for drug crimes and two years in Folsom State Penitentiary on a burglary conviction.

"That's the greeting I get from my own sister?" Hennisten said.

"Quit calling me your sister," Strayer said, appraising him.

Though six years younger, Hennisten looked at least twenty years older. He was an inch or two taller than Strayer, reed-thin, and wore greasy collar-length hair over a drooping mustache and goatee. Like her he was half-Korean, but his father had been of Hispanic origin, unlike her Nordic father, and as a result he had a much swarthier complexion, and they shared no other common features. He was attired in filthy, ill-fitting thrift-store clothing and smelled as if he hadn't bathed in weeks. He was trembling, though it wasn't from cold, his eyes were sunken, his face was strained, and he kept shifting his weight from one foot to the other, apparently unable to stand still.

"Maybe you are only my half sister," Hennisten said, "but technically we're still family."

"You aren't my family," Strayer said, "you're a homeless drug addict and a convicted felon. For your information, I'm prohibited by departmental regulations from fraternizing with drug addicts and felons, whether they're related to me or not. How did you find out where I live?"

"Farnham's a small town," Hennisten explained. "I get around."

"I'll ask you again," she said. "What do you want?"

"I thought maybe we could go inside and talk? Catch up a little?"

"By 'catch up,' you're referring to using my shower, raiding my refrigerator, crashing on my couch, and trying to bilk me out of some of my hard-earned cash for your next fix, right? Is that what you had in mind?"

"Gimme a break, Lee," Hennisten said. "I'm really hurtin' right now."

"Not my problem," Strayer said. "Unlike you, Robbie, I have a job. A job that kicked my ass today and will be waiting to kick my ass again at zero-dark-thirty tomorrow. So if you'll excuse me, I'm going inside to an early bunk."

"Please, Lee," Hennisten begged. "I wouldn't be here if I didn't have it bad tonight. I'm in serious pain, man. You gotta help me out. I'm desperate. You don't want me to do somethin' stupid, do you?"

"So it's my fault," she said, "if you break into another car or commit another burglary to feed your dope habit? Is that what you're telling me?"

"I'm just sayin' . . ."

"Tell it to someone who gives a shit," Strayer cut him off. She produced her money clip, took out a twenty, and handed it to him.

"I could use a little more," Hennisten said, hungrily eyeing the clip as she stowed it.

"That's all you're getting," Strayer said. "And you're only getting this because I'm too tired to argue with you. Don't plan on getting anything more from me, ever."

"Thanks, Sis," he said.

"Don't call me that," she said. "And don't ever come back to my home. If I see you in this neighborhood again, I swear I'll arrest you. And the next time I catch you lurking in the bushes, so help me God, I'll pull the trigger."

"Whatever you say," he said, caressing the twenty-dollar bill. She could tell by his glazed eyes he was no longer listening. His mind was already heating up a glass pipe.

"Get lost," she said.

Hennisten started to walk away, then stopped and turned around. "Hey, Lee," he said.

"What now?" Strayer said, with no attempt to hide her exasperation.

"I heard somethin'," he said, "in one of the places I . . . do business. Nobody knows you and me are related, ya know? Some guys were talkin' about you. Talkin' about doin' you. For payback on account of that dude you smoked in the trailer park."

"I heard," Strayer said.

"I hear a lotta guys talkin' smack," Hennisten continued, "tryin' to sound badass. Most of 'em are full of shit. These dudes ain't." His jaundiced eyes darted nervously to the ground. "They know where you live."

"I wonder how?" she said. "I'll bet that information is probably worth a lid of heroin or an eight ball of crank, don't you think?"

"Just thought you should know," he said sheepishly. "You might want to watch your back." He turned and began to shuffle off again.

"Thanks for the head-up," Strayer said, after he'd gone.

CHAPTER TWENTY-ONE

The knock on the door startled everyone.

"Don't nobody move!" Skink ordered, waving his pistol. "Duane!" he called upstairs. "Somebody's at the door."

Skink was seated in the kitchen. Hector and Margaret were sitting together on the couch in the main room where he could keep an eye on them. It was well past the dinner hour, and night had fallen.

Mims and Skink spent the day keeping watch over their hostages in alternating shifts. After Margaret cooked them a meal of steak, eggs, and hash browns, Mims prompted Skink to shower, shave, and don his new clothes first. He now wore an oversized plaid shirt, denims, and slightly too-big work boots reluctantly provided by Hector. Skink was even able to obtain an actual sling for his injured arm, left over from when Hector was recovering from rotator cuff surgery several years previously.

Once Skink had cleaned himself up and returned downstairs, Mims bound Hector's and Margaret's hands behind their backs with a roll of duct tape he found in a kitchen junk drawer. When Skink inquired about the need to bind the older couple, Mims answered that Skink couldn't be trusted to stay awake.

With Hector and Margaret bound on the couch, and Skink guarding them, it became Mims's turn to clean himself up. He showered, shaved, and helped himself to some of Hector's hair gel and cologne. Then he exchanged his filthy prison attire for trousers, a T-shirt, a hoodie, and hiking boots that Margaret told him belonged to her son-in-law. The T-shirt and hoodie were a little snug through the chest and shoulders, but the trousers and boots fit well.

Mims and Skink spent the remainder of the afternoon taking alternating naps in the master bedroom upstairs. Mims let Skink sleep first, while he stayed downstairs monitoring their captives. When Skink asked for one of the pistols, Mims declined, explaining he had to first clean the guns since they'd been dunked in the creek.

While Skink slept, Mims occupied himself by field stripping and cleaning one of the .40 caliber pistols using a rag and a can of WD-40 he also found in the drawer. He then detail stripped the components of the slide assembly on the other. This was easy to do with Glock handguns, and accomplished with only a small Phillips-head screwdriver discovered in the same drawer where he'd found the duct tape and aerosol solvent. In this manner, he kept one of the weapons ready for instant use at all times while cleaning the other.

He'd taken Hector's Remington shotgun, before Skink went upstairs to shower, and locked it inside the cab of the truck outside. The box of shells he tossed into the well.

Late in the afternoon, four hours after Skink went to sleep, Mims ordered Hector to go upstairs and rouse him.

He aimed his Glock at Margaret, and told him if they both weren't down in one minute, he'd shoot her.

Once Hector and a sleepy-eyed, groggy, and feverish Skink rejoined them, Mims removed their bonds, allowed the couple to use the bathroom, and then ordered Margaret into the kitchen to make coffee. Then he re-duct taped Hector's hands and gave Skink more ibuprofen. When the coffee was finished, he bound Margaret and put her back on the couch alongside her husband.

"Who were those two women I saw leave here earlier?" Mims demanded.

Neither Hector nor Margaret answered.

"You can tell me now," Mims said, putting the barrel of his gun against Hector's head, "while your husband is still breathing, or you can tell me over his corpse. It's all the same to me. I know they're coming back, so you might as well tell me who they are. I'm going to find out eventually."

"Our daughters," Margaret finally said.

Mims withdrew the Glock and returned it to his waistband. "I guessed as much. There's a family resemblance. And the kids?"

"Our grandchildren," Margaret said.

"When are they returning?"

"We don't know for sure," Hector said. "You'd better not hurt them."

Hector's last sentence wasn't a plea, it was a statement. He scowled up at Mims from the sofa.

Mims smiled back at him. "Wake me if anybody shows up," he told Skink. "Otherwise, don't bother me for at least four hours. I'm ready to drop. Can you manage that?"

"Sure, Duane."

"Sit at the kitchen table," Mims said. "And keep an eye on them."

"What's wrong with the big easy chair?" Skink complained.

"If you sit in the recliner you'll nod off," Mims answered. "If you nod off," he pointed at Hector with his pistol, "old Hector there will kick your teeth in, take your gun, and shove it up your ass, even with his hands tied. Won't you, Hector?"

Hector said nothing, looking into the barrel of Mims's gun. Margaret closed her eyes and silently prayed.

"I ain't gonna let that happen."

"See that you don't," Mims said, lowering the pistol. "Because if you fall asleep while you're supposed to be on watch, I'll shoot you myself."

"Jeez," Skink said. "Quit bein' an asshole and get some sack time, will ya? Don't worry, I'll stay in the kitchen if it'll make you feel better."

Mims gave Skink one of the Glocks and disappeared upstairs. Skink stuck the pistol in his waistband and turned on the radio, which was already tuned to a twenty-four-hour news program. Then he sat heavily down at the kitchen table, sipped coffee, and gingerly rubbed his shoulder and arm.

"Your friend seems a little edgy," Hector said.

"He ain't really my friend," Skink said. "I only met him yesterday."

"You can't exactly call yourselves strangers," Hector said, "if you're kidnapping people together, can you?"

"I s'pose you could call us partners," Skink said.

"Are you going to kill us?" Margaret blurted.

"Hush, Marge," Hector said.

"Nobody's gettin' killed," Skink said. "Not by me, anyway. Duane won't neither, unless you do somethin' stupid."

"Are you sure about that?" Hector chided. "It's your life if you're wrong."

"What's that supposed to mean?"

"It means," Hector said, "if he kills us, he'll have to kill you. He can't have a witness running around, can he?"

"Nice try," Skink said, wagging his good finger at Hector. "I know what you're doin'. You're trying get me and Duane to go against each other. It ain't gonna work."

"Why don't you both take the truck and go?" Margaret said. "Nobody's stopping you. It's got a full tank of gas, and your partner already has the keys. There's no reason for you two to stay. We don't have a cell phone, and the phone lines are down, so you know we can't call the authorities even if we wanted to. You could be miles away before anyone starts looking for you."

"Ain't nobody gonna be lookin' for us," Skink said smugly, grinning through his corroded teeth. "The fire already seen to that."

"You got what you wanted," Margaret implored. "We fed you, cleaned you up, and gave you new clothes. Please leave us alone?"

"We ain't goin' nowhere until Duane gets some shut-eye," Skink said. "After that, we'll see what happens?"

"I know what happens," Hector said. "Your partner will kill us."

"That ain't likely."

"How do you know?" Hector challenged. "You said you just met him a day ago. What do you really know about him?"

"I know he saved my bacon," Skink said. "If it hadn't been for him, I'd have been burned to a crisp on the road."

"Do you know what he was in jail for?" Hector asked.

"He wasn't in jail," Skink corrected, "he was in prison. There's a difference. Folks that ain't never been incarcerated don't know that. I was in jail, headin' off to prison. And no, I don't know what Duane was in for."

"Maybe you should ask," Hector said.

"Maybe you should shut up," Skink said. "All this jabberin' is makin' my headache worse."

"You don't look so well," Margaret said. "You have a fever. Are you all right?"

"No," Skink said. "I ain't all right. I've got a busted collarbone, a splittin' head, a bellyache, I feel like lukewarm shit, and you two are annoying the livin' hell outta me."

He removed the Glock from his waistband and set it on the table. "I told you once to shut up. If I have to say it again, I'll be wakin' up Duane with gunshots."

The rest of the afternoon passed in silence, with the only conversation coming from the radio. The twenty-four-hour news program, while intermittently covering a number of global, national, and regional topics, largely focused its broadcast on the Farnham Fire in the same way a hurricane or major earthquake dominates the news cycle.

In the three days since its eruption, the Farnham Fire had burned an estimated ninety thousand acres and was still burning uncontrollably and uncontained. Though not as severe yet as the 2018 Camp Fire, the most destructive in California's history, the comparisons were being noted by radio pundits at every opportunity.

More than three thousand structures had been destroyed, mostly in Tuckerville and Drayton, and over ten thousand people had been displaced either through evacuation or loss of their homes. The confirmed death toll was currently listed at fifty-three, though expected to rise, with hundreds of people still unaccounted for.

The only good news the radio offered was that meteorologists were predicting a slight potential for precipitation in the coming days. But for the present there was no end in sight to the extremely low humidity and gusting winds that were generating the firestorm conditions. Both the governor and the president had declared states of emergency in the region.

Afternoon drifted into evening. Skink stayed awake, listening to the radio and drinking coffee. The pain in his right arm and the throbbing in his skull kept him alert.

"I should make dinner," Margaret offered, not long after darkness fell. "We all need to eat something. Especially you, since you're not feeling well." Hers were the first words spoken by someone other than on the radio in almost four hours.

"When Duane wakes up" was all Skink said. A short time later they were startled by the knocking on the door. He alerted Mims, who emerged from the stairwell with his pistol in his hand.

"Someone's at the door," Skink announced.

"Did you hear a vehicle drive up?" Mims asked, his face hardening, "or were you asleep?"

"I wasn't asleep," Skink retorted hotly. "There wasn't no car, I swear."

Mims turned to the couple bound on the couch. "Who is it?"

"I don't know," Hector answered. "We don't get many visitors out here."

Margaret looked at her husband. The fear in her eyes asked the question they both couldn't. Was it Mary retuning? Marjorie and the kids?

Mims grabbed a kitchen knife and cut the tape binding Margaret's wrists. The knocking steadily continued.

"Get up," Mims ordered. Hector and Margaret both rose shakily to their feet. Hours of sitting motionless had numbed their legs. She began rubbing the circulation back into her wrists.

"Take the old man into the kitchen," Mims told Skink, "and stay out of sight." Skink picked up his gun and prodded Hector from the living room.

"You're going to answer the door," Mims said to Margaret. "We'll hide in the kitchen. Don't think we won't be watching you. Whoever it is, get rid of them. No tricks. If you try anything, your husband gets shot. Then you'll get it and whoever's at the door. Got it?"

Margaret nodded. "Got it," she said.

"Get going," Mims said. He, Skink, and Hector waited in the kitchen.

She slowly walked to the door, trying to erase the fear and worry from her face. The knocking persisted.

Margaret opened the door. Standing before her were two small children in makeshift Halloween costumes. "Trick or treat!" they said.

"It's only the Dixon kids," Margaret said over her shoulder, relieved it wasn't either of her daughters. "They're alone. Dell and Carly aren't with them."

Brandy Dixon, age ten, was wearing crudely applied lipstick, clown-like eye makeup, and an adult's sequined dress that hung loosely over her T-shirt. On her feet were flip-flops that revealed unclipped nails and filthy feet.

Travis Dixon, age six, was wearing a cardboard mask of Iron Man cut out from the back of a cereal box. Neither of his ragged shoes had laces. Both were undersized for their ages, and were unwashed, malnourished-looking, and holding empty plastic grocery bags.

"Who are they?" Mims whispered to Hector.

"They're our neighbor's children."

"How close do they live?"

"A mile down the road," Hector whispered back.

"Did you two walk all the way from your place alone in the dark?" Margaret asked the two children.

"It wasn't dark when we left," Brandy said. "We wanted to go trick-or-treating."

"Where are your folks?"

"Dad's gone again," Brandy said. "Mom's sleeping like she always does."

Margaret knew that instead of "sleeping," Brandy's mother Carly was more likely passed out due to alcohol, drugs, or both.

"I'm Iron Man," Travis declared, lifting his mask to reveal a dirty face and a bruised cheek.

"What a scary costume you have," Margaret said. "You two wait here, while I get your treats." She left them on the porch and went into the kitchen.

"What are you doing?" Mims demanded.

"They're harmless children," Margaret answered. "Their parents, Del and Carly, are unemployed dope addicts who live in a trailer not fit for animals. The poor things probably haven't had a decent meal, or a bath, in days."

"Why did they come here?" Mims said.

"We're their closest neighbors," she said. "They come here every once in a while, usually when there's no food in the house or one of their parents are hitting them. Brandy is practically raising little Travis by herself. We've had to call the sheriff's office more than once because they showed up unfed or neglected."

"Things are tough all over," Mims said. "Get rid of them."

"I can't just get rid of them," Margaret said. "Whenever they've come here before, either me or Hector has driven them home in our truck. You can't expect us to send a pair of small children off to walk home alone in the dark?"

"I expect you to get rid of them, like I told you," Mims said. He jabbed Hector again in the ribs with the gun, causing him to wince in pain. "Unless you want me to get rid of your husband?"

"Let me drive them home?" Margaret pleaded. "I'll come right back, I promise. Brandy said her father's gone, and her mother's likely passed out on drugs. Your partner can come with us, if you want. No one will see the truck. I'll drop the kids off a ways from their house. I can be back in fifteen minutes."

"Not a chance," Mims said.

"I can drive *her* home," Skink suggested, failing to mention the boy, Travis. As he spoke, he craned his neck to more closely observe Brandy as she stood in the doorway in her makeshift costume.

Skink's face flushed, his eyes brightened, a vein had distended in his neck, and his stare fixated squarely on the little girl.

"Margaret can tell 'em I'm a friend of the family," he went on excitedly. "I'll get 'em home safe."

"No," Mims said flatly, "you won't."

"I was only lookin' out for the kids," Skink said.

"Sure you were," Mims grunted.

Margaret and Hector also stared, but not at Brandy Dixon. They gaped in revulsion at Skink, who leered hungrily at the young girl.

"I'll send them away," Margaret said, grabbing a handful of granola bars, two bags of cookies, a pair of water bottles, and a flashlight. She left the kitchen, returned to the door, and placed the items in their bags.

"Here's your treats," Margaret said. "You have to go home now."

"Can't you drive us?" Brandy asked.

"No," Margaret said. She took Brandy by the arm. "I can't. Not tonight. The truck . . . doesn't work. You'll have to run along home by yourselves. Use the flashlight, and you'll be all right."

"I'm tired," Travis said.

Margaret glanced over her shoulder to the kitchen. She saw her husband's apprehensive face, Mims's hard face, and Skink's aroused face.

"Listen to me, Brandy," Margaret said sternly. "Take your brother's hand and run home as fast as you can. Don't stop and don't come back. Not for anything. I mean it. Now go!"

Before the confused and frightened children could say anything, Margaret nudged them through the doorway and closed the door.

Almost immediately, the knocking resumed. Margaret looked anxiously back toward the kitchen and found Mims holding up his pistol and shaking his head.

Margaret opened the door again to find Brandy and Travis still on the porch. Travis was crying, and Brandy looked about to start. "Please give us a ride home," she begged.

"GET OUT OF HERE!" Margaret yelled at them. "Run! Get going! Don't come back, you hear?"

The terrified children ran off, sobbing, and disappeared down the gravel driveway into the night. Margaret watched them vanish into the darkness. After she lost sight of them, she put her face in her hands.

Mims, Skink, and Hector came out of kitchen. Hector rushed over and put his forehead against his wife's, since he was unable to put his arms around her.

After a moment she lowered her hands and closed and locked the door. She turned toward Mims and Skink.

"You're monsters," she said, wiping away tears on the back of her wrists. "The both of you. It's no wonder you were locked up."

"Can't argue with that," Mims said.

CHAPTER TWENTY-TWO

Mary knocked twice and the door opened. She stepped into the motel room and closed the door behind her.

"What the hell's been keeping you? I've been waiting here for hours."

"I couldn't get away," she said. "Marjorie was driving the kids back to Granite Bay to go trick-or-treating, but she pulled over along the side of the road in Farnham."

"What for?"

"I don't know," Mary said. "Looked like she was having a spat with Joel."

"Did they see you?"

"I don't think so."

"You want a beer?"

"Sure," Mary said.

Tad Guthrie walked over to the mini-fridge and pulled out two cans of beer from a twelve-pack inside. Seven empty cans were already on the table.

"I see you've had a productive afternoon," Mary said, accepting the beer and gesturing to the empties.

"You're the last person on the planet who should be giving me crap about drinking," Tad said, popping open his beer. "Besides, what the hell else am I supposed to do in this dirtwater town? It isn't like I can go out to a restaurant or bar. I'm stuck here in this shitbox motel room. If Marjorie or the kids spot me, I'm toast."

"Restraining orders have a way of doing that," Mary said, lighting a cigarette.

"So what progress have you made? Will she talk to me?"

"What do you think I am," Mary said, "a miracle worker? I just hooked up with Marjorie and my folks for the first time in over year last night. I've got to ease into this prodigal daughter gig slowly."

"I'm not paying you to move slowly," Tad said. "I'm paying for results. I'm on a clock, Mary. I've got to get her to drop those charges and soon. Dad's lawyer says the longer this thing goes on, the less likely he'll be able to convince the deputy district attorney to back off."

"What the hell do you expect me to do?" Mary said. "Walk up to her and say, 'Hi, Marjorie. We haven't spoken in more than a year, and the last time we did we were at each other's throats, but hey, would you mind dropping all the charges against your asshole husband for beating the shit out of you and forget about the divorce?' How do you think that would go over?"

"You told me you could get her to come around," Tad insisted.

"And I can," Mary said, "but it isn't going to happen overnight. I need a few days to soften her up and get back into her good graces. You'll have to be patient."

"Easy for you to say," he said. "You're not looking at between nine months and four years in a cell."

"Maybe you should have thought about that before you punched out your wife."

"It wasn't like that," he said into his beer.

"Then tell me what it was like?" Mary asked. "Because I saw her face with my own two eyes. She doesn't need a Halloween mask tonight. You fucked her up good, Tad. She may be a stuck-up bitch, but she's still my sister."

"I only hit her once," he said glumly.

"That makes it better how?" Mary said, putting out her mostly unsmoked cigarette in one of the empty beer cans. "You outweigh her by at least a hundred pounds."

"You make me sound like a total asshole."

"The shoe fits," Mary said. "We both know you don't really give a shit about patching things up with Marjorie. And you never cared about your kids. The divorce doesn't mean anything to you. Your daddy's gonna pay for it all, even the alimony and child support. This is all about keeping your sorry ass out of jail."

"I don't want to talk about it," he said.

"I'm sure you don't," Mary said, as she removed her T-shirt shirt and unfastened her bra. She let both drop to the floor. "So, what do you want to do?"

"What we've been doing since you were in high school," Tad said, unbuckling his belt and unzipping his trousers.

CHAPTER TWENTY-THREE

Marjorie brought the Range Rover to a halt next to her father's truck, turned off the engine, and rubbed her eyes. She was exhausted, and she was relieved to finally be back at her parents' home for the night. She noticed Mary's rented Lincoln was absent.

Both Jennifer, still in her Princess Ariel costume, and Joel, in the tattered shirt and zombie makeup he'd applied himself, were asleep.

Once they left the house in Granite Bay earlier that afternoon, Marjorie drove to Mark and Kristen Gould's house. Kristen gladly allowed Marjorie to store the items in her Range Rover inside their garage.

This included not only Marjorie's and the kid's important records and photographs but the photos and documents she and her mother preemptively packed up from her parents' home. She wanted the stuff out of the SUV so she'd have room for everyone in the event they all had to evacuate the rural farmhouse together in one vehicle. Her father's truck couldn't seat them all, and who knew if Mary and her fancy rental car would even be around to help if and when they had to flee the encroaching fire?

While her friend was certainly gracious to let her store the items, Marjorie was forced to endure a series of uncomfortable questions. Not to mention plenty of too-long stares associated with her battered appearance.

After an early dinner at In-N-Out, one of Joel's favorite places to eat, Marjorie helped Jennifer into her costume in the parking lot while her brother decorated his face with realistic-looking latex scars and splattered himself with fake blood. She thought Jennifer was going to be frightened by her brother's macabre getup, but discovered she was not only unafraid, but giggled when he proudly displayed his ghoulish handiwork for her approval.

"You look silly," Jennifer said.

"I'm supposed to look scary," Joel informed her. In response, she giggled even more.

Marjorie drove back to their old neighborhood, parked her car down the block from the house, and spent the next couple of hours escorting her children as they went door-to-door in search of candy.

She encountered a number of her former neighbors and exchanged awkward greetings with more than a few. Marjorie was grateful when daylight finally yielded to the hazy sky and smoke and helped conceal her face in the comforting blanket of darkness.

When the trick-or-treating finally waned, and the throngs of costumed children began to gradually return to their homes, a weary Marjorie herded her children to the car for the hour-long drive back to rural Farnham County. By the time she turned off the dirt road into the long, gravel, driveway of her parents' house, both of her kids were slumbering.

Jennifer didn't wake up as Marjorie unbuckled her

from the car seat and took the sleeping Disney princess into her arms. Joel, only half-awake himself, followed his mother up the porch steps. Jennifer made him leave their trick-or-treat bags, filled with Halloween goodies, in the car.

The door opened before Marjorie could knock. Her mother met her in the doorway wearing an expression she'd never seen before. Margaret Hernandez's normally genial eyes appeared frightened, sick, and worried all at the same time.

"Are you all right, Mom?" Marjorie asked, as she entered the house with Jennifer in her arms and Joel on her heels. "Is everything okay?"

"Everything's fine," a gruff voice whispered in her ear.

Marjorie whirled as the door closed behind her. Standing at her back was someone she hadn't noticed because he'd been concealed behind the opened door. He was a tall, husky man she didn't recognize. The man was staring at her, and wearing clothes she instantly recognized as belonging to Tad. He grabbed Joel in a headlock and placed a pistol to the boy's head. Joel's eyes widened.

"Be cool," Mims said to Marjorie, "and nobody has to get hurt."

"What do you want?" the terrified Marjorie asked.

"Right now," Mims said, "only for you to be quiet and sit down on that couch. Take your mother and children with you."

His eyes roved up and down Marjorie's body, lingering at her breasts and hips. "I'll let you know when I want something else."

Mims released Joel and pushed him away. Margaret guided her grandson into the living room and sat on the couch, as she was directed, with her arms protectively around him. Marjorie, still carrying Jennifer, joined them.

"I'm so sorry," Margaret said, looking at her daughter through tortured eyes. "There was no way to warn you. There's two of them in the house. They've had us here at gunpoint since you left."

Marjorie watched in horror as her father stepped into view from the kitchen. His hands were bound behind his back. Next to him was a skinny, shave-headed, tattooed man in his twenties with his right arm in a sling and poking a pistol into Hector's side. The thin man's face was shiny with sweat, and he looked pale and weak.

"Dad!" she exclaimed. Joel started to get up from the couch, but Margaret restrained him.

"Stay where you are," Hector said. "I'm all right."

"Everybody's going to be all right," Mims said, "as long as you do exactly as we say."

"Who are you?" Marjorie demanded.

"Who we are isn't important," Mims said. "All you need to know is that we're in charge."

"Yeah," Skink spoke up from across the room, "we're in charge. And don't you forget it."

"Stop pointing that gun at my grandpa," Joel said.

"What are you gonna do if I don't." Skink laughed. "Bite me and turn me into a zombie?"

"Take it easy, Joel," Hector said to his red-faced grandson. "I'm okay. Just stay back. I don't want you to get hurt."

"Better listen to your gramps," Skink said, grinning through his infected teeth. "I've seen a few zombie movies. I'd have to shoot you in the head, or else you'll rise up from the grave and eat me."

"You're pretty tough with that gun," Joel taunted. "I'll bet without it you're a total pussy."

Skink's corroded grin faded. He switched his aim from Hector to Joel.

Margaret and Marjorie both said "No!" at the same time.

"Put it down," Mims ordered Skink.

"I will when that kid stops givin' me lip," Skink said.

"Lower the weapon," Mims said.

"But he said . . ."

"I don't care what he said," Mims said. "He's a kid. Put down the gun. I'll tell you when and where to point it."

Skink's lower lip curled into a pout, but he lowered his pistol. He scowled at Joel. Joel returned the scowl and gave him the finger.

"What's your name?" Mims asked Marjorie.

Marjorie didn't answer.

"I know it's either Marjorie or Mary," Mims said. "Your mother already told us about you and your sister's visit. You might as well tell me which sister you are. I can always look at your driver's license."

"Marjorie."

"How'd your face get banged up, Marjorie?"

"That's none of your business."

"Do you or the kids have cell phones? A laptop?"

"The kids don't," Marjorie said. "They're too young. My iPhone and laptop are in my bag. Neither of them will do you any good out here."

"If you please," Mims said, taking Marjorie's purse and emptying the contents on the coffee table, "I'll make sure they don't."

Mims examined her personal effects and removed the

cell device, laptop computer, and vehicle remote. The Range Rover utilized push-button door locks and ignition and had no keys. Mims also picked up the prescription bottle containing her antibiotics and read the label.

"What're these for?" Mims asked.

"An infection," Marjorie said.

Mims tossed the bottle to Skink. "Take a couple of those," he said. "Then take everyone except Marjorie into the basement."

"Why do we have to go down there?" Hector demanded. "Why can't you let us stay upstairs in our rooms?"

"You might get out of your rooms," Mims answered.

"We won't," Hector said. "You have my word. It's dark and uncomfortable down there. At least let the children remain upstairs?"

"No dice," Mims said. He nodded to Skink, who'd given up trying to open the childproof lid of the prescription drug bottle one-handed.

"Okay," Skink said. He tossed the bottle on the table and opened the basement door. "Everybody downstairs," he ordered, waving his gun. He pointed it at Marjorie. "Except for you, foxy lady."

"Oh no, you don't," Marjorie said. "I'm not letting my children out of my sight."

"Suit yourself," Mims said. "If you want your kids to see what you and me are going to be doing up here on the couch, that's your business."

"You leave my mom alone!" Joel jumped up with his fists clenched.

"You can point your gun at the kid now," Mims said to Skink. Skink complied, moving his pistol from Marjorie to Joel. A venomous smile lit his face.

Joel boldly faced Skink. "I'm not afraid of you," he said.

"Good for you, zombie-boy," Skink said. "Makes it easier for me to pull the trigger."

"Please?" Marjorie begged Skink. "Don't shoot. He's just a child."

"Tell him to put down the gun," Hector said to Mims.

"Maybe I will," Mims shrugged, "and maybe I won't. That all depends on Marjorie."

"You filthy son of a bitch," Hector said.

"You have no idea," Mims said. "What's it going to be, Marjorie?"

Several long seconds passed before Marjorie answered. "Take Joel and Jennifer downstairs," she finally said to her mother.

"But Marj . . ." Margaret protested.

"Do it!" Marjorie snapped. Her raised voice finally awakened Jennifer. The girl lifted her head from her mother's shoulder and looked around the room, blinking. "What's going on, Mom?" she asked.

"Nothing," Marjorie said to Jennifer, handing her confused daughter over to Margaret. "Go downstairs with Grandma and Grandpa. You're going to stay in the basement with them for a while. You can go back to sleep."

"But Mom . . ." Joel protested.

"Do as I say," she told her son. "Look after your sister."

"Who're the men?" Jennifer asked, still partially asleep.

"They're nobody," Marjorie said. "Don't give them a thought. Good night." She kissed her daughter on the forehead. She kissed Joel, too.

Margaret carried Jennifer, took Joel's arm, and they

headed through the kitchen to the basement stairs. Skink kept the gun on them as they filed past.

"I'll need a lantern," Margaret said, "and some candles and flashlights. The lights are out, remember? I'd also like to take the radio."

"You can take a lantern and flashlight," Mims said, "but forget the candles and radio." Margaret picked up a battery-powered lantern, and Joel a flashlight.

"If you touch so much as a hair on my daughter's head," Hector warned Mims.

Mims waited until Margaret, Jennifer, and Joel disappeared down the basement stairs. Then he switched his pistol to his left hand and punched Hector in the mouth. Hector's head snapped back and he slid down the wall, unable to use his hands to break his fall since they were taped behind his back. He groaned but remained conscious.

"Dad!" Marjorie exclaimed. She rushed over to him.

"I'm getting tired of reminding people who's in charge," Mims said.

With Marjorie's help, Hector wriggled himself to his feet. Blood trickled from his mouth. He faced Mims.

"You hit like a girl," he said, looking Mims in the eye. "I'll be damned if I'm leaving my daughter alone with you."

Mims drew back his fist for another blow. "Stop it!" Marjorie said, stepping between them. "Leave him alone."

"What's it going to be, Marjorie?" Mims asked.

"Hey," Skink cackled, "that sorta rhymes."

"Shut up," Mims told him.

"Go downstairs and watch over Mom and the kids," Marjorie said to her father. Tears ebbed from the corner of each bruised eye, but her face remained otherwise impassive. "I'll be all right."

"Take the old man downstairs," Mims ordered Skink. "Once he's there, you can cut his hands loose. There's no way out of the cellar. I already checked."

"What if he tries to jump me?" Skink asked. "Can I shoot him?"

"He won't try anything," Mims assured Skink. "He knows what'll happen to his daughter if he does."

Skink followed Hector down the basement steps, taking a kitchen knife with him. Hector looked back at his daughter as Skink prodded him along. There were tears in the corners of his eyes.

Skink came back up a minute later, winded and sweating from mounting the steps.

"They're all down in the cellar," Skink panted. He tossed the kitchen knife on the table. "Just like you wanted."

Mims closed the basement door and threw the dead bolt, locking it. "Go upstairs and get some sleep," he said to Skink.

"How come you get to go first?" Skink complained, as he leered at Marjorie.

"You'll get your turn," Mims said. "Do as I say for now. You need to lay down before you fall down."

"I want to lay down," Skink said, pointing his gun at Marjorie, "with her."

"Go upstairs," Mims said. "Do as I say."

For a moment it looked as if Skink was going to refuse. But then he lowered his eyes and gun and headed for the stairs.

"Whatever you say, Duane," Skink said sarcastically. "I'll be a good boy and take a nap upstairs while you stay down here and have fun with the pretty lady." He slowly disappeared up the stairwell.

"Are you going to rape me now?" Marjorie asked, once she and Mims were alone. She looked at him in defiance and revulsion. "Is that the plan?"

"Something like that," Mims said.

"You're an animal."

"Your mother called me a monster," Mims said. "Maybe you're both right." He leveled his pistol at her chest. "Get undressed."

"There's something you might want to know before you touch me," Marjorie said. "That bottle of antibiotics in my purse? It's for a sexually transmitted infection."

"Claiming to have a venereal disease," Mims said, clicking his teeth. "Nice try. Did you learn that old trick at a college rape-prevention seminar? I'll bet the prescription's really for bronchitis."

"I'm not lying," Marjorie said. "I have chlamydia."

Mims silently appraised her for a long minute. "I believe you," he finally said, a nasty smile spreading across his face. "You were sleeping around on your husband, weren't you? Caught a bedbug and infected him, right? Is that why he rearranged your face?"

"It's the other way around," Marjorie said.

"It doesn't matter," Mims said. His smile vanished, and a darkness fell over his features. "There're things short of rape. Things you can do to me. Things I'll bet you're good at." He raised the pistol to her face. "Take your clothes off."

"Maybe I'd rather be shot."

"What makes you think I'd shoot you?" Mims said. "Maybe I'll make you decide which of your kids to shoot."

Marjorie's shoulders slumped. She hung her head, nodding to herself in defeat. She slowly began to unbutton her blouse. Tears that had begun slowly now fell steadily. Her face remained stoic, however, as she unfastened the buttons. The top of her shirt draped open.

"I don't know what you're blubbering about," Mims taunted. "I'll bet you didn't have any trouble getting undressed for the guy who beat you up. I promise I won't do any worse to you than he did."

Marjorie stopped unbuttoning and looked up. "What do you know about it?"

"I know domestic violence when I see it," Mims said. "I've seen it plenty. The man who did that to your face is the father of those two kids, isn't he?"

"Go to hell," she said.

"That's certain," Mims said. "Hurry up and get those clothes off." Marjorie reluctantly resumed unbuttoning.

By the time she undid the final button, Mims had undergone a transformation. His mouth had opened slightly, his breathing had become heavier, and he stared at her transfixed. His eyes locked on her breasts and the flat plane of her belly. He seemed almost hypnotized.

"Take your shirt off," he said, his voice reduced to a hoarse whisper.

She slipped off her blouse, revealing her full breasts, the bra that contained them, and the taut abdomen beneath it. Mims stepped closer. This was the nearest he'd been to a woman undressing in almost ten years, and he couldn't remember when he'd been close to one as beautiful.

"Let down your hair," he whispered.

Marjorie released the band that contained her ponytail. Her dark shoulder-length hair plummeted.

She momentarily contemplated fighting him for the gun but abandoned the thought as quickly as it arose. Mims was a full head taller than her and weighed close to what her husband weighed, which was over one hundred pounds more than she did. But he didn't seem soft like Tad was.

There was something else about the manner with which he carried himself, and gave orders, and the way he held his gun compared to the other man, that made her abandon the idea of trying to physically challenge him. He'd been formally trained, she was sure of it. Either in the military, the police, as a security guard, or in the martial arts. She instinctively knew if she tried to resist, he would easily overpower her. Perhaps he might grow angry and take out his anger by hurting the children or her parents?

Marjorie knew if she was to survive and protect her family, her only course of action was to endure this man's foul desires.

She continued to stare insolently at Mims and tried to prepare herself for what was about to transpire. She steeled herself, determined to suffer through whatever she had to in order to safeguard her loved ones.

With his left hand, Mims placed his pistol in his belt. With his right he reached out for her. To her surprise he didn't touch her breasts or even her bare skin. He touched her hair.

He moved to stand behind her. He was very close, and she felt his breath on her ear and the back of her naked neck. He was wearing her father's aftershave, and a lifetime of pleasant childhood memories triggered by that agreeable scent were instantly soiled.

Marjorie stood motionless as Mims gently took a

handful of her hair in his fist. First, he fondled it, then he brought it to his nose and inhaled it, and finally, to her disgust, he put it into his mouth.

She closed her eyes, trembling in revulsion. His breathing became more rapid, and he made moaning sounds as he tasted her hair.

"Kneel down," he said as he spat out her hair.

Marjorie opened her eyes and slowly complied. Once she knelt, the Glock pistol in his belt was directly in front of her face. She looked up and saw Mims smirking down at her, daring her to try and take it.

After a moment he took out the gun and held it down at his side. "Unbuckle my belt," he said, "and take it out. You know what to do with it." He put the gun against the side of her head. "If I feel teeth, you feel a bullet."

Marjorie angrily wiped her tears away and reached for Mims's belt with both hands. She began to unlatch the buckles.

The crunch of tires on gravel sounded outside. The glare of headlights reflected through the front window.

Mims stepped away from Marjorie and went to the window. She stood up. He parted the blinds with his pistol and peered out.

"That'll be your sister," Mims said. "Don't just stand there," he ordered. "Get your shirt on and open the door."

CHAPTER TWENTY-FOUR

Mary Hernandez tossed her cigarette and mounted the porch steps. She knew it was late enough that her parents, sister, niece, and nephew were probably already in bed. As if to confirm her assertion, she looked up and found no lights flickering in the upstairs windows. Downstairs, she detected a faint glow filtering through the blinds. She guessed somebody must be up since there were at least a few candles lit or one of the battery-powered lanterns was still switched on.

Mary wasn't tired, though she realized she should be exhausted. Despite spending most of the afternoon and evening in bed, she got little sleep. She did, however, consume two beers, a half-pack of cigarettes, a significant amount of marijuana, and another line of methamphetamine. Tad Guthrie partook of everything along with her but the cigarettes.

Mary knew her father had cold beer in the refrigerator. She figured on helping herself to a couple in the hope of taking the edge off her accelerated metabolic state. She doubted her parents or the kids would recognize that she was under the influence of booze, pot, and speed, but figured Marjorie might suspect if her nosy sister was still up and around.

She found the front door unlocked, which surprised her. She remembered her father almost always kept the door secured. She recalled how she'd arrived after the drive from Sacramento the night before needing to urinate badly and had to pound on the locked door to get inside to the bathroom.

When she opened the unlocked door and entered, she was further surprised to find Marjorie standing alone in the hallway to greet her. The buttons on her shirt were strangely misaligned, and there was an odd look on her bruised face. Her expression seemed to be a combination of dread, guilt, and fear. It also looked as if she'd been crying.

"You didn't have to wait up," Mary said, grateful the light was dim. The only illumination in the house was from a candle in the kitchen and a battery-powered lantern on the coffee table in the living room. She didn't want her dilated pupils to give her illicit drug use away. "I stopped obeying curfews in high school."

"I'm sorry, Mary," Marjorie said, understanding all too well how her mother must have felt when she and her children arrived earlier.

"What have you got to be sorry about?" Mary asked, confused.

"Me," Mims said, stepping from behind the front door for the second time that evening. He poked Mary in the kidney with the Glock.

"What the fuck?" Mary exclaimed.

Mims closed the door, locked it, and forced Mary and Marjorie into the main room at gunpoint.

"What the hell is going on?" Mary asked her sister. "Who is this asshole?"

"There's another one upstairs," Marjorie said. "Mom, Dad, and the kids are down in the basement."

"In the basement?" Mary said. "Who are these guys? What do they want?"

"You'll have to ask them yourself."

Mims took Mary's handbag from her and motioned for the two women to sit on the couch. Once they complied, he emptied the contents of her purse onto the coffee table along with Marjorie's. Among her cigarettes, cell phone, and keys was the thick roll of cash given to her by Tad Guthrie.

"That's my property," Mary protested, as Mims pocketed the cash, keys, and phone.

"Not anymore," Mims said.

"Whaddya know?" Skink's voice said from across the room. "Another foxy lady come to join the festivities. By the looks of her, this one likes to party."

While Mims was sifting through the contents of Mary's purse, Skink had emerged unnoticed from upstairs. He'd come down to investigate the sound of voices. He hadn't slept at all, due to the increasing pain in his neck and shoulder and the advance of his fever and chills. His legs were unsteady and his face pallid, and he was forced to lean against the wall as he ogled the two women.

"You'd better sit down," Mims said to him, "before you fall down."

"I ain't gonna fall down," Skink said. He went into the kitchen on rubbery legs, opened the refrigerator, and collected a beer.

"You all right?" Mims asked him.

"To be honest," Skink said, as he opened the beer, came into the living room, and plopped himself heavily on the couch opposite Marjorie and Mary, "I've felt better." His sentence ended in a coughing fit.

"You want some more painkillers?"

"Nope," Skink said, holding his beer aloft. "Got all the painkiller I need right here."

"Help yourself," Mary said mockingly, "why don't you?"

"Don't mind if I do," Skink said as he stared at her. "Might just help myself to somethin' else, while I'm at it."

"In your dreams," Mary said.

"Hey," Skink said, noticing Mary's personal effects scattered on the tabletop. "Smokes."

He put his pistol in his waistband, reached out a shaky left hand, and picked up the pack of Marlboros and a butane lighter. "You know how long it's been since I had a cigarette?"

"Like I give a shit," Mary said.

Skink flipped open the cigarette box's top to shake out a smoke. "Hello," he said, withdrawing the small glass jar secreted inside. "What have we got here?"

He unscrewed the cap with his rotting teeth and brought the jar to his nose. His sickly face instantly broke into a grin. "Looks like Christmas came early," he said. He directed his tarnished smile at Mary. "I knew you were my kind of gal the second I laid eyes on you."

"Fuck you," Mary said to him.

"That's definitely on the agenda," Skink said. He poured a quantity of the brown, paste-like powder onto the back of his slung right hand, raised it to his nostrils, and inhaled deeply.

He closed his eyes, twitched once, and let out a huge breath. Instantly perking up, he wiped his nose and held out the jar of methamphetamine to Mims. "Help yourself," he said. "It's quality shit."

"Not my cup of tea," Mims said.

"Suit yourself," Skink said. "Just means there's more for me." He turned to Mary. "I'd offer you some, honey, but it looks like you've already partaken." He capped the jar, pocketed it, and lit a cigarette.

"My folks don't allow smoking inside the house," Marjorie said to Skink.

"You hear that?" he said to Mims. "They don't allow smoking in the house." He giggled as the crank sped its way through his respiratory system to his brain, kicking his metabolic state into overdrive. "I guess that makes me a bad boy, doesn't it?"

"What's wrong with him?" Mary said.

"Busted collarbone," Mims said. "I think it's getting infected and causing a fever. That little pick-me-up he just found in your purse isn't going to help."

"Can't hurt," Skink said with a grin.

"Jesus," Marjorie said as she turned to Mary. "I can't believe you brought that shit into our parents' house."

"I'd say that's the least of our worries right now," Mary said.

As disappointed as she was with her sister bringing methamphetamine into their family home, Marjorie was silently grateful Mary arrived when she did. Had she not, Mims would undoubtedly be in the process of sexually assaulting her at this very moment.

"Actually," Skink declared to no one in particular, "I'm starting to feel pretty good."

He looked anything but. His face was sunken and his eyes were hollow, although they now featured extremely dilated pupils, and he was sweating profusely.

"Nothin' like a cold beer," Skink announced. He chugged the entire bottle in one long gulp. When he finished, he belched and tossed the empty bottle to the floor.

Mims, Mary noticed, didn't look much better. She couldn't know that he'd had less than four hours' sleep in the last thirty-six hours. All she knew was that he had flat, hard, emotionless eyes and was clearly the member of the gun-wielding duo who was calling the shots.

"Hey," Skink said to Mary, "why don't you be a Sweet Home Alabama, go into that kitchen, and grab me another cold one? And while you're at it, why don't you bring one for everybody? It's a party, ain't it?"

"Why don't you get it yourself, asshole?"

"Easy," Marjorie said to Mary. "Just do what he says."

"Better listen to your sister," Skink said. He drew his pistol again.

"If you think I'm afraid of your bony tweaker ass," Mary said to Skink, "you're mistaken. Gun or not, you're nothing but a punk-ass bitch." She pointed her chin at Mims. "Just like your boyfriend over there."

Skink's smile vanished. "You need to watch your mouth," he said.

"And you need to go piss up a rope," Mary retorted.

"Don't provoke them," Marjorie said.

"I'm not afraid of getting shot," Mary said. "Not by these gutless creeps."

"It isn't you they'll shoot," Marjorie insisted. "You don't know what happened before you got here. What they threatened to do."

Mary looked from her sister to Mims, who stood impassively observing the exchange, and back to Skink. "You threatened our parents? A harmless old couple?"

"No," Marjorie answered. "Joel and Jennifer."

Comprehension struck Mary like a thunderbolt. "That's why you were up here alone," she said, "and everybody else is downstairs locked in the basement? They were both gonna do you, weren't they? They told you they'd shoot the kids if you didn't let them have their way? Is that it?"

"Him," Marjorie said, pointing to Mims. "He was going first. The other one was going to go second."

"Sloppy seconds," Skink griped. "That's what I was gonna get."

"A couple of real tough guys," Mary said.

"You'd best figure out what your family already learned," Mims said. "We're in charge. Which means we do what we want around here."

"Yeah," Skink echoed, "we do what we want around here." He sucked in a long drag from his cigarette for emphasis. "We're in charge."

"I guess that means I'll have to fetch you that beer, won't I?" Mary said.

"Now you're startin' to get the picture," Skink said, exhaling smoke.

Mary got up from the couch and entered the kitchen. When she opened the refrigerator and reached inside for two bottles of beer, the appliance's door momentarily blocked her from view. She snatched a paring knife from the butcher's block on the counter and slipped it into her hip pocket. Then she put a beer in each hand and closed the door with her foot.

When the refrigerator door closed, Mary was startled to find Mims standing next to her. Unfortunately for her, the door also blocked her view of him approaching. His pistol was pointed at her head.

"Did you know," Mims said, "that in a typical household the kitchen is the room containing the most deadly weapons?"

She didn't answer. Mims extended his arm and placed the muzzle of the Glock against her forehead. "Put down the bottles, slowly, and place that knife on the counter."

Mary did as she was told. "Get back to your sister," Mims ordered. Mary hastily returned to the couch with Marjorie.

"That was a stupid thing to do," Marjorie said. "Are you trying to get us killed?"

"Leave me alone," Mary said,

"Cover them," Mims told Skink, as he unlocked the basement door.

"What about the beers?" Skink said.

"Forget the beers and do what I say," Mims said irritably. He opened the basement door. "Send up the old lady," he called down into the darkness.

"What for?" came Hector's voice.

"Send her up," Mims shouted, the first signs of anger creeping into his tone, "or I'll come down and get one of the children instead."

A moment later Margaret arose from the stairs. Mims closed the door, locked the dead bolt, grabbed her roughly by the hair, and dragged her out to the living room. She cried out in pain as both Marjorie and Mary instinctively started to rise from the sofa to go to her.

"Sit down!" Skink ordered, waving his gun. "Put your butts back on that couch or I'll shoot."

Marjorie and Mary sat down and watched helplessly as Mims forced their mother to her knees, released her, and stepped back. He aimed his pistol at her head, execution-style.

"No!" Marjorie shrieked, as she again tried to rise to her feet. Mary struggled to restrain her. Skink assumed a two-handed hold on his gun. He aimed directly at Marjorie, thrashing to escape her sister's arms.

"You'd better keep your sister on a leash," Skink said around his cigarette, "unless you want her to catch a bullet."

"If you know any prayers," Mims said to Margaret, "now's the time."

Margaret crossed herself, closed her eyes, and softly began to recite the Hail Mary.

"No!" Marjorie shouted again.

"Do you know why you're going to die?" Mims asked Margaret. She ignored the question and continued to pray. "Because you raised disobedient daughters, that's why."

"No!" Marjorie shouted a third time, as Mary struggled to keep her from rushing to their mother. "Leave her alone! We'll do whatever you say! Please?"

"What's it going to be?" Mims asked Mary. "Are you both going to get with the program, or do I open up your mother's noggin?"

"You're in charge," Mary said, as Marjorie stopped

struggling and both women looked up at Mims. "We get it. We'll do whatever you say." Marjorie silently nodded through her tears.

Mims lowered his gun. "Get back downstairs," he told Margaret. He strode into the kitchen, unlocked the cellar door, and held it open.

She could barely stand, but Margaret struggled to her feet and staggered into the kitchen. When she looked back at her daughters, as she descended the stairwell, her eyes were distant and unfocused. Mims closed the door and relocked it behind her.

He collected the beers and returned to the living room. Skink was still covering the women with his handgun.

Mims opened one of the beers and placed it on the table before Skink. Then he opened the bottle containing the antibiotic prescription and placed a pair of tablets on the counter next to the beer. Skink returned his gun to his belt, removed the cigarette from his mouth, and reached for the pills and beer.

Mims placed his pistol in his waistband and opened the other beer. He took a swig and met the sisters' defeated gazes.

"What just happened to your mother," Mims said, "is as nice as I get. If there are any more doubts about who's running the show, or any more tricks like that stunt in the kitchen with the blade, I'll end somebody's life. That's a promise. Only next time, it won't be the old lady. So help me, I'll put a bullet to the little girl."

"Don't worry," Mary said, as her older sister hung her head. "We'll play nice."

"I know you will," Mims said.

Across the room, Skink's corroded grin reappeared. He swallowed the pills, washed them down with a swallow of beer, and continued to leer at the women. "We're gonna have us a real good time tonight, aren't we, Duane?"

Mims took another swig before answering.

"A real good time," he echoed. "I believe we've earned it."

CHAPTER TWENTY-FIVE

The basement was dark, even with the lantern. On a cot against one wall, under a wool blanket, slept Jennifer. Joel refused to sleep. Like his grandparents, he was worried and frightened for his mother and aunt. They were alone upstairs with the two gunmen.

The basement door opened and Hector, Margaret, and Joel looked up to find Marjorie coming down the basement steps alone. She supported herself on the railing as she descended, as if her legs might possibly fail her. She was trembling, and her bruised face was pale and tear-streaked.

Hector gently released Margaret, whom he and Joel had been comforting since she'd returned to the basement in a nearly catatonic state. Having to impotently watch her walk up the stairs by herself, when called up by Mims, was the most dreadful, heart-rending thing he'd ever witnessed. At that terrible moment, he was unsure if he would ever see his wife alive again.

He waited, expecting to hear a gunshot and trying to keep up a stoic face for Joel's benefit. When the basement door opened again after what seemed like hours, but was only minutes, and a shell-shocked Margaret came down the stairs, Hector was flooded with relief.

Once seated, Margaret broke down. "Mary's home," was all she could say between sobs. "They've got both our girls."

Hector and Joel held Margaret until she eventually calmed. He gave her aspirin from a first-aid kit stored in the basement and made her drink a bottle of water.

Less than an hour later, the basement door again opened. That's when Hector met his eldest daughter halfway down the stairs. He and Joel escorted her to a seat at the folding table next to Margaret, where she hugged her son.

"Are you hurt?" Hector asked.

Marjorie shook her head. "No," she said. "I'm all right, thanks to Mary. At least for now."

"What do you mean, 'thanks to Mary'?"

"She made a deal with them," Marjorie said. "She agreed to . . . to let them . . ." Her voice trailed off. "But only if they'd leave me alone. That's why they let me go."

"Oh my God," Margaret said, putting her face in her hands. "My poor Mary."

"She said she'd let them do whatever they wanted," Marjorie continued, "if they promised not to harm any of us."

Hector sat heavily down. He clenched his fists as he stared off into the darkness.

"Are the men hurting Aunt Mary?" Joel asked.

"Yes," Marjorie said, her voice a whisper. She held her son tighter.

Several minutes passed with only the sound of Margaret's subdued crying to break the silence. Finally, Hector stood up.

"Come with me, Joel," he said to his grandson. "I need you to give me a hand. We've got work to do."

CHAPTER TWENTY-SIX

After a fitful, mostly sleepless night in an endless string of mostly sleepless nights, Strayer rose earlier than usual. A light sleeper since the summer she enlisted, she was plagued by bouts of insomnia. One of the many reasons she habitually worked out was to ensure her body was tired enough at the end of each day to facilitate at least a little slumber each night.

Unfortunately, she couldn't exhaust her mind through physical exercise. The dreams, visions, and nightmares she routinely experienced during what slumber she got always seemed to find a way to rouse her from truly restful sleep.

Strayer donned her workout attire and shouldered her bag. She cracked the door and scanned the vicinity of her apartment complex before venturing out. Lieutenant McDillon's admonition about potential reprisal by the Mexican Mafia, coupled with her half brother's cryptic warning, "They know where you live," were still fresh in her mind.

Strayer kept her car keys in her left hand, her .45 in her right, and her head on a swivel as she walked from her apartment to her parked car. It was still at least an hour before dawn, and the smoke-filled air was already stuffy and thick. It irritated her nose and throat and stung her eyes and lungs.

There was a film of ash on her car, like everything else in Farnham County. As she fired up the engine, Strayer wondered how much more territory the fire had consumed since last night, and more important, how close it was getting to the town of Farnham.

Strayer turned on her car radio, hoping for an update on the fire during the short ride to the station. But all she got before she guided her car into the departmental parking lot was a string of commercials.

Strayer went directly to the gym. There were a number of other deputies in the facility getting in a pre-shift workout. Most were from the Custody Division, some from the Patrol Division, and except for her, none from Investigations. There were also a few current S.W.A.T. deputies and at least two former S.W.A.T. deputies, like her. One of them was Colby, who nodded a greeting.

Strayer stretched and began warming up with sets of burpees. A number of deputies surreptitiously checked her out. She sensed it, as always, but ignored them.

She knew she was considered attractive. Her muscular and curvaceous physique, the result of tae kwon do training and regular strength and cardio workouts, did little to dispel the perception.

Today was supposed to be a run day for her, but the toxic air quality prevented Strayer from exercising outdoors. Across the room at the power rack was Meyers. He wore baggy shorts, fingerless gloves, and a cutaway wifebeater, which offered a view of the steroid-induced acne that flourished on the landscape of his broad, thick, and hairy back and neck. He had earbuds in both ears and was bobbing his head in time to music thankfully inaudible to everyone else in the gym. Between his sets of squats, he played air guitar. When he noticed Strayer enter, he removed the buds and sauntered over.

Colby was jogging on a treadmill. "How's Investigations treating you?" he asked her.

"No complaints," Strayer answered, "yet. Only been there a day. Too early to complain. How's Patrol going?"

"Same as it ever was," he said. "Refereeing domestics, shagging false alarm calls, and scratching out traffic tickets and cold reports. My wife's glad I got assigned to day shift, but I'm not. Too many regular folks out and about in the daytime. Give me crooks over law-abiding citizens any day. They're easier to deal with."

"Any word on what the team's doing?" Strayer asked.

"They've got all the S.W.A.T. deputies out in the fire zone," he said, "just like we thought. The firefighters have requested their help in case they run into looters."

"Sure wish we were with them," Strayer said.

"Spilled milk." Colby shrugged. "I heard you made a nice collar on your first day on the third floor. Some guy who burned his three-year-old niece."

"He was a righteous creep," Strayer acknowledged. She jumped up to a horizontal bar and began doing behind-the-neck pull-ups.

"I heard you beat the shit out of him," Meyers interjected. "Buddy of mine working intake said when the guy was booked into the jail, he looked like he'd been hit by a truck."

"Was somebody talking to you?" Colby said. Strayer ignored Meyers and continued her pullups.

"Gotta love Deputy Deadeye Strayer," Meyers chuckled, disregarding Colby's query. "Her last day on S.W.A.T. she kills a guy, and on her first day in Dicks she puts one in the emergency room. She's like the female version of Dirty Harry."

He laughed at his own joke, and looked around the gym for approval. "That's what I'm gonna call you from now on, Strayer. Dirty Harriet."

"Why don't you do me a favor," Strayer said between pull-ups, "and don't talk to me at all?"

"Do me the same favor," Colby said.

"Why don't you fuck off?" Meyers said to Colby.

"Snappy comeback," Colby said. "You have a rapier wit."

"Rape what?" Meyers said. Colby rolled his eyes.

Strayer finished her fifteenth pullup, lowered herself to the ground and immediately began doing push-ups. Meyers moved to stand over her.

"Guess what else I heard?" he said, loud enough to ensure everyone else in the gym could hear. "I heard the local Mexican gangs put out a hit on Dirty Harriet, here. Put out a hit on all of us, actually. Word's coming into the Gang Unit they want to take out a Farnham deputy to even the score for Machado."

"You afraid, Meyers?" Colby said. "Worried a teenaged gangbanger with a twenty-five-caliber Lorcin is going to punch your ticket?"

"I ain't afraid of no Mexican gangsters," Meyers scoffed. "Bring 'em on, I say. Actually, I wanted to thank Deadeye for stirring them up. Gives the rest of us a chance to catch up to the number of notches on her gun."

"That's enough," Strayer said, springing to her feet. "I come here to work out, not get harassed by a brain-dead juice-monkey."

Everyone else in the gym stopped what they were doing. Colby stepped off the treadmill. Strayer put her hands on her hips and stepped in close to Meyers. She looked up at him with her blue eyes flashing. All other eyes in the gym were on her.

"I don't know why you get off on riding me," she said to Meyers, "and I don't care. But it's going to end. Starting now."

"What's the matter?" Meyers said. "Afraid of a little kidding?"

"What you do to me isn't kidding," Strayer said. "There's another name for it, and I'm not going to take it anymore. I'm warning you to leave me alone."

"Or what?"

"Give it a rest, Meyers," Colby said. "Just do like she says and leave her alone."

"Yeah," another S.W.A.T. deputy spoke up. "Leave her alone, man. You want to get brought up on harassment charges?"

"Shut up," Meyers said to no one in particular. "This is between me and her."

"What is?" Strayer said. "You act like we have a relationship. I don't like you, Meyers. You're an asshat. I don't want to talk to you, and I don't want you near me. Why can't you understand that? Have the steroids shrunk your brain along with your balls?"

"Watch your fucking mouth," Meyers said, his face turning red. He loomed over her, at least eight inches taller than her own five-foot-eight height.

"Or what?" Strayer said, feeding him back his own words. She took a step back, assumed a wider stance, clenched her right fist, and made a blade of her left.

"Are you picking a fight with me?" Meyers said incredulously.

"You picked the fight," Strayer shot back, "when I came into the room."

"You're kidding?" Meyers said. "I'd crush you."

"Then step into the ring and do it," Strayer said. "What's the matter? Afraid of a little girl?"

"Let's take this down a notch," Colby said, "both of you. This is getting out of hand."

"He's always been out of hand," Strayer said, her voice rising, "and everybody knows it. It isn't just the roids, either. Will somebody please tell me why I have to take his shit? Because he's a member of the boys' club, and I'm not? Is that the reason?"

Most of the deputies in the room suddenly found things on the ceiling, or at their feet, to notice.

"Meyers's just an asshole," one of the other S.W.A.T. deputies finally spoke up. "He's always been like that. He fucks with everybody. Don't take it personally."

"Don't let him get under your skin," another deputy added.

"Don't worry," Strayer said, "I won't. Not anymore."

She turned her attention back to Meyers. "One way or another, you're never putting your mouth on me again. The next time you talk shit to me, I'll beat you like a rented mule."

"In your dreams," Meyers said. "You're lucky I'm a . . ."

"Bully?" Strayer cut him off. "A coward? Because that's

what you are. You start a fight with somebody half your size but won't finish it."

"We both know what would happen if I took you on," Meyers said.

"Sure, we do," Strayer said. "I'd kick your teeth in like that punk I arrested yesterday."

"More like I'd put your ass in the hospital," Meyers said hotly. "If you think I won't fuck you up because you're a chick, think again."

More than a couple of the other deputies in the gym cringed when Meyers used the word "chick." Several walked out.

"What I think," Strayer said, "is you're a big, stupid, dope-using, misogynistic douchebag who likes to push women around because deep inside you know you're really a weapons-grade pussy."

"Keep it up, Deadeye," Meyers said through tight lips. "See what happens."

Meyers was losing his temper and everyone could see it. His plan to tease and humiliate Strayer had backfired, and he was now being teased and facing humiliation himself. The flush on his face had spread to his body, and the veins on his arms, legs, and neck were distended like writhing snakes.

"Don't let my gender stop you," Strayer said. She appeared to be losing her temper as well.

"You'll be singing a different tune after I mess you up," Meyers said.

"Big talk," Strayer said, "from a little bitch."

"That's enough," Colby said to both of them. "Everybody calm down. Neither of you need this. Do you want the duty sergeant down here? How about I.A.?"

"Ask him," Strayer jutted her chin at Meyers. "And while you're at it, ask him what illegal drugs he's got on board? Dianabol? Ox? Deca? GH? Test? Maybe a little meth to pep up the morning workout? I don't mind I.A. coming down to the gym. Bring 'em on, I say. There isn't any dope in my system or any needles in my locker. I'll take a piss test, and let them search my locker, right now. How about you, Meyers? You willing to take a drug test?"

The fire in Meyers's eyes quickly faded. He took a step back and glanced nervously around the room with a weak grin on his red, perspiring, face.

"Can you believe her?" he asked. Every other deputy in the room turned away and resumed their workouts. "Who does she think she is?"

"Somebody you shouldn't have fucked with," Strayer said. "Start swinging or start walking."

"Get out of here," Colby said to Meyers. "Before this goes to a place you don't want it to."

"Like I need this bullshit," Meyers said, in a vain attempt to retrieve his dignity. He turned away from Strayer, picked up his gym bag, and started for the door.

"Hey, Meyers," Strayer called out as he opened the door. He stopped in the doorway but didn't turn around.

"If you ever say another word to me that isn't work-related," she said, "it's on."

"I'm real scared," Meyers grunted but walked out.

Strayer finished her workout in silence. When she left the gym after a session on the heavy bag and thirty minutes on a treadmill and headed for the locker room, Colby was waiting for her in the hallway.

"What the hell was that all about?" he asked her. "Are you trying to get suspended and lose your star?"

"I guess I wasn't up for Meyers's usual bullshit today," she said as they walked together down the hallway.

"I'm not buying it," Colby said. "Meyers is always an asshole. I've seen you endure his alpha male gorilla chest-beating routine a dozen times before. But I've never seen you almost lose it like you did just now. Are you okay?"

"It's been a rough couple of days," Strayer admitted, "on top of some rough weeks, months, and years. I can't explain why he triggered me today. Maybe I'm just wearing down. Hell," she sighed, "I don't know."

"Forget it," he said. "It was kind of fun watching him squirm."

"I don't want to make him squirm," Strayer said. "I don't want anything to do with him. I just want to be left alone."

"Hang in there," Colby said, giving her a reassuring pat on the shoulder. "We've been squad mates for three years, and I've seen you face a helluva lot more than Meyers's crap. You're just going through a rough patch, that's all. You'll be all right. One step at a time, one day at a time, right?"

"Right," she said with a weak smile. "A rough patch ten years long."

"Have you got somebody to talk to?" Colby asked. "Sounds like maybe now might be a good time for you to check in with someone who has your best interests at heart? Get some perspective, you know? Everybody needs a little help now and then." He released a grin. "Even a badass like you."

Strayer knew Colby, who was several years older than she was, to be a solid deputy, a proficient tactical officer, and a happily married family man. Though they weren't good friends, he'd never made a pass at her, which was something she couldn't say about most other deputies, whether married or not. She also knew he was referring to professional counseling.

Most deputies eschewed counseling and refused to participate in it unless mandatory, like the post-shooting psychological evaluation, despite the fact that such services were provided at no cost to all sworn personnel. Law enforcement officers in general feared the stigma attached to availing themselves of mental health services, often choosing instead to suffer in silence or numb themselves with alcoholic beverages, drugs, sexual promiscuity, or other risky, self-destructive behaviors. Strayer knew that when it came to counseling, she was no different.

"I've been to counseling before," Colby said, "and I'm not ashamed to admit it. I'm also not afraid to say it helped. Not just in my career, but in my marriage and with my overall health. Why don't you give it a try?"

"I don't know," she mumbled.

"What have you got to lose?"

"Come to think of it," she said, "there is someone I could probably talk to. Maybe I'll think about giving her a call."

"What can it hurt?" Colby said. "Who knows? It might even make you feel better?"

"I'll mull it over," she said. "No promises."

"Not asking for one. I sure would've enjoyed seeing you kick the shit out of Meyers."

"What makes you think he wouldn't have kicked the shit out of me?"

"Not a chance," Colby said. "You'd have buried him. Especially since if it looked like you were getting into trouble I'd have snuck up behind his big dumb ass and clobbered him in the back of the head with a dumbbell."

"Is it possible to clobber a dumbbell with a dumbbell?" she asked. He laughed.

"Thanks for the pep talk, coach," she said as they parted.

After she showered, but before she fully dressed, Strayer dug through her locker. She came out with the soft body armor she'd worn when she was working in the Patrol Division.

Designed to be worn concealed under a duty uniform, the ballistic vest was tailored to her body and rated IIIA by the National Institute of Justice. It was light, flexible, comprised of woven Kevlar, and able to withstand impacts from .44 Magnum bullets and all lesser threats. She hadn't donned it in nearly three years, ever since assigned to a tactical team, because the vests issued to S.W.A.T. deputies were worn outside their fatigues.

Tactical ballistic vests were constructed of heavy, ballistic, ceramic plates and rated to withstand impact from 7.62-millimeter, military-grade rifle ammunition and all lesser threats. Tac vests also weighed a ton and couldn't be concealed beneath clothing, unlike soft body armor.

Strayer put on the vest, her dress shirt, and finally her summer-weight sports jacket. She'd never worn body armor under anything but her uniform, and wanted to see if it was noticeable under her civilian clothes.

After checking her appearance in the full-length mirror, she satisfied herself the body armor was inconspicuous. She wasn't relishing the notion of wearing the uncomfortable ballistic vest in the current heat of the Indian summer, but relished the notion of getting shot without it even less.

She clipped her .45 onto her right hip, the two spare

magazines on the opposite hip, and her seven-point deputy sheriff's badge on her belt in front of the pistol's holster. Then she pocketed her knife and handkerchief, closed her locker, took in and let out a deep breath, and reluctantly headed for the stairs.

Strayer was disappointed in herself that she'd allowed her temper to get away from her. The confrontation with Meyers in the gym left her mentally and emotionally drained and filled with self-doubt.

It also left her dreading her second day in the Investigations Division.

CHAPTER TWENTY-SEVEN

The sound of his cell phone ringing brought Tad Guthrie grudgingly awake. He sat up in bed as the ringtone blared, magnifying the pain in his already throbbing head. It took a moment for his eyes to focus and his brain to process where he was. He reached out clumsily for the device amid the beer cans, overstuffed ashtray, vodka bottle, and bong surrounding it on the motel nightstand.

"Yeah," he mumbled.

"Teddy? Are you still in bed?"

"I was before you called," he said, looking at the clock radio. The luminous face read 7:41 A.M. "What do you want, Dad?"

"Where are you? I've been calling since last night. Why didn't you answer your phone?"

"It's better if you don't know," Tad said, not wanting to admit he'd switched off his phone yesterday afternoon after Mary arrived in his motel room.

"Vince Holloway phoned last night. He told me your arraignment's been moved up. It's scheduled for the day after tomorrow."

"The day after tomorrow?" Tad said, sitting up. "Can't he get me an extension?"

"No. He told me the date's been set. That's not all he told me."

"What else?"

"Vince wanted me to pass along a message. He said he doesn't want to know what you're up to, but whatever it is, you'd better do it fast. If you're going to convince a certain somebody whose name I won't say over an open line to back off, you'd best get it done. You're almost out of time."

"Why the rush? I thought we had some breathing room?"

"So did Vince, but he was wrong. He didn't anticipate the political winds."

"Political winds? What the hell are you talking about?"

"The district attorney is on the warpath because of the election in a few days. According to Vince, he isn't pleased with his polling numbers. As a result, he's launched a last-minute campaign blitz designed to highlight his tough-on-crime credentials. Which means he isn't inclined to let any of his deputy D.A.s cut plea bargains right now. Especially on open-and-shut domestic violence cases that guarantee slam-dunk convictions. Vince told me to tell you if somebody doesn't have a change of heart in the next day or so, before the election and decide to refuse to cooperate with the prosecution, the chances of your case being dropped are going the way of the dodo bird."

Tad's headache began to throb harder.

"I don't know where you are," Dr. Guthrie's voice continued, "but you'd better come back to Sacramento right away. You and I need to meet with Vince again and come up with a plan."

"I've already got a plan," Tad retorted. "I just have to move up the timetable, that's all."

"What are you going to do?"

"You don't need to know," Tad said. "So long, Dad. If you try to call me again, you may not get through. Cell service around here is pretty shitty. I'll call you as soon as I can."

Tad ended the call and immediately punched up Mary Hernandez's number. The automated message from her cell carrier, which answered instead of her, advised him the number he'd called was outside the service area or that service was temporarily interrupted. That's when his hung-over mind remembered something he already knew; that even without the Farnham Fire, there was no cell service at her parents' house.

Though he didn't want to admit it, Mary had been right when she accused Tad of not really caring whether he got divorced from her sister. She'd also been right about how little he cared about his kids. As far as he was concerned, Marjorie could have full custody of Joel and Jennifer. They were nothing to him now but numbers on a monthly child-support check that his father was going to write.

But Tad cared about his freedom; he cared a lot. And he knew he couldn't wait for Mary to convince her sister to speak with him any longer. If he was going to stay out of jail, it was up to him.

"Son of a bitch," Tad grumbled as he got out of bed and headed for the shower.

CHAPTER TWENTY-EIGHT

When Strayer walked into the Investigations Division briefing room, the place was packed with detectives, but no one noticed her enter. All eyes were locked on the wall-mounted television, which was airing a local news broadcast.

". . . continues to burn unabated. Cal Fire has confirmed that as of this morning, the Farnham Fire is less than five-percent contained. The fire has consumed well over one hundred thousand acres, most of that in the Farnham National Forest and surrounding areas. A Cal Fire spokesperson said the continuing hot, dry weather the Western Sierra Nevadas are experiencing, coupled with the late-afternoon high winds, have combined to create the perfect conditions for stoking the wildfire. We go now to Ken Estrada, on the scene with Cal Fire, near the fire-ravaged town of Tuckerville."

The camera switched to a view of a reporter in a windbreaker wearing a surgical mask tucked below his chin. Thick smoke swirled around him, and in the background, there was an array of tents, several emergency vehicles, and dozens of firefighters and law enforcement personnel from a number of different agencies milling about.

"I'm here at the staging area for Cal Fire," the reporter said, "where along with other journalists, I've just received a briefing by a spokesperson for the Farnham County Coroner's Office. At this time, I'm sad to report, at least sixty persons have died as a result of the Farnham Fire. Hundreds are still missing, and authorities tell me they believe at least some of those listed as missing are presumed dead. I say presumed, because we're being told that due to the intense heat the fire generated, as well as the extremely high winds, it's not impossible that the remains of some of the missing, if indeed they perished in the fire, as is feared, may never be recovered. The sheriff is asking anyone seeking or having information regarding missing persons associated with the Farnham Fire to call the number you see now on your screen."

Benavides finally noticed Strayer and winked an acknowledgment to her. He was standing with Sergeant Simpson in the back of the room. Both held coffee mugs. She sidled over.

"What's so fascinating?" Strayer whispered to Benavides.

"Keep watching," he whispered back. "Something of interest to a lot of senior deputies is coming up. The newscaster played a teaser before the last round of commercials."

". . . among the dead is a local firefighter, who perished from injuries sustained battling the blaze only last night," Estrada droned on. "But coroner's deputies tell us the greatest majority of fatalities so far occurred within the first twenty-four hours of the fire, when a group of motorists stuck in a traffic jam on Highway 50 became trapped in their vehicles as the firestorm swept over them. Survivors had to abandon their cars and flee for their lives on foot as a wall of wind-driven flames seventy-five to one hundred feet high descended upon them. It's been reported, but not confirmed, that most of those motorists lucky enough to survive did so by immersing themselves in a nearby creek as the firestorm overtook them."

"Can you imagine?" Benavides said to Simpson. "That must have been a terrifying ordeal."

"Glad I wasn't there," Simpson said as she sipped coffee.

Estrada's reporting went on. "Coroner's deputies tell us the exact death toll from the highway incident is at this time impossible to tabulate. According to a coroner's spokesperson, the firestorm overtaking the convoy of stranded vehicles was magnified exponentially by a gasoline tanker that ignited, adding to the inferno's intensity. He told us that temperatures in the vicinity of the exploding tanker could have reached as high as eighteen hundred degrees Fahrenheit."

The reporter continued. "To give our viewers some perspective on how hot that is, a commercial crematorium, which reduces the human body to fine ash, typically generates in the range of fourteen hundred degrees. Firefighters told this reporter that some of the automobiles near the exploded tanker were reduced to lumps of molten metal. The coroner's spokesperson told us that heat in the vicinity of the exploded gasoline tanker was so fierce that remains of some victims who perished near it might never be recovered. This news can only contribute to the heartbreak of those anxiously awaiting word of the fate of their missing loved ones."

"That's one hot fire," Benavides whistled.

"Among those missing and presumed dead," the TV reporter said, "were two on-duty correctional officers who were transporting a pair of inmates from the California Correctional Medical Facility in Solano County to Folsom Prison. What's left of their vehicle was found adjacent to the exploded gas tanker. The identity of those correctional officers is being withheld pending notification of next of kin."

"Here it comes," Benavides said to Strayer, pointing to the screen with his mug.

"One of the two inmates being transported by those correctional officers, also now listed as missing and presumed dead, was Duane Audie Mims."

The screen changed from the live image of Ken Estrada to a picture of a tall, husky, clean-shaven man with a military haircut. He was posing in front of a flag and wearing the uniform of a Farnham County deputy sheriff. The photo was dated fifteen years before and wore the caption FILE PHOTO.

"Some of our viewers may remember Duane Audie Mims," Estrada's voice continued without his image, "infamously known as the 'Middle Fork Rapist.' Mims was convicted of the murder of twenty-year-old Sierra College student Pamela Gardner, as well as multiple sexual assaults, during a crime spree that terrorized the Farnham County area a decade ago."

The TV image switched to the high school yearbook picture of Gardner, an extremely pretty blond girl with an infectious smile.

"A Farnham County deputy sheriff at the time he committed his offenses," the broadcast continued, "Mims perpetrated his crimes while on duty and was linked through DNA to more than half a dozen rapes in addition to Gardner's murder."

"I went to the academy with that dude," Benavides said to Strayer. "You wouldn't remember him. He was before your time."

The reporter's voice narrated on. "Mims was serving a life sentence at the California Correctional Facility at Folsom. A representative from that agency told our producers he'd been receiving treatment for an undisclosed medical condition at their facility in Solano County. There is no word yet on the identity of the other inmate, also missing and presumed dead, who likely perished in the blaze along with Mims and the two correctional officers transporting them."

The screen switched from the yearbook photo of Gardner to one of Mims in an orange jumpsuit. He was wearing restraints and being escorted from a courtroom.

Strayer realized why the television was captivating the attention of so many of her fellow deputies. Anyone in the room with more than a dozen years on the department would have worked with Mims.

"I hope Mims is burning in hell right now," a senior Property Crimes detective said.

"How appropriate," an older female Property Crimes detective said. "Not even his ashes are left."

"I hope he died screaming," a veteran Narcotics detective said.

"Couldn't happen to a more deserving guy," another detective remarked.

"Evidently justice delayed," a fourth detective chimed in, "doesn't necessarily mean justice denied."

"Karma's apparently not only a bitch," another female detective said, "she's a hot bitch."

Strayer barely heard them. She stared blankly at the TV screen. The room was unexpectedly spinning, her ears were ringing, her heart was pounding in her chest, and she felt dizzy.

"I've got to go to the restroom," she mumbled and abruptly left.

Strayer departed the Investigations Division and jogged down the vacant third floor hallway to the women's restroom. She burst through the door and made it into one of the stalls just in time.

After she finished vomiting, she flushed the toilet and went over to the bank of sinks. There she washed her face with cold water, rinsed her mouth, and stared for long minutes at her reflection in the mirror. The dark circles she'd been cultivating over the past sleepless nights were on full display.

Strayer didn't expect to see Mims, nor the face of the young woman he murdered, Pamela Gardner, if only as images on television. She certainly didn't anticipate the severity of her involuntary physical reaction. She closed her eyes and shook her head, trying to dispel the memories.

Sergeant Simpson entered the restroom. "I thought I might find you in here," she said. "McDillon's waiting on you to start his briefing. You're the guest of honor, remember?"

It was only after she spoke that Simpson realized Strayer was in some distress. Her newest Juvenile Unit deputy was leaning over the sink with her head down. The faint scent of vomitus wafted across her alert nose.

"You okay?"

"I'm all right, Sarge," Strayer nodded. "I'll be five by five in a minute."

"You sure?"

"Yeah," Strayer lied. "Probably just a stomach bug."

"I'll stall McDillon," Simpson said. "But don't take too much longer."

"Don't bother," Strayer said, standing up. "I'm right behind you."

By the time they got back to the briefing room, they found the television had been switched off and every seat was taken. People were lined up in the back against the wall. Lieutenant McDillon was at the podium, and behind him stood Undersheriff Torres and the sergeant in charge of the Gang Unit. Strayer and Simpson made their way in and returned to the vacant spot against the wall next to Detective Benavides.

"Nice of you to join us," McDillon said as Simpson and Strayer entered. He made an elaborate gesture of first checking his wristwatch and then looking up at the clock above on the wall, which read 8:04 A.M.

"What a jerk," Benavides muttered, loud enough for most around him to hear.

"At least he's consistent," Simpson answered.

"Now that we're all here"—McDillon peered over his glasses at Strayer as he addressed the room—"we can begin. I'll start off with a piece of good news, because frankly, there's plenty of not-so-good news today, and we could use a little. The good news is that Amalia Gallantes, the young girl who was hit by gunfire during the shoot-out at the Pleasant Pines Trailer Park, is being released from the hospital this morning and is going home. I'm told she lost her spleen but is otherwise going to make a full recovery."

The deputies in the room spontaneously broke out into applause.

"Now for the bad news," McDillon continued, once the clapping subsided. "In addition to the fire, which you all know is still burning uncontrolled . . ."

"I'm smoking a pack of cigarettes a day right now," a detective shouted from the back of the room, "and I don't even smoke." Laughter erupted.

"You aren't the only one in Farnham County sucking in fumes," McDillon said, "but at least you haven't lost any loved ones or your home." The laughter quickly faded.

"As I was saying," McDillon resumed, now looking sternly over his glasses at the detective who'd interrupted him, "I've got some bad news. The ballistics report on the slug that struck Amalia Gallantes is in, and it ain't good. The bullet that hit her was a five-five-six fired from one of our S.W.A.T. rifles."

The room got silent. "The department is issuing a press release later this morning after the daily fire briefing. We expect some blowback from the community."

"Ya think?" Simpson whispered to Benavides.

"How about a lawsuit?" Benavides whispered to Simpson.

"That's the understatement of the year," Simpson whispered back.

"Deputies confronted by citizens expressing their opinions about the shooting are reminded not to engage in public debate and refer all queries to the departmental press information officer. Any questions before we move on?"

"Are there going to be protests again?" the sergeant in charge of the Crimes Against Persons Unit asked.

"We are anticipating protests here at the department," McDillon answered, "after word about the origin of the bullet hits the presses. There's a mob of reporters waiting to ambush Amalia and her family in the hospital parking lot as we speak, no doubt to get her family's reaction to the news. As you all know, we've recently experienced several spontaneous demonstrations and protests since the Pleasant Pines incident. Expect them again today."

"We've got a plan in place to deal with protestors," Undersheriff Torres spoke up. "It shouldn't be a problem."

"Tell that to the sheriff," Simpson whispered to Benavides. "It's his reelection that's on the line."

"Any more questions?" McDillon asked. No one spoke up.

"Moving on," McDillon said. "Some of you may have heard rumors about a 'hit' being put out on our deputies by Hispanic gangs associated with the Mexican Mafia. Unfortunately, that scuttlebutt might be true. Sergeant Brandonmire will fill you in."

McDillon yielded the podium to a thin man of medium height in his early forties, wearing a T-shirt and jeans, whom Strayer recognized as the Gang Unit's supervisor. She'd interacted with him and his detectives occasionally during her stint in the Patrol Division, and knew he had a reputation as a competent deputy. Before he signed on with the Farnham County Sheriff's Department, he worked for almost ten years in the California Department of Corrections' Gang Unit at San Quentin.

"Good morning," Brandonmire said. "Ever since the death of Ernesto Machado, the department has been receiving sporadic reports claiming the Mexican Mafia is looking for payback. There's buzz that a contract, officially sanctioned by La Eme, has been put out on anyone wearing a Farnham County star. Thanks to our local press, which believes identifying individual law enforcement officers and exposing them to retribution from criminals is a great way to sell newspapers, some of those threats have been specifically directed against Deputy Strayer."

Strayer felt all eyes in the room move toward her. It took effort to appear indifferent, especially since her stomach was still roiling and her mind racing from seeing the news report about Mims.

"Most of the intelligence coming to us," Brandonmire continued, "is filtering in from the usual sources, such as gang members who are in custody and looking to shave time or confidential informants working off dope beefs with our Narcotics and Gang Units. What we're hearing would normally be chalked up to nothing more than the usual macho posturing all gangs put on after one of their own is taken out by law enforcement. While we take any threat to our deputies seriously, we get them regularly enough that most can be swallowed with a grain of salt."

Brandonmire stepped to the side of the podium and rested an elbow on it. He looked like a community college instructor teaching sociology, not a career undercover detective addressing his colleagues. Behind him, Undersheriff Torres and Lieutenant McDillon stood with their arms folded.

"But we've recently received intel," Brandonmire said, "coming in from several outside agencies. These sources include the DOJ, CDC, and ATF, and indicate the alleged hit might well be legitimate this time. Informants within the

Mexican Mafia are telling their handlers in these agencies that a contract has been put out on Deputy Strayer, straight from the top of La Eme. This information also includes a general threat against all Farnham County deputies."

Brandonmire stepped back and turned the podium over to McDillon.

"In light of these threats," McDillon said, "all deputies, regardless of what division they're assigned to, are being advised to exercise extra officer-safety precautions. This briefing is officially for the purpose of notifying you of the elevated threat level, which goes for off duty, as well. For the foreseeable future, I want all detectives within my command working in pairs. No exceptions."

A grumble permeated the room. "That's going to slow the division's work down significantly," the Narcotics sergeant spoke up. "I don't know about the other units, Lieutenant, but our cases are already backed up."

"I realize you all have heavy caseloads," McDillon responded, addressing everyone, not only the Narcotics supervisor, "and that most of your investigative work is performed on an individual basis. I'm also fully aware that doubling up during routine investigative tasks will back you up a bit further."

"A bit further?" another detective scoffed. "How about doubling the time it'll take to clear a case?"

"I'd rather our division got less work done," McDillon answered, "than lose a deputy."

The grumbling among the detectives grew louder.

"This comes straight from the sheriff," Torres interjected, "and isn't negotiable. So unless any of you would like to be on the receiving end of disciplinary action, don't be caught working alone out there. If you are, I can guarantee a suspension."

"Nothing like a pep talk to motivate the troops," Benavides whispered to Simpson.

"All right," McDillon said, signaling the end of the briefing, "unless there's anything else, let's hit the street. Work in pairs at all times and look out for each other. We need to be safe out there."

"Who's 'we?'" Benavides again whispered to Simpson. "Does McDillon really think he's gonna get shot behind his desk?"

Deputies began to file from the room.

"I want all the unit supervisors to stick around," McDillon announced over the din of their departure. "You, too, Deputy Strayer."

"Here we go again," Simpson said.

Chapter Twenty-nine

Tad Guthrie gave his horn three long blasts, the final one lasting for twice as long as the previous two, and punched the steering wheel in frustration. His car had been stuck at a dead stop, along with a long line of other vehicles, for nearly an hour.

Dead-stopped traffic was something Tad would have been accustomed to in the Bay Area or Sacramento region but was unexpected on a two-lane, country road in rural Farnham County. Due to the heavy smoke, he couldn't see more than a few car lengths ahead. The smoke, which had blanketed the sky and air for over three days now, was becoming thicker.

Tad left the motel in a Buick, having chosen to travel to Farnham County from Granite Bay in a rental car instead of his beloved Porsche. One glance at the Porsche, and Marjorie and her family would instantly know he was in the area. He was pretty sure there weren't any other Miami Blue 718 Caymans in the farming community of Farnham, California.

Suddenly there was an insistent knock on the driver's window. He looked up to find a Farnham County deputy sheriff standing alongside his motionless car. The deputy was wearing fatigues, a reflective vest, and a dust filter over his mouth.

Tad rolled down the window. The scent of smoke instantly filled his car. "Good morning, Officer," he said.

"It's Deputy," the deputy's muffled voice said, "not Officer. What's with the horn, buddy?"

"I'm sorry," Tad said. "I'm frustrated, that's all. I've got family a few miles down the road, and I'm worried about them. I guess it's making me irritable."

"You ain't alone," the deputy said, "but honking your horn isn't going to get things moving any faster, and it's pissing people off. One of those people is me. Can't you see the road's blocked?"

"For how long?"

"However long it takes," the deputy said. "If you haven't heard, the fire is moving closer to Farnham. They announced a voluntary evacuation this morning. All the roads are clogged with emergency vehicles trying to get in and folks trying to get out. So lay off the horn, okay?"

"I apologize," Tad said. "I won't do it again."

"I know you won't," the deputy said. "Because the fastest way for me to get off this lousy traffic post and out of the smoke is to arrest somebody. I hear the air in the county jail is nice and clean."

"You can't arrest me for honking my horn, can you?"

"Try me," the deputy said.

"No, thank you," Tad said. "Have a nice day, Deputy."

"Same to you," the deputy said, and walked away.

"Asshole," Tad muttered, as he rolled up the window. Still frustrated, he tried his cell phone again. It showed no service, as expected, just as it had since he left the Farnham town limits almost an hour ago.

Ten agonizingly slow minutes later, the vehicles ahead of him finally began to move. Tad put the Buick back into gear and crept forward. Within another few minutes the traffic was flowing semi-normally again.

The smoke was indeed getting thicker, Tad thought, and he remembered what the deputy told him about the fire moving closer to town. He wondered how close the blaze was to his in-laws' house, and if Marjorie and their children were still there. Perhaps they'd elected to voluntarily evacuate like the deputy said.

Tad couldn't help but wonder what would happen to the charges against him if Marjorie perished in the fire. He could only assume they'd be dropped. He made a mental note to ask his father to ask Vince Holloway that very question when he was next able to make a phone call.

He also wondered where Mary was.

She'd angered him with her excuses about needing more time to massage Marjorie into agreeing to meet with him. Hadn't he made it clear to her that time was the one thing he didn't have?

Tad should have known, better than anyone, about Mary's drug-dependency issues. After all, he was the one who'd given her the first taste of cocaine when she was still in high school. If anyone should have been aware of how erratic and unreliable Mary Hernandez could be, it was Tad Guthrie.

Tad quickly discovered teenaged Mary like coke; she liked it a lot. Almost as much she liked to drink, smoke cigarettes, and spark weed without her parents' knowledge.

But what she liked to do most of all, he soon learned, was bang him behind her big sister's back.

The bad-little-sister-getting-back-at-her-goody-two-shoes-big-sister dynamic was almost too clichéd for him to believe, at first. But Tad had never been one to turn down a good time, or a good lay, and his girlfriend's underage sister was too ripe a fruit not to be plucked. Before he knew it, what was supposed to be nothing more than a brief fling never ended.

Mary's appetite for cocaine eventually graduated into meth use and grew along with their illicit relationship. He continued to see her, off and on, all the time he was dating Marjorie. In fact, Tad and Mary actually knocked boots on his and Marjorie's wedding day, only hours before the ceremony. That old superstitious chestnut about not seeing the bride before the nuptials didn't mention anything about not seeing the bride's sister.

As the years went by, he and Mary found ways to hook up, though not always regularly. When Mary dropped out of college, after her first stint in rehab, he didn't see her for many months. But she would eventually reach out to him, usually when she needed money. And when she did, she always found Tad ready, willing, and able to accommodate her.

Even when Marjorie was pregnant with Joel, and then Jennifer, Tad ensured Mary knew which city and motel he was staying at when he was traveling on business. Hiding money from his wife had never been a problem, thanks to his father, and she never once suspected the true nature of his relationship with her younger sister or for how long it had been going on. The fact that Marjorie and Mary weren't close and saw each other only once or twice a year

at the occasional family function, made it all the easier
for Tad and Mary to conceal their illicit, sporadic, and on-
going relationship.

When Mary texted him a few weeks before his arrest,
she hadn't seen Tad in over eight months and her own
family in well over a year. He thought it ironic that over
the years she encountered him more routinely than her own
sister or parents. He felt it made their forbidden reunions
even more exciting.

Mary looked a little rougher since the last time he'd
seen her, and it was evident she was once again losing
control of her habits. She needed money, of course. Like
always, Tad gave it to her.

What Mary gave him, which he didn't discover until
the night he was arrested, was chlamydia.

Tad made the familiar turnoff from the two-lane black-
top to the unmarked gravel road leading to the Hernandez
home. He still had several miles of unpaved ground to
cover but was glad to leave the other vehicles behind. His
mind wandered to the countless times over the years
he'd driven this very road with his wife and children while
visiting his in-laws.

A mile or two later Tad passed the landmark of the
Dixon property, which told him he was only a mile away
from his destination. The Dixons—Delbert, Carly, and
their two children, Brandy and Travis—were his in-laws'
nearest neighbors. Their house, if it could be called that,
was a ramshackle trailer in the midst of a trash-strewn,
grassless yard.

Three quarters of a mile from the Dixons' place, Tad
turned off the gravel road into an almond orchard. He'd
planned to park deep within the rows of trees to keep the

vehicle from being spotted from the road. With the smoke as thick as it was, however, he decided it wasn't necessary to enter the orchard more than a hundred feet to render the Buick unseen.

Tad got out of the car, mentally kicking himself for not thinking to bring a protective dust mask like the one worn by the deputy and others he'd seen back in Farnham. The acrid air stung his nostrils and lungs and made his eyes water. He removed the pint bottle of vodka from the cargo pocket of his khaki trousers, uncapped it, and took a long drink. The vodka burned his throat but steadied his nerves.

Marjorie didn't know it, but he'd actually been off the wagon for months. He'd kept his drinking from her by developing the discipline to only imbibe when away from home on business. He also smoked marijuana and snorted cocaine while traveling, usually when in her sister Mary's company.

There were a couple of times during the past few weeks, after coming home from a business trip, when he was certain Marjorie would have noticed he was hung over. But each time he blamed his condition on jet lag and she bought it. Tad comforted himself in the knowledge that ever since he'd met her, Marjorie generally only saw what she wanted to see.

Tad pocketed the vodka bottle and began his hike. All he had to do was cross the road, traverse a quarter of a mile through a patch of dense, familiar woods, and he'd be at the back door of his in-laws' house. It was only mid-morning, and he tentatively hoped the house was intact and his family was still there. He half expected to find the farmhouse burned down and Marjorie gone.

Or dead.

It wasn't that Tad wished for his wife to perish in the fire, and he certainly wouldn't have killed her himself. But Marjorie was determined to send him to jail, maybe for a year or more. There was no way he was going to let that happen. The two short stints he'd already spent in jail—six hours on a DUI arrest a couple of years ago, and three horrifying days this past week—had convinced him he would never survive if locked up for any real length of time.

While he didn't specifically yearn for his wife's death, Tad was acutely cognizant of how many of his troubles would disappear if she were to succumb to the fire.

He knew he was taking a huge risk in attempting to contact his wife while under a restraining order, but he had no choice. He was confident, as always, in his ability to bend Marjorie's will to his own, and he was sure he could persuade her to revoke the criminal charges against him.

Of course, he'd also try to convince her he wanted to make amends and repair their marriage, which wasn't true, and merely a ruse to entice her to do what he wanted. Once she dropped the charges, as far as Tad was concerned, she and their two brats could go to hell. He'd gladly divorce her then and leave them all in the dust. Marjorie, Joel, and Jennifer would become nothing more than another monthly check written by his father.

Emboldening him further on his mission was the knowledge that even if Marjorie or her parents wanted to call the sheriff's office and report the restraining-order violation, there was no way to do it. The landlines were down, and there'd never been cell coverage in that region.

Tad had it all thought out, or so he believed. If Marjorie absolutely refused to engage him in conversation, and insisted on pressing charges for violating the protective stay-away order, the excuse he would offer through his attorney when he got back was that his paternal concern for his children's safety during the fire emergency had overridden his fear of arrest. He was certain Vince Holloway could convince a judge that the exigency created by the Farnham Fire, coupled with his inability to contact or locate his children, should vindicate his actions.

In any case, Tad had come to the conclusion he had no choice and nothing to lose. Mary hadn't delivered the goods, despite the money he'd given her and the rental car he'd provided. He could no longer count on her to broker a meeting with her sister, as if he ever could, and was almost out of time. It was now up to him to reach out to Marjorie and persuade her to drop the charges on his own.

As Tad crossed the gravel road, he coughed and lifted his shirt to cover his mouth and nose. He entered the woods and began to make his way through the smoke toward the Hernandez property.

CHAPTER THIRTY

The pounding on the basement door was loud and insistent. It went on for almost a minute before Skink answered.

"Quit beatin' on that door," he said in a raspy voice. "Whaddya want?"

Skink had been lying on the couch in the living room in a state of mild delirium, not quite asleep but not entirely awake, when the thumping on the basement door roused him from his intoxicated semiconsciousness. During the night he'd consumed an entire pack of cigarettes, five bottles of beer, and most of a bottle of rum he found in the kitchen while rifling through the cabinets. He'd also inhaled two more lines of methamphetamine from the jar he found in Mary's purse.

The contrasting combination of alcoholic beverages and stimulant drugs, in concert with his high fever and worsening pain, gradually rendered Skink almost delusional. By early morning, when he finally collapsed on the couch in a pseudo-hallucinogenic state, he barely knew where he was or whom he was with. He tossed and turned until well after sunrise, moaning aloud in the throes of nightmares.

It took a long time for the sound of the pounding on the basement door to pull Skink out of his stupor. He struggled slowly off the couch, got his unsteady legs under him, and staggered into the kitchen as Mims's voice from upstairs pierced his ears and resonated inside his throbbing skull.

"Do something about that noise!" Mims yelled down.

"I'm on it," Skink yelled back, as the sound of his own voice made his head throb even more.

Mims had taken Mary Hernandez upstairs shortly before midnight. Skink expected him to bring her down sometime during the night, and give him his turn with her as she'd agreed. But as the night wore on, and Skink became more intoxicated and detached from reality, neither Mims nor the girl returned.

The last thing Skink's dope- and booze-flooded mind remembered before he crumpled on the couch was being pissed off at Mims for not keeping his word and letting him have a go at Mary. But he also remembered being vaguely aware that even if Mims had brought the woman down, he'd have been unable to perform anyway due to his level of intoxication.

In any case, Skink felt cheated. Unable to get it on or not, he was supposed to be given the opportunity to at least try. That was what Mims told him, and that was the deal they made with the woman to keep them off her older sister and from harming anyone else. A bargain that in retrospect seemed to benefit only Mims.

"You have to let us out," Margaret's voice came from behind the basement door. "The children need to use the bathroom. So do we. We need to eat, too."

"Go back downstairs," Skink mumbled. "I'll let you out later."

"We can't wait until later," Margaret insisted. "You have to at least let us use the bathroom."

"Shut up and go back downstairs," Skink said through the door. Now that he was fully awake, his headache had intensified, and the pain in his right shoulder, neck, and arm had become excruciating. He felt dizzy and sat heavily down on one of the kitchen chairs. He was afraid if he didn't, he might fall.

"No," Margaret said. "Let us out!" The pounding on the door resumed.

Skink drew his gun and pointed it at the kitchen door. "Quit thumpin' on that door," he screeched, "or so help me, I'll start puttin' bullets through it." The pounding continued unabated.

"What the hell is going on?" Mims said, entering the kitchen. He was barefoot and wearing only trousers and a T-shirt. His Glock was in his waistband.

"They won't stop beatin' on the door," Skink said.

"Put that gun away," Mims said. Skink set his pistol down on the kitchen table and used his good hand to cover his left ear.

Mims drew his own pistol, unlocked the bolt, and opened the basement door. Margaret stood at the top of the stairwell, her fist poised to strike the door again.

"What's the problem?" he asked.

"As I told your partner," Margaret said, "we have to use the bathroom. We also have to eat. Stretching our legs wouldn't hurt, either. We've been cooped up in that cellar all night."

"All right," Mims said. "One at a time, the kids first.

When one is finished in the bathroom and returns to the basement, another can come up. When everybody's done, you'll stay up here in the kitchen, by yourself, and make breakfast."

"Thank you," Margaret said. "But if you don't mind, Marjorie will have to go along with Jennifer. She's only a little girl, and she's scared."

"I'll allow it," Mims said, "but everybody else comes up alone." He stepped back. "Get moving."

Margaret returned downstairs, and Marjorie made her way up holding Jennifer's hand. The kindergarten-aged girl looked terrified and about to cry.

"Where's Mary?" Marjorie asked, as they passed through the kitchen.

"If I were you," Mims said, "I'd save my worrying for me and my kids."

"Don't fret about your sister," Skink chided. "Duane took good care of her last night. Just like I'll be takin' care of you tonight." He opened his mouth to laugh, again revealing his decayed teeth.

Marjorie ignored the comment.

"You haven't got any weapons on you?" Mims asked. "Something you might have found down in the basement."

"No," Marjorie said.

"I'll have to check."

Marjorie stood like a statue, with her jaw set and eyes forward, while Mims ran his hands over her body. Though she was wearing only a short-sleeved blouse and a pair of jeans, his hands lingered far too long over her buttocks, crotch, and breasts. Jennifer watched in confusion, while Skink stared and cackled, as her mother was "searched."

"Done?" Marjorie said as Mims stepped back.

"You're clean," Mims said. He motioned her forward.

Marjorie escorted Jennifer into the downstairs bathroom and closed the door. Mims turned to Skink, who'd laughed himself into a coughing fit that hadn't ended. He was now bent at the waist and appeared ready to vomit.

"You look like shit," Mims said. He put his gun back into his belt, opened the bottles of ibuprofen and antibiotics, and poured a few of each into his hand. He set the pills, along with a glass of water, on the table before Skink.

Skink looked up at him through bleary, livid eyes. "I don't need no goddamn pills," he snapped, sweeping the water and tablets to the floor. The glass shattered.

He reached into his shirt pocket and withdrew the small jar of methamphetamine. Glaring hotly at Mims, he opened the cap with his teeth and poured out another glob of the powder on the web of his slung right hand. Mims noticed the tips of the fingers were blue and the hand itself was swollen and red.

"Got everything I need right here," he said, "courtesy of your girlfriend." He lowered his head and inhaled the meth.

"That's not going to make you feel better," Mims said.

"What do you know about how I feel?" Skink challenged. His face reddened, his eyes watered, and he shook his head back and forth like a dog shaking off water.

"You've barely eaten anything," Mims said, "you've hardly slept in days, you've got a broken arm and a serious infection, and you've been drinking and snorting crank all night. You can't go on much longer that way. That's what I know."

"You worry too much," Skink said. "We're ghosts, remember? We can do whatever we want."

He giggled, in stark divergence from his rage only a moment before. Mims presumed the bipolar emotional range he was exhibiting was a result of the effects of sleep deprivation, his injury and fever, and the substances he'd ingested.

"In fact," Skink went on, "I don't know why the hell we're still here. There ain't no reason we couldn't take one of them cars outside and be on our way. Leave this redneck, shithole county behind us in the rearview mirror."

"You're not thinking straight," Mims said. "We might be free for now, but we're hardly off the hook. The fire's got this region surrounded on three sides. Which means there's only one way for us to go; west, straight back toward Folsom. All the roads in that direction are littered with cops and firefighters. Chances are we'd hit a road-block or traffic jam. Even if we weren't recognized, we'd likely end up right back where we started—on foot and running for our lives."

Mims shook his head. "No," he continued, "our best option is to wait here for now. This place is ideal. It's remote, we've got plenty of food and water, and we can ride out the fire in comfort until the emergency is over and we're officially declared dead. Then it's off to wherever we want to go at our leisure, without ever having to look over our shoulders again."

"What if the fire makes it out here, Mister Smarty-Pants?" Skink said. "Then what?"

"Then we'll evacuate," Mims said, "but not before we have to. If and when we go, we'll bring a few of these people along with us, as an insurance policy, just in case we run into any cops."

"Hostages," Mims said, licking his teeth. "Now I get what

you're doin'. That's the real reason you're keepin' these folks alive, ain't it? In case we need 'em for hostages?"

"I thought you knew that," Mims said.

"Uh . . . sure I did," Skink lied. "I was thinkin' the same thing."

"I'm glad we're on the same page," Mims said, aware Skink was lying. "I'm hoping the fire might miss us entirely, but hope isn't a strategy. We need to have a contingency plan, and these people are it. Either way, whether we leave with or without them, you couldn't travel right now if you wanted to. You're a mess."

"I appreciate your concern for my well-being," Skink said as he capped the jar and returned it to his pocket. "Always lookin' out for your pal Skink, aren't you?" He wiped his runny nose on his sleeve. "Where was that consideration last night, while you were upstairs doin' the horizontal boogie? I seem to remember somethin' about me gettin' a whirl with the tattooed lady?" His mood darkened again.

"You were in no state," Mims said. "Don't blame me. You did it to yourself."

"I surely am grateful," Skink said, his eyes bulging and veins distended in his neck and temples, "for decidin' what's best for me and what's not. That was real thoughtful of you, Duane." He jabbed his good left finger in the air at Mims like a gun. "You're a true-blue friend."

The sound of a toilet flushing sounded, and Marjorie and Jennifer came out of the bathroom. Marjorie hurriedly guided her daughter between Mims and Skink in the kitchen and started back down the basement stairs.

"Lookin' good, Marjorie," Skink said, staring at her backside. "Gonna be gettin' a real close look tonight."

Joel emerged from the basement next.

"Good mornin', Zombie Boy," Skink said to Joel. "Did you sleep well down there in the dark?"

Joel eyed the Glock sitting on the kitchen table. Skink noticed.

"You like my gun?" he said. "Go ahead, boy. Pick it up. You know you want to. You'd like nothin' more than to snatch up that pistol and blow my brains out, wouldn't you?"

"Get moving," Mims said to Joel, who scurried off to the bathroom. He turned to Skink. "Cut the crap, and mind your weapon."

"What's the matter?" Skink said. "You don't like me fuckin' with the hostages? I guess you're the only one who gets to do that, huh? Literally."

"I'm getting tired of your mouth," Mims said.

"And I'm gettin' tired of takin' orders," Skink retorted. "I can give 'em, too. You ain't the only one with a gun, ya know?"

"I know," Mims said.

"Best you don't forget it," Skink said.

"I haven't," Mims said evenly, "and I won't."

After a few minutes, and Joel exited the bathroom. "Everything come out all right, Zombie Boy?" Skink taunted.

Joel silently returned to the basement, and Hector came up. Skink picked up his pistol.

"Where's Mary," Hector demanded.

"I already told your other daughter not to worry about her," Mims said. "Same advice goes for you."

"I want to see her."

"Okay," Mims shrugged. "Go use the bathroom. She'll be downstairs when you come out."

Hector went into the bathroom. Mims started for the stairs.

"What do you expect me to do while you're upstairs?" Skink said, irritated and confused that Mims was apparently going to leave him alone with Hector in the bathroom and the basement door wide open.

"If I were you," Mims said, "I'd watch ole' Hector pretty closely. But you don't have to take my advice. I wouldn't want you to interpret my suggestion as an order."

"Fuck you," Skink said. "Just hurry up."

Hector came out of the bathroom several minutes later, as Mims and Mary materialized at the stairs. Mary was wearing her T-shirt with no bra, jeans, and was barefoot and carrying her high-tops. Her hair was messed up, and both of her wrists were raw and bore the marks of being bound. The left side of her face, from the hairline to the corner of her mouth, was one continuous bruise. Her left eye was swollen almost shut.

"Good God," Hector said when he saw his youngest daughter. He stared angrily at Mims, who leveled his pistol at the older man's torso with a blank face.

"You really did a number on her mug," Skink chuckled. "She looks almost like her big sister, now. Whyen't you slug her on the other side of her face and give her another shiner to match?" He laughed at his own joke. "Then they'd look identical."

"Okay," Mims said to Hector, "you've seen her. Back downstairs." He prodded Mary toward the basement. "You, too."

Hector allowed Mary to pass him, and waited until she

disappeared down the stairs. "I need to listen to the radio," he said to Mims.

"No."

"We don't know exactly where the fire is. The only way to find out how close it's getting is to hear the news broadcasts."

"We'll listen to it from up here," Mims said, "and let you know if the fire gets any closer." He moved his gun from Hector's stomach to his head. "Get your ass back down those stairs."

CHAPTER THIRTY-ONE

"Call me when you're ready to get picked up," Simpson said to Strayer as she got out of the car. "It's close to lunchtime. I'm going for a bite to eat, so take all the time you need."

Strayer got out of Sergeant Simpson's unmarked Charger and headed into Dr. Wozniak's office. She'd been driven to Folsom by her supervisor, with a brief stop at the Farnham County Hospital emergency room on the way.

Strayer had stormed out of Lieutenant McDillon's office after the morning meeting. She'd lost her temper, and knew if she hadn't left at that moment she would have said or done something resulting in a suspension or worse.

McDillon kept all five of the Investigations Division supervisors, and Deputy Strayer, in the briefing room once the main meeting ended. That's when he announced that until further notice Strayer was forbidden to leave the administration building alone, and even then could only assist other detectives with their criminal cases. She would not be assigned any criminal cases of her own.

Strayer's caseload was to be restricted to statutory

offenses and administrative duties, like truancy checks and child welfare inspections, and she would be allowed to conduct those outside of the building only with Sergeant Simpson's express permission, on a case-by-case basis, and when accompanied by another detective.

Before Strayer could protest, McDillon went on to explain that this change in her assigned duties was only temporary and being done for her protection.

This new, humiliating revelation, delivered while she was still stewing over her earlier beef with Deputy Meyers in the gym, suffering the lingering aftereffects of the news report announcing Mims's death, and coming in the wake of the Machado shooting, being removed from S.W.A.T., and being involuntarily transferred to Investigations, pushed Strayer to the limits of her composure. She felt like screaming, crying, and punching McDillon in the mouth all at once.

Evidently the internal struggle to maintain her self-control was visible on her face, and Strayer felt six pairs of eyes awaiting her reaction. She stared straight ahead, meeting no one else's gaze, as she'd learned to do in the army when standing at attention.

"Do you have a problem with this policy, Deputy Strayer?" McDillon asked.

"When I do, Lieutenant," Strayer said through clenched teeth, "you'll be the first to know." She turned and headed for the briefing-room door.

"Where do you think you're going?" McDillon called after her from behind the podium. "This meeting isn't over. No one's been dismissed."

"I'm going to the bathroom," Strayer said. "Or am I prohibited from doing that alone, too? Maybe you'd like to send someone along with me to hold my hand while I pee?"

Before McDillon could respond further, Strayer exited the briefing room. It took effort for her to keep from delivering a backhanded middle finger on the way out.

When Strayer entered the women's restroom for the second time, she didn't feel the urge to vomit. She was boiling over with rage, flooding from a well of anger she didn't realize she possessed. She stared at her visage once more in the mirror, as she'd done earlier, but this time the face staring back at her wasn't pale with nausea. Her face was flushed, and the piercing blue eyes returning her intense stare were blazing in frustration.

All of a sudden, a fist lashed out and struck the mirror, shattering it. The blow was an expertly delivered straight-left, and landed squarely on the refection of Strayer's face. It wasn't until she saw the shards of glass and droplets of blood in the sink that she realized she'd thrown the punch.

"Are you done?" Sergeant Simpson's voice said.

Strayer turned to find her supervisor had again entered the restroom behind her.

Strayer didn't answer. Her tempest had passed, evaporating in the explosive release of punching the mirror. She silently rinsed her knuckles and applied a paper towel to quell the bleeding.

"That's what they want," Simpson said, "you know. For you to get pissed off and quit. You'd solve their problems with you for them."

"I've never quit anything in my life," Strayer said.

"So you're not a quitter?" Simpson said. "Big deal. That won't matter if you do something stupid to get yourself fired instead."

"Like punching out inanimate objects?"

"Or getting into brawls in the departmental gym," Simpson said.

"News travels fast," Strayer said.

"What did you expect? You called out another deputy in front of twenty witnesses. He also happened to be the biggest deputy in the room. Did you think it wasn't going to get around?"

She took Strayer's hand and examined it. "That was a nice punch," she said. "You're the heavyweight champion of the world at coldcocking bathroom fixtures. But now you're going to need a couple of stitches. Come with me."

Before Strayer could object, Simpson led her from the restroom. They took the stairs down to the rear exit and headed from there into the secure parking lot. Simpson got into her vehicle and motioned for Strayer to take the passenger seat.

"I thought I wasn't supposed to leave the building?" Strayer said sarcastically.

"Without your supervisor's permission," Simpson said. "I'm your supervisor, remember?"

As they drove from the administration building, they noticed a crowd of about fifty protestors being photographed by several reporters assembled at the front steps. Undersheriff Torres, flanked by a pair of unformed deputies, was trying unsuccessfully to address them.

As she drove, Simpson dialed her cell phone. "Benny?" she said, when the other end was answered. "I need you to work some of your magic. There was a little accident in the women's restroom up on the third floor. Can you have one of your buddies at the corporation yard get on it? It needs to be done fast, discreetly, and without a work order. It's worth a case of beer, and I ain't talking Old Milwaukee."

Simpson ended the call. "Benny knows everybody working for the county," she explained, "and everybody knows him. He'll have that mirror replaced within the hour. McDildo will never even know it happened."

"Thank you," Strayer said.

"Don't thank me yet," Simpson said.

Five minutes later they were in the emergency room. Simpson spoke to the receptionist, and a few moments later an attractive woman in scrubs came out and gave her a hug. Simpson told her what they needed, and the woman motioned for them to follow.

"My wife is a physician," Simpson explained to Strayer, "who used to work at this hospital. I know a few people."

Strayer was led into a vacant treatment room. "I'm Dr. Joan Crandall," the woman introduced herself. She smiled mischievously. "Me and Tasha go way back, before she and her wife got married."

She squinted at Strayer. "Didn't I see you in here yesterday, with Benny Benavides and a prisoner with a renovated face?"

"I told you everybody knows Benny," Simpson said.

Strayer reluctantly nodded. "I'd ask you what the other guy looked like," Crandall said, examining her damaged left hand, "but the mirrored glass shards in your knuckles tell me it wasn't a person you slugged."

"Let's just say Deputy Strayer had a moment of reflection," Simpson said, "and leave it at that."

"It's a good thing you two weren't here about half an hour ago," Crandall said. "The Gallantes girl was released.

Place was crawling with reporters. They surely would have noticed you."

"I've got to make a phone call," Simpson said to Strayer. "I'll leave you in Joan's capable hands."

After Simpson departed, Strayer waived the numbing agent. Dr. Crandall removed several tiny shards of glass, cleansed and stitched two cuts, and closed a pair of smaller ones with Steri-Strips. She completed the treatment by covering her handiwork with a bandage. Simpson returned just as she was finishing up.

"Good as new," Crandall announced. "The stitches will dissolve on their own. No need to come back"— she smiled at Strayer—"unless you want to see me again."

"Thanks," Strayer said, flexing her fingers. "I should be fine."

"Drat," Crandall said, snapping her fingers.

"If it's not a problem," Simpson said to Crandall as they left the ER, "this one's off the books?"

"Not a problem," Crandall said. She gave Simpson another hug. "You girls stay out of trouble, you hear?"

"Unlikely," Simpson said. She pointed a thumb at Strayer. "Trouble's her middle name."

A little more than an hour later, Simpson pulled the unmarked Ford to a stop in front of Dr. Wozniak's office. The forty-mile drive to Folsom took longer than expected, due to the heavy civilian traffic flooding out of the Farnham County area and the large number of emergency vehicles heading in.

Strayer tried to phone Benavides while on the journey, to check on the status of the restroom repair and on McDillon's mood, but as expected they lost cell coverage as soon as they were outside the Farnham town limits.

"How'd you know to bring me here?" Strayer asked, once at Wozniak's office. She suspected the destination as soon as they departed Farnham.

"I know Dr. Wozniak," Simpson said. "I've used her myself. I sure as hell wasn't going to take you to one of the departmental psychologists and have the entire sheriff's department find out about it."

"So you're not just my supervisor," Strayer said, "you're now my shrink?"

"I don't have to be a shrink to see you need to talk to somebody," Simpson said. "Helen Keller could see that from a thousand yards in full dark."

"I've already got an appointment to see Dr. Wozniak," Strayer said. "Next week."

"At the rate you're going," Simpson said, "you won't last a week."

"What if I don't want to see her today?"

"Not negotiable," Simpson said. "I've already covered your ass, at risk to my own job, twice. Benny is doing it right now. Do you remember when I told you that McDillon would think nothing of squashing me and my other detectives if we get in the way of him squashing you? I wasn't bullshitting. You owe me."

"It's like that, huh?"

"Damn straight," Simpson said. "You've got two choices. Either get your butt into Wozniak's office right now and work out your shit, or from here on out you're on your own. The next time you fuck up and McDillon or Torres or anybody else comes gunning for you, I'm strictly a noncombatant."

"Does Dr. Wozniak know I'm coming?"

"I called her from the ER."

"I guess I'll be talking to Dr. Wozniak today," Strayer said, opening the car door.

"Good idea," Simpson said.

CHAPTER THIRTY-TWO

"You should eat something," Marjorie said to Mary as she held out a plate of food.

"I'm not hungry," Mary said without looking up.

Mary sat in one corner of the basement floor with her forehead on her knees and her legs folded into her chest. Marjorie knelt next to her.

"Is there anything I can do?" she asked.

"Do you have a cigarette?" Mary said, looking up.

"No."

"Then there's nothing you can do," Mary said and returned her head to her knees.

After the bathroom break, Margaret was forced to go upstairs and cook. She made a large pan of spaghetti, with garlic bread and a salad, from the makings she'd intended for a family meal before their kidnappers arrived. After she fed the two gunmen, she was allowed to bring food down for those in the cellar.

Everyone ate but Mary. Before the meal, while Margaret was upstairs preparing food and Marjorie tended to Jennifer, Hector and Joel continued their clandestine work in the back room.

The stone cellar actually consisted of two rooms. A narrow passage led from the main room into a smaller secondary room that housed the home's propane-powered furnace. When Mims briefly checked out the basement after he and Skink initially entered the house, all he found in the secondary room was four flat walls, the furnace apparatus, and ducting. At the time of his hasty search he was only concerned with ensuring there were no other occupants in the basement and satisfying himself there were no windows or other ways out.

Had Mims looked a bit closer, he might have noticed that three of the walls in the smaller back room were stone, and the other wall, behind the furnace, consisted of horizontal wooden slats.

Like most houses built shortly after the turn of the twentieth century, the home at one time featured a coal-powered furnace. The secondary room was once the coal repository. Coal was originally delivered by horse-drawn wagon, and eventually by truck, and shoveled or poured through a concrete-lined opening along one side of the house.

By the time Hector and Margaret Hernandez purchased the home, one of the previous owners had long since removed the coal-powered furnace and replaced it with a modern, propane-powered, appliance. The coal chute and bin were boarded up in the basement and capped outside at ground level with a heavy metal hatch secured by a hasp and padlock.

Since the previous night, Hector and Joel had been hard at work. Joel held a flashlight while Hector pried off the horizontal boards using a rusty tire iron he located among some old tools in the basement. Working carefully to avoid sound, the pair removed the slats and entered the former coal bin. Hector examined the chute's cover, which was several feet above his head.

While there was no ladder in the basement, there were several sturdy, self-standing, six-foot-tall industrial shelves Hector had purchased from a hardware store in Farnham years ago and assembled for added storage in the cellar's main room. With Margaret and Marjorie lending a hand while Jennifer slept, he and Joel removed all the items from one of the shelving units. They meticulously rearranged the items on the other shelves to accommodate the transfer, and Joel helped him quietly move the empty shelf into the second room and into the coal bin.

Hector covered the heavy-duty, four-level, shelf with an old blanket to muffle sound. With Joel to steady it, he placed it beneath the hatch and climbed up.

Hector could now easily reach the hatch. Pushing upward, he slowly raised the heavy cover. The hatch broke through decades of sediment and dead leaves until its progress was stopped after a little less than two inches by the hasp and padlock. Though he couldn't see through the emerging crack due to the darkness, he felt air on his face, and the heavy scent of woodsmoke from the Farnham Fire filled his nostrils.

There were no bolt cutters, or a hacksaw, in the box of old discarded tools in the main part of the basement, but Hector found a rusty hacksaw blade lying in the bottom of the tray. He also found a single twelve-gauge, 00 buck shotgun shell inside the toolbox, which he pocketed.

Donning a pair of old gloves to protect his hands, Hector got to work. Wedging open the hatch cover with a stack of gardening magazines, he discovered he could just get a blade through the gap and aligned with the padlock. But due to the limited length of the saw blade and the distance from the opening of the hatch cover to the lock's shackle, he could only manage very short strokes.

Hector worked through the evening and into the night. He switched hands frequently to alleviate the cramping in his fingers, wrists, forearms, and shoulders which was exacerbated by the awkward sawing angle and abbreviated cuts.

Sometime after midnight, Hector sent Joel to sleep on the cot along with Jennifer. At three A.M., he became too exhausted to continue the tedious sawing and fell asleep on the basement floor. By his best estimate, he'd cut through approximately one-third of the shackle on the rusty old padlock.

Margaret cried herself to sleep worrying about Mary, alone with the men upstairs. She slumbered on a make-shift mattress comprised of old tarpaulins and a tent. The children slept together on the cot. Marjorie dozed while seated at the folding table, rising frequently to check on her children or when startled awake by her own nightmares.

Hector was awake again by six A.M. and back at work on the padlock. Joel joined him with his flashlight a little after eight, and they worked together all morning. They halted work and replaced the horizontal boards covering the coal chute and bin just before Margaret went up the stairs to pound on the door and demand access to the bathroom.

Once the bathroom break was over, and the meal was concluded, Hector and Joel returned to the coal chute and resumed their task. Margaret remained upstairs, and

Jennifer napped on the cot. Marjorie again approached Mary.

"How're you doing?" she asked her sister in a hushed voice.

"You're kidding, right?" Mary said, giving her older sister a disgusted look.

"That eye looks painful."

"You would know," Mary said.

"About last night," Marjorie said, "I wanted to tell you . . ."

"Forget it," Mary cut her off. "Didn't you accuse me of banging bikers and carnies? That would mean I'm used to it, right?"

"Is that what happened," Marjorie said, "up there?"

"What do you think happened?" Mary retorted.

"I don't know," Marjorie said. "I only asked because I care."

Mary looked like she was going to launch another snarky retort but didn't. She rubbed her eyes, gingerly touching the swollen one.

"The big guy, Duane," she began, "took me upstairs. He made me . . . do stuff to him. But he couldn't get hard. He tried to penetrate me, but he couldn't. Big, tough badass with a gun is a limp noodle." She laughed bitterly. "I guess it made him mad, so he hit me. Like it's my fault he's got no lead in his pencil."

Marjorie sat down on the floor next to Mary and put her arms around her sister. Tears began to leak from Mary's eyes, but her face remained hard and her voice remained even.

"He bound my wrists with electrical cord and tied me to the bed. Then he lay down next to me and slept. All night. He never touched me again. When the morning came, he brought me downstairs, and here I am."

"I'm sorry," Marjorie said. "I'll never forget what you did. The sacrifice you made for us. For me."

"Don't be grateful," Mary said. "I'm not worth it."

"Of course you are," Marjorie said, pulling her sister closer. "What makes you say such a thing? Sure we've had our differences, and we don't always see eye to eye, but I never doubted that you love me. And I hope you always knew that I love you. You're my baby sister."

Mary burst into sobs. She buried her face in Marjorie's chest and cried, her body trembling with the increasing intensity of her weeping.

"I'm sorry," she wept. "Please forgive me."

"What in the world is there to forgive you for?" Marjorie asked, confused. She rocked her sister gently, patting her back as she cried. "Like I tell my kids," she said, "if you haven't done anything wrong, there's no need to apologize."

"We're all going to die," Mary blurted.

"No," Marjorie said, "we're not. If they were going to kill us, they'd have done it by now. Besides, Dad's going to get us out of here."

"You're wrong," Mary said, regaining her composure and wiping her eyes. "You don't know what I know. I saw something in that Duane guy's eyes last night. Something empty. A hole in a person like I've never seen before, not even in rehab, where everybody is the walking dead. He's not going to let us escape. He's going to kill us. All of us. I'm certain of it."

"We'll just have to make sure that doesn't happen," Marjorie said, "because I'm not going to let either one of those bastards hurt my kids. No way. Not as long as there's a single breath left in my body. The same goes for Mom and Dad and you. You're my family, and I'll do whatever it takes to protect you."

Hector and Joel emerged from the back room. Hector was holding a bloody handkerchief to one of his hands.

"What happened?" Marjorie said.

"Cut my knuckle," he said. "It's not bad, but it's bleeding. I need to bandage it up."

Marjorie retrieved the first-aid kit and began to tend to her father's injury. "How's it going?" she asked.

"I'm about halfway through," Hector said. "Those old-time padlocks are made of pretty hard steel. If I had a hacksaw, instead of only a dull, rusty hacksaw blade, I'd have been through it by now."

"How much longer?"

"At this rate," he said, "a few more hours, at least."

"Let's hope we have a few more hours," Marjorie said, thinking about what Mary said.

"Something's been bothering me," Hector said, as Marjorie bandaged his fingers. "I can't figure out where I've seen that Duane guy before, but I'm positive I have. I sure wish I could remember."

"Don't worry about him right now," Marjorie said. "Focus on cutting through that lock and getting us out of here."

The basement door opened. Hector hid his hand behind his back.

He needn't have. Margaret came down alone, bearing several cold sodas and a bag of ice. The door closed behind her, and they heard the *click* of the dead bolt.

Margaret handed the ice pack to Mary and a soda to Joel. The rest of the beverages she placed on the table.

"Are you okay?" Hector asked, hugging his wife.

She nodded. "They didn't hurt me. They had me clean up the kitchen and start tonight's meal."

"Did they say anything about what they're going to do? Marjorie asked. "Are they planning to leave anytime soon?"

"They didn't say much," Margaret said, "to me or each other. I get the feeling they aren't getting along. The skinny one with the tattoo is drinking a lot of beer and smoking cigarettes, and keeps sniffing drugs into his nose. He doesn't look well at all."

"I hope he dies," Joel said.

"Joel," Margaret admonished her grandson. "You don't mean that."

"Yes, I do," Joel said.

"Did you learn anything else?" Hector asked.

"They've got the radio on in the living room," Margaret said. "I could hear it when I was in the kitchen. The fire's getting closer. The news said it was more than halfway from Tuckerville to Farnham, which means . . ."

". . . it's only a couple of miles from here," Hector finished.

"That's not all," Margaret said. "The weather forecast is calling for another bout of high winds later this afternoon and into the night. But it also said there was a possibility of rain."

"Did the radio have any other news?" Hector said.

"Only that they've announced emergency evacuations in Farnham and the outlying areas."

"Outlying areas," Marjorie said. "That's us."

"Did either of them say anything about what they intend to do if the fire reaches us here?" Hector asked.

"I asked them that very question myself," she answered.

"Duane didn't say anything," she continued. "He doesn't say much. The other one, who Duane calls Skink, just laughed, and told me not to worry. He said the fire would take care of everything."

"I stand corrected," Mary spoke up. "When I said they were going to kill us, I was wrong. They're not going to kill us. They're going to let the fire do it for them."

CHAPTER THIRTY-THREE

"It's nice to see you again, Deputy Strayer," Dr. Wozniak said. "I wasn't expecting you so soon. Please come in and have a seat."

Strayer entered and sat down.

"May I offer you anything?"

Strayer shook her head. Wozniak sat down on the couch opposite her with a diet soda and straw, kicked off her shoes, and tucked her legs under her skirt.

"Aren't you going to ask me about my hand?" Strayer said.

"I don't have to," Wozniak said. "I already know how you injured it. I also know you were nearly involved in a fight with a fellow deputy this morning and threw up in the women's restroom, and that yesterday you beat a child-abuse suspect to the tune of a busted nose, broken jaw, and several missing teeth."

Strayer's eyebrows lifted. "Sergeant Simpson has been a regular patient of mine for years," Wozniak said, answering the unspoken question. "You should be grateful she cares enough about you to take an interest in your well-being. I presume it's why you're here now."

"It's not like she gave me a choice," Strayer said.

"Are you saying you don't want to be here?"

"Not especially," Strayer said.

"I see," Wozniak said. She set down her soda and stood up. "Then there's no point in wasting any more of your time. Or mine. Good day, Deputy Strayer."

"I don't understand?" Strayer said.

"What were you expecting?" Wozniak said. "Waterboarding? For me to hold you down and try to help you against your will?"

"Who said I needed any help?" Strayer said.

"Deputy Strayer," Wozniak said, "if you can't see that you're in crisis, nothing I say is going to convince you. I've been around too long to believe everyone can be saved. Some casualties can be, others can't. That's just how it is. You were a soldier. You've experienced combat. You should know this better than anyone."

"What are you saying?" Strayer stood to face Wozniak.

"The last time you were here," Wozniak said, "you insisted you weren't suffering from post-traumatic stress disorder."

"That's right," Strayer said. "And you agreed with me."

"Actually, I didn't. I merely pointed out that I never said you had post-traumatic stress disorder. In truth, you're as textbook a case as I've ever seen."

"That's ridiculous," Strayer said.

"Is it?" Wozniak said. "Since you're on the way out, and probably won't be back, I'll do you the honor of being blunt. I've found with soldiers, like we are, frankness works better than tiptoeing around a problem."

"Your point is?"

"I believe," Wozniak said, "based on what limited information I know about you, that you are in fact suffering from a severe case of PTSD."

"What makes you think that?"

"How about I list off some symptoms" Wozniak said, "and you can decide for yourself if they apply to you?"

"Go ahead."

"You live a Spartan, isolated life," Wozniak began. "You're a loner, and don't encourage or sustain even superficial social relationships. I doubt you've been intimate, with a friend or lover, for a very long time. You work out a lot and are always in training."

"Training?" Strayer said. "For what?"

"In preparation to meet your next enemy. You're constantly reinforcing your physical, mental, and emotional armor."

Strayer's face went slack, though she didn't realize it.

Wozniak continued. "You maintain a constant level of alertness for danger. This state of mind is clinically known as hypervigilance, and it takes effort to maintain. Over long periods of time it can be extremely damaging to the body. I assume you sleep poorly, and subconsciously relive in dream states your past battles and traumas."

Strayer felt the room beginning to warm.

"You chose to become a soldier quite young, not exactly a typical profession for a young woman even in today's society. This leads me to believe that while you certainly experienced any number of critical incidents while deployed, the underlying trauma that was the genesis of your disorder occurred before you enlisted. If I had to guess, I'd say it was a catastrophic event you suffered and survived while you were a little girl or perhaps as a teenager. I suspect you were hard-wired for post-traumatic stress disorder long before you ever got into a combat zone."

Beads of perspiration broke out over Strayer's forehead.

"After your military service," Wozniak said, "you consciously or subconsciously chose to work in an occupation where hypervigilance is commonplace. Many within the law enforcement profession suffer from post-traumatic stress disorder. Your own state of chronic hypervigilance and symptoms of post-traumatic stress disorder would be camouflaged and normalized among others around you who behave similarly and are similarly afflicted. It's a defense mechanism, the perfect way to hide in plain sight."

Strayer found she couldn't meet Wozniak's eyes, which seemed to be boring into her. She examined the bandage on her left hand.

"You didn't stop there," Wozniak said. "Not satisfied with merely being a patrol deputy you sought S.W.A.T. duty, an even more high-risk position. As a S.W.A.T. deputy, you would be exposed to even greater levels of risk and more intense releases of adrenaline."

"Adrenaline?"

"Adrenaline is a drug as potent as any other," Wozniak explained, "and just as addictive. Many PTSD sufferers have become addicted to adrenaline, among other substances, and are driven towards environments that feed their addiction."

"I'm not admitting I have any of those symptoms,"

Strayers said, her voice suddenly dry and raspy, "but if I did, what would cause them?"

"There can be any number of causes," Wozniak said. "Symptoms usually manifest themselves in the aftermath of a traumatic event and worsen over time. In your case, I suspect shame over a past trauma, or series of traumas, is the probable cause. That, and perhaps a misguided belief that you somehow brought your suffering on yourself, or deserved it, coupled with guilt that you survived."

"If I did have PTSD," Strayer said, fully sweating now, "hypothetically, how would I get rid of it?"

"You can't, really," Wozniak said. "Not entirely. You can, however, learn to manage it. PTSD is like cancer, or alcoholism, as I mentioned earlier. One might quit drinking, or have their cancer go into remission, but there's always the potential for relapse. Post-traumatic stress disorder is much the same. It can be managed, and quite successfully, but only if the person experiencing it is committed to their healing and willing to do the necessary work."

"What's the first step?" Strayer asked.

"Unburdening yourself," Wozniak said. "Jettisoning the shame and guilt. Getting it out."

"I don't know how," Strayer said, finally looking up to again meet Wozniak's eyes. Her voice was barely a whisper.

"Why don't you sit down," Wozniak said, guiding Strayer back to the couch, "and we can talk about it?"

Chapter Thirty-four

Tad Guthrie stumbled from the woods behind the Hernandez house frustrated, disheveled, abraded, and out of breath. He'd spent well over an hour lost between the almond orchard where he'd parked his rental car and his in-laws' home.

Under normal conditions, it would have taken him less than fifteen minutes to navigate the quarter-mile-long stretch of forest. But the smoke, which seemed to be getting thicker and more dense by the minute, had rendered visibility only a few yards. As a result of the smoke-fogged air, and the stinging, eye-watering effects it had on his vision, he quickly became disoriented in the heavy brush and began wandering in circles.

Adding to his vexation and discomfort was the temperature, which had risen again into the upper nineties. In addition to the heat, being lost, and the suffocating smoke, a steadily increasing wind had erupted that added swirling dust to the nearly unbreathable atmosphere. Tad coughed and gasped as he staggered through the brambles and briars.

When he finally emerged from the woods into his

in-laws' familiar backyard, which he located through sheer luck, he was sweat-soaked, dust-caked, bug-bitten, covered in scratches, exhausted, and pissed off.

Tad had originally planned to remain in the woods and observe the property from a position of concealment before attempting to contact anyone inside. He'd hoped to locate and signal Mary, after he spotted her rented Lincoln parked next to Marjorie's Range Rover and their father's old truck. He knew she wasn't allowed to smoke in the house, and figured it wouldn't be long before she came outside for a cigarette.

But in his overheated and irritated state, with his throat and lungs on fire, eyes watering, and skin itching from insect bites and abrasions, Tad abandoned the idea of waiting for Mary's next cigarette break. He was determined to get inside the comfort of the house as quickly as possible.

Dusting himself off as best he could, he headed across the yard to the front door. Tad stopped momentarily to examine each of the parked vehicles, finding them all locked. He decided to look inside to determine if any of them had been packed for a quick departure.

When he wiped away the layer of ash covering the windshield of the truck, he was surprised to see a shotgun lying on the seat until it occurred to him that his father-in-law might have secured the weapon there because the children were visiting.

Tad was relieved. At least Hector can't shoot me, he thought.

Ruminating between what he was going to say to Marjorie and pondering the fresh air and cold water waiting inside the house, Tad took another quick swig of vodka. Then he stashed the bottle and mounted the porch steps.

* * *

The knock on the door brought Mims quickly from the kitchen into the main room. He found Skink struggling to get up from where he'd been lying, semiconscious, on the couch.

"Who is it?" Mims asked, drawing his own gun.

"I don't know," Skink said. He shook his head to clear it. "I didn't hear no car drive up."

Mims carefully cracked a blind and peered out. He saw a tall, heavyset man in his mid-thirties with salon-styled hair. He was sprinkled with dust and ash, and wearing a perspiration-stained Lacoste shirt, khaki trousers, and filthy deck shoes without socks. The man knocked again on the door and tried the knob, which was locked.

Mims's first thought was that the man on the porch might be a stranded motorist who'd made it to the old farmhouse on foot from a disabled car. "Keep an eye on the door," he ordered Skink. Then he went into the kitchen, unlocked the basement door, and opened it.

"Marjorie," Mims called down. "Get up here. Now."

"What do you want with her?" Margaret demanded.

"Tell her to get her ass upstairs," Mims said, "or I'll come down there and bring up one of her kids instead."

Marjorie appeared on the stairs with an apprehensive look on her bruised face.

"Hurry up," Mims snapped, as she tentatively climbed the steps.

Once Marjorie entered the kitchen, Mims quickly patted her down. Then he took her by the arm and led her to the living room window. The insistent knocking on the front door continued.

Mims parted the blinds with his pistol. "Do you know who that is?"

Marjorie's shoulders slumped, but she didn't answer.

"Tell me," Mims said, realizing she recognized him. "Who is he?"

"It's my husband, Tad," Marjorie said, as she peeked through the slats.

"Were you expecting him?"

"No," she said, stepping back from the window. "Definitely not. I have a restraining order against him, and he knows it. He's prohibited from coming here. That's the reason I brought the kids out to my folks' house in the first place."

"Evidently your husband isn't afraid to break the law," Mims grunted. "Why is he here?"

"If I had to guess," Marjorie said, "he came to try and convince me to abandon the divorce and drop the criminal charges against him. He did that before."

"Get rid of him."

"How?"

"Tell him to go away," Mims said, "through the door. Don't open it."

"I can't," Marjorie said. "I'm not supposed to have any contact with him."

"I don't give a damn about your restraining order," Mims said, grabbing her roughly by the arm and putting his gun against her throat. "Get rid of him, or I will. My way is permanent."

Marjorie reluctantly nodded as Mims released her. He moved to the side of the doorway, to the same place he'd hidden to ambush Marjorie and Mary when they'd each entered the home.

Mims gestured for Skink to go into the kitchen, but the skinny convict was already en route. Once he tucked himself out of view, Mims prodded Marjorie again with his gun.

"Go away," Marjorie said through the door. "You're not supposed to be here."

"Open up," Tad's voice answered.

"No," she countered. "You're in violation of a restraining order. You can be arrested. Get out of here, before I call the sheriff's department."

"You won't," Tad argued, "because you can't. The phone lines are down and you don't have cell service out here."

"What do you want?"

"I only want to make sure you and the kids are okay," Tad lied. "The fire's getting close. Can't you tell the smoke's growing heavier?"

Actually, Marjorie had noticed the heavier smoke when she looked out the window a moment before. But she wasn't fooled about the real reason Tad had shown up.

Mims poked Marjorie with his pistol. "We're fine," she said through the panel. "We can pack up and leave whenever we want. You're not supposed to be here, Tad. Go away."

"I'm not going away until you talk to me," Tad's voice said.

"I've got nothing to say to you. Now or ever."

"Open the door, Marjorie," Tad said.

"No," she said. "I won't."

"It's hot and smoky out here, and it hurts my throat to holler through this door. Open up."

"No," she said.

"Then I'll kick it in."

"If you do," Marjorie said, looking sideways at Mims, "you'll be shot."

"Nice try," Tad said, "but I know you're lying. Your dad's old shotgun is locked in his truck. Last chance, Marjorie. Open the door and let me in, or I'll kick it down and come in anyway."

"I'm warning you," Marjorie said. "Don't do it, Tad. Don't come in here."

"Step back," he said through the door.

Mims nodded to her, and Marjorie retreated several steps. An instant later the jamb splintered and the door burst open.

A red-faced and panting Tad stood in the open doorway. He glared at Marjorie with clenched fists.

"You shouldn't have come in," Marjorie said.

"You should've opened the door," Tad said smugly.

"You should listen to your wife more often," Mims said, stepping from behind the door.

Before Tad could turn to see who the voice behind him belonged to, Mims grabbed his coiffed hair and yanked violently downward. At the same time, he planted his heel behind one of Tad's knees.

The hair-pull takedown, executed just as he'd been taught at the sheriff's academy over two decades before, sent Tad sprawling to the ground on his back. The impact knocked the wind out of him and launched a fireworks display before his eyes.

When his vision finally cleared, several blinks later, Tad looked up to find a man he'd never seen before standing over him with a pistol pointed at his face.

CHAPTER THIRTY-FIVE

"Where am I supposed to start?" Strayer asked.

"Wherever you want," Dr. Wozniak said. "But I suspect you already know where."

"Yeah," Strayer said.

Seventeen-year-old Leanne Strayer stepped off the rural school bus along with two dozen other students who also resided in the Sierra Vista Mobile Home Park. The trailer park, the largest in Farnham County, was a little more than five miles outside the Farnham town limits.

It was Friday afternoon, and unlike the other students on the bus, Strayer wasn't relieved the school week had ended. She much preferred to be at school than at home. She was especially anxious this particular Friday because there was only one week of school left until summer break.

A junior at Farnham High, Strayer had a busy weekend ahead of her. In addition to her regular homework and studying for next week's end-of-year exams, she was also studying in preparation for her general equivalency diploma. She was scheduled to take her GED test on the first Monday after summer break began.

Along with her studies, she had also arranged to babysit on Saturday night and Sunday afternoon. Strayer was employed by a number of families with small children within the park, and had a reputation as a responsible and reliable babysitter. The money she generated through her regular babysitting gigs was all that sustained her, since the meager sum her mother received through public assistance was largely squandered on cigarettes and alcoholic beverages.

Strayer wound her way through the park and the maze of trailers until her mother's single-wide unit came into view. Her shoulders slumped when she recognized the dented multicolored Pontiac Grand Am sitting in the driveway. The car belonged to her mother's current boyfriend, Karl. He was the most recent in an endless string of boyfriends, a result of her mother's pathological inability to be alone.

Strayer had hoped that when Donnie Hennisten left earlier that spring, taking his son, her half brother Robbie, back with him up north, that her mother might at least wait a few weeks before introducing another man into their lives. But such hope was always in vain. One man would no sooner leave, or be kicked out, than another would be introduced. The Strayer trailer was a veritable revolving door of strange men.

The men her mother dated always possessed the same general qualities. All were heavy drinkers, like she was, few had steady jobs, and rarely did they have their own places to live. Which meant that shortly after meeting a new man, her mother would inevitably invite him to reside in the tiny trailer along with them.

They would stay a week, or a month, or in Hennisten's case, a year, but eventually they would leave, or be kicked out, and Strayer's mother would dutifully go out and find another.

Karl was more repugnant than most of the previous boyfriends, a reflection of her mother's rapidly deteriorating appearance and health. Once strikingly beautiful, the river of booze and mountain of smokes Ji-eun "Junie" Strayer had consumed since her husband's death, when Leanne was only a toddler, left her a shadowy remnant of her once-vibrant self. She spent her days smoking, drinking, and watching daytime television, rarely leaving the trailer during daylight hours.

But each night, Junie Strayer was off to the Squirrel Cage. The Squirrel Cage was a hole-in-the-wall combination gas station, bar, and diner less than a half mile down the road from the Sierra Vista Mobile Home Park. There she would drink and smoke the night away and invariably attract the men she would later bring back to her trailer and into her daughter's life.

Strayer entered the trailer, which as usual was stiflingly hot and reeked of stale cigarette smoke. Her mother, still clad in her bathrobe, was seated in the kitchen. Karl was seated on the worn couch, his obese body taking up most of it. Both were smoking, and the television was tuned to a game show.

"Hey, Leanne," Karl greeted her, his unshaved face brightening. He made no effort to hide the leer he directed at Strayer's legs. "Lookin' good. I always said, there's nothin' hotter than a Eurasian gal. Ain't I always sayin' that, Junie?"

Strayer's mother didn't respond, staring blankly at the television. Strayer ignored Karl, gave her mom a quick hug, and opened the refrigerator.

"What happened to my Dr Pepper?" she asked, as soon as she noticed the bottle was gone. "I bought that yesterday for after school today."

Her mother looked away and extinguished her cigarette. Strayer looked accusingly at Karl.

"I got thirsty," Karl said with a shrug.

"That was mine," Strayer said.

"There was nobody's name on it," Karl grunted.

Strayer glared at her mother and shook her head. She set down her backpack in the kitchen and had started to enter the bathroom when the odor stopped her. The scent from Karl's most recent deposit almost made her gag.

"God," Strayer gasped. "Mom," she called out in exasperation, "could you please teach your boyfriend to flush a toilet?"

From the other room, Karl laughed. "You like it?" he taunted. "One of my better productions. I really took the Browns to the Superbowl on that one."

Since she needed to urinate, Strayer had no choice but to use the facility. When she emerged a moment later, after holding her breath while relieving herself, she found Karl had risen from the couch and was withdrawing her laptop computer from her backpack.

"Hey!" Strayer shouted. She rushed over and tried to snatch the computer away from him, but he wouldn't release it.

"That's mine!" she said, struggling for the device. "Give it back!" She looked to her mother, who merely lit another cigarette and sat passively with her chronically blank face.

"I want to use the internet," Karl said.

"Not on my computer," Strayer said through clenched teeth. She tugged on the laptop with all her might, finally wresting it free.

"Your mom said I could," Karl whined. "Ain't that right, Junie?"

"I don't care what she said," Strayer insisted, wrapping both arms protectively around the laptop. She turned to her mother. "The school gave me this computer to do my homework, Mom. It's not for your creepy boyfriends to use."

"I say he use," she said without emotion, in her thick Korean accent.

"See," Karl said smugly. "I have permission."

"It's not hers to give," Strayer said.

"You need to learn to mind your momma," Karl said.

"You need to butt out," Strayer said, returning the laptop to her backpack. "Don't talk to me, stay away from me, and keep your greasy, fat paws off my stuff."

"You should show a little respect for your elders," Karl said. "I've half a mind to turn you over my knee."

"Don't even think about it," Strayer said dismissively. She turned again to her mother. "Did you sign the papers yet?"

"What papers?" her mother said.

"You know what papers," Strayer said in frustration. "The army papers I brought home last week. You promised you'd look them over."

"I forgot."

"Mom! You promised!"

"Don't want sign papers," she said. "Want you here with me. You no go to army."

Strayer was referring to the military enlistment documents she'd obtained with the help of an army recruiter. Since she was only seventeen, she needed the signature of a parent or guardian to enlist.

Earlier in the year, two of her mother's boyfriends ago, Strayer vowed to find a way out of the trailer park. She knew she had to escape the life of squalor inflicted upon her by her mother's pathetic neediness as soon as possible. But with no money for college, nor even any saved to support herself if she was to move out of the trailer and try to live on her own, she sought the advice of a high school guidance counselor.

Her guidance counselor, accustomed to assisting rural students like Strayer who were penniless and without family support, recommended that she consider enlisting in one of the branches of the military. But only after she graduated high school the following year.

Strayer decided she couldn't wait another year. She refused to become collateral damage from her mother's self-destructive lifestyle or be subjected any further to the degenerate men her mother brought into their home. She knew she had to find a way out on her own. The more she thought about military service, the more the idea appealed to her.

Not only would she be free of her mother and the dregs of humanity she associated with, in the military Strayer wouldn't have to constantly worry about where her next meal was coming from. She'd be fed, clothed, and housed, not to mention have access to medical and dental care, which she currently didn't have, and be trained in a military occupational specialty that could lead to not just a job but potentially a career. When she found out that she would also be able to pursue her college education while on active duty via online courses, at no cost, her mind was made up.

She loved her mother, but suffered no delusions about who her mom was or how she was going to end up. Strayer had been sleeping with a kitchen knife under her pillow since the age of twelve, after she woke up one night to find one of her mother's boyfriends standing in her room in his underwear.

He ran when she screamed, but ever since that night she realized her mother had always put her own selfish wants above her daughter's needs and safety. Strayer had no second thoughts about leaving home or abandoning a parent who had essentially abandoned her long ago.

Strayer discovered that no branch of the military would accept an underage recruit without a high school diploma, and rarely with only a general equivalency diploma, or GED, regardless of her age. But with a high SAT score, which she had, and a letter of recommendation provided by her high school counselor attesting to her good character, maturity, and excellent scholastic record, she obtained a waiver that would allow her to enlist with only a GED if she agreed to continue her education while in the military, something she'd planned to do anyway.

She began studying for the general equivalency diploma shortly after Christmas. When she turned seventeen in April, she took the Armed Services Vocational Aptitude

Battery, or ASVAB test, and scored well. She planned to complete her junior year at Farnham High School, obtain her GED within a week thereafter, and enlist in the army, forgoing her senior year. The only thing standing in her way, since she was underage, was her mother's written permission on the enlistment documents.

"I no sign. Want you here."

"Mom," Strayer said, "it's time for me to move on." She looked over her shoulder at Karl. "You don't need me here anymore. You have a boyfriend. Why don't you sign the papers and let me go?"

"Want you here. No go."

Strayer grabbed her backpack and huffed off to her room. She closed the door, opened the window, and began unpacking her books and computer, opting to get an early start on her homework as a way to calm herself. She intended to remain in her room until after dark, when her mother and Karl would drive off in his car to the Squirrel Cage for an evening of more drinking and smoking. For her dinner, she'd saved an apple and half a sandwich from her school lunch, minus the Dr Pepper she'd been so looking forward to. A moment later, a knock sounded on the door.

Thinking it was her mother, Strayer opened the door to find Karl standing in the doorway.

"I didn't know you was thinkin' about joinin' the army," he said.

"That's because it's none of your business," Strayer said. She tried to close the door, but he stepped in and blocked the jamb with his huge body.

"I was in the navy once," he said, "for a couple of months. I got a medical discharge out of boot camp."

"There's a shocker," Strayer said. "If you'll excuse me," she went on, trying to close the door, "I've got homework to do."

"You know," Karl said, "if you asked me nice, I could maybe talk to your mom about signin' them papers for ya?"

"You've known her three weeks," Strayer said. "I don't think so. Besides, like I already told you, it's none of your business."

"You might try bein' a little nicer to me," Karl said, ogling Strayer's figure. "Could be, there's a way we might help each other out."

"Get out of my room," Strayer said, pushing him out and closing the door.

Afternoon became evening, and Karl and her mother departed shortly after sunset. Relieved to see them go, Strayer left her room, opened the windows to air the stale cigarette smoke from the trailer, and continued her homework and studies at the kitchen table where the light was better.

A little before midnight, Strayer finished her homework and studies. She washed her face and retired to her room, undressing and climbing into bed in only her T-shirt and panties. She fell instantly asleep, exhausted from her hectic week.

Sometime after 2:00 A.M., according to her alarm clock, she heard the rickety clatter of Karl's Pontiac drive up. Strayer didn't have to see Karl and her mother stumbling up the metal steps to know they were both intoxicated. She could tell by the racket they made as they entered the trailer.

Strayer had heard the drunken clamor of her mother

coming home in the early morning hours too many times to remember, and with too many different men. She buried herself deeper under the covers and tried to go back to sleep.

CHAPTER THIRTY-SIX

"I warned you not to come in," Marjorie said.

Tad sat on the couch with his hands duct-taped behind his back. His pockets had been emptied, and his personal possessions were added to the contents of Marjorie's and Mary's purses scattered on the living-room table. All except the pint bottle of vodka, which Mims handed to Skink.

"You could have told me why."

"I did," Marjorie said. "I told you not to come in or you'd be shot, didn't I?"

"I thought you meant by your dad."

"Did I say it was my dad who was going to shoot you?"

"Shut up," Mims said, "both of you."

"What are we gonna do with him?" Skink asked. He was seated on the opposite couch, counting the thick wad of money from Tad's wallet.

"We'll put him down in the basement," Mims answered, "same as the others."

"I don't want him near me," Marjorie said, "or my children. He's not supposed to be near us."

"You already told me that," Mims said. "I didn't care then, and I don't care now."

"Fine with me if they want to be apart," Skink said. He unscrewed the vodka bottle with his good left hand. "He can go down into the cellar, and she can stay up here and keep me company."

"Bad idea," Mims said. "There's too many of them now. I want everybody downstairs, in one place, where they can be contained."

"That's bullshit," Skink said. He took a long slug of vodka, spilling some over his chin. When he finished, he pointed the bottle at Mims. "You had your fun with the younger one. It's my turn. I want what's comin' to me, and I want it now."

"Not a good time," Mims said. "Maybe later tonight, after you've rested."

"I don't think you heard me, Duane," Skink said, standing shakily up. He set the vodka bottle on the table and tucked his good left thumb into his belt over the pistol nestled there. "I wasn't askin'."

"Don't be a fool," Mims said.

"That's pretty good advice," Skink said. "Because I'm done bein' a fool, your fool. I ain't takin' no more orders from you, and I wasn't askin' your permission to get my dick wet. Me and Marjorie are gonna get acquainted, same as you and her sister Mary did. If you've got a problem with that, I reckon you'd best look to your pistola."

Mims, Marjorie, and Tad all watched Skink. His skin was jaundiced, he was sweating profusely, his eyes were sunken and his pupils dilated, and his entire body seemed to be twitching, even though he was standing still. The combination of sleeplessness, heavy methamphetamine and alcohol ingestion, and the increasingly obvious signs of infection from his broken collarbone left him looking like a frayed wire about to spark and beget a fire. His left hand hovered over the Glock in his belt, a tremor visible in his tattooed fingers.

"Your call," Skink challenged. Every inch of him was primed to draw his gun. "Stand aside, and let me have my way with Marjorie, or go for your gun."

"Fine," Mims said, backing down. "If you feel that strongly about it, go right ahead. Take her upstairs, though, will you? I don't particularly want to watch."

"What's going on?" Tad said. He looked incredulously from Marjorie, to Skink, and then to Mims. "Did he just say they raped Mary? And they're going to rape you?"

"Your husband's a smart one." Skink chuckled at Marjorie. "He catches on real quick."

"No way," Tad said standing up. "I won't allow it."

Skink walked over to Tad and kicked him in the groin. It wasn't a powerful kick, because he was so weak, but it was enough. Tad fell to his knees, gasping in agony. Skink kicked him again, this time in the stomach. Tad fell forward on his face.

"Just like we did to them two prison guards, eh Duane?" Skink cackled. He finished his sentence with a coughing fit, which didn't end until he was forced to lower himself to the couch, depleted from the exertion of kicking Tad.

Mims shook his head at Skink in disgust. "Get up," he said to Tad, hauling the semiconscious newcomer to his feet. He began to steer him toward the basement door.

"Let's go," Skink said to Marjorie. With effort he pushed himself off the couch, drew his gun, and waved it at her. "You know the drill. You treat me right, and make me feel extra special good, or I'll put a bullet into one of your kids." He laughed again and pointed his chin at Mims. "Ain't that the deal Duane gave you?"

Marjorie hung her head and slowly began to climb the stairs. Skink steadied himself against the wall, took out the jar of methamphetamine, poured another glob onto the back of his gun hand, and snorted. Then he retrieved the vodka bottle, released an anemic rebel yell which ended in another coughing fit, and followed Marjorie up the stairs.

Chapter Thirty-seven

"Am I doing this right?" Strayer asked.

"You're doing just fine," Dr. Wozniak said.

"I've never spoken about any of this," Strayer said. She rubbed her face with her hands. "Not to anyone."

"I know," Wozniak said.

Strayer sensed a presence in the room before she was fully awake. She opened her eyes and found the hulking shadow of Karl looming over her. She tried to scream, but a thick, nicotine-stained, hand instantly clamped over her mouth.

He collapsed on top of her, his massive weight pressing her deep into the mattress. The air in her lungs was expelled through her nostrils, and her screams came out no louder than a squeaky hinge. Karl smelled of beer, cigarettes, and rancid sweat. His trousers were already pulled down to his knees, and she could feel his erection jabbing against her leg.

"You're gonna learn to respect the man of the house,"

Karl whispered into her ear, flicking his tongue as he spoke. "Oh yeah, you're gonna get a real hard lesson tonight."

The hand not clamped like a vise over her mouth snaked its way across her breasts, down her stomach, and beneath her panties. His foul, alcohol-sweet breath was hot on her face.

With one hand on her mouth, and the other at her crotch, Karl didn't bother to restrain Strayer's hands. She was so much smaller and weaker than him, he thought, and besides, as far as he was concerned, any struggle she put up only added to the fun. As a result, and because he was distracted by his state of arousal, he didn't notice one of her hands slide under her pillow.

Strayer snatched the serrated kitchen knife and began to slash and stab. She got in three good strikes on Karl's neck, shoulder, and face before he roared like a wounded beast and flung himself off the bed. He stumbled backward, his pants around his ankles, and fell on his butt in one corner of her small room.

Strayer stood over him, the knife poised above her head. Karl had a long gash on his cheek, a longer one across his drooping pectorals, and a superficial stab wound in one meaty shoulder.

"No!" he begged as he cowered, his hands covering his head. "Don't cut me no more!"

The lights in the short hallway came on, and Strayer's mother came stumbling into the room. Clearly intoxicated, she stared blankly up at her daughter standing over her boyfriend with a raised knife and an enraged expression on her face. Then she stared down at Karl, quivering on his butt in the corner with a bloody face and his now-flaccid penis exposed.

"What happen?" she asked in her Korean accent.

"What do you think happened?" Strayer shouted. "Your boyfriend just tried to rape me."

Her mother continued to stare vacantly, unable to process what she was seeing and hearing.

"I did not," Karl sputtered. "That girl of yours is crazy. She attacked me for no reason."

"Get out," Strayer said to Karl. "Get out of this trailer."

"Just hold on a minute," Karl said. "I shouldn't have to be put out . . ."

"GET OUT!" Strayer shrieked, cutting him off. She reached out and slashed Karl's forearm with the knife.

"Don't!" Karl howled. "No more!"

"Then get out," Strayer repeated, "or I swear I'll carve you into little pieces!"

"Okay," Karl said. He got to his feet, pulled up his trousers, and waddled toward the door, trying to put pressure on his multiple wounds as he made his way out.

"If you ever come back," Strayer said, as Karl hastily grabbed his things, "I'll kill you."

"That bitch is crazy," Karl said, as he opened the door and staggered down the steps to his car. "You hear me, Junie? Your daughter's crazy! I'm callin' the sheriff. We'll see what they have to say about a teenage girl takin' a knife to me for no reason?"

Several porch lights on nearby trailers flicked on. Doors and windows opened as aggravated neighbors investigated the early-morning commotion at the Strayers' mobile home.

"Call the sheriff," Strayer said. "Go on. When I tell them what you were trying to do to me, we'll see which one of us they believe. Especially with you drunk and your blood all over my bed. Go on, call 'em."

Strayer's last remark got Karl's attention as intoxicated and sliced up as he was. There was no way she could have known, but he was already a registered sex offender in Tuolumne County. In a "his-word-versus-her-word" contest with the teenaged Strayer, he knew he would lose.

"Aw, go to hell," Karl mumbled, squeezing his fat frame into his car. "The both of you!" He fired up his claptrap car and drove off.

Strayer led her numb mother back into the trailer. She stood in the kitchen in a stupor, staring vacuously at her daughter. "What happen?" she asked again.

"Go to bed, Mom," Strayer said. "You're drunk. We can talk about it in the morning."

Her mother wordlessly stumbled back into her room, as if attempted rapes and stabbings were everyday occurrences in her home.

Strayer sat down wearily at the kitchen table. Though covered in blood, none of it was hers. She was trembling, and it took a moment for her to realize she was still clutching the bloody knife.

She threw it in the sink and rose to her feet. Physically and emotionally drained, she pushed herself up from the table and went into the bathroom to clean herself up.

Strayer had just come out of the shower and donned a clean T-shirt, panties, and shorts when there was a loud knock on the door. She peered through the kitchen window and saw a tall man in a Farnham County Sheriff's

Department uniform standing on the trailer's tiny metal porch.

Strayer opened the door. "Can I help you?" she asked meekly.

"My name is Deputy Mims," the man said. "There's been a report of a disturbance."

CHAPTER THIRTY-EIGHT

"Daddy!" Jennifer cried, when she saw her father coming down the stairs.

Margaret and Mary immediately noticed what the young girl did not; that Tad was having difficulty walking and leaned heavily against the railing as he slowly descended.

Mims cut the duct tape binding his hands before releasing him into the basement, but the kicks to his groin and gut left him light-headed, in pain, and unsteady on his feet. Margaret and Mary guided Tad to the table, where he sat heavily down.

"What's wrong with Daddy?" Jennifer asked, about to cry.

"It's all right," Margaret soothed her granddaughter, "your daddy doesn't feel well. He'll be okay soon." Mary went into the secondary room to fetch Hector and Joel, while Margaret opened a bottle of water and placed it on the table before Tad.

"Where's Marjorie?" Margaret asked.

"Huh?" Tad groggily mumbled. He looked up at her through bleary, unfocused eyes.

"Your wife," Margaret said, this time with more insistence. "Where is Marjorie?"

Hector, Joel, and Mary reentered the main cellar. Tad noticed the water bottle. He poured water over his face, then brought it to his parched mouth and gulped.

"Where's Marjorie?" Margaret asked a third time.

"Upstairs," Tad murmured between gulps, sputtering water down his shirt front.

"We know that much, you idiot," Hector said. He slapped the bottle from Tad's hands and grabbed him roughly by the collar. "What are they doing to my daughter?"

"I don't know," said Tad indignantly.

"You don't know?" an enraged Hector shouted. He shook Tad violently, dragging him from the chair and then slamming him to the floor. He stood over him, his gloved hands transforming into fists.

Jennifer started to cry, and Margaret rushed to her. Joel looked from his grandfather to his father, confused and alarmed.

"Same thing they did to Mary, I guess," a terrified and bewildered Tad shrugged. He covered his head defensively with his hands as he lay cowering on the cold basement floor. "How the hell should I know? I was busy getting my ass kicked." He pointed to Mary. "Ask her what they're gonna do to Marjorie. They already did it to her. She can tell you."

"You asshole," Mary said, looking down at Tad in disgust. "What are you doing here, anyway?"

"I couldn't wait on you forever, could I?" Tad blurted.

Margaret looked up sharply from comforting the now-sobbing Jennifer. Her eyes narrowed as she appraised Tad, whose face suddenly flushed, and Mary, whose face suddenly paled.

"I ought to kick your teeth in," Hector said.

"What did I do?" Tad pleaded.

"Calm down," Margaret said to her husband. "You're frightening the children."

"I don't understand," Joel said, bewildered. "Why is everybody so mad at Dad?"

"This is all your fault," Hector began, pointing an accusing finger at Tad. "All of it. If you hadn't hurt Marjorie she wouldn't be here. The children wouldn't be here. None of this would be happening to them, only to me and my wife." His eyes flared, and his body trembled with rage. "You brought this down on them. Because of you, my grandchildren are in danger and my little girl is upstairs getting . . . being . . ."

"That's enough," Margaret said to her husband. "Please, Hector?"

Hector looked at his wife through tortured eyes, then turned away. He fell to his knees and buried his face in his hands. The sound of his muffled crying mingled with Jennifer's.

Joel struggled to keep from crying, too. Mary noticed, and wrapped her arms around him. She glared past the boy at Tad, who lay on the floor with a vexed look on his face.

CHAPTER THIRTY-NINE

Skink prodded Marjorie ahead into the master bedroom at gunpoint. The march upstairs winded him more than he anticipated, and he paused at the top of the stairs to catch his breath. His heart was pounding in his bony chest like a drum, and he knew the methamphetamine was only partially responsible for his hyper-accelerated state. The other factor contributing to his excitement was the anticipation of what was about to transpire.

He knew the meth he'd been steadily ingesting was probably responsible for the raging erection he was currently sporting, and for diminishing the sensation of his throbbing headache and the agony in his shoulder, neck, and right arm. Skink was aware that his steadily increasing pain, kept at bay only through the consumption of booze and crank, would soon overwhelm the anesthetizing effects of even those substances. For the moment, he didn't care. All he could think about was Marjorie.

Even with her blackened eyes, Skink thought she was extremely pretty. And he couldn't remember the last time he'd seen a real-live woman with a body like hers. He thought she looked like the nude models he'd seen in pornographic magazines. He couldn't wait to see her without clothes on.

He was almost grateful Duane got to have his way with Mary first, leaving Marjorie for him. Mary was pretty hot, he had to concede, in a punk-rock, party-girl sort of way, but compared to her older sister there was no contest.

Marjorie walked into her parents' bedroom and turned around. She and Skink appraised each other at arm's length. Skink beheld a beautiful, dark-haired, woman with a resigned look on her battered face. Marjorie saw a skeletal, sweating, tattoo-covered man with one swollen, discolored arm in a sling, seemingly barely able to stand on his own two feet.

Skink stared back at her with glazed, hungry eyes.

"This is what I've been waitin' for," he said. His eyes roved over her. "I'm gonna give it to you proper, you can count on that."

"I want to get this over with," Marjorie asked. "What do you want me to do?"

"Get your clothes off," Skink said with a grin. "I tell you what to do after that."

"If you promise not to hurt me," Marjorie said, "I'll make it really good for you."

"I ain't makin' any promises," Skink said, jittery with overstimulation. "I guess we'll just have to wait and see how good you are, won't we?"

Marjorie removed her blouse and tossed it on the bed. Skink's eyes were riveted on her breasts.

"Take off the damn bra," he said excitedly. "I wanna see 'em."

She reached both hands behind her back to unfasten her brassiere.

"Hurry up," Skink demanded impatiently. His sweating had become more pronounced, if that was possible, and he looked about ready to burst out of his own skin.

"It's stuck," Marjorie said. "I can't unsnap it." She lowered her hands, turned her back to Skink, and flipped her hair forward. Stepping backward into him, she said, "Can you unfasten it for me?"

"Hold still," Skink said in frustration. The intense throbbing in his head was competing with the throbbing in his crotch. All he could think about was freeing Marjorie's magnificent bosom from the restraints of her malfunctioning bra. He put his pistol into his belt and grabbed the bra's dual fasteners with the thumb and forefinger of his only functioning hand.

"Almost got it," he said.

The instant Marjorie felt Skink's clammy hand on her nearly naked back, she struck.

Pivoting with all the power and speed she could muster, honed from countless trunk-twists during innumerable Zumba classes at her local fitness club, Marjorie slammed her right elbow into Skink's face. No sooner did she feel the crunch of his nose than she pivoted the opposite direction, and tackled him.

She expected Skink to resist, but the stunning blow to his head, coupled with his already weakened condition, deflated the emaciated convict like a popped balloon.

Skink weighed only a few pounds more than Marjorie, and her own weight and momentum shoved him backward onto the bed. This was intentional, as she wanted to avoid the sound of his inert body crashing to the floor. She didn't want to alert Mims downstairs to the fact that she was no longer a passive captive.

Skink lay immobile on the bed. Marjorie plucked the pistol from his belt. Hastily donning her shirt, she checked his condition.

Skink's nose was broken and bleeding profusely, but he was unconscious. By the looks of him, he would remain that way for some time. Marjorie guessed the ease with which she'd knocked him out had less to do with her single blow to his head and more to do with his level of intoxication and weakened condition.

Marjorie examined the pistol. As a young girl, she and Mary had been taught to shoot using their father's Remington pump-action shotgun. She had never before held a handgun, much less fired one.

She grasped the weapon, keeping her finger off the trigger until she was ready to fire as her father had once taught her. She crept quietly from the bedroom and carefully began to descend the stairs. She held the gun before her in both hands, like a talisman.

CHAPTER FORTY

"I'm not sure I can go on," Strayer said. "I'm not . . . ready."

"Do you think you'll be more ready tomorrow?" Dr. Wozniak asked. "Or next week? How about next year?"

"What's talking about it going to do?"

"In order to purge your demons," Dr. Wozniak said, "you have to face them."

Deputy Mims stepped into the trailer without being asked. "What's your name?"

"Leanne Strayer."

"How old are you?"

"I just turned seventeen."

"Where are your folks?" He looked around, spotting the blood spatter on the kitchen floor and the trail leading down the mobile home's narrow hallway.

"My dad died when I was little. My mom's passed out drunk in her room."

"Anybody else live in this trailer?"

"No," she said. "Just me and my mom."

"What happened here tonight?" Mims said, as he began following the blood trail through the hallway. He paused to peer into her mother's open bedroom door. He found the tiny Korean woman lying facedown, fully clothed and snoring heavily. He closed the door.

"What was reported?" Strayer asked, afraid of what else to say.

"Got several calls about a loud argument," Mims said. "One of the callers mentioned something about someone having a knife."

"Yeah," Strayer said, "there was an argument here."

"What about the knife?"

Strayer didn't answer.

"By the amount of blood," Mims said, "I'd say it was quite an argument." He reached out and touched Strayer's wet hair. "You just took a shower, didn't you?"

"So?"

"Funny time of the night to be showering, wouldn't you say?"

"I suppose," Strayer said, looking away.

"You weren't washing off blood," the deputy asked, "were you?"

Strayer refused to meet the big deputy's eyes.

Mims didn't let go of her hair. He ran it through his fingers, fondling it. Once he finally let go, he brought his fingers to his nose, closed his eyes, and inhaled. He remained that way, to Strayer's bewilderment, for several long seconds.

When he finally opened his eyes, Mims reached for the portable transceiver microphone clipped to his lapel. "Code four," he radioed. "No other units needed."

"Ten-four," the dispatcher's voice repeated back. "Code four at the Sierra Vista Trailer Park."

"I presume that's your room?" Mims asked, pointing to the end of the hallway where the blood trail led.

"You don't have to go in there," Strayer said, her voice belying her nervousness, "do you?"

"Why don't you tell me what really happened here tonight?"

"Do I have to?" Strayer asked.

Instead of answering, Mims pushed past Strayer and walked into her room. He flicked on the light switch, revealing the mass of fresh blood on her bed and along the walls and floor leading out the doorway.

"It looks like somebody was slaughtered in here," Mims said. "I want the truth, young lady, and I want it now. Tell me what happened, or I'm taking you in."

"It wasn't my fault," Strayer began, pleading and beginning to cry at the same time. "I was asleep. I wasn't doing anything to anybody. Mom and her new boyfriend came home, drunk, like always. All of a sudden I woke up and he was in my bed."

She broke down, crying harder. "He put his hand over my mouth. He put his fingers in my underpants. Then he tried to . . ." Her voice trailed off.

"And you had a knife?" Mims asked.

Strayer nodded, unable to speak. After a moment, she collected herself enough to go on. "I always keep a knife under my pillow. Some of Mom's boyfriends have tried stuff with me before. Before tonight, I never had to use it."

"Where's the knife now?"

"In the kitchen sink."

"You're a brave girl," Mims said. He closed the door

behind him. Then he reached out and again took a handful of Strayer's hair. He once more closed his eyes.

Confused, Stayer wiped her eyes, looked up at the tall deputy, and slowly pushed his hand away.

Deputy Mims opened his eyes. He looked down at Strayer, nodded to himself as if affirming a decision, and then grabbed her.

CHAPTER FORTY-ONE

Marjorie could hear the radio playing below her, in the main room, as she descended the stairs. When she reached the next-to-last step, she stopped and carefully peeked around the corner of the stairwell.

Mims was seated on one of the couches. The radio was resting on the coffee table along with his pistol. He appeared to be dozing as he listened to a news broadcast. His eyes opened and shut intermittently, and his head occasionally bobbed up and down.

". . . received official word from the Farnham County Sheriff's Department and the State of California's Office of Emergency Management," the stern voice of a female radio announcer droned on. "At this time, mandatory evacuation orders are now in effect in the Town of Farnham and surrounding areas. Farnham is the largest community to be threatened by the fire since the destruction of the rural communities of Drayton and Tuckerville. Thousands of Farnham County residents have already been displaced by the out-of-control wildfire, which has consumed over one hundred thousand acres and continues to burn out of control."

Marjorie could feel the tension within her body and struggled to control the shudder in her breathing and the tremor in her hands. She took several deep breaths, calmed her mind, and steadied her resolve.

When Mims's eyes drooped again, she stepped off the stairs and entered the hallway. The radio news report covered the sound of her footsteps on the hardwood floor.

". . . we go now to our Weather Center and meteorologist Nancy Sanchez," the radio announcer said.

"In what could be welcome news to firefighters battling the Farnham Fire, as well as thousands of Farnham County residents displaced by its massive path of destruction," a different woman's voice broke in, "we're currently tracking a weather system that is traveling south with the jet stream and could be heading our way. As most Californians know, November is the traditional start of the rainy season. With the arrival of this new system, it looks to be right on time."

The weather report continued. "At this time of the year, the summertime trough over the West Coast gradually transitions into a ridge as Northern Hemisphere storms become more active. These storms, usually forming in the Gulf of Alaska or to the east over north America, are picked up by the jet stream. The stream then strengthens and shifts southward over the northern Pacific Ocean. This shift eventually moves the storms toward the West Coast."

Mims remained immobile, with his eyelids shut and his chin on his chest, as Marjorie slowly advanced. She aimed the pistol directly at him and moved her forefinger to the trigger. She gripped the gun so tightly her forearms ached, and the weapon's front and rear sights swayed and weaved before her eyes. She entered the main room from the hallway and halted before reaching the couch.

"What does all this meteorological jargon mean to us, here in California?" Sanchez asked her audience. "It could potentially mean rain in the Upper Sierras as early as this evening, and possibly in the region of the Farnham Fire by later tonight. This can only be good news to the emergency services personnel battling the blaze and to the hard-hit residents of Farnham County. A Cal Fire spokesperson said this coming storm system, and the desperately needed rain it would bring, could be the unexpected break everyone has been praying for. Because without rain, the fire could go on for weeks, much like the infamous Camp Fire in 2018, which started at almost exactly this time of year and burned for over seventeen days, becoming the most destructive wildfire in California history."

"Wake up," Marjorie heard herself say in a voice she barely recognized as her own.

Mims slowly raised his head. He blinked up at her, standing over him with a pistol aimed at his face.

"Don't you move," she said.

A smile spread across Mims's face. "I knew you were too much woman for Skink," he said.

"You're going to do as I say," Marjorie said.

"Why?" Mims said. "You aren't going to shoot me."

"Don't be so sure," Marjorie said.

"I know you, Marjorie. You don't have it in you."

"Don't try me," she said.

Marjorie began to back up toward the kitchen. She wasn't comfortable moving closer to Mims and attempting to take the pistol from the coffee table, and there was no way she was going to allow him to pick it up and toss it away. Even with a gun in her hands he was too big, too confident, and she was too scared.

Also, she wasn't sure how much longer Skink would remain unconscious upstairs. As frail as he was, she still didn't want him coming down to double-team her. She decided her best course of action was to have her father join her from the cellar. Together they could deal with the two kidnappers.

"I'm going to open the basement door," she said, still aiming the gun with both hands at Mims. "If you move or try to touch that gun on the table, I'm going to shoot you."

"Sure, I'll play along," Mims said congenially. "But I'm telling you, you're not going to shoot me."

"Precipitation projection models," meteorologist Sanchez continued broadcasting, "are looking good. The system we're tracking might bring as much as two inches of rainfall to the Sierras by morning. Back to you."

"Thank you, Nancy," the previous announcer's voice continued.

Marjorie let go of the pistol with her left hand, keeping her focus, and the gun, trained on Mims. She unlocked the basement door and opened it. Mims sat smiling in the couch, both of his hands on his knees.

"Mom," Marjorie yelled down the basement stairs.

"Marjorie?" her mother's voice called back.

"Get Dad," she ordered. "Have him come up here. Hurry."

"What's going on?"

"Just do it!" she barked at her mother. She returned both hands to her gun. "Don't you move," she said to Mims.

"You said that already," Mims said. "Don't worry. I'm not going anywhere."

A moment later Hector emerged cautiously from the stairs. His eyes widened when he saw his eldest daughter holding the Glock on Mims.

"Where's the other one?" he asked.

"Upstairs," she said. "He was knocked out a few minutes ago. I don't know about now."

"Good afternoon," Mims said pleasantly to Hector.

"Take it," she said, handing the pistol to her father. He accepted the gun and covered Mims.

"I knew you didn't have the nerve to pull the trigger on me," Mims taunted. "You like me too much. You're looking forward to finishing what we started last night as much as I am."

"Go to hell," Marjorie said.

"I have the nerve to shoot you," Hector said, "you son of a bitch."

"I know you do," Mims agreed. "You'd drop the hammer on me in a heartbeat. Except you aren't going to shoot me any more than your daughter was."

"You're wrong about that," Hector said. He'd removed his garden gloves before leaving the basement and was holding the pistol on Mims in a solid, two-handed, grip.

"I'm not wrong," Mims said, standing up. He looked down at his Glock on the coffee table.

". . . estimates of the financial impact of the fire," the radio droned on, "are already in the tens of millions of dollars . . ."

"Don't touch that gun," Hector said.

"Or what?" Mims said. He reached out and switched off the radio.

"I mean it," Hector said. "Get away from that gun."

"This gun?" Mims asked, picking up the Glock.

Hector pulled the trigger.

CHAPTER FORTY-TWO

"Try to relax," Dr. Wozniak said. "You're not there, and it's not back then. You're here, with me, now."

"I know," Strayer said. Her voice was as hollow as her eyes. "But it feels like it just happened."

"That's because you're bringing it out. Perhaps for the first time, consciously, since it occurred. Those memories can trigger a powerful emotional response."

"What should I do?"

"Don't stop," Dr. Wozniak said. "Get it out. Use your law enforcement training, Deputy Strayer. Just recount in chronological order, as you've been trained to do, what transpired next."

"Okay," Strayer said, taking in a deep breath.

The last thing Strayer remembered, before she passed out, was knowing she was going to die. The deputy grabbed her by the throat with such savage force that he lifted her entirely off the ground. The next thing she knew she'd been spun around and slammed face-first into the bloody sheets covering her own bed.

With the breath knocked out of her for the second time that night, Strayer was convinced her death was imminent. She couldn't even gasp for air as her face was jammed into the pillow. She felt her shorts and panties being torn off and tried to struggle, but the viselike hand forcing her head into the bedding almost completely encircled her neck.

Strayer felt his tongue on her neck, and realized he was scooping her hair into his mouth. Seconds later, which felt like hours, she passed out, and darkness mercifully descended.

When she awoke, sputtering and coughing, Deputy Mims was standing over her. She was naked, and lying on her back. Her throat was on fire, and she didn't know how long she'd been unconscious. Mims was buckling on his gun belt.

Looking down at her impassively, Mims re-clipped the shoulder microphone of his portable transceiver to his lapel. He turned his head, activated the push-to-talk switch, and said, "Ten-eight."

"Ten-four," the female dispatcher's dispassionate voice replied. "Back in service."

Strayer tried to sit up. She was still heatedly coughing and feared she might vomit. Mims drew his service pistol, pushed her back down onto the bed, and placed the barrel of the weapon against her forehead.

Strayer's eyes widened in terror and she stopped coughing. Mims thumbed back the pistol's hammer with an audible *click*.

"I'm going to leave now," the big deputy said matter-of-factly. "Whether I return depends on you."

Strayer stared at the gun, afraid to move.

"If you ever breathe a word about this to anyone," he continued, "I'll be back. Nobody would believe you anyway. I'm a decorated law enforcement officer and you're a half-breed, teenaged slut who stabbed somebody in a trailer park."

A single tear eked from the corner of each of Strayer's eyes, but otherwise she was as immobile as a statue.

"But if you do begin talking," Mims went on, "I'll know about it. I'll hunt you down and end you. Your mother, too. You think about that, Leanne Strayer, before you start running your mouth."

Mims decocked his pistol and holstered it. Then he turned and walked out of the trailer.

Strayer didn't move for many minutes after she heard the sheriff's cruiser drive away. Once the sound of the vehicle faded, she curled into a fetal position and began to cry uncontrollably.

It would be the last time Strayer cried until more than ten years later.

"What happened next?" Dr. Wozniak asked. She normally wouldn't have spoken herself, preferring her patient to continue at their own pace without prompting, but Strayer hadn't spoken for more than fifteen minutes. She was folded at the waist, with her head on her knees, and had spent that time sobbing with an intensity she didn't know she possessed. When she eventually quieted, she remained in her seat with her head on her forearms staring at the floor between her legs.

"I can't remember the last time I cried like that," Strayer said, regaining her composure and sitting up. Wozniak handed her the box of tissues. "Or cried at all."

"It's been said that crying is the soul's pressure release valve," Dr. Wozniak said.

"I didn't even cry at my mom's funeral," Strayer said. She wiped her eyes and blew her nose. "I didn't cry at the funerals of any of my friends who got it in Afghanistan, either." She shook her head. "Everybody else in my unit thought I was a stone badass. I wasn't. I was just numb."

"Having some of your emotional responses frozen, and others, like anger, for instance, amplified after suffering extreme trauma is normal," Wozniak said. "It's the mind and body's way of protecting us from processing heavy-duty things before we're ready. The bad news is that many of our good emotions get anaesthetized with the painful ones we're trying to suppress. The good news is that those emotions aren't dead; they're just hibernating. Once the trauma is processed the emotional synapses reawaken. It's one of the reasons we sometimes feel better after a good cry."

"I feel like shit," Strayer said. She helped herself to more tissue.

"I expect so," Wozniak said. "It'll pass."

"To answer your question about what I did next," Strayer said, resuming her disclosure, "I split."

"Split?"

"Yeah. When my mother woke up, hung over, the next morning, she found me waiting for her in the kitchen. I was a wreck. I didn't sleep the rest of the night. I spent the time cleaning myself, and my room, up."

"Were you badly hurt?"

"I was in pain, bleeding down there. I was okay otherwise. I packed my stuff, and when Mom came into the kitchen, I jumped her."

"You attacked your mother?"

"That's right. I had the enlistment papers on the kitchen table and the knife I'd used on Karl in my hand. I told my mother if she didn't sign on the dotted line, I'd kill her."

"And she believed you?"

"She signed the papers."

"What if she hadn't signed?"

"I honestly don't know," Strayer admitted. "After what happened to me that night, and the mental and emotional state I was in, I'm not sure what I would have done. Anyway, it didn't matter. I left that day and never went back. I stayed with a friend until the end of the school year a week later. I took my finals and my GED test, which I passed, and shipped out to the army. The next time I saw my mom was at her funeral."

"And you never told anyone about what happened that night?"

"You're the first."

"When did you learn about what became of Deputy Mims?"

"The following autumn," Strayer said. "I was nearing the end of my advanced individual training at Fort Leonard Wood. Deputy Mims's arrest made national news. Since I was in military police school, it was a hot topic among the trainees. One of my instructors even fostered a discussion about it in class."

"A deputy sheriff from California getting arrested for a string of rapes and an on-duty murder would make the news, all right," Wozniak agreed. "If I recall the case, he pulled over a young college student who was driving home for Thanksgiving break?"

"That's right," Strayer said. "He put her in his patrol car, drove her to a secluded area, and tried to rape her. She fought him, and he ended up killing her in the struggle. Her strangled body was found within days. They made Mims on DNA. After he was arrested, many victims came forward. I'm sure there were a lot of others, like me, who didn't."

"How did the news affect you?"

"When I heard," Strayer said, "it put me into a tailspin. I almost didn't complete my training."

"You blamed yourself for that student's murder, didn't you?" Wozniak asked.

Strayer only nodded.

"And you still do?"

This time, Strayer's nod was barely perceptible. "During the class discussion," she said, "my instructor showed us a picture of the murdered girl from her high school year-book. Her name was Pamela Gardner. I've been seeing her face, in my sleep, every night for ten years. When I saw it again today on the news at the department, along with Mims's picture, I freaked out."

"You realize how irrational your guilt is, don't you?" Wozniak said. "Had you reported what Deputy Mims did to you, it's almost a certainty no one at the sheriff's department would have believed your story. He would have still been free to do what he did to his other victims, as well as to that young college student. And he undoubt-edly would have made good on his threat to come after you and your mother."

"Maybe," Strayer said. "Maybe not. What if . . ."

"We don't get to live in the 'what if' world," Wozniak interrupted. "We have to live in the real world. You were a teenaged girl. You don't have the right to take responsibility for what a monster like Duane Mims did. His crimes weren't your fault."

"That's easy to say," Strayer said.

"I realize that," Wozniak said. "It's the reason you've been punishing yourself all these years."

"Punishing myself?" Strayer said.

"Do you really think it's a coincidence," Wozniak asked, "that with all the different places you could go after your military service ended, and all the different law enforcement agencies you could have chosen to work for, you ended up back in Farnham working for the sheriff's department?"

Before Strayer could answer, the door to Dr. Wozniak's office burst open, and Sergeant Simpson stormed in.

"Excuse the interruption, Doc," Simpson said, "but we gotta go, Strayer. Farnham's under a full evacuation order, including the sheriff's department. Let's move."

Chapter Forty-three

Hector's pistol didn't fire. It didn't even make a *click*. He hastily retracted the Glock's slide, thinking it didn't have a round chambered. A .40 caliber, hollow-point bullet ejected from the weapon. He released the slide, aimed it at Mims again, and pulled the trigger. The gun still didn't fire.

Hector racked the slide once more and ejected another live bullet, as his alarm at the malfunctioning weapon morphed into dread.

"It's loaded, all right," Mims said, a wicked grin spreading across his face. "But it won't fire without this." He produced a metallic, spring-wrapped, cylinder about the size of a Q-tip from his hip pocket and tossed it to the ground at Hector's feet.

"You removed the firing pin while you were cleaning the guns," Hector said. His voice became drained of emotion, and he let the useless pistol fall from his hands. "I even watched you do it, yesterday, when I was tied up on the couch. Your partner was asleep upstairs."

"That's right," Mims said. "Do you really think I'm stupid enough to let that junkie shithead have a functional firearm?"

"All this time," Marjorie asked her father, "Skink's gun didn't work?"

"Evidently Duane wasn't taking any chances," Hector nodded. "Not even with his own partner."

"My gun still works perfectly, though," Mims said cheerfully.

"I'm sure it does," Hector said. He tilted his head and squinted, appraising Mims. "I remember now where I know you from. It was on the TV news. It's been a long time, but I knew I'd seen you somewhere before. You're Duane Mims, aren't you? You're the deputy who killed that college girl about ten years back and committed all those rapes?"

"Jeopardy!" Mims said, as he shot Hector. He fired twice. Both rounds struck the older man in the upper chest.

Marjorie screamed as her father collapsed. She knelt beside him, wailing.

"What's going on up there?" Margaret's terrified voice called from the basement. "Were those gunshots? Marjorie? Hector?"

Mims walked past Marjorie and Hector to the basement door and closed and locked it.

Hector choked and gagged as Marjorie sobbed and tried to apply pressure to the growing crimson patch on her father's chest. Hector blinked and spat an enormous amount of blood. His body began to convulse, and he reached up weakly with both hands, placing them over his daughter's. He looked into her agonized eyes.

"I . . . love . . . you," he said. He gripped Marjorie's fingers, squeezed them tightly as he winced in one final gasp, and went limp. His eyes remained open as he stared through her at the ceiling.

Marjorie bent over her father, hugging his body. Her own body was racked with grief.

Mims nonchalantly retrieved Skink's inoperative pistol, the firing pin, and the two fresh cartridges Hector ejected from the gun while attempting to shoot him. Then he returned to the couch and sat down.

While Marjorie cried over her dead father, Mims replaced the two cartridges he'd fired from his pistol with the two he'd recovered from the floor. Then he stuck his freshly loaded weapon into his waistband, unloaded Skink's gun, and began to disassemble the slide.

By the time he'd returned the firing pin, reassembled the weapon, and reinserted the magazine, Marjorie had slowly pushed herself off her father's corpse and stood to face him.

"You murdering bastard," she seethed as she stared at Mims through hate-filled eyes.

"I think that's been established," Mims said. "But if you have any doubts, why don't you ask your father?"

Marjorie charged at him, howling in rage. He stood and sidestepped her reckless attack, spun her around, and put her in a choke hold from behind. He applied pressure to her neck and lifted her nearly off the ground. Her furious scream instantly ceased along with her intake of air. She was essentially paralyzed.

"That's the kind of spirit I like in a gal," Mims whispered into her ear. "It really gets my engine going, you know what I mean?" He sucked in a mouthful of her hair.

A loud pounding began on the basement door. Mims ignored it, closing his eyes and savoring Marjorie's hair in his mouth until the heavy, insistent, thumping finally snapped him out of his reverie.

He released Marjorie, who was almost ready to pass out.

Lost in the scent and taste of her hair, Mims had forgotten how hard his forearm was clamped around her neck or for how long. She folded to her knees, gasping for breath.

Mims picked up the other pistol and went back into the kitchen, where he angrily opened the dead bolt and opened the door. He found Margaret at the top of the stairs with Mary on the step behind her. Both wore anxious expressions.

"Send up Tad," Mims ordered.

"What happened up here?" Margaret asked. "We heard shots." She craned her neck and looked past Mims, through the kitchen, into the house. She spotted her husband's body on the floor. A dazed Marjorie knelt nearby, massaging her neck.

Before Margaret could scream, Mims clamped a hand around her throat and put his pistol against her forehead.

"You're forgetting who's in charge again," Mims said, as Margaret moaned in grief and horror through his fingers. "Don't make me remind you with a bullet."

Mary moved up and supported her mother above her. "Don't shoot," Mary pleaded. "Please."

"Then send up Tad like I ordered."

"Tad!" Mary called over her shoulder. "Get up here, now!"

"What for?" Tad's nervous voice emitted from the darkness below.

"Get your useless ass upstairs!" Mary shouted.

Mary took her weeping mother and began to guide her down the stairs as Tad passed her on the way up. Mary wouldn't look at him.

"Come on," Mims coaxed Tad with his pistol. Tad nervously emerged from the stairwell with his hands raised.

"Holy shit," he exclaimed when he saw Hector. "Are you going to shoot me?" He seemed about to cry.

"Not if you do what I say," Mims said. Tad vigorously nodded.

"Marjorie," Mims said, "get downstairs with your mother. Move."

A numb Marjorie gained her feet, walked past her dead father, and headed past Tad and Mims toward the basement with her head hung. Once she entered the stairwell Mims closed the door and secured the dead bolt.

Tad couldn't take his eyes off Hector. He'd never seen a dead body except at a funeral once, and certainly not a freshly murdered one.

"You're going to go upstairs," Mims said, prodding Tad with his pistol, "and bring Skink down."

"Skink?"

"The other guy with me. Skinny dude, covered in tattoos?"

"Yeah, Skink, right," Tad muttered, still hypnotized by his father-in-law's corpse.

Mims slapped Tad across the face, bringing him out of his stupor. "He's knocked out. Bring him down here. And hurry up. If you're not back in five minutes, I'll come up shooting."

"Where upstairs is he?"

"How the hell do I know?" Mims said. "Get going."

Tad scurried up the stairs. Mims opened the refrigerator and helped himself to a cold beer.

After taking a long sip, he stuck his gun into his waistband with its mate and pushed the refrigerator from the wall. He carefully examined the gas hookup. He knew it led to a main line that further led to the propane tank outside, just like the stove, washer, and dryer.

Remembering he'd seen a box of tools on the steps of the rear porch, Mims went outside and found an adjustable wrench. Then he went back into the kitchen and confirmed the fittings for the stove and refrigerator were the same diameter. He adjusted the wrench to match, and set it aside on the kitchen table.

Mims suddenly realized it had been longer than five minutes since he'd sent Tad to fetch Skink. He also realized he could hear no noise emanating from upstairs, like the sounds created by one man laboring to carry another or the boots of an unconscious person scraping across the floor.

He ran to the stairs and ascended them two at a time with one of the Glocks back in his hand. When he got to the top floor, he immediately smelled the strong odor of smoke. Mims checked the master bedroom first, and found Skink lying faceup on the bed. There was dried blood on his face, his nose was broken, his good left arm was askew over his head, and he was loudly snoring.

The next thing Mims noticed was that one of the windows in the master bedroom was flung fully open, with the curtains waving in what was clearly a powerful breeze. He dashed over, parted the dangling curtains, and looked out.

Three things caught Mims's immediate attention. The first was that the smoke was much thicker than it had been even a few hours ago. Visibility was limited to only a couple of dozen feet. The second was the orange tint to the smoke covering the entire eastern horizon. He'd witnessed a glow like that while chained in a prisoner transportation van with Skink, just before a firestorm overtook them.

The third thing Mims saw, for only a fleeting instant, was Tad's back as he ran away. He disappeared into the smoke, heading for the same woods he and Skink had once come out of.

PART THREE
HEAT

CHAPTER FORTY-FOUR

Sergeant Simpson drove back to Farnham as fast as possible given the dense smoke, reduced visibility, and heavy traffic. Fortunately, the vast majority of vehicles on the highway were heading west, away from Farnham and the encroaching wildfire. Simpson's unmarked Dodge Charger, with its siren blaring and the dash and grille's tricolored emergency lights flashing, was going east. The road in that direction featured very few automobiles.

"Sorry to cut your session with Dr. Wozniak short," Simpson apologized, once they were out of Folsom and speeding down the road toward Farnham. "While I was eating lunch, Lieutenant McDillon called. He told me mandatory evacuation orders had just been issued for Farnham. He was pissed as hell that I wasn't around, and that we'd left the county without telling him."

"I hope you're not in too much trouble on my account," Strayer said.

"Trouble's your middle name, remember?" Simpson said with a grin. "McDipshit will get over it."

"The entire town of Farnham is being evacuated?"

"It ain't like nobody saw it coming," Simpson said. "The fire's been progressing steadily west since it broke out. Rain's supposed to be in the forecast, and everybody was hoping we'd get it before the blaze reached Farnham, but that didn't happen."

"What did the lieutenant say about the evacuation?"

"He told me everyone's days off have been canceled and everybody wearing a badge is officially on duty until further notice."

"I guess that means us," Strayer said. Her mind was only partially involved in the conversation with her supervisor. The remainder of her thoughts were still lingering in Dr. Wozniak's office, struggling to process what she'd unexpectedly divulged.

"I spoke with Benny, too," Simpson went on. "He told me it's a madhouse back at the station. They've got all the people they can muster trying to move computers, records, and anything else that isn't nailed down. It's all being loaded onto trucks headed for Folsom."

"How far is the fire from Farnham?"

"Less than a couple of miles now. There are pockets the fire supposedly hasn't reached yet, but all indications are that almost everything from the Farnham National Forest all the way to the town has been burned up. Farnham's fixin' to go into the oven next."

"What about your family?" Strayers said. "Don't you live in town?"

"My wife packed up the important stuff and is taking our daughter west," she said. "We have friends in the Bay Area who can put them up. We might even pass them on the way into Farnham. How about you? Do you need to go home and rescue anything?"

Strayer didn't own much, but all of her important personal, military, financial, and scholastic documents were in her apartment, as well as what few photographs and items of memorabilia had belonged to her parents.

"I wouldn't mind stopping by my apartment," Strayer admitted. "It'd take me less than five minutes to pack up my laptop and grab a few pictures and documents."

"We'll swing by your place on the way to the station," Simpson agreed.

They drove without speaking for a while. The only sound punctuating their silence was the hollow wailing of the siren and the noise of the vehicle's laboring engine.

"How'd it go with Dr. Wozniak?" Simpson finally asked.

"I'm not sure," Strayer said. "I've got some stuff to sort out."

"Don't we all," Simpson said. "Without her help a few years back, I don't think I'd have held it together." She turned her head from the road briefly and looked directly at Strayer. "Wozniak's good people. She solid, you know?"

"I don't have experience with any other psychiatrists to compare her with," Strayer said, "but if I had to say, I'd call Dr. Wozniak the no-bullshit kind."

"Ain't that the truth," Simpson said. "Are you going to see her again?"

"Yeah," Strayer said after a long pause. "I think I am."

"Good answer."

"Thanks for taking me to see her today," Strayer said. "That's another one I owe you."

"Forget it," Simpson said. "This one's on the house.

Besides, I was only looking out for my workplace. At the rate you were going, you'd have busted every mirror in the station by sundown."

Slightly less than half an hour later, due to the speed of their code-three run, the duo entered Farnham. Strayer gave Simpson directions to her apartment. The Juvenile Unit supervisor parked in a vacant spot a short walk from her door.

"I'll just be a couple of minutes," Strayer said.

"I'll go in with you," Simpson offered. "More hands make short work."

Both women got out and started down the sidewalk toward Strayer's front door. The smoke and haze were thick, and swirling ash was heavy in the dense air. Still contemplating her session with Dr. Wozniak, a distracted Strayer fumbled in her pocket for her keys.

"GUN!" Simpson yelled. She stepped forward, elbowed Strayer behind her, and drew her pistol.

The preoccupied Strayer stumbled, not expecting a shove by Simpson. She looked up just as her sergeant's warning registered and saw two figures emerge from the hedges in front of her apartment. They were the same hedges her half brother had surprised her from.

Both men were Mexican. One was short and looked to be in his early thirties. The other was younger, in his late teens or early twenties, but much taller. They each sported tattoos and a gun. The shorter one brought an AK-47 to his shoulder, and the younger man raised a black semi-automatic pistol with an extended magazine protruding from its grip. The distance between the gunmen and the two deputies was no more than a couple of car lengths.

Simpson and the man with the AK-47 fired simultaneously. Each got off multiple shots before they both fell.

The tall man with the high-capacity pistol began firing a second later. He walked towards Strayer holding his gun in one hand, sideways, gangster style. He unleashed a torrent of shots as fast as he could jerk the trigger.

Off balance, Strayer reflexively let her martial arts and S.W.A.T. training take over and didn't try to remain upright. Instead she allowed herself to drop to one knee, drawing her .45 in one, smooth, motion. Ignoring the not-unfamiliar sound of bullets zipping past her, she brought up her pistol, thumbed down the safety, and found the weapon's front sight. The instant the sights intersected with the torso of the tall gunman advancing on her, she squeezed off three rapid shots.

The tall gunman crumpled straight to the ground like a marionette with its strings cut.

Keeping her weapon trained on his now-motionless form, Strayer stood and advanced. The gunman was dead. All three of her rounds had struck him, with the final bullet entering his right eye. She switched her focus to the other gunman.

The older gunman was unsuccessfully trying to push himself up, but all of the rounds fired from Sergeant Simpson's .40 caliber Sig Sauer had struck him in the chest. One of those projectiles severed his spine just below his armpits. Strayer didn't think he had much time left. She kicked his rifle away and turned her attention to Simpson.

The Juvenile Unit supervisor was lying on her back, bleeding but conscious. Her assailant's first few shots missed, but his last struck her in the right thigh. It didn't appear to Strayer to have severed the femoral artery, but the wound was hemorrhaging badly. Strayer had seen her share of 7.62x39 wounds in Afghanistan, and knew arterial bleeding when she saw it. Thankfully, she didn't see it now.

"You're going to be all right, Sarge," Strayer said, holstering her pistol. "Looks like it missed the artery. Put pressure here," she said, guiding Simpson's hands to the wound. "I'm going to call for an ambulance and get the med kit out of the trunk."

"Are they both down?" Simpson asked through gritted teeth.

"One's confirmed KIA," Strayer said. She looked back at the older gunman, the one who'd exchanged shots with Simpson. He'd stopped moving, and his eyes were open and didn't blink. "The other one's getting there."

"Tell me something, Strayer?" Simpson said. She forced a smile to mask the pain. "Your middle name really is 'Trouble,' isn't it?"

"I'm beginning to think so," Strayer said.

CHAPTER FORTY-FIVE

Mary held her mother, who'd collapsed to her knees on the cellar floor and was sobbing hysterically. Marjorie sat at the small table holding Jennifer as the five-year-old cried in concert with her grandmother. She stared off into space, with unfocused eyes and her face blank, as she comforted her daughter.

Joel, in an effort to hold back his own tears, picked up the pair of work gloves Hector had removed before being called up from the cellar. He returned to the furnace room, climbed the improvised shelf-ladder, adjusted the flashlight, which was beginning to dim, and picked up the dull, rusty hacksaw blade.

Crying and sawing at the same time, he resumed his grandfather's work on the padlock through the gap in the coal chute hatch. As a result of Hector's relentless efforts, the quarter-inch-diameter shackle had been cut more than three-fourths of the way through.

Mims burst through the back door and sprinted toward the woods, heading for the spot in the smoky haze where he'd last seen Tad flee. He cursed to himself as he ran. He knew if Marjorie's husband got away and reported that he and Skink were alive, any chance he'd have to escape pursuit by the authorities would vanish with him.

Duane Audie Mims was supposedly burned to ashes by the Farnham Fire. If word got out he wasn't dead, given his heinous crimes and the notoriety of his arrest and conviction, a nationwide manhunt would inevitably ensue. A manhunt that he knew, based on his own law enforcement experience, he'd have great difficulty evading. The best way for Mims to keep from returning to prison was to continue being a person nobody was looking for—an already dead man.

The smoke was very thick now, and the ash particles swirling in the wind were becoming larger. Some of the particles were still burning, and bits of flaming tinder fell all around. Several of the trees in the wood line behind the property were already in flames, ignited by falling embers generated by the encroaching wildfire.

Mims could barely breathe, and the stinging in his eyes only made it more difficult to see. What was worse, the high winds were making it difficult to hear. His best chance of locating the fleeing Tad was by the noise he made as he lumbered through the heavy timber.

Pausing to halt the din of his own movement, he cupped both hands behind his ears to amplify his hearing and filter out the howling wind. He was rewarded by the faint but sharp cracks of twigs being snapped and broken as someone stomped pell-mell through the brush. He headed in the direction of the noise, which appeared to be less than fifty feet away, at a trot.

The clatter of movement in the woods ahead got louder

as Mims progressed, and soon he could hear a man cursing. He slowed his own movement to a walk, enabling him to better muffle his footsteps and dodge the twigs and branches flicking at him in the dense brush. He wanted to avoid committing the same mistake as his quarry and give away his presence.

Mims needn't have worried. As he continued, he realized Tad was thrashing, stomping, and cursing his way through the thickets with apparently no grasp that the sounds he was making were leading his former kidnapper straight to him. He squinted through the smoke, and the vague outline of a man materialized ahead.

Drawing his pistols, Mims closed in. He could see Tad clearly now. His shirt was torn in several places, and his face, arms, and neck were littered with abrasions. He'd fallen multiple times and was covered in ash and dirt.

"Motherfucker," Tad swore, as he stumbled on a root and nearly fell. He was out of breath and coughing, and Mims could tell by his posture he was already nearly exhausted.

"That's far enough," Mims said, stepping out of the smoke. Both of his Glocks were leveled.

Tad whirled around to face Mims, a terrified expression on his face. "Please," he begged, sagging to his knees, "don't kill me."

"You're a real family man," Mims said. "Ran off and left your wife and children to save your own skin."

"What was I supposed to do?" Tad whined. "Getting myself killed wouldn't do them any good, would it?"

"You make me sick to my stomach," Mims said.

"Please," Tad repeated, clasping his hands and beginning to cry, "don't kill me. I don't want to die."

"I'm not going to kill you," Mims said. "Get up."

Tad couldn't know it, but Mims had every intention of ending his life. He just didn't want Tad's body left out in the woods, separated from the others, and to have to carry his carcass back.

"Where are we going?" Tad asked, relieved he was still alive. He struggled to his feet.

"Back to your family," Mims said. He nudged Tad ahead with his guns.

"Which way?" Tad said. "I'm lost in all this smoke."

"That way," Mims said, thinking that Tad would be lost even without the smoke. He pointed toward the direction from which they'd come.

With Tad blundering ahead at gunpoint, still tripping and cursing, the pair marched back through the woods. When they got to the wood line at the edge of the property, and the silhouette of the house became dimly visible again through the smoke, a multicolored flashing glow could be seen illuminating the haze in the area near the front of the house. As they drew closer, the glow became pronounced enough to identify.

Mims instantly recognized it as the emergency lights of a police vehicle. It was a Farnham County Sheriff's Department cruiser, parked near the other three vehicles in the gravel driveway.

Tad instinctively raised both arms to wave, and opened his mouth to shout, when a thick arm encircled his neck from behind. He was flung violently backward, as what felt like a python closed around his windpipe.

Theodore "Tad" Guthrie was unconscious within seconds and dead within a minute thereafter.

CHAPTER FORTY-SIX

"What do you suppose Duane is doing with Tad?" Mary asked in a hushed voice. "He's been upstairs a long time."

"I don't know," Marjorie said glumly, "and I don't care."

Margaret had been placed on the cot, with a wet cloth over her forehead and eyes, to try and calm her. Jennifer lay down with her, and the two clung to each other under a blanket. Neither was asleep, but both had cried themselves into a state of exhaustion. Mary and Marjorie spoke in hushed tones in the opposite corner.

"You don't mean that," Mary said.

"The hell I don't," Marjorie said. "Dad was only half-right when he blamed Tad. Some of this is his fault, but most of the blame is mine."

"How do you figure?"

"If I hadn't come out here to get away from my shitty marriage," Marjorie said, "Dad would still be alive and my kids wouldn't be in danger. I brought this on them."

"That's bullshit," Mary said. "None of this is anyone's fault except those two bastards upstairs."

Mary couldn't help but think, however ironically, that there was some truth in her sister's words. If Marjorie and her children hadn't sought refuge at their parents' rural Farnham County home, she wouldn't have come out, at Tad's prompting, either.

"The fire's getting close," Marjorie said, changing the subject. She didn't want to think about her father. She tried to force the image of him falling, shot twice through the chest, from her mind. His final words still rang in her ears, and his blood was still on her hands.

"I know," Mary said. "The smoke smell is growing stronger, even down here in the basement."

"I heard on the radio," Marjorie said, "when I was upstairs, that it might rain soon. Maybe even later tonight."

"Rain won't matter," Mary said, lowering her voice even more. "Unless we get out of here, we'll be dead long before then."

"How can you be sure?"

"They crossed a line when they murdered Dad," Mary said, "and they know it. Even if they were thinking about letting us live, they sure as hell aren't now. We're witnesses. In for a penny, in for a pound. The penalty's the same whether they kill one of us or all of us. They're going to kill us, all right. They have to."

"If what you're saying is true," Marjorie said, "then Duane is going to have to kill Skink, too." She briefly related what transpired upstairs, detailing how Mims had removed the firing pin from Skink's pistol. She also mentioned her father recognizing Duane, just before he was shot, as a former deputy sheriff who'd been convicted of rape and murder.

"It all fits," Mary said. "If he was a deputy, like Dad said, he'd know the law. He's also the one who shot Dad, which makes Skink another potential witness against him if they're caught."

"What do you think he has in mind?"

"Skink gave it away," Mary said, "when he told Mom, the fire would take care of everything. Duane's going to keep us all down here trapped in the basement. Skink, too, when he wakes up, I'll wager. If the Farnham Fire doesn't do us in on its own, he'll torch the place before he splits to make sure."

"How much time do you think we have?"

"Not long," Mary said. "He has to take off before the fire gets here." She gripped her older sister's arm. "We've got to get out of this cellar."

"I'll check on Joel," Marjorie said. She got up and disappeared into the second room.

"Are you going to tell her?" Margaret asked.

"What?" Mary said. She thought her mother was asleep, along with Jennifer, who was now snoring.

"I heard every word you said," Margaret stated. She removed the damp cloth from her eyes and sat up, careful to avoid waking her granddaughter.

"What are you talking about?" Mary said.

"I'm talking about you and Tad," Margaret said. "I can't believe I didn't figure it out sooner."

"You're crazy," Mary said, averting her eyes.

"And you're lying. We both know it. You can't fool your own mother. Not any longer. I know what you've done. I can see it in your eyes. I just don't know for how long it's been going on. I'm almost afraid to know."

"I'm not going to entertain this nonsense," Mary said. "We just lost Dad. You're upset and not thinking right. We're all upset. But to accuse me of—"

"The truth," Margaret interrupted. "You need to fess up and tell Marjorie. Ask for her forgiveness. You don't want to die with this on your soul."

"What soul?" Mary said. "I'm the black sheep, remember? The bad sister? At least that's what everybody in this family keeps telling me."

"What you are," Margaret said softly, "is what you do. Those choices belong to you. If you want to blame me or your father or even Marjorie for the things you've done, that's your choice. But you can't lie to yourself. We've all got a reckoning coming"—she gently stroked Jennifer's hair as she slumbered—"maybe sooner than you think."

"Thanks for the sermon," Mary said, staring glumly at the floor. "Even if I wanted to tell her, do you really think now's the time?"

"How much more time do you think we have?" Margaret said. She lay back down on the cot, put her arms protectively around her granddaughter, and closed her eyes.

Marjorie entered the furnace room and tapped Joel on the leg. He was lying on top of the shelves above her. What little light coming in from the small gap between the coal chute and the hatch illuminated his face, which was wrinkled in concentration. The flashlight, on the last vestiges of its dying batteries, was barely flickering.

"How's it going?" she asked.

"This old saw blade is so dull," Joel answered. "It's hard to get more than tiny, little, strokes in, too. Also, I'm not a strong as Grandpa." He paused for a second, as mention of his grandfather sent a wave of emotion through him.

"How much longer?" Marjorie asked.

"Thanks to Grandpa," he said, resuming his sawing, "not very long. He cut most of the way through. Maybe another hour?"

"Listen to me," Marjorie began. "What I have to tell you is important."

"I hear you," Joel said, as he continued cutting.

"The instant you cut through that lock, you come and tell me, okay?"

"Of course, Mom."

"You're going to take Jennifer out through that hatch, and you're going to run. Get her to the road and follow it west. Do you know which way is west?"

"Sure," Joel said. "It's back the way we came, towards town."

"That's right. Take Jennifer and keep going. Stay with her, don't stop, and don't look back, no matter what you see or hear at the house."

"What about you and Grandma and Aunt Mary and Dad?"

"Don't worry about us," Marjorie said. "Your responsibility is to get your little sister to safety. This'll be the most important thing you've ever done."

"You want me to just leave you?"

"You must do as I say," she said. "The men upstairs will kill you and Jennifer if they catch you. Your only chance to get away is if they're occupied back here. Do you understand what I'm telling you?"

"I think so."

"There's no thinking to do about it, son. If you don't do exactly as I say, you'll not only die, but Jennifer will die, too."

"Okay," he said, "I'll do what you say."

"Promise me. You have to swear."

"I promise." He momentarily stopped cutting again. "While me and Jennifer are getting away," he asked, "what are you gonna be doing to occupy them?"

Marjorie took out the shotgun shell from her pocket, and wiped away as much of the blood on it as her blood-stained shirt would allow. Her father, in his dying act, had discreetly thrust the cartridge into her grasp while she held his hands.

"Whatever I have to," Marjorie said, as she pocketed the shell.

CHAPTER FORTY-SEVEN

Detective Benavides was helping Strayer rinse blood from her hands with a bottle of water provided by one of the ambulance crews when Undersheriff Torres, flanked by Lieutenant McDillon and Sergeant Brandonmire, approached them.

The ambulance that took Sergeant Simpson to the hospital had departed only moments before, and the shooting scene in front of Strayer's apartment was still fresh and chaotic. The first patrol deputies to respond were cordoning off the area with yellow crime scene tape, and a coroner's deputy had covered the bodies of the two dead gunmen with plastic tarps. Detectives and crime scene technicians were just arriving.

"We really didn't need this right now," Torres said to Strayer without any greeting.

"You think I did?" Strayer retorted.

"If you'd been around this morning," Torres continued, "you'd know we have a full-scale evacuation going on in Farnham. Every deputy who isn't helping the citizenry bug out is helping to pack up and move critical resources from departmental headquarters. If you didn't notice,

Deputy Strayer, we're a little shorthanded today. We needed a deputy-involved shooting like I need another ulcer."

"Don't tell me," Strayer said, wringing her hands dry and pointing to the two tarpaulin-covered bodies with her chin. "Tell them."

"I'm not in the mood for your insubordination," Torres said.

"And I'm not in the mood to get my ass chewed for not getting killed," Strayer shot back.

"Maybe if you'd remained in the station," McDillon said, "at your desk like you were ordered to, this wouldn't have happened?"

"That's brilliant, Lieutenant," Strayer said wearily. "If I'd stayed in the station all day, the only thing that would have happened differently is I'd have been alone when I came home tonight. The ambush still would have gone down, but it would have been two against one. I'd be dead, and your troubles would be over, right?"

"That's enough," Torres said.

"You've got that right," Strayer said. She turned, stepped over the bodies of the two men who tried to murder her, keyed open her front door, and entered her apartment.

"Where does she think she's going?" Torres demanded.

"Home, I think," Benavides said. Torres and McDillon both scowled at him.

Brandonmire walked over to the nearest body, lifted the tarp, and made a cursory visual examination, paying special attention to the tattoos. He did the same for the other body, then knelt and examined their weapons. When he finished, he returned to McDillon and Torres.

"They're both La Eme," he said. "The older one is inked

as a shot caller, but the younger guy isn't fully tatted out yet. He was probably trying to make his bones today. They were packing serious hardware, too. One of the weapons is an AK, probably stolen from the same batch as the gun Machado used, and the other is a nine-millimeter Glock with a thirty-round mag. It was a sanctioned hit, all right."

"Put the word out," McDillon said. "Let all units know the Mexican Mafia has officially declared war on us."

"Right away," Brandonmire said, heading to his car.

"What are you going to do about Strayer?" Torres asked McDillon. "Are you going to just let her walk out on you in the middle of a shooting investigation? She hasn't even provided her initial verbal report yet, has she?"

"She has not," McDillon acknowledged, unable to hide his elation. "And this time, Sergeant Simpson isn't around to cover for her."

"I'll leave you to handle things here," Torres said, not wanting to witness the impending fireworks display between Deputy Strayer and Lieutenant McDillon, who was clearly relishing the prospect of grilling her. "I've got a lot to do back at the station with the evacuation going on."

"Come with me," McDillon ordered Benavides. "You're going to be my witness."

"Why don't we just wait until she comes out?" Benavides suggested. "She's had a rough day, Lieutenant. Maybe she needs a few minutes to collect herself. If you didn't notice, she almost got killed a little while ago. I'm sure she won't be long."

"I don't have a few minutes," McDillon said. "Let's go, Detective."

"This oughta go well," Benavides muttered to himself as he followed in McDillon's footsteps.

McDillon pounded on Strayer's door. "This is Lieutenant McDillon," he called out, loud enough for a number of the other sheriff's department personnel at the crime scene to look up from their tasks.

The door opened and Strayer stood in the doorway. She'd removed her bloodstained sports jacket and shirt, and was clad above the waist in only her T-shirt and ballistic vest. She was drying her damp face with a towel.

"You're required to provide an initial verbal report to your immediate supervisor as soon as possible after any significant on-duty critical incident," McDillon said officiously. "Since your supervisor, Sergeant Simpson, is indisposed, I'm your next ranking superior. I want that report."

"I figured," Strayer said calmly.

"I can take it inside," McDillon said, stepping forward. "I'm sure you don't want your report overheard by bystanders." Strayer stopped him with a hand on his chest.

"I don't care who hears what I have to say," Strayer said. "You don't enter my home without a warrant. I'll be out in a minute, as soon as I get dressed."

"I want your report now," McDillon insisted.

"I guess you'll just have to wait," Strayer said, "won't you?" She closed the door as Benavides and several other deputies struggled to hide their grins.

It was closer to ten minutes later when Strayer, wearing a clean shirt and new sports jacket, emerged from her apartment.

"Report," McDillon ordered. "Now, if you please?"

"Sure, Lieutenant. Two Mexican Mafia gangsters tried to murder me. Can I go now?"

"Don't be impertinent," he quipped. "Give me the details."

"I was walking to my apartment from the parking lot with Sergeant Simpson," Strayer began. "She was going to help me pack some of my personal effects. Two men, one armed with a military rifle and one with a semiautomatic pistol, were hiding in the bushes. Sergeant Simpson spotted them first. They fired first. We returned fire. Simpson got the one with the rifle, I took out the one with the pistol. Sergeant Simpson sustained a gunshot injury. I called it in and rendered first aid."

"Anything else?"

"Yeah," Strayer said. "Two things. First off, this apartment complex has security cameras. They should have captured the incident and when the two gunmen first showed up and hid out to lay in wait for me."

"And the second thing?"

"For the record, Sergeant Simpson saved my life. Had she not done what she did when she did it, I'd be dead. I'm officially nominating her for the departmental Medal of Valor. That's all I have to say at this time."

"What about—?"

"What part of 'that's all I have to say' don't you understand, Lieutenant?" Strayer cut him off. "I'll provide a more detailed statement to the shooting investigation team. I'm done talking."

A frustrated McDillon wanted to question her further, but knew she'd met the requirements of providing an initial verbal report. "I'll need to confiscate your weapon," he said, putting out his hand.

"Not a chance," Strayer said. "I'm familiar with the procedure requiring a deputy to turn over their weapon as evidence after a shooting, but I'm not going to be left unarmed because of a damned rule." She pointed to the corpses on the sidewalk. "The Mexican Mafia already tried to punch my ticket once. Do you think they're going to stop trying because those two losers failed?" She shook her head. "You'll get my gun when I get a replacement, and not before."

"I'm ordering you to turn over your weapon, Deputy Strayer," McDillon said. This time, every deputy and technician at the scene looked up.

"If you want my gun," Strayer said, "you're going to have to take it."

"Are you refusing a direct order?" McDillon said, elevating his voice to ensure others heard him.

"No," Strayer said coolly. "All I'm saying, Lieutenant, is if you want my gun, you'll have to take it." A thin smile appeared on her face. "I hope you brought a lunch."

McDillon's face reddened. For a brief moment, it actually looked as if he might reach out and attempt to remove Strayer's pistol from its holster. But an instant after his arm started forward, he checked himself, evidently deciding that putting his hands on the young female deputy might bring unwanted legal repercussions, if not immediate physical injury.

McDillon stood glaring at Stayer, who met his stare with her hard blue eyes and a neutral expression. Her smile had vanished. She was practically daring him to relieve her of her weapon.

"Enough," Benavides said, stepping between them. "With everything going on right now in Farnham, do we really have time for a pissing contest?" Before either McDillon or Strayer could answer, he took Strayer by the arm and led her away.

Benavides and Strayer got all the way to his unmarked sedan before the furious McDillon turned and stormed off to his own car, ignoring the snickers of deputies and technicians as he departed.

Benavides quickly opened the passenger door and gently but firmly shoved Strayer into the seat. She didn't protest. Then he scurried around the car, slid behind the wheel, and drove off.

"What's the hurry?" Strayer asked, as they sped from the apartment complex.

"I wanted to get you out of there," Benavides said, reaching down and switching off the car's Motorola two-way transceiver, "before Lieutenant McDickhead gets over his embarrassment and realizes he forgot to order you on administrative leave."

No sooner had Benavides spoken than Strayer's cell phone vibrated. She checked the screen, and sure enough, it was McDillon calling. She held it up for Benavides to see.

"I wouldn't answer that," he said, "if I were you."

"Not planning to," Strayer said, silencing and pocketing the phone. A moment later, Benavides's phone rang. His ringtone was Ennio Morricone's famous theme from the classic spaghetti western *The Good, the Bad and the Ugly.* He didn't answer and held up the phone for Strayer to see.

"McDillon," she confirmed. "Calling you to order me back to the station, no doubt, since he can't reach me."

"Bad connection," he said, pocketing his phone.

CHAPTER FORTY-EIGHT

Skink was roused to wakefulness by an excruciating headache. The ache inside his skull, and on his face, ejected him from the merciful bliss of slumber and launched him into agonizing consciousness with an involuntary groan. When he brought his good left hand to his mouth, it came away covered in a mixture of dried and fresh blood.

It took a moment for the pain to subside and for his alcohol- and drug-numbed mind to grasp where he was. He sat up abruptly, releasing a shudder of torture in his throbbing shoulder and neck.

Marjorie was gone. A quick check at his belt, and around the bed on which he sat, and Skink realized his pistol was gone along with her.

He pushed himself off the bed and staggered into the bathroom. The face staring back at him in the mirror had changed since he last saw it. In addition to the red, sunken eyes, hollow cheeks, and jaundiced complexion, he could add a broken nose and missing teeth to his features.

Skink gagged and vomited a mouthful of blood and teeth into the sink. He ran cold water over his face, cursing

Marjorie as he rinsed his damaged gums and washed his face.

After dunking his head under the faucet to further wake himself up, Skink toweled his face, leaving a bloody smear on the fabric, and reached into his pocket for the jar of methamphetamine. He emptied the remainder of the jar's contents onto the back of his hand and inhaled the last of the powdery paste.

The meth stung worse than usual as it passed his shattered septum, causing Skink to emit a growl through what was left of his infected teeth. Within seconds the rush hit him. The pain faded, and he became more alert. At least as alert as he could be, given his depleted physical condition and rapidly diminishing mental acuity.

Skink shook his head sharply a few times, trying unsuccessfully to clear it. He knew he had to find Marjorie and retrieve his gun. He was afraid of what Mims would do when he found out he'd lost them both.

If he hadn't found out already.

Skink stumbled out of the bedroom on shaky legs and headed for the stairs.

Mims pushed Tad's heavy, limp, body off as quietly as he could, picked up his guns, and silently knelt. The two uniformed men hadn't looked in his direction as they examined the three vehicles parked in the driveway. Fortunately, he'd been able to silence Tad before he'd alerted them.

He and Tad saw the men getting out of the sheriff's cruiser at the same time, giving Mims only a split second to drop his pistols and wrap his arm around the younger man's neck to prevent him from hailing them.

Mims initially applied what is known as a carotid restraint, a law enforcement technique he'd been trained to use in the sheriff's academy decades before. The carotid restraint, also known as the bilateral vascular restraint, could render a victim unconscious in scant seconds, conveniently silencing them at the same time.

If applied correctly, the technique safely induced fainting by compression of the carotid arteries, jugular veins, and the stimulation of the vagus nerve. But if not released immediately after fainting occurs, and the applying arm is moved from bilateral pressure on the sides of a person's neck to direct pressure rearward into the windpipe, the restraint becomes a choke hold. Suffocation and death can quickly result.

Mims was fully aware of the lethal difference between a carotid restraint and a choke hold when he transitioned from the former to the latter. He dropped to the ground onto his back with Tad on top of him, wrapped his legs around his struggling victim, and within seconds felt him go limp.

Keeping maximum pressure on Tad's throat for a full minute afterward, Mims crushed his windpipe and choked the life out of him. Then he carefully let go of the body, retrieved his discarded pistols, rose to a kneeling position, and observed the two men mount the porch steps together and approach the door. Both wore goggles and particle filter masks over their noses and mouths.

One of the men was a firefighter. He wore a baseball cap and windbreaker bearing the logo of the Farnham

County Fire District. He bore no weapons, carrying only a flashlight and a fire axe.

The other man was a sheriff's deputy. He was a full head taller than the firefighter, had a very large build, and was clad in fatigues, a tactical vest, and a thigh-holstered sidearm.

Mims squinted through the swirling smoke and burning embers, which had only become thicker since he'd left the house in pursuit of the fleeing Tad. Off to the east, the orange glow had dramatically increased in intensity. He thought he could actually see flames beginning to flicker through the impenetrable haze.

The big deputy began pounding on the door. "Sheriff's department," he announced, momentarily lowering the mask. "We're here to help you evacuate. Is there anyone inside?"

The firefighter peered through the window and shook his head. "Blinds are closed," he said in a muffled voice. "Can't see a thing inside."

"You'd think with all the cars out front," the deputy said, "somebody would be in there." He knocked and announced again.

"We might as well go ahead and bust in and make sure," the firefighter suggested. "By the looks of things, the fire's gonna burn down this house anyway." He extended the fire axe to the deputy. "Your turn," he said.

"Might as well," the deputy agreed. "There could be a shut-in, or maybe a deaf person, in there." He returned his mask to his face and accepted the axe from the firefighter. "We only have one more place on the list to check after this, don't we?"

"Yeah," the firefighter said. He withdrew a piece of

paper from his pocket. "The Dixon residence. It says on the map it's a mobile home about a mile down the road."

"Looks to me like the fire may have already reached that far," the deputy said, scanning the orange haze to the east. "That place might already be torched."

"Let's hurry up and get this house cleared," the firefighter said. "Then we'll make a good-faith effort to check on the Dixon place. If the fire's too close, we'll call it a day and head back to Farnham."

"Sounds like a plan," the deputy said, raising the axe.

CHAPTER FORTY-NINE

"How're you holding up, kiddo?" Benavides asked.

"I've had better days," Strayer admitted. "Thanks for bailing me out back there. Another minute and I was going to—"

"—kick the shit out of your commanding officer?" Benavides finished her sentence. "I know. You forget I've seen you do it before."

"Anyway, thanks."

"Don't mention it," he said.

"Any word on Sergeant Simpson?"

"I spoke to the paramedics just before they loaded her into the ambulance," Benavides said. "I know one of them pretty well."

"Is there anybody employed by Farnham County you don't know?" Strayer asked.

"Not really," he admitted. "That's what happens when you're as old as me and have been around as long as I have."

"What'd your friend the paramedic say?"

"Tasha will be all right. She's gonna have a hitch in her

giddyup for a while, but she should be back in the saddle in no time."

"She saved my life," Strayer said.

"I heard you tell that to the lieutenant. What you didn't tell him was that you saved hers, too." He gave Strayer a wink. "Don't think she doesn't know it."

Ennio Morricone's classic western theme once again sounded from within Benavides's pocket. This time, after checking the screen, he answered. "It's Paula Robeson, from Child Protective Services," he explained to Strayer, as he switched the phone's speaker on.

"Hiya, Paula," he greeted her, "how're things in Folsom?"

"Not as bad as I hear in Farnham," Robeson's voice answered. "I understand there's an evacuation underway. Are you okay? How about your family?"

"I'm fine," he said. "I already sent my wife and kids off to her mother's in Yuba City."

"Good to know," Robeson said. Her tone changed. "This isn't a social call, Benny. I need your help."

"What's up?"

"Do you know Karen Underhill?"

"Isn't she with CPS here in Farnham County?"

"That's right," Robeson's voice said. "She just transferred over there from Sacramento County a few months ago. She has a couple of kids in her caseload she's concerned about. They haven't attended school in several days. They live somewhere out in rural Farnham County, in a trailer without a phone."

"What're their names?"

"Brandy and Travis Dixon. Brandy is ten years old, and Travis is six."

"I'm familiar with the family," Benavides said. "CPS

has taken the kids into protective custody before. Both parents are dopers. They neglect the kids even when they're around."

"Karen's repeatedly called your dispatch center," Robeson explained, "and is getting the runaround. They keep telling her that deputies have been assigned to help evacuate residents in rural areas of the county, but can't confirm if anyone has been out to the Dixon place yet. She asked if a deputy could go out there now, but was told there aren't any deputies available due to the fire emergency and evacuation."

"You want me to go out and check on the kids for her?"

"Could you? Karen called me out of desperation, knowing I have contacts in Farnham County. I'm sorry to bother you, but she's really worried about those two kids. She didn't know who else to call."

"Consider it done," Benavides said. "Should take me less than an hour to get there and back. Once I leave the town limits, though, cell coverage drops. I'll won't be able to call you back until I return to Farnham."

"Thanks, Benny. I owe you a big one for this."

"I'll be in touch," Benavides said, signing off and putting down his phone. He conducted a U-turn and steered the sedan toward the highway onramp.

"With everything that's going on," Strayer said, "we're actually going to leave Farnham and go gallivanting off into the county to conduct a bullshit kiddie welfare check?"

"Don't knock child welfare checks," Benavides scolded. "I know you're a badass S.W.A.T. operator, but looking out for kids is the most important work we do."

Strayer realized by the set of Benavides's jaw, the spark

in his eyes, and the way he gripped the steering wheel that she'd touched a nerve.

"Get something straight," Benavides continued, his voice hardening. "All those gangsters and gunmen and dope dealers your S.W.A.T. buddies go after chose their life. Right or wrong, they deserve what's coming to them. Children don't get to make those choices. For better or worse, they're forced to suffer the consequences of the choices their parents make. In some cases, like the Dixons, their so-called parents make some pretty shitty choices. If those two kids are stuck out in the fire zone, left to fend for themselves, what the hell else have we got to do that's more important?"

"I guess I never thought of it like that," Strayer said.

"Welcome to the Juvenile Unit," Benavides said, shaking his head. "What we do may not be as cool as being a tactical deputy, or as glamorous as being a narcotics or homicide detective, but to the children we're sworn to protect, it's damned important duty. Many of the kids we deal with have nobody looking out for them except an overworked and underpaid social worker like Paula Robeson or Karen Underhill, or a broken-down old deputy like me. So yeah, if it's not too much of an inconvenience for you, we're going out into the county to conduct a 'bullshit kiddie welfare check.' Unless you'd rather go back to the station and fly a desk with Lieutenant McDillon breathing down your neck?"

"By all means," Strayer said, "let's go check on those kids."

Chapter Fifty

"Whoa there," Mims called out to the two men on the porch. "Please don't bash in the front door." He walked nonchalantly across the yard toward the house. Both of the Glock pistols were concealed in his waistband, one in front and the other in back, under his hoodie.

The big deputy lowered the fire axe. He and the firefighter turned to face Mims as he approached.

"Are you the resident here?" the deputy asked, pulling his filter mask aside.

"No," Mims answered, as he reached the porch steps. "Just a guest. The house belongs to my wife's parents, Hector and Margaret Hernandez. I'm only visiting."

"Did you know there's a wildfire bearing down on you only a short distance from here?" the firefighter asked. "It's heading this way. You should have evacuated hours ago."

"I know," Mims said as he mounted the steps. "Tell me something," he smiled when he reached the top, "do either of you have any luck getting your in-laws to do what you tell them to do?" He shook his head and grinned. "Me either," he answered his own question. "I don't know about yours," he went on, "but my in-laws are stubborn has hell."

"I hear that," the firefighter chuckled.

"Be that as it may," said the deputy, who was unmarried and didn't have any in-laws, "we've got to get you people out of here. This entire area has been officially declared a disaster area. A state of emergency is in effect, along with a mandatory evacuation."

"As you can see by our vehicles," Mims said, pointing to the red gas can in the back of Hector's truck, "we're packed up and ready to go. There's no need to wait for us."

"We'll help you load up your folks," the firefighter offered.

"That won't be necessary," Mims said. "I'm sure you boys have other homes to check. Thanks for your concern, but we'll be okay."

"Actually," the deputy said, handing the axe back to the firefighter, "we can't leave until we've made sure all the residents here have been evacuated and there's nobody still on the property. That's what 'mandatory evacuation' means."

"Take my word for it, Deputy," Mims said. "We're fine."

"What did you say your name was?" the deputy asked.

"Guthrie," Mims said, recalling the last name on Tad's driver's license. "Tad Guthrie." He extended his hand. "I live in Granite Bay."

"I'm Deputy Wayne Meyers," the big lawman said. "This here is Firefighter Greg Letourneau." The men shook hands all around.

"Who else besides your in-laws are in the house?" Meyers asked. He noticed for the first time the jamb surrounding the door's handle was splintered. Someone had recently kicked in the door.

"Nobody," Mims lied. "My wife and kids left yesterday. I only stayed on to help pack up her parents." He moved his right hand under his hoodie, ostensibly to scratch his belly. "We're going to caravan out together. Each of us will be driving one of the vehicles."

"What happened to the door?" Meyers asked.

Before Mims could answer the front door swung open. Everyone looked over to find Skink's emaciated, tattoo-covered, and sweating frame standing shakily in the doorway.

"I heard voices," he announced, as if that explained everything.

Deputy Meyers immediately went for the Sig Sauer .45 at this thigh. He'd just cleared the holster when the .40 caliber slug fired from Mims's pistol struck him in the face. He specifically aimed at the gargantuan deputy's head because of the heavy ballistic vest he wore. The huge body slumped to the porch, his pistol clattering next to him.

Firefighter Letourneau dropped his flashlight and axe, instinctively raised both hands protectively in front of his face, and yelled "No!" as he, too, was shot. The bullet entered through the middle of his dust mask. Mims couldn't tell if he was wearing soft body armor under his windbreaker, so he aimed at the head to be sure. The firefighter, dead before he hit the ground, joined the deputy crumpled on the porch.

Skink stood in the doorway, flinching with each shot. While he'd been with Mims when he attacked the corrections officers, eventually resulting in their deaths, and had found Hector's body, cringing as he stepped over it lying on the floor after he came downstairs, this was the first time he'd actually witnessed Mims kill anyone.

"Holy shit, Duane," he muttered. He stared, wide-eyed, at the bodies on the porch. "You don't fuck around, do you?"

"Generally not," Mims said, as he fired another round each into the downed men's heads for extra measure. Skink winced again with each shot.

"Where the hell have you been?" Mims demanded. He put the Glock back into his waistband and picked up the Sig Sauer 1911 pistol that had belonged to the now-deceased deputy.

"That Marjorie bitch slugged me and got away," he said sheepishly.

"I figured as much," Mims said. "Where's your gun?" He pushed past Skink into the house to get out of the smoke.

"I . . . I don't know," Skink stuttered. "I think she might have taken it." He followed Mims back inside and closed the door.

"She took it, all right," Mims said, "and gave it to her father." He pointed to Hector's body lying on the floor.

"Is that why you shot him?" Skink said.

"He aimed your gun at me and pulled the trigger," Mims explained. "What would you do?"

"Shoot him, I guess," Skink said sheepishly.

"Good thing I already took the firing pin out of your gun."

"You did what?" Skink sputtered, as his dope-addled brain tried to fathom what he'd just heard. "When did you do that?"

"Just after we got here," Mims answered, "while you were showering."

"But that means . . ."

"That's right," Mims interrupted. "It means you were shooting blanks all this time. Don't worry," he continued, "I put the firing pin back in place. Your gun works like a charm, now. Just ask those two dudes on the porch."

"Can I have it back now?" Skink asked in a timid voice.

"I don't think so," Mims said. He switched the deputy's pistol to his left hand. With his right fist he punched Skink directly in the collarbone.

Skink emitted a guttural shriek and collapsed in agony. Mims walked over to the basement door, unlocked it, and opened it. Then he returned to the moaning, gasping, and writhing Skink and grabbed him by his shirtfront. He dragged the feebly struggling convict to the top of the stairs and hurled him bodily down into the basement.

After re-closing and relocking the cellar door, Mims went outside. He strode to Hector's pickup truck and took the ten-gallon gas can from the bed. Then he returned to the house, lugged the heavy container upstairs, and went from room to room pouring out the contents.

CHAPTER FIFTY-ONE

Marjorie and Mary heard the faint crunch of gravel above them. The muffled closing of two vehicle doors followed.

"That's a car," Mary said.

"Quiet," Marjorie silenced her. She listened for several seconds more, then went into the furnace room where Joel had stopped cutting on the lock. He lay motionless on the shelf with his ear tilted toward the gap in the coal-chute hatch.

"I just heard a car drive up," he whispered.

"I know," Marjorie said, as she climbed the shelves to join him. "We heard it, too."

The chute was on the side of the house nearest the road, placed there by the home's builder a century ago to facilitate coal delivery. Even without the smoke from the wildfire limiting their view through the two-inch gap in the hatch, Marjorie and Joel couldn't see around the corner of the house where the vehicles were parked.

The faint and indistinct sounds of male voices could be heard emanating from around the corner. Looking up simultaneously, Marjorie and Joel also detected footsteps above them in the house upstairs. A few moments later they were startled to hear a pair of gunshots. Two more quickly followed.

"Were those shots?" Joel asked.

Marjorie didn't answer him. Instead, she craned her neck to peer through the gap and squinted at the lock. "How close are you to cutting through?"

"Just a little bit," he said. "Maybe another half hour?"

She could see the long-necked padlock had been cut almost all the way through. There was still approximately one-tenth of an inch of the shackle's stem remaining.

"We don't have half an hour," Marjorie said, trying to keep her fear and dread, which erupted like a volcano at the sound of the shots, from contaminating her voice. She clambered down the shelves.

"Wait here," she said to Joel, as she dashed into the main cellar.

"Were those gunshots?" Mary asked, with no effort to hide the fear in her own voice. She was kneeling next to the cot in the fading light of the battery-powered lantern. Her mother and niece were awake and sitting up.

Marjorie ignored her sister's question, lifted Jennifer out of the cot, and handed her to Mary. "Put her shoes on. Hurry up!"

Mary scrambled to comply as Marjorie snatched the lantern from the table. She dumped the contents of the box of corroded old tools out onto the floor. She was looking for a hammer, and a chisel, awl, or flathead screwdriver. She found an ancient, five-pound hammer and a Phillips-head screwdriver. She tossed the screwdriver aside, knowing its tip wouldn't do.

"Mama," Jennifer said, watching her mother frantically dig through the pile of tools, "what are you doing?"

"You're going to go with your brother," Marjorie answered, without looking up from her search. "You must do exactly as he says."

Marjorie finally found an old wooden-handled, long-necked, flathead screwdriver. It was covered in rust, and one corner of its tip was broken off.

"What's going on?" Margaret said. "You're scaring your daughter. Me, too."

"Get up, Mom," Marjorie said. "We're getting out of here."

The basement door above them abruptly opened and Skink came tumbling down the steps, screaming as he rolled. He landed on his back at the base of the stairs as Marjorie stood protectively in front of her family. The door above them closed again.

Marjorie raised the hammer, prepared to defend herself if Skink attacked, but she needn't have. He lay sobbing on the floor through his bloody mouth, unable to get up.

Skink's involuntary plunge broke his ankle and split open a nasty gash on his forehead. His once merely broken collarbone had become a compound fracture during the somersault down the stone stairs. A jagged shard of bone now protruded through his skin between his neck and shoulder.

Mary pounced on Skink, straddling his chest. He howled in pain. She got in two punches to his face before Marjorie restrained her, pulling her enraged sister off the injured convict.

"Shit," he moaned weakly, once Mary had released him, "it hurts. It hurts bad. Help me, please?"

"Take Jennifer into the back room with Joel," Marjorie told her mother. "We'll be there in a minute." Margaret covered Jennifer's eyes and led the girl away.

"Where's Mims?" Marjorie demanded, once her mother and daughter were gone.

"Ughhh," Skink groaned. "I'm all busted up. You gotta help me."

Marjorie kicked him in the ribs. "Where's Mims?"

"Upstairs somewhere," Skink said, after he curled in to a fetal position. "Please don't hurt me no more."

"What's he doing?"

"I dunno," Skink grunted. "After he shot those two deputies, he threw my ass down here with you. Your guess is as good as mine as to what he's up to."

Mary pulled back her foot to kick him, but Marjorie stopped her. "What did you do to get sent to prison?"

Skink stared up at the faces of the two women looking down at him, failing to detect even a glimmer of mercy. He averted his bleary eyes and didn't answer.

Marjorie nodded to her sister, and Mary kicked Skink in his right arm, near the protruding bone. He convulsed, and his piercing scream lasted for several long seconds.

"Answer the question," Marjorie said. Mary cocked her foot again.

"They say I killed a kid," Skink exclaimed, holding out his left hand in protest. "But I didn't. It wasn't me, I swear. The rug rat was my old lady's daughter. Somebody else must've come into the apartment and . . ." He looked away again.

"Go on," Marjorie said. "Tell us the rest." Mary nudged his injured shoulder with her toe.

"Okay," he relented, panting, "I'll tell you. Just don't

kick me no more. Somebody busted in . . . and . . ." His voice trailed off. His eyes darted nervously from Marjorie to Mary.

"Spit it out," Mary hissed.

"They raped and strangled the girl," he said. "My old lady was at work. I was passed out, wasted, on the couch when it happened."

"How could you sleep through someone breaking into your apartment?" Mary scoffed.

"I was comin' off a crank bender," Skink said. "I hadn't slept in almost a week. I totally crashed. I don't remember nuthin' from that night."

The repulsion on the faces of the women standing over him was stark. "It wasn't me," he insisted, reading their disbelief. "I don't care what all that DNA bullshit said. The cops lied. I didn't do it."

"Keep an eye on him," Marjorie told Mary, as she disappeared into the back room with the hammer and screwdriver.

CHAPTER FIFTY-TWO

"This is the Dixon place," Benavides said. He made a left turn from the county road they were traveling on to a private dirt road marked only with a leaning mailbox.

"I don't see anything," Strayer said, squinting through the windshield.

It wasn't hard to understand why. The smoke was extremely heavy and the windswept air was swirling in a blizzard of ash and falling embers, making visibility beyond a few dozen feet nearly impossible.

Compounding the problem was the lateness of the afternoon. The sun, hidden behind a thick layer of clouds and an equally impenetrable layer of smoke from the Farnham Fire, had brought twilight several hours early. Had Benavides not known where the dirt road leading to the Dixon property was from his previous visits, they'd have driven right past the mailbox without seeing the turnoff. The orange glow to the east, where the wildfire was rapidly approaching, provided the only illumination besides the headlights of the unmarked sedan.

Benavides drove another fifty yards over the bumpy road, and a dilapidated mobile home gradually came into view. It was resting aboveground on cinder blocks, and over half of its roof was a blue plastic tarpaulin. There were no vehicles parked on the property.

He stopped the car, leaving the engine running, and retrieved a flashlight from the glove box.

"You ready?" he asked.

"Right behind you," she said.

When Strayer and Benavides got out of the car, they were immediately struck by a blast of heat and a fierce, hot wind. The crackling sounds of burning brush and timber was loud enough to rival the wind's roar. Dust and debris peppered them. While they couldn't actually see the fire, both knew it was very close.

"We haven't got much time," Benavides shouted to Strayer. Shielding their eyes, they made their way across the trash-strewn yard to the trailer.

"Sheriff's department!" Benavides announced, pounding on the door with his flashlight. "Anybody inside?"

The door opened slightly. A tiny, frightened, face peered out at them.

"Travis?" Benavides said. "Is that you?"

The face nodded. Benavides pushed the door open and Strayer followed him in, closing the door behind her.

The trailer's interior was dark and filthy. The overwhelming odor of rancid food and un-disposed-of trash competed with the smell of smoke. Benavides scanned the cramped trailer with his flashlight, finding refuse and garbage in every corner.

Six-year-old Travis Dixon stood before them. His malnourished body looked as if he hadn't been fed or washed in days.

"Where're your folks," Benavides asked, "and your sister?"

"Daddy's gone," Travis said. "Brandy's in the bedroom with mom. She's sleeping."

Benavides knelt down to face level to speak further with Travis. He handed Strayer the flashlight and motioned for her to check out the bedroom.

Climbing over mounds of waste, Strayer navigated the narrow hallway and entered the only bedroom in the small trailer. Like the main room and hallway, it was filled with trash. She panned the flashlight beam around.

In the center of the room was a soiled mattress. Curled up next to a woman who was lying supine on it was a little girl. She was barefoot, as dirty as her brother, and her long hair was matted and clumped.

"Brandy Dixon?" Strayer said. "Is that you?"

The girl, who appeared much younger than her ten years, looked up but didn't move. Strayer had seen a thousand-yard stare identical to hers before, many times, in Afghanistan.

"Mama's not feeling well," Brandy said softly. "She's asleep."

As soon as Strayer neared the bed, she realized the woman was not only dead, but had been in that state for several days. The necrotic scent of decomposing flesh was also familiar to Strayer from her combat tours. She couldn't know for sure, but if she had to guess, the woman had succumbed to a drug overdose. There were several discarded needles lying on the rubbish-covered floor.

"Come with me, Brandy," Strayer said, reaching for the girl. "We have to go now."

"I can't leave Mama," Brandy said. "She'll be all alone when she wakes up."

"It's okay," Strayer said. "Let your mama sleep."

"Who are you?"

"My name's Leanne," Strayer said. "I'm a sheriff's deputy."

Brandy didn't resist when Strayer reached down and picked her up. The girl was much lighter than she should have been. She hugged the deputy with a strength that surprised Strayer, and she felt the girl's frail body trembling in her arms.

When Strayer got back to the main room, Benavides was holding Travis.

"Where's Carly?" he asked, referring to the children's mother. Strayer merely shook her head.

"Let's get out of here," Benavides said. When he opened the trailer door, he and Strayer were met with a sight that momentarily shocked them.

While they were inside the trailer, the wind-fueled fire had fully advanced onto the Dixon property. A wall of flame twenty feet high was overtaking the yard and completely blocked the private road they'd driven in on. Flames licked at the sheriff's car.

"Follow me!" Benavides yelled, and dashed from the trailer. Strayer ran out behind him. They sprinted to the vehicle, high-stepping over burning patches of grass, each carrying a terrified child in their arms.

Benavides opened the rear door and tossed Travis Dixon inside as Strayer did the same with Brandy from the opposite side of the vehicle. After he and Strayer had scrambled in themselves, Benavides put the car into gear and floored it, turning away from the road and guiding the sedan over the burning yard and away from the rapidly encroaching tide of fire.

As the unmarked sheriff's car swerved and bounced over the uneven terrain, Strayer leaned across the front seat and struggled to buckle the children into their safety belts. When she finally got both of the Dixons secured, she returned to her own jostling seat and buckled herself in.

Strayer looked back but saw nothing through the rear windscreen but thick smoke and flames. She realized the trailer they'd just abandoned was engulfed.

"That was a close one," she finally said.

"Whaddya mean?" Benavides grinned. He lowered his voice. "This was nothing but a 'bullshit kiddie welfare check.'"

"All right," Strayer relented, "you win. I was wrong."

"Like I said before"—he winked—"welcome to the Juvenile Unit."

"Do you have any idea where we're going?" she asked, as the car bounded across a series of open fields and finally came to rest on a different dirt road. Once on flat ground, Benavides kept the gas pedal pressed, trying to put as much distance between them and the fire as possible.

"We can't go back the way we came," Benavides said over the roar of the engine, "that's for sure. Wherever this road leads, we'll have to take it."

"So we're lost?" Strayer said.

"Don't worry," Benavides said. Like Strayer, his face was covered in sweat and soot. "I'll eventually figure out where we are."

"Who's worried?" Strayers said sarcastically. "It's not like we're lost in the middle of a raging wildfire."

"I know where this road goes," Travis said from the back seat.

"Where's that?" Benavides asked.

"This is the road to Hector and Margie's house," he said triumphantly.

CHAPTER FIFTY-THREE

Mims emptied half of the ten-gallon can upstairs and the other half downstairs. Then he went to the porch and dragged the bodies of the deputy and firefighter through the front door and placed them next to Hector Hernandez's corpse in the main room. He carefully removed the dust mask from Deputy Meyer's head, taking pains to avoid contaminating it with more blood than was already on it. His goggles had been shattered by the bullets entering his skull. So, unfortunately, were the firefighter's.

The deputy had been going for his pistol, and Mims was forced to shoot hastily, but the firefighter was empty-handed when he was executed. Mims cursed himself for not having the presence of mind to aim more carefully and preserve his protective eyewear.

Out of breath from the exertion of moving the bodies, Mims rested on the couch while he filled his pockets with the plentiful cash from Marjorie and Mary's purses and Tad's wallet. He resisted the impulse to take credit cards, knowing they could be traced.

His original plan, which involved keeping at least one of his captives alive as a potential traveling hostage, had changed with Tad Guthrie's arrival. He'd initially planned to kill Skink along with the hostages, making it appear, if any of their remains were even left to examine after the fire, that the escaped convict had committed the murders of the Hernandez and Guthrie families. That was the only reason Mims kept the degenerate drug addict alive and allowed him to tag along in the first place.

The only problem with Mims's plan to blame the killings on Skink was it would raise the question; if Skink survived the firestorm on the highway and escaped, wouldn't the authorities presume Duane Audie Mims had escaped as well?

But when Tad Guthrie arrived, and Mims learned of the restraining order his wife Marjorie obtained prohibiting her estranged husband from contacting her, he hatched an even better plan. One that would also account for the deaths of the firefighter and deputy. Mims's law enforcement–trained mind realized Tad would make the perfect fall guy.

A deranged husband, whose capacity for violence against loved ones had already been established by the condition of his wife's face and furious at his spouse and children for abandoning him, had shown up at his in-law's home in violation of a protective order and wiped out the entire family. Such tragedies were technically called familicides and occurred all too often somewhere in America. Mims knew the investigators at the Farnham County Sheriff's Department would easily conclude such a scenario took place once Tad Guthrie's body was found at the scene. He'd also be blamed for the deaths of the deputy and firefighter, presumably ambushing them when they arrived to help evacuate the residents. After his killing spree, of course, Tad would then have taken his own life. Suicide by perpetrators of familicide was not uncommon.

Mims chose to take the keys to Mary's Lincoln. As a rental, it would take the longest to be reported unreturned or stolen. With the chaos of the Farnham Fire and its aftermath, it could be weeks before anyone thought to look for the vehicle. By then, with a bit of luck, he'd be well across the southern border and deep into Mexico.

Mims was fluent in Spanish, like many California law enforcement officers, and had little doubt he could find both refuge and employment with one of the cartels. He was confident his training, background, skill set, and complete lack of remorse would make him a valuable asset to one of the many drug lords who were the real rulers of America's southern neighbor.

He went into the kitchen and rinsed the dust mask, then cleaned it with a paper towel. Picking up the adjustable wrench he'd left on the table, Mims reached behind the stove and unfastened the nut linking the appliance to the gas line. A rotten-egg smell immediately began to fill the kitchen.

He next pushed the refrigerator aside and detached that appliance's gas line as well. The rotten-egg smell became stronger, joining the scent of gasoline and woodsmoke that had previously pervaded the home.

Mims left through the front door and walked across the yard, through the swirling smoke and burning embers, until he came to Tad Guthrie's body. He put on the dust filter, covering his nose and mouth.

He paused to look around. The sky was dark, even with the intense orange glow, and Mims could hear the crackle of the fire, churning up timber and brush, over the sounds of the wind. He realized, with some satisfaction, that the wildfire would reach the house within minutes after he departed. By then the structure would be filled with propane and would not only burn, but go up in a mushroom cloud like the gas tanker next to the prisoner van.

Mims rolled Tad onto his back. He drew the deputy's .45 from his belt, thumbed down the safety, and knelt next to the body. He pressed the muzzle against Tad's temple and fired. Finally, he placed the weapon in Tad's lifeless right hand, completing the final staging of his twice-modified, but nonetheless still satisfying, plan.

He dug the Lincoln's keys from his pocket and was walking back toward the parked vehicles, when he noticed movement up ahead, near the house. He wiped his stinging eyes and peered through the smoke.

Mims realized, with mounting fury, that his plan had gone awry. He watched as the two Guthrie children, Joel and Jennifer, ran off into the haze. They were followed a moment later by the old lady, Margaret Hernandez, who was moving much more slowly.

Chapter Fifty-four

Marjorie lay on top of the shelves. She'd slipped the old screwdriver through the gap and wedged its broken tip, as best she could, into the cut in the padlock's shank made by her father and son. Taking the hammer, she prepared to strike.

Margaret was below her, holding Jennifer's hand. Joel lay next to her on the shelf, aiming the dimming flashlight at the screwdriver for his mother.

Marjorie started to hit the screwdriver with the hammer but stopped herself, realizing the angle at which she lay gave her no leverage to apply force. It was too awkward for one person to hold the screwdriver in place and utilize the hammer at the same time. She was afraid all she would do was make a loud noise and fail to chisel through the padlock's stem.

Joel instantly grasped his mother's dilemma. "I can hold the screwdriver," he offered.

"No," Marjorie said. "I'll hold it. You've got better eye/hand coordination than me, and you know how to swing from baseball practice. I want you to use the hammer."

"But if I miss," Joel protested, "I'll smash your hands."

"Don't think about that," Marjorie said. She handed him the hammer, noticing his blistered and bleeding hands. His grandfather's gloves were too big for him, and he'd been forced to discard them during the night. The young boy had been working as desperately as her father to save his family.

"Hit it as hard as you can, Joel. I don't want to have to do this more than once."

"Okay," Joel said, accepting the hammer. "Here goes."

Mary rushed into the room, halting their endeavor. "Gas," she exclaimed. "I smell gas. It's coming from up-stairs."

As soon as Mary ran from the cellar's main room into the furnace room to warn the others, Skink sat up. He bit his lip to quell a scream as an excruciating bolt of agony ripped through his shoulder.

Like Mary, he could easily detect the growing smell of gas filtering into the basement from above. He knew immediately what Duane had done, and that very soon the house was going to become a crematorium.

Woozy with pain, Skink posted his left arm to steady himself. He knew he had to find a way out. His hand ended up among the tools scattered on the basement floor when Marjorie overturned the old toolbox. He fumbled among them until his fingers wrapped around the Phillips-head screwdriver.

* * *

"Do it!" Marjorie commanded Joel. "Remember, hit as hard as you can." She closed her eyes and began to pray.

Joel took in a breath, closed one eye, and focused on the end of the screwdriver like a sniper aiming through a telescopic sight. He swung the hammer with every ounce of skill and strength his years of swinging a Little League bat had given him.

The hammer struck the screwdriver squarely on the end, launching it through Marjorie's hands. The blade easily broke through the remaining portion of the padlock's shackle.

Marjorie's adult-sized hand was too thick, but Joel reached his fingers through the gap and wriggled the broken lock off the hasp. She quickly rolled over onto her back, planted her feet, and leg-pressed the coal chute's metal hatch open.

Whatever fleeting moment of elation Marjorie experienced in opening the hatch was extinguished by the growing smell of decayed eggs, and the knowledge that any moment the house could go up in ball of fire.

"Take your sister," Marjorie commanded Joel, as she hastily climbed down the shelves. She grabbed Jennifer, kissed her, and handed the girl up to her brother.

"Run," she told them. "Grandma and I will be right behind you. Don't wait for us. Head for the road, like I told you, away from the fire."

Joel nodded and said, "I love you, Mom." He and Jennifer climbed through the hatch and were gone.

"You're next," Marjorie said to her mother.

"No," Margaret said. "You and Mary should go first. I couldn't—"

"Get your ass up there!" Marjorie snapped at her mother, cutting off her protests. "We haven't got time for this!" She guided Margaret up the shelves, steadying her as she clumsily climbed the improvised ladder.

"What about him?" Mary said, pointing to the main room with her thumb. She was referring to Skink.

"What about him?"

"Are we just going to leave him to die?"

"That's what he'd planned for us," Marjorie said.

"We're not him," Mary said.

"You're right," Marjorie conceded, knowing she couldn't abandon Skink to his death. "He's not very big. If we work together, we should be able to get him out. But we've got to hurry."

After watching their mother vanish through the hatch, Marjorie followed Mary back into the main cellar. The odor of propane that met them there was strong. The battery-powered camping lantern was still on, but just barely. Skink was no longer lying on the floor.

Before either could react, Skink lunged from out of the darkness and plunged the Phillips-head screwdriver hilt-deep into Mary's stomach.

"Mary!" Marjorie cried out, and instinctively started toward her sister.

Mary gasped, clutched her abdomen with both hands, and fell forward. Skink withdrew the screwdriver and blocked Marjorie's path.

Skink's eyes were maniacally bright, and he was twitching. The effects of the methamphetamine he'd ingested had kicked in again and given him a second wind. He stood before Marjorie, grinning through his toothless mouth, and waved the screwdriver back and forth menacingly. The fresh blood from the gash on his forehead had mixed with the dried blood from his shattered nose, covering his face in crimson. It lent him an almost demonic appearance in the fading light of the lantern.

"You're gonna get me outta here," he hissed.

"What makes you think I'd help you do anything?" Marjorie said, looking down at her sister and fighting back tears.

"I ain't gonna burn," he said. "No way. I almost burned up once, along with Duane. You're gettin' me outta here, all right."

The distinct sound of a gunshot sounded outside. Skink looked up, momentarily distracted by the noise.

That's when Marjorie attacked.

CHAPTER FIFTY-FIVE

The unmarked sheriff's sedan, piloted by Benavides, motored over the narrow dirt lane. He was driving far too fast for the road conditions and limited visibility, but he and Strayer knew he had no choice. The nebulous orange glow emanating from the east, which had characterized their journey from Farnham to the Dixon property, was gone. It had been replaced by an all-too-visible wall of flame that paralleled the road, which was for the moment acting as a temporary firebreak.

"I sure hope this road leads someplace besides another neighbor," Strayer said.

"I'll drive us as far as I can," Benavides said.

"What happens when we run out of road?"

"I guess we'll be hoofing it," he answered with a tight grin.

In the rear seat behind them, Brandy Dixon stared catatonically out the window with no expression. She may as well have been out for a Sunday drive. Travis Dixon's unwashed six-year-old face reflected the tension in Strayer's.

"I see a house up ahead," Benavides said, slowing the sedan. "Cars, too."

"That's Hector and Margie's house," Travis announced from the back seat.

As the structure came into better view, Strayer recognized one of the vehicles. "That's a sheriff's car!" she exclaimed, pointing through the windshield.

"So it is," Benavides said. "Maybe we'll catch a break."

As they neared the house, an older woman emerged from the darkness and smoke. She was running toward them, away from the house, and frantically waving her arms. She wore a desperate look on her face, and mouthed words Strayer and Benavides couldn't hear from inside their vehicle.

"Stop the car," Strayer said. Benavides complied. Strayer opened the passenger door and stepped out, as the woman lurched forward and collapsed onto the hood of the sheriff's sedan. All around them the wind blew and the fire crackled.

". . . gun!" the woman yelled, out of breath and with unrestrained terror in her voice. "We've got to help Marjorie! He's got a gun!"

"Calm down," Strayer said, instantly alert at the word "gun." Benavides also stepped out of the car. "Who's Marjorie? Who has a gun?"

"His name is Mims," the woman panted. "Back at the house," she gasped. "Duane Mims."

Strayer and Benavides exchanged incredulous glances over the roof of the car. Both drew their sidearms.

"Mims?" Strayer said. "He's alive?"

"How else would she know that name?" Benavides said.

Before either of the deputies could question the panicked woman further, a bullet struck the windshield, followed by several more. Strayer pushed the woman to the ground, as even more rounds impacted the car's hood and grille. Benavides, on the other side of the sedan, grunted and fell.

Strayer looked up, as she lay protectively over the woman, in the direction the shots came from. She saw a tall, shadowy figure moving through the smoke and darkness. He was wearing a dust mask over his face and holding a pistol.

Strayer raised her .45 and fired two three-shot strings before her pistol emptied and the slide locked back. She realized she'd forgotten to reload her gun with a fresh magazine after the earlier shooting incident at her apartment.

The figure with the gun vanished again into the murky gloom as Strayer dumped the Sig Sauer's empty single-stack magazine and reloaded from one of the spares on her belt. She wondered whether she'd hit the gunman, and if it was, in fact, actually Mims?

While she certainly doubted she'd struck their attacker with her hasty return fire, Strayer couldn't help but know, deep in her gut, that the tall, ghostly figure she'd just witnessed was indeed Duane Mims.

CHAPTER FIFTY-SIX

Marjorie struck out with a powerful front kick that landed directly in Skink's solar plexus. The skinny convict, who weighed only a couple of pounds more than Marjorie and was balanced on one leg as a result of his broken ankle, was thrown backward across the cellar and crumpled to the floor.

One of Marjorie's favorite workouts at the upscale health club she belonged to in Granite Bay was a fitness class entitled Retro Tae Bo. The class was taught by a fit young woman who held a 1st Dan in tae kwon do and featured music from Top 40 artists of the '90s like Snoop Dogg and the Backstreet Boys, when Billy Blanks's exercise videos were at the height of their popularity. While the workout was health-oriented, and not a self-defense class, it was based on martial arts moves such as lateral kicks, roundhouse kicks, and of course, front kicks.

Instead of continuing her attack, Marjorie retreated into the furnace room. For the second time since he'd been hurled down the stairs in to the basement, Skink was forced to curl himself into a fetal ball of agony. He could barely breathe and lay writhing on the ground.

Marjorie reemerged from the furnace room, this time carrying the five-pound hammer Joel had used to shatter the cut-away padlock.

Skink, sensing her approach, looked up to find Marjorie looming over him with the hammer raised above her head. Her face was a portrait of primal rage.

"No!" he begged, dropping the screwdriver. "You can't!"

"The hell I can't," Marjorie said through closed teeth. She brought the hammer down with all her might.

It wasn't really the face of a hammer that came crashing down on the crown of Skink's forehead. It was a lightning rod, channeling all of the trauma, abuse, wrath, anguish, shame, maternal fear, and grief she'd experienced over the past several days.

Marjorie raised the hammer and struck two more times. With each successive strike, she was peppered with blood.

Spent, Marjorie dropped the hammer and turned to Mary. She knelt and cradled her little sister's head in her lap. Mary's face was slack and her complexion pale, and her lips were turning blue. She stared past her sister through eyes unfocused and tearing. The front of her shirt was soaked in blood.

"Oh, Mary," Marjorie said, with quivering lips.

"I'm . . . sorry," Mary whispered, her voice almost inaudible. Marjorie lowered one ear to her sister's mouth. "For . . . Tad."

"I told you already," Marjorie comforted her, "you don't have anything to be sorry about. Even if you did, I forgive you. I love you."

Mary smiled. Then she emitted a bubbling gurgle from deep in her throat, twitched for an instant, and died.

Marjorie desperately wanted to remain on the cellar floor holding her sister and to release the torrent of sobs poised at the back of her throat. But concern for Jennifer, Joel, and her mother made her swallow her grief and stifle her tears.

She stood up, dashed back through the furnace room into the coal bin, and was clambering up the shelves when she heard the gunshots.

CHAPTER FIFTY-SEVEN

Strayer's stunned mind scrambled for footing. Visions flashed like exploding camera bulbs inside her head.

Her unexpectedly potent reaction that morning to seeing Mims's image on television. Recollections of her conversations with Dr. Wozniak. The picture of Pamela Gardner. The gunfights at the trailer park and at her apartment. The flight, just now, from the Dixons' trailer.

The uncontrollable barrage of memories and emotions unnerved her. They competed with the visceral images of her long-ago encounter with Mims, threatening to overwhelm her composure.

She was snapped out of her frozen state by a pair of children, a boy and girl about the same ages as the Dixon children, who came running up to the car from out of the smoke. Both were out of breath, and immediately went to the older woman.

"Grandma!" the little girl said. They all held each other.

"Stay here," Strayer told the trio, "and stay down." She had more pressing matters to contend with than sorting out details of the newcomers' identities. Mims was out there, armed and hiding, in the smoke and darkness. If that weren't enough, she noticed the fire had now crossed the dirt road and was advancing on the lawn toward the house.

She went around the car to Benavides, who'd sat himself up. His left arm lay useless against his chest, a bloodstain decorating the shoulder of his jacket. He held his pistol in his right fist.

"I'm okay," he said before Strayer could ask. "It isn't too bad."

"Let me see," Strayer said, starting to open his coat.

"Forget it," Benavides waved her off. "There isn't time. We've got to get these people out of here before Mims comes back."

"Agreed," Strayer said. She scanned the surrounding area, which was fruitless due to the nonexistent visibility caused by the heavy smoke and fading light. Mims was nowhere to be found. She helped her partner into the driver's seat.

"Get in the car," she shouted to the woman and children. Covering with her pistol, Strayer guided them into the vehicle. She put the two new kids in back with the Dixons, and was helping the woman into the front seat, when Benavides abruptly cursed.

"What's wrong?"

"The engine won't start," he explained. "One of Mims's bullets must have damaged something under the hood." He slammed his pistol butt against the steering wheel in frustration. "This ride's dead in the water."

"I'll check the patrol car," Strayer said. Keeping her gun up, she ran over to the sheriff's cruiser. She found the doors unlocked, but no keys in the ignition. Not only couldn't she start the car, she couldn't operate the Electro-Loc holding the vehicle's AR-15 rifle, either.

"No luck," she said, when she returned to Benavides. "The deputy must have the keys on him."

"Speaking of the deputy," Benavides asked, "where do you suppose he is?"

"If I had to guess," Strayer said, "Mims already got him." Benavides nodded.

Strayer looked at Benavides. He was still conscious but in no condition to walk, much less flee a murderous gunman and an approaching wildfire on foot.

"Stay here and protect these folks," Strayer told him, patting him on his uninjured shoulder.

"Where're you going?"

"To get Mims," she said, "before he gets us."

CHAPTER FIFTY-EIGHT

Mims moved in a crouch with a Glock in each hand. He'd circled completely around the property, giving the house a wide berth in case it blew. He was heading back to the front from the opposite direction. He had no choice but to return there, because that's where the vehicles were parked.

Mims knew he didn't have much time. He could see the fire advancing across the yard and knew the house was filling up with propane from the big tank outside. Burning embers fell like rain, and he suspected the structure could ignite and explode into flames at any moment.

He'd watched the unmarked sedan drive up while hidden behind the patrol car. He originally intended to wait until the occupants got out and gun them down at point-blank range like he'd done to the uniformed deputy and firefighter.

But just as the car stopped in the driveway, far enough away to be barely visible in the swirling smoke, Mims saw the hysterical Margaret Hernandez run toward the vehicle. When the two plainclothes deputies got out of their car to greet her, he clearly heard Margaret speak his name.

Incensed, Mims opened fire. Though not at a distance where he'd normally have trouble making accurate shots, the haze and smoke made his targets little more than indistinct shapes. He fired multiple times, swinging the barrel of his pistol first at the male deputy, then at the female deputy, and lastly at Margaret Hernandez, operating on the chauvinistic assumption that the male deputy would be the better shot.

He heard several of his bullets *tink* against the unmarked sedan, and watched in satisfaction as the blurry outlines of all three of his targets fell from view.

As he was approaching to confirm the kills, the female deputy suddenly popped up and cut loose with a volley of gunfire of her own. Mims threw himself to the ground and rolled as one of her bullets grazed his hip. He was forced to scramble to his feet and retreat. As he backed away into the smoke, he took little comfort knowing they could no longer see him. He couldn't see them anymore, either.

Once behind the house, Mims checked his injury. The slug had torn through his trousers and creased a furrow through the meaty portion of his left hip and buttock. It wasn't a serious wound, but it bled, and hurt, and he cursed himself for his impetuousness in advancing too soon on what he presumed were a pair of incapacitated deputies and a harmless old woman.

Mims was livid. Not only did law enforcement personnel now know he was alive, his hostages, whom he'd hoped would be immolated when the house went up in flames, had gotten loose. While he didn't consider Marjorie Guthrie, her sister Mary, the grandmother, or the children an immediate threat since they were afoot in a wildfire, their survival and freedom jeopardized his plans to remain anonymous and escape justice.

It was too late to contemplate that now. There was no time left to hunt them all down and eliminate them, especially with at least one armed deputy still alive and about. Mims knew he had to reach the luxury car and get away before the house blew up or he was shot again. He patted his pocket, reassuring himself the keys to Mary's rented Lincoln were still there.

As Mims cautiously proceeded around the far side of the house, he noticed the open coal hatch. This had undoubtedly been the means by which his hostages escaped. Once again, he cursed himself. How could he have missed the coal chute when he searched the basement?

It didn't matter now. Mims put his self-criticism aside, along with the growing ache in his hip, and focused all of his energy on getting to the Lincoln. To do that, he knew he had to find, and kill, the female deputy.

Though Mims didn't know it, Marjorie Guthrie had emerged from the cellar only a moment before he'd discovered the open coal hatch. She'd traded the scent of rotten eggs for the suffocating smell of woodsmoke and made her escape.

Marjorie tried not to think about the many gunshots she'd heard while down in the basement. Her mind refused to let her believe that Mims had somehow caught her mother and children and executed them.

She went directly to her father's truck. Swinging the bloody hammer, which she'd brought with her from the basement, Marjorie shattered the driver's door window.

Then she dropped the hammer to the ground, reached through the window, and grabbed the Remington shotgun that had been locked inside the vehicle by Mims.

Racking the pump back to open the ejection port, Marjorie reached into her pocket and retrieved the solitary shotgun shell her father had given to her before he died. She inserted it into the chamber, slammed the pump forward, and ensured the safety behind the trigger guard was switched off.

"Fire with the finger," her father's words came back to her from more than twenty years past, "and safety with the thumb. That's how you do it with a Remington, Marjorie."

Marjorie shouldered the weapon and looked around. She saw nothing but smoke, ash, burning embers, and darkness locked in battle with light from the advancing flames.

"Mims!" she hollered at the top of her lungs. "Duane Mims! Come and get me, you son of a bitch!"

CHAPTER FIFTY-NINE

When Strayer heard the woman's voice shouting Mims's name, she stopped in her tracks. The voice was coming from somewhere behind her, back near the driveway.

Like Mims, Strayer was stalking her way through the smoke, darkness, and burning debris. She held her pistol in a two-handed Weaver stance and was "duckwalking," a slang term tactical operators coined for the short-stepped gait they used to steady their aim while moving.

She headed off in the same direction she'd last seen Mims before he vanished. Strayer had gone about fifty steps along the side of the house when a body, lying on the ground, materialized before her.

The corpse belonged to a heavy-set man in his thirties. Most of his facial features were eradicated by a large-caliber gunshot wound to his right temple. A pistol was nestled in his lifeless right hand.

Strayer instantly recognized the unique weapon as a Farnham County Sheriff's Department–issued S.W.A.T. pistol; a Sig Sauer 1911 .45, identical to hers. Clearly the firearm had been the property of the deputy, undoubtedly assigned to the S.W.A.T. Unit, who'd arrived in the patrol car to assist with the evacuation of the residents. She wondered which deputy it was.

Realizing a dead body holding a S.W.A.T. firearm didn't bode well for the gun's owner, Strayer pried the pistol from the cadaver's hand and examined it. When she saw the name on the magazine's baseplate, her eyebrows lifted.

Most deputies, whether assigned to S.W.A.T. or any other unit, marked the baseplates of their pistol magazines with their names or star numbers to avoid mixing them up with mags belonging to other deputies. The name on the weapon in Strayer's hands was MEYERS.

Strayer press-checked the pistol to ensure it was loaded, flicked up the safety, and removed the magazine. It was only one round short of its full capacity of eight cartridges. She reinserted the magazine, placed the pistol in her empty holster, and resumed her search.

She'd progressed another few yards when she heard the woman shout Mims's name, along with the epithet that followed. Strayer immediately turned one hundred and eighty degrees and began heading back the way she'd came.

The shouting woman, whoever she was, was trying to draw Mims to her. That was good enough for Strayer. She decided to make a beeline for the voice in the hope of intercepting him on his way to the woman.

Strayer knew she didn't have a choice.

The wildfire was closing in fast, and Strayer figured following the siren call of the woman's voice was her best chance of nailing him. It beat tramping aimlessly around in the darkness and smoke, waiting to be overcome by a forest fire or ambushed by a homicidal former deputy sheriff.

Strayer advanced slowly, scanning over the glowing tritium dot of her pistol's front sight. She struggled to keep from coughing, which would give away her position. Her eyes watered and stung as she strained to see through the dust, ash, and smoke.

Mims suddenly appeared. He surfaced from out of the smoke, ninety degrees to her right and less than a dozen feet away. He was still wearing the dust mask, and his Glock was aimed directly at her.

Strayer swung her pistol around but wasn't fast enough. Mims already had her dead to rights. He fired three times. All three of the .40 caliber slugs struck her in the center of her chest.

Strayer stumbled backward and her pistol fell from her grasp. She landed on her back and didn't move.

Mims walked over and stood above her. Strayer looked up at him, motionless.

"You aren't half-bad looking," he commented, pulling down his dust mask with one hand while continuing to aim his pistol at her with the other. "Too bad I had to kill you."

"Hey asshole," came a voice from the smoke behind him. "Over here."

When Mims pivoted to face the voice's owner, he found Marjorie Guthrie pointing a shotgun at him from only a few feet away. Unlike Strayer, he didn't even try to bring his gun up against someone who already had the drop on him.

"Drop it," Marjorie commanded. Mims opened his hand and released the pistol.

"Are you really going to shoot me," Mims asked, "in cold blood?"

"Like you did my father?" she asked.

Marjorie stepped forward and pressed the barrel against Mims's chest.

"Killing's not in your nature, Marjorie," he said, looking down at the barrel. "And gunning down an unarmed man certainly isn't your style."

"I wouldn't be so sure," she said. "I just killed your partner with a hammer."

Mims's eyebrows jumped. He noticed the blood spatter on her chest and face.

"I'm impressed," he said. "I didn't think you had it in you. Just like I don't think that shotgun is loaded." He smiled. "You're bluffing."

"Call it," she said.

"Where's your sister?" Mims asked. His smile widened. "She's the friendly one."

"She's dead, you bastar—"

Marjorie's words were cut short as Mims darted out a hand and grabbed the shotgun. He deliberately waited until she was talking, to reduce her reaction time, as he'd once been trained. He swung the barrel up and away as she fired.

The shotgun boomed. The 00 buckshot charge, consisting of nine .33 caliber lead balls, missed his head by inches.

Mims jerked the weapon from Marjorie's grasp, then butt-stroked her in the stomach. She gasped, folded, and sunk to her knees.

He tossed the shotgun away, then opened his mouth, put his fingers in his ears, and jiggled his head, trying to shake off the effects of the thunderous blast going off so close to his skull.

"You bitch," he cursed, as his ears rang. "I didn't think it was loaded."

He drew the second Glock from behind his back.

"Goodbye, Marjorie Guthrie," he said.

Marjorie knelt before Mims with her arms folded across her abdomen. She looked up at him in defiance. He leveled his pistol at her head.

"Drop the gun," a voice commanded.

Mims looked over his shoulder to find Strayer aiming a pistol at him.

"Drop the gun," Strayer repeated. "I won't tell you again."

Mims's shoulders slumped, and for the second time he let his pistol fall. "You're wearing body armor, aren't you?"

"Yep," Strayer said. She struggled to one knee, keeping her weapon leveled at Mims.

"I should have known," he said remorsefully, "and capped you in the head. Where'd you get the second gun?"

"Found it in a dead man's hand," she said, "over yonder."

"That was her husband," he chuckled, pointing to Marjorie. "He was a real hero." His eyes narrowed, and he stared at Strayer.

"Do I know you?"

"Ten years ago," she said. "I was in high school. You were on duty. You attacked me in my mom's mobile home."

"Oh yeah," Mims recollected. A lurid grin lit his face. "Now I remember."

"Put your hands on top of your head," Strayer ordered. "Turn around and facc mc."

Mims shrugged and complied. "If you're going to

arrest me, Deputy," he said, "you'd better do it quick. We're all about to become kindling."

"Who said anything about arresting you?"

"You're not going to shoot me." Mims laughed and pointed his chin at Marjorie, "any more than she was."

"Oh yeah?" Strayer said.

"I'm unarmed," Mims scoffed. "You're a deputy sheriff. You can't just kill me."

"You're right about that," Strayer said. "You can't kill someone who's already dead."

Seven .45 slugs, rapid-fired from Deputy Meyers's pistol, entered his torso. The eighth and final bullet pierced his forehead.

Duane Audie Mims jerked and shuddered with each successive impact. He fell forward onto his face and was dead before he hit the ground.

CHAPTER SIXTY

"I thought he'd killed you," Marjorie said.

"Me, too," Strayer said, as Marjorie helped the deputy to her feet. Strayer didn't show it, but her head was spinning, and she was woozy from the impacts of the three .40 caliber bullets, which felt like three strikes from a baseball bat. She rapped weakly on her chest. "The body armor saved me."

"Thank heaven you were wearing it," Marjorie said.

"Actually," Strayer said, shaking her head at the irony, "the thanks go to the Mexican Mafia." Collecting herself, she discarded Meyers's empty gun, recovered her own pistol, and looked around at the burning landscape.

"The fire's almost on us," Strayer coughed. "We have to get out of here."

"I can't leave," Marjorie said. "I have to find my children."

"Boy about ten," Strayer asked, "and a girl about half that age?"

"You've seen them?"

"They're with my partner. Come with me."

Holding each other for support, the two women stumbled through the smoke toward the front of the house. Marjorie's Range Rover unexpectedly pulled up to meet them.

"Get in!" Benavides shouted from behind the wheel. Margaret Hernandez, Joel and Jennifer Guthrie, and the two Dixon children were in the back seat and rear compartment of the sport utility.

"Hurry up!" Benavides yelled at them. "I just found out the gas line is busted! The house is going to blow!"

Marjorie hastily piled into the back seat with her mother and the children, and Strayer got into the front seat. The vehicle sped off.

"Wait!" Margaret protested. "We can't leave without Mary!"

Marjorie put her arms around Margaret. Looking into her mother's eyes, she shook her head.

"Oh, no." Margaret buried her face in her daughter's chest. "Not my Mary, too?"

"Where's Dad?" Joel asked, instinctively knowing the answer.

Marjorie gestured with her eyes to her mother and daughter, who were both crying in her arms. "We'll talk later," she said solemnly. Joel hung his head and nodded.

"Hold on," Benavides announced. "It's going to get rough."

He switched the vehicle into four-wheel-drive mode and gunned the SUV across the burning lawn toward the dirt road.

Strayer looked back. No sooner had the Range Rover reached the county road than the house exploded. The structure erupted into a flaming, mushroom cloud–shaped fireball, which enveloped all of the other vehicles near the house. An instant later, another, larger, mushroom cloud joined the first, as the exterior propane tank blew.

"Jesus, Joseph, and Mary," Benavides said, as the dual concussions rocked the car. "That was close."

"Out of the frying pan," Strayer said, pointing to the road ahead.

The wildfire raged all around them as far as they could see. Flames licked at the vehicle from both sides of the dirt road, as the Range Rover raced from the burning farmhouse. Benavides was driving as fast as he dared, through a maelstrom of flames and smoke.

"Which way is away from the fire?" Strayer asked.

"From where we are right now," Benavides said, "anywhere. All we can do is head toward Farnham and hope to make it out of the fire zone before the tires blow or the engine gives out."

They drove in silence for many long minutes, at breakneck speed, through the seemingly endless corridor of fire. The only sounds punctuating their desperate flight were the crackling roar of the fire outside, the howl of the wind, the labored chug of the smoke-clogged, oxygen-starved engine and Margaret Hernandez's mournful weeping.

The temperature inside the car was becoming uncomfortable, and the air thin, making Benavides and Strayer silently question the temperature and oxygen levels outside. They both knew if the vehicle gave out, it was all over.

If the car became undrivable, there was no way they would make it out of the raging inferno on foot. The only reason they were still alive was because they were cocooned in the protective shell of the Range Rover. How much longer that vehicle would protect them was anyone's guess.

The dashboard warning lights blinked on, the thermometer moved into the red, and smoke from under the hood began to join the smoke generated from the wildfire. The starving combustion engine, pushed to its limits and clogged with smoke, ash, and debris, struggled to function.

"Do you still have your service weapon?" Benavides whispered to Strayer. She nodded.

"Me, too," he whispered.

She understood what her partner was implying. The fate they would all suffer if the Range Rover gave out would be slow deaths in excruciating agony. It would be Benavides's and Strayer's responsibility, should that eventuality occur, to end the suffering of the others before ending their own lives. The engine began to grind and pop.

Margaret sat up and wiped her eyes. "Would anyone like to pray with me?" she asked.

"Why not?" Benavides said.

"Go ahead, Mom," Marjorie said.

"Hail Mary," Margaret began, "full of grace, the Lord is with thee."

Brandy and Travis Dixon didn't know the words to the prayer, but they clambered over the back seat and sat in Marjorie's and Margaret's laps. Joel and Jennifer hugged their mother and grandmother as they prayed along with them.

"Blessed art thou . . ."

The engine sputtered as the cylinders misfired. One of the tires blew, and then another, rocking the car. Benavides struggled to keep the vehicle on the road. The motor whined, the Rover started to slow, and the smoke emanating from under the hood turned from gray to white.

Benavides looked at Strayer and shook his head. She bit her lip and nodded once.

"You know," he said, "even though we didn't work together very long, I thought we made a pretty good team."

"I thought so, too," she said.

"Even if 'Trouble' is your middle name," he chuckled.

"Go to hell," Strayer said with a grin. Another tire blew.

"I think we're already there."

The engine died. The Range Rover gradually rolled to a halt.

". . . pray for us sinners," Margaret continued, "now, and at the hour of our death. Amen."

Once the vehicle stopped, the temperature inside the Range Rover's cabin became more noticeable. It crept its way from uncomfortable to nearly unbearable. Margaret began leading the others in the Lord's Prayer.

Strayer wiped perspiration from her forehead and once more met Benavides's eyes. Beads of sweat had formed on his face, and his left shoulder was soaked in blood. His right hand had moved from the steering wheel to beneath his coat, where she suspected it was wrapped around the grip of his holstered pistol. He leaned over and put his mouth against her ear.

"Do it quick," he whispered. Behind him, everyone continued to hold hands and pray. "Headshots," he went on. "Kids first. I'll get the Dixons and the old lady. You get the other three."

Strayer nodded once more.

"What's that?" asked Brandy Dixon, who'd been silent up until then. She pointed to an ash smudge on the windshield.

"What's what, honey?" Margaret said.

"That," she said, still pointing to the windshield. By then, several more ash smudges appeared on the filthy glass.

Soon those smudges were joined by many others. A rhythmic staccato began to beat a steady drumbeat on the metal roof of the vehicle.

"Is that—" Margaret said.

"—rain," Marjorie finished the sentence. "It is! It's raining!"

"I don't believe it," Benavides said.

Within a minute, it wasn't merely raining, it was pouring. A torrential downpour had commenced, drenching the landscape.

Benavides opened the driver's door and stepped out into the deluge. Everyone else clambered out to join him.

"I've never been so happy to see rain," Strayer said, "in all my life."

"It is November, after all," Benavides said, cradling his injured arm. "Isn't November supposed to be the official start of California's rainy season?"

All around them, steam and smoke rose from the rapidly extinguishing wildfire. Strayer turned her face skyward and allowed the cleansing shower to wash over her.

Marjorie hugged her mother, who was busy hugging Joel, Jennifer, Brandy, and Travis.

"It isn't just the start of the rainy season," Margaret said to Benavides, looking up from embracing her daughter, grandchildren, and the two orphans. "I prayed to my Hector and Mary for deliverance, and they answered my prayers. It's a miracle, Deputy. A heaven-sent miracle."

"You'll get no argument from me," Benavides said.

"I'll take it," Strayer said.

CHAPTER SIXTY-ONE

Strayer entered the administration building and took the stairs up to the third floor. It was the first time she'd been back to the department in over a week.

Strayer, Detective Benavides, Margaret Hernandez, Marjorie, Joel and Jennifer Guthrie, and Brandy and Travis Dixon were rescued within with a surprisingly short time. A little more than an hour after the first major rainstorm of the season began snuffing out the Farnham Fire, a truck full of firefighters from the California Department of Forestry and a Ford Explorer belonging to the Farnham County Sheriff's Department found the stranded motorists.

As it turned out, they were searching for a missing Farnham County S.W.A.T. deputy named Meyers, who along with a firefighter named Letourneau, had failed to report in.

Not long after the rainfall started, while everyone else was both grieving and rejoicing, Strayer began rendering first aid to her partner. She made Benavides get back into the car and sit down, despite his protests, fearing the rain and drop in temperature might possibly induce shock. She placed her handkerchief over the gunshot wound in his shoulder.

"I'm sure glad we didn't have to—"

"Don't say it," Strayer cut him off. "Never speak of it again."

Benavides nodded.

As she was applying the handkerchief compress, Strayer noticed for the first time that the Range Rover's center console surrounding the starter button was torn up and the wiring underneath exposed.

"Excuse the pun," Strayer said, "but did you hot-wire this car?"

"One-handed, too," Benavides proudly declared. "Didn't I tell you I'd been arrested as a kid for stealing cars?"

Marjorie separated herself from the children, who were hungrily devouring Halloween candy from the trick-or-treat bags they'd discovered inside the vehicle. Even Margaret partook. Marjorie approached the two deputies.

"May I have a word with you alone?" Marjorie asked Strayer.

Benavides took over for Strayer, who was applying the compress, and signaled for her to go with Marjorie. "Is there a Baby Ruth in those bags?" he called out to the kids.

Strayer and Marjorie walked a short distance from the car. The rain streaming down muffled their voices.

"About what happened back there," Marjorie began, "with Mims—"

"Don't worry," Strayer interrupted. "When I get back to the department, I'll do the right thing. I'll turn myself in."

"For what?"

"Mims was right," Strayer said. "I'm a sworn law enforcement officer. I can't just gun someone down. Even a criminal like him. Especially if they're unarmed."

"Is it true?" Marjorie asked.

"Is what true?"

"That he raped you? Back when you were in high school?"

"Yes."

"He tried to rape me, too," Marjorie said. "And he abused my sister, who's dead now. He also murdered my father, and my husband, and tried to slaughter my mother and children by trapping them in the fire."

"I'm sorry," Strayer said. "But I still have to report what I did."

"I was going to kill him myself," Marjorie said. "I just couldn't get it done."

"I won't ask you to lie," Strayer said.

"You saved my life," Marjorie said, reaching out and taking Strayer by the shoulders, "and the lives of my family. As far as I'm concerned, Mims was still holding his gun when you fired. That's my story, and I'm sticking to it. Are you going to make a liar out of me?"

Strayer looked down at her feet.

Marjorie let go of Strayer's shoulder with one hand and lifted the deputy's chin to meet her eyes.

"Hasn't Duane Mims ruined enough lives?" she asked.

The rain prevented Marjorie from seeing Strayer's tears.

"By the way," she said, sticking out her hand, "my name's Marjorie. Marjorie Guthrie."

"Leanne Strayer."

They started to shake hands, but Marjorie let go and pulled Strayer to her.

"Thank you," Marjorie said, as she hugged Strayer fiercely. "Thank you for saving my children."

When their rescuers got them back to Farnham, they discovered the rain began to fall when the fire was less than a hundred yards from the WELCOME TO FARNHAM! sign at the town's eastern limit.

Everyone except Strayer was taken to the hospital. She insisted on having the uniformed deputy drive her to the station.

She walked into the Emergency Operating Center, which was packed with deputies, civilian employees, technicians, and command officers, including Lieutenant McDillon, Undersheriff Torres, and the sheriff. Everyone stopped what they were doing and watched as the filthy, soaking-wet deputy strode up to the map table, which was surrounded by the sheriff and his command staff. The room abruptly silenced.

Strayer wordlessly set her pistol on the table. Then she removed her jacket, and to everyone's astonishment, her shirt. She took off her body armor, which had three .40 caliber bullets embedded in the shock plate, and tossed it next to her gun. She turned to face McDillon.

"Here's my initial verbal report," she began. "Detective Benavides and I went out into the county to rescue a pair of abandoned children. We got trapped by the fire. Duane Mims was there."

An excited murmur spread across the room. The sheriff held up a hand, and the room again quieted.

"Duane Mims?" McDillon asked. "You're telling me Duane Mims is alive?"

"Was," she said. "I shot him. He tried to kill me and a family he'd been holding hostage. But not before he murdered several other people, including Deputy Wayne Meyers. Anything else I have to say, I'll say on the record to the investigators."

The murmuring grew loud again.

"I presume I'm now officially on administrative leave,"

Strayer said. "I'm going home." She abruptly turned from the sea of incredulous faces and began to walk out.

Strayer stopped halfway to the door and turned around again. "By the way," she asked, "does anybody have a gun I can borrow? Unless something changed while I was gone, there're still some gangsters gunning for me."

She walked out past wide eyes and dropped jaws.

During the time she spent at home on administrative leave, Strayer rested, worked out every day in the gym at her apartment complex, and met with her Deputy Sheriff's Association attorney to prepare for her formal statement, which was scheduled for a week later. Normally a deputy was interviewed within seventy-two hours after a shooting incident, but she had two of them to account for, and the department more than had its hands full in the wake of the Farnham Fire and impending election.

Strayer also visited Dr. Wozniak every day.

A week later, she donned one of her suits, strapped on the third Sig Sauer 1911 she'd been issued in as many weeks, and reported to the department.

She spent several hours in one of the Interview and Interrogation rooms in the Investigations Division providing her accounts of the shoot-out at her apartment and the incidents that took place at the Dixon trailer and Hernandez home.

When eventually asked if Mims was holding a gun on Marjorie Guthrie and preparing to execute her at the time she fired her weapon, which clearly implied the investigators had already interviewed Marjorie, Strayer hesitated before answering.

After a long moment, she finally said, "Yes."

Strayer walked out of the Interview and Interrogation room and found Sergeant Simpson and Detective Benavides waiting for her in the bowling alley. Benavides had his arm in a sling, and Simpson was on crutches.

"How'd it go?" Benavides asked.

"How do you think?" Strayer retorted. "Like a root canal, only less fun."

"Are you all right?" Simpson asked.

"I think so," she said. "The lead detective told me, off the record, that I was within policy and the law. Now all I have to do is get my fitness-for-duty evaluation over with and I'm back to work."

"Dr. Wozniak?" Simpson said.

"Yep. As it turns out, I was scheduled to see her tomorrow anyway."

"That's great news," Simpson said.

"That's not the only great news," Strayer said. "Undersheriff Torres told me the sheriff is in a good mood since he got reelected. Evidently, he feels he picked up a few votes on account of the way I handled the Mims thing. He told McDillon to tell me I could go back to the S.W.A.T. Unit whenever I'm ready."

"Congratulations," Benavides said, though his smile drooped. "I'm happy for you. I'm glad you got what you wanted."

"When do you go back?" Simpson asked.

"I don't," Strayer answered.

"Huh?"

"I turned down the transfer. I've decided to stay in the Juvenile Unit." She looked at Benavides and Simpson. "If that's okay with you guys?"

"I dunno," Benavides said, his trademark smile returning. "Frankly, Strayer, you're a helluva lot of trouble."

"Give her a break, Benny," Simpson said. "After all, it is her middle name."

AUTHOR'S NOTE

As the reader has undoubtedly surmised, there is no Farnham County, Town of Farnham, or Farnham County Sheriff's Department. These entities, as noted in the disclaimer at the beginning of this novel, are entirely fictional. Tragically, the effects of firestorms during California's notorious wildfire season, as depicted in this story, are not.

This novel is predicated on the premise that a human body can be cremated beyond recovery or identification during a California woodland firestorm. There are those who contend (I have heard from such naysayers) that the disintegration of humans, under circumstances other than those created by an industrial incinerator, is impossible. I respectfully beg to differ.

As any experienced firefighter can assure you, such destructive potential exists. While a S.W.A.T. team member deployed to anti-looting duty in the first hours of the 1991 Oakland Hills Fire, and continuously for many weeks thereafter, I personally witnessed such effects firsthand.

The combination of drought, abundant fuel in the form of dense woodlands, grasslands, and man-made structures and materials, in concert with gale force winds such as the Monos, Santa Anas, and Diablos, funneled and magnified through canyons, valleys, and mountainous passes, can easily generate enough heat to not only incinerate people to ash, but can reduce vehicles to little more than furniture-sized lumps of metal. Such events, like the Oakland Hills Fire or the more recent Camp Fire, the worst in California's history, can create a furnace easily as destructive to human remains as any industrial crematorium.

ACKNOWLEDGMENTS

I wish to express my heartfelt gratitude to the following individuals for their support in the writing of this novel:

Gary Goldstein. My friend, editor at Kensington Publishing, and the fellow who suggested I write this story. I only wish I could create a character as wise, salty, and true as him.

Scott Miller. My friend, literary agent at Trident Media Group, and a man of honor who always keeps the faith.

The Calaveras Crew. Sidehackers all, and men to ride the river with.

The Usual Suspects. If it takes a village, ours is the "Village of the Damned."

Lastly, and most important, my wife, Denise, daughter, Brynne, and son, Owen. They are the greatest blessings ever bestowed on a fellow. I am humbled every day. Today, tomorrow, and forever; you know the rest.

Connect with

U s

Visit us online at
KensingtonBooks.com
to read more from your favorite authors, see books
by series, view reading group guides, and more.

Join us on social media

for sneak peeks, chances to win books and prize packs,
and to share your thoughts with other readers.

facebook.com/kensingtonpublishing
twitter.com/kensingtonbooks

Tell us what you think!

To share your thoughts, submit a review,
or sign up for our eNewsletters, please visit:
KensingtonBooks.com/TellUs.